Praise for the novels of Ace Atkins

INFAMOUS

"Compulsively readable . . . [Atkins] takes a revisionist look at the life and times of Machine Gun Kelly and the very bad woman who stood behind him . . . Bullets fly, gore puddles, and, as the denouement approaches, oh how those pages turn. Atkins, who loves his characters colorful, makes readers love them too, and it doesn't much matter whether they're naughty or nice."
—*Kirkus Reviews*

"Atkins brings to vivid life the henpecked George and the bloodthirsty Kathryn as he convincingly conjures up a past era."
—*Publishers Weekly*

"Kathryn [Kelly] is a force of nature, a preening, determined-not-to-be-poor-again shopaholic, a celebrity-obsessed Lady Macbeth."
—*Booklist*

"[An] evocative portrait of a criminal . . . An insightful look at ambition, the seduction of fame, the beginnings of the FBI's power, and a multi-tiered society of criminals . . . *Infamous* is immersed in the atmosphere of the Great Depression."
— *South Florida Sun-Sentinel*

"This tough, boisterous, lustful tale of a would-be playboy miscast as a villain compares to the best of Max Allan Collins or Elmore Leonard and will appeal to adult readers who like their gangster stories based on fact." —*Library Journal*

DEVIL'S GARDEN

"*Devil's Garden* is a remarkable book that succeeds on every level. As a riveting detective story, it is great entertainment. As a historical novel, it transports the reader. Atkins's prose, at once muscular and lyrical, is good from the first sentence to the last. He has solidified his place alongside Dennis Lehane and George Pelecanos as one of our most important literary crime novelists."
—*San Francisco Chronicle*

continued . . .

"With enviable ease, Atkins brings to life Hammett, Arbuckle, William Randolph Hearst, and other real figures of the period. Those familiar with the historical case will be impressed by how well the book meshes fact and fiction. Genre fans who enjoy the grim realism of James Ellroy's post–World War II Los Angeles will find a lot to like in Atkins's Prohibition-era San Francisco." —*Publishers Weekly* (starred review)

WICKED CITY

"The author paints a visceral portrait . . . Atkins is a proud torchbearer of a literary tradition that includes William Faulkner . . . There's nothing derivative about this novel, only the emergence of a great new voice in American fiction." —*Chicago Sun-Times*

"[Atkins's] unflinching, graphic storytelling echoes the best of James Ellroy and James Crumley . . . A solid piece of crime fiction, not a history lesson." —*South Florida Sun-Sentinel*

"Atkins has been making a name for himself with highly descriptive, noirish tales set in the Deep South and based on real events. With his latest taking place in the real Phenix City, he has conjured up a time and setting that literally smells of swamps and sweat, tobacco and gunpowder." —*Rocky Mountain News*

"You don't just read *Wicked City* . . . You absorb each highball of bourbon, each plume of smoke, each peek at a pastie-covered nipple until you're woozy off words that dance and dart and catch you cold, like a sucker punch to the chin . . . What elevates Atkins's prose to greatness . . . [is] his ability to let these characters breathe in a way that few authors could ever imagine. He doesn't so much write them as unleash them upon the page." —*The Tampa Tribune*

WHITE SHADOW

"Keep an eye on Ace Atkins, he can write rings around most of the names in the crime field." —Elmore Leonard

"A sweeping page-turner anchored in a beautifully wrought time and place." —Laura Lippman

"Mesmerizing . . . Wonderful detail of character and history . . . [A] tour de force from one of the best crime writers at work today." —Michael Connelly

"Ace Atkins has done a superb job of re-creating old Tampa, a place whose underworld was as dangerous and debauched as Chicago's in its prime." —Carl Hiaasen

"*White Shadow* is a big, poetic, and muscular novel, as sleek and tough as the stylish characters that inhabit its pages. Ace Atkins writes like a crime beat reporter jacked on passion and ambition. A bravura performance." —George Pelecanos

"Ace Atkins makes 1950s Florida as cool and hip as tomorrow in this outstanding novel. It's a stunning achievement and sure to be a book of the year." —Lee Child

"*White Shadow*, based on the unsolved, real-life throat slashing of a retired bootlegger named Charlie Wall, succeeds both as a first-rate historical novel and as a superb crime story. The book packs the emotional wallop of Dennis Lehane's *Mystic River*. It is as gritty as James Ellroy's *L.A. Confidential*. And yet, the prose is as lyrical as James Lee Burke's *Crusader's Cross* . . . With *White Shadow*, Atkins has found his true voice." —The Associated Press

INFAMOUS

ACE ATKINS

BERKLEY BOOKS, NEW YORK

THE BERKLEY PUBLISHING GROUP
Published by the Penguin Group
Penguin Group (USA) Inc.
375 Hudson Street, New York, New York 10014, USA
Penguin Group (Canada), 90 Eglinton Avenue East, Suite 700, Toronto, Ontario M4P 2Y3, Canada
(a division of Pearson Penguin Canada Inc.)
Penguin Books Ltd., 80 Strand, London WC2R 0RL, England
Penguin Group Ireland, 25 St. Stephen's Green, Dublin 2, Ireland (a division of Penguin Books Ltd.)
Penguin Group (Australia), 250 Camberwell Road, Camberwell, Victoria 3124, Australia
(a division of Pearson Australia Group Pty. Ltd.)
Penguin Books India Pvt. Ltd., 11 Community Centre, Panchsheel Park, New Delhi—110 017, India
Penguin Group (NZ), 67 Apollo Drive, Rosedale, Auckland 0632, New Zealand
(a division of Pearson New Zealand Ltd.)
Penguin Books (South Africa) (Pty.) Ltd., 24 Sturdee Avenue, Rosebank, Johannesburg 2196,
South Africa

Penguin Books Ltd., Registered Offices: 80 Strand, London WC2R 0RL, England

This is a work of fiction. Names, characters, places, and incidents either are the product of the author's imagination or are used fictitiously, and any resemblance to actual persons, living or dead, business establishments, events, or locales is entirely coincidental. The publisher does not have any control over and does not assume any responsibility for author or third-party websites or their content.

PRINTING HISTORY
G. P. Putnam's Sons hardcover edition / April 2010
Berkley trade paperback edition / April 2011

Berkley trade paperback ISBN: 978-0-425-23901-8

The Library of Congress has catalogued the G. P. Putnam's Sons hardcover edition as follows:

Atkins, Ace.
    Infamous / Ace Atkins.
        p. cm.
    ISBN 978-0-399-15630-4
    1. Kelly, Machine Gun, 1897–1954—Fiction.   2. Criminals—United States—Fiction.   I. Title.
    PS3551.T49154   2010   2009044498
    813'.54—dc22

PRINTED IN THE UNITED STATES OF AMERICA

10   9   8   7   6   5   4   3   2   1

This book is for

DORIS ATKINS and CHARLIE WELCH

I'm leading a trail that is crooked,
My foes lurk 'round every bend;
I know someday they will get me,
I dread to think of the end.

—GENE AUTRY, "GANGSTER'S WARNING"

Everything is funny as long as it is
happening to someone else.

—WILL ROGERS

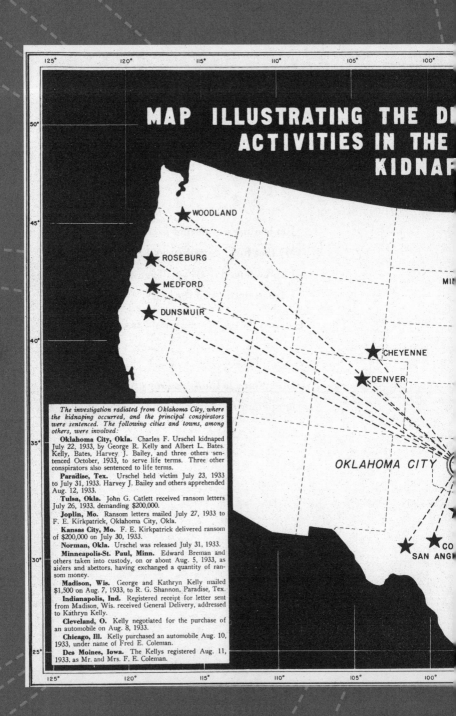

MAP ILLUSTRATING THE DI
ACTIVITIES IN THE
KIDNAF

★ WOODLAND

★ ROSEBURG

★ MEDFORD

★ DUNSMUIR

★ CHEYENNE

★ DENVER

OKLAHOMA CITY

★ CO
SAN ANG

The investigation radiated from Oklahoma City, where the kidnaping occurred, and the principal conspirators were sentenced. The following cities and towns, among others, were involved:

Oklahoma City, Okla. Charles F. Urschel kidnaped July 22, 1933, by George R. Kelly and Albert L. Bates. Kelly, Bates, Harvey J. Bailey, and three others sentenced October, 1933, to serve life terms. Three other conspirators also sentenced to life terms.

Paradise, Tex. Urschel held victim July 23, 1933 to July 31, 1933. Harvey J. Bailey and others apprehended Aug. 12, 1933.

Tulsa, Okla. John G. Catlett received ransom letters July 26, 1933, demanding $200,000.

Joplin, Mo. Ransom letters mailed July 27, 1933 to F. E. Kirkpatrick, Oklahoma City, Okla.

Kansas City, Mo. F. E. Kirkpatrick delivered ransom of $200,000 on July 30, 1933.

Norman, Okla. Urschel was released July 31, 1933.

Minneapolis-St. Paul, Minn. Edward Breman and others taken into custody, on or about Aug. 5, 1933, as aiders and abettors, having exchanged a quantity of ransom money.

Madison, Wis. George and Kathryn Kelly mailed $1,500 on Aug. 7, 1933, to R. G. Shannon, Paradise, Tex.

Indianapolis, Ind. Registered receipt for letter sent from Madison, Wis. received General Delivery, addressed to Kathryn Kelly.

Cleveland, O. Kelly negotiated for the purchase of an automobile on Aug. 8, 1933.

Chicago, Ill. Kelly purchased an automobile Aug. 10, 1933, under name of Fred E. Coleman.

Des Moines, Iowa. The Kellys registered Aug. 11, 1933, as Mr. and Mrs. F. E. Coleman.

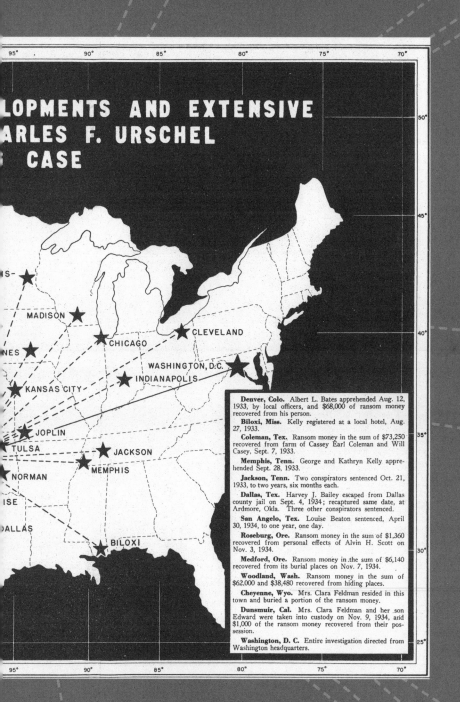

LOPMENTS AND EXTENSIVE
ARLES F. URSCHEL
CASE

Denver, Colo. Albert L. Bates apprehended Aug. 12, 1933, by local officers, and $68,000 of ransom money recovered from his person.

Biloxi, Miss. Kelly registered at a local hotel, Aug. 27, 1933.

Coleman, Tex. Ransom money in the sum of $73,250 recovered from farm of Cassey Earl Coleman and Will Casey, Sept. 7, 1933.

Memphis, Tenn. George and Kathryn Kelly apprehended Sept. 28, 1933.

Jackson, Tenn. Two conspirators sentenced Oct. 21, 1933, to two years, six months each.

Dallas, Tex. Harvey J. Bailey escaped from Dallas county jail on Sept. 4, 1934; recaptured same date, at Ardmore, Okla. Three other conspirators sentenced.

San Angelo, Tex. Louise Beaton sentenced, April 30, 1934, to one year, one day.

Roseburg, Ore. Ransom money in the sum of $1,360 recovered from personal effects of Alvin H. Scott on Nov. 3, 1934.

Medford, Ore. Ransom money in the sum of $6,140 recovered from its burial places on Nov. 7, 1934.

Woodland, Wash. Ransom money in the sum of $62,000 and $38,480 recovered from hiding places.

Cheyenne, Wyo. Mrs. Clara Feldman resided in this town and buried a portion of the ransom money.

Dunsmuir, Cal. Mrs. Clara Feldman and her son Edward were taken into custody on Nov. 9, 1934, and $1,000 of the ransom money recovered from their possession.

Washington, D. C. Entire investigation directed from Washington headquarters.

Saturday, June 17, 1933

They'd barely made it out of Arkansas alive after nabbing Frank "Jelly" Nash inside the White Front Café, a known hangout for grifters, thieves, and assorted hoodlums vacationing in Hot Springs. At first, Nash had made a real show of how they had it all wrong and that his name was really Marshall, and for a second it seemed plausible until old Otto Reed—the sheriff they'd brought along—ripped the toupee off Nash's bald head and then started for the mustache. "That's mine. That's mine," Nash had said. They'd ditched the plan to drive to Joplin after almost losing Nash at a roadblock of crooked cops. And now the old bank robber was seated across from them, riding the Missouri Pacific all-nighter out of Fort Smith, wearing a shit-eating grin, confident his hoodlum buddies would spring him.

Special Agent Gus T. Jones of the U.S. Department of Justice checked his gold pocket watch.

It was three a.m.

Four more hours until they'd meet the Special Agent in Charge in Kansas City, where he, his partner Joe Lackey, and Sheriff Reed would hand off the son of a bitch for a short trip back to Leavenworth, from where he'd escaped three years before.

Jones would want a shower and a shave and some sleep, but first he wanted a meal at the Harvey House, a big plate of eggs and bacon with hot coffee, served by a lilac-scented Harvey girl who'd flirt with him despite Jones being fifty-two years old and needing a pair of bifocals to read the menu. He'd call Mary Ann, find a hotel, and then ride the rails back to San Antonio, where he worked as the Special Agent in Charge.

"If you let me go, I'll just tell people I escaped," Nash said. "To my grave, I'll tell people I hopped out the crapper window."

Jones filled his pipe from a leather pouch and dusted loose tobacco from his knee.

He stared over at Joe Lackey—a good fella, for a Yankee—who sported a gray fedora over his Roman nose and small brown eyes. Jones still preferred a pearl gray Stetson, the same kind required when he'd been a Ranger and later worked for Customs years back, riding the Rio Grande on the lookout for revolutionaries, cattle rustlers, and German spies.

The night flew past.

The seats in the train jostled up and down, metal wheels scraping against rail, anonymous towns of light and smoke flying by the window, just slightly cracked. Joe Lackey crossed his arms across his chest, his chin dipping down to his red tie in short fits of sleep. Sheriff Reed sat closest to the window and watched the lean-tos, farmhouses, and hobo jungles ablaze with oil-drum fires whiz by, exchanging a glance or two with Nash. The old bandit would give him the stink eye and turn his head, disappointed that Jones would be so hardheaded as not to take a bribe.

"How'd you find me?" Nash asked, his bald pate stark white. Face beet red from the sun. "Doesn't matter much now."

Jones looked at him across the haze of pipe smoke with a wry smile. Jelly Nash was chained to a bunk and couldn't even scratch his ass.

"But you're not going to tell me."

"Guess not," Jones said.

"Hey, where'd you get those boots?"

"El Paso."

"You still got a horse?"

"Why don't you get some sleep."

"Just making some conversation."

"You got a lot of friends in Arkansas."

"Sorry about that," Nash said. "I thought that roadblock was my ticket out."

"So did I."

"Probably be some friends waiting on me in Kansas City."

"I doubt it."

"You want to put some money down?"

"You wanna fill me in?"

"People talk."

Jones stood as the train shifted onto another track, and he found purchase on an overhead rail. He emptied his pipe out the open window, feeling the hot summer wind on his face. Without much thought, he fingered the loose bullets in his right pocket, keeping the .45 revolver in a holster under the hot coat, despite the Justice Department's policy about agents not carrying weapons.

"I think a federal cop is a screwy idea," Nash said.

"Who asked you?"

"What makes you all any different from those goons in Spain or Germany?"

"I'd like to know what makes a con so damn stupid as to return to the prison where he escaped. If you hadn't busted them boys outta Lansing, you might be sleeping on satin sheets at some hot pillow joint."

"That wasn't me."

Joe Lackey raised his head and knocked up the brim of his fedora from his eyes with two fingers and said, "Sure thing, Jelly. Sure thing."

Jones looked over at his old buddy Otto Reed and watched him sleep.

Sheriff Reed looked ancient, out of step off a horse, out of place with the times. They only brought him along because he'd know Nash on sight. The old man was cut from the same cloth as Jones's mentor, old Rome Shields back in San Angelo, who'd taught Jones to fight and shoot after his father's heart had been pierced by an Indian's arrow.

Jones clicked open his gold timepiece again, feeling the heft of his holstered gun.

Frank Nash watched him, looking like a circus clown with that naked white head and reddened face, smiling at Jones, knowing. Slats of light shuttered his profile as they passed under a wooden bridge and came out again in moonlight.

Jones didn't like the look. It was the kind that always made him fold a hand.

HARVEY BAILEY KNEW THE MEET WAS ON THE LEVEL, A little diner right around the corner from Union Station in Kansas City, Verne Miller sending the signal that Jelly Nash needed a friend. And, brother, there was a lot you could say about Jelly Nash, but that bald-headed son of a bitch was there for Harvey when Harvey was serving a ten-stretch for bank robbery in Lansing, helping bust him out last month with a set of .38s smuggled into boxes of twine. Harvey, Jim Clark, "Mad Dog" Underhill, and a few more thieving sonsabitches walking out with the warden pretty as you please, Underhill holding him with a garrote like it were a leash.

Jelly Nash.

That was all Verne Miller had to say, and there was Harvey sitting beside a redheaded woman in a red dress at the counter. The woman wanted some eggs and bacon after a little late-night action with Harvey, who'd picked her up at a colored joint where they'd watched Cab Calloway and his orchestra till three o'clock. When Miller walked in the door, the woman kept studying her nails, not even noting the two men were friends. Of course she didn't know Harvey was married and had a kid, or even his real name. He'd told her that he was a traveling salesman of women's nightgowns, wondering if the action could've been better if she'd known she was with the dean of bank robbers, the gentleman bandit who'd been knocking over jugs for more than ten years. She surely had read about some of his work, two million in cash and stocks from the National Bank and Trust in Lincoln a couple years back, or the U.S. Mint in Denver in '22.

She'd liked his gray hair, his tailored navy suit and crushed-felt hat, and his jokes at the hotel when they'd finished up the first time and he'd hummed "I've Got the World on a String" as they cooled down under the sheets.

At the diner, he handed the gal some bus fare, patted her backside, and she was gone, the girl knowing the score as much as he did. Harvey moved onto a stool close to Miller and smiled as a goofy-looking fella in a paper hat refilled their coffee and seemed to be real impressed that Jean Harlow was in town, asking if they knew she was a hometown girl.

Miller just looked up from his coffee, and the boy shut his mouth and headed back to the kitchen.

"You sure know how to make friends."

Miller shrugged.

Harvey had known Miller for years. He was a retired bootlegger, a part-time bank robber, and a full-time button man for the Nitti Syndicate in Chicago and the Jew Outfit in New York. Miller had been a war hero who'd come home from the trenches to be elected sheriff somewhere in South Dakota. And then he decided to take a nice cut of the county purse for himself and was run from town. Harvey met him after all that, when they'd been running whiskey down from Canada into Minnesota.

He was blond-haired and gray-eyed, movie-star handsome, a stone-cold killer who hated foul language—most of all when you used the Lord's name in vain.

"Goddamn, it's good to see you," Harvey said.

Miller shifted his eyes to him. He'd yet to take off his gray hat.

The two men sat in front of the plate glass of the diner, the small space feeling like a fishbowl, brightly lit in the middle of the night. Miller shuffled out a cigarette from his pack of Camels and tossed the rest to Harvey.

"So what's the score?"

"They got Jelly in Hot Springs at Dick Galatas's place," Miller said.

"That was kinda showy, wasn't it? Prancing around Hot Springs like nobody would see him."

Miller shrugged. "Two federal agents and some old sheriff."

"What time?"

"Seven."

"Who's meeting them at the station?"

"Guess we'll find out."

"You got guns."

"I got guns."

"We got help?" Harvey asked.

"Working on it."

"How's it looking?"

Miller shrugged.

"Goddamn."

"I don't like that kind of talk, Harvey."

"I got a gun," Harvey said. "A helluva gun that was supposed to help with some bank work, make some dough, and get me out of this lousy racket."

"I can handle a Thompson."

"I don't want trouble," Harvey said. "I don't want any trouble. This can be as smooth and easy as we like."

"I don't like trouble," Miller said, squashing out his cigarette. "I hate it."

"Jesus, I just wanted to make a little dough and cash out," Harvey said. "And this doesn't do nothing but turn up the heat on all us."

"It's a square deal."

"Am I arguing?"

THE MISSOURI PACIFIC STOPPED ONCE IN COFFEYVILLE AND rolled on through Roper and Garnett, curving east to Osawatomie and Leeds. The gray morning light hit the side of unpainted barns leaning hard into the wind and brushed across the windows of the train car. Jones watched Frank Nash startle himself with a hard snore and come alive with a start, reaching for a gun—like a man on the run was apt to do—but only getting a few inches and finding bound wrists.

He looked up at Jones, and Jones winked back.

Jones fingered bullets into the cylinder of his .45, spinning the wheel and clicking it back into frame. Joe Lackey was in the washroom shaving with a straight razor he'd bought from the negro porter.

"How 'bout some breakfast?" Nash asked.

"I hear they make a mean slop of grits in Leavenworth," Sheriff Otto Reed said. Reed was a pleasant man with a stomach large enough to provide a good rest for crossed arms. He chuckled a bit at his own joke, and Jones smiled back at him.

Nash said, "Otto, sometimes you can be a true, authentic asshole."

"Think of me when you're being cornholed, Jellybean."

Nash looked like he'd sucked a lemon.

The light turned gold and hot, shining over endless rows of green cornstalks about to ripen in the high summer. Nash began to complain about the manacles hurting his wrists and asked if he could please put his hairpiece back on because he knew the *Star* and Associated Press would be waiting when he got off the train.

"Come again?" Jones asked.

"You know, that reporter fella who chatted you all up in the station and knew who I was and where we're going? Yes, sir, I bet my story is all across the wire."

Jones looked over at Sheriff Reed, and Reed said he didn't know what he was talking about. Lackey came out of the head, drying off his face with a little towel and then sliding back into a wrinkled shirt, knotting his tie high at the throat.

"Did I miss something?" Lackey asked.

KANSAS CITY UNION STATION WAS A BIG, FAT STONE CATHE-dral with a sloping roof and Greek columns, a weigh station, a purgatorial crossroads where tracks from all over creation mishmashed and met and then bent and whipped out to the next turn, the following bend. Big, wide schedule boards, shoeshine stands, soda fountains, and fancy clocks, and even a Harvey House restaurant that Harvey had always liked because of the name.

They could turn right back around, head out of the city, and rob a dozen banks, fattening their rolls and leaving Jelly Nash to his own mire of shit. Sure he'd been a good egg and come through with those .38s, but sending along some guns while you sit back and read the newspapers on the crapper ain't the same as putting yourself out there, waiting outside a train station, sweating from worry, with barrels aimed at detectives and federal agents. Harvey wasn't so sure that Nash would go that far, truth be told.

"Where'd you get the Chevy?" Harvey asked.

"Does it matter?"

"Gonna be tough with just two," Harvey said, spotting the entrance where they'd watch and wait, windows down in all this heat.

"Says who?" Miller asked. "That Thompson's a beaut."

"Belongs to George Kelly," Harvey said. "Kit bought it as an anniversary gift."

"And he let you borrow it?"

"Hell, I said I'd give it back."

"George Kelly," Miller said, smiling as much as Verne Miller ever smiled. " 'Machine Gun' Kelly."

"I know, I know," Harvey said. "You remember that little bank in Ottumwa? He got so scared he puked all over himself."

"He's getting a name."

"I don't want a name. Gettin' a name gets you killed. If I hadn't been so damn stupid carrying those bonds with me, I'd never been pinched."

"Next time don't play golf with Keating and Holden."

Harvey slid into a parking space by the entrance and killed the engine. Two black sedans pulled by the doors, four men gathered and talked. Two of them held shotguns. One showed a badge to a porter when the porter gave some back talk.

"We take 'em after they got Nash," Miller said.

"Frank Nash ain't worth this, brother."

"Lansing must've been a special place."

Harvey leaned into the driver's seat and lit another cigarette. He'd burn through three more before he'd see those boys leading Frank Nash out in handcuffs. "Verne, you are the most honorable bastard I ever met."

THE TRAIN BACKED INTO PLATFORM 12 A LITTLE AFTER seven.

Jones and Joe Lackey were on their feet. Sheriff Reed unlocked Nash's handcuffs, let him affix the curly brown toupee back on his head, and then locked the cuffs back in front of him.

"How do I look?" Nash asked.

"Like some squirrel crawled onto your head and died," Lackey said.

Nash ignored him and lifted his hands to use a little finger to smooth down a thin mustache while Lackey walked out first. From the window, Jones could make out a handshake with a clean-shaven young man in a blue suit and neat tie, the kind of style that mirrored all those endless memos from J. Edgar himself. Jones eased up a bit, still feeling good with the gun under his arm.

He reached for the broken-in Stetson on the rack, slid it onto his head. From down on the platform, Lackey gave a wave.

"C'mon, Jelly," Jones said. "Let's go."

"Only my friends call me Jelly, and you're no friend of mine."

"Get goin', shithead," Jones said. "How's that?"

Reed snatched Nash's elbow. Jones led the way.

He walked down onto the steps. The black locomotive still hissing and spitting, worn out in the hot morning. He scanned the station, not finding much but that kind of simple action; the quiet rhythm you find at all train stations, coming and going, women in hats, men looking at the big board. The place was endless, as large a station as Jones had ever seen, fashioned of brick and marble, with tall windows that were downright religious. He'd always imagined purgatory would be a place like this, a big, sprawling train station with people filtering through, but so large that you could never find your way out.

Lackey introduced him to the young agent.

The kid pumped his hand and smiled and told Jones he'd read all about him in *True Detective*, about the trouble at that Indian reservation, all those dead women, and what an honor it was to work with him. He looked to be about twelve years old, hair parted neat across one side, eyes eager, and hands nervous as he accepted the key from Sheriff Reed and took custody of Frank Nash.

"Merry Christmas," Jones said. "I sure will miss your company, Jelly."

"Go fuck yourself," Nash said.

"Is it just you?" Jones asked the young agent.

"No, sir."

The young man nodded to the front entrance of Union Station and three men in suits walking toward them. He pushed Nash ahead, placing a .38 in the small of his back and nervously telling the old train robber that he'd blow out his spine if he tried any funny business. Frank Nash just laughed at that and said, "Oh, all right, kid. Nothin' from me."

More introductions.

Two beefy Kansas City detectives and the Special Agent in Charge.

"We got a car waiting outside," the KC SAC said. "The detectives here will follow us to the prison just in case."

"Just in case what?"

"An ambush," he said. "Their car is armor plated."

They were a group now, and Jones could feel the nervousness around him, scanning the big openness of the station, looking for any quick movement, a face covered by a newspaper, the point of a barrel around a corner. The light bleeding through the high-walled windows yawned white-hot on the marble floors.

When they passed a little booth for the Travelers Aid Society, a woman gave a big smile, looking at old Frank Nash, the curly toupee on his head and chained wrists, and said, "Well, I'll be. It's 'Pretty Boy' Floyd!"

Jones looked over at Lackey, and they had a laugh, before emerging from the big cavern and out on the street and to the waiting car.

The two detectives walked ahead, watching the street, guns at the ready.

They handed Joe Lackey a shotgun they'd brought in from the trunk of the armored car. Jones placed his big revolver in his coat pocket while the young agent and the two beefy detectives walked Frank Nash out of Union Station and crossed the big open platform to the parking lot. A long row of windows showed folks eating up breakfast at the Harvey House, and Jones promised himself he'd come back just as soon as the bastard was delivered and locked away.

The lot had filled with automobiles and people hustling through the big wide doors to the station. A metallic voice from a public-address system read off the morning trains set to leave. A gaggle of nuns emerged from a taxi, and a fat nun opened a coin purse to count out change into the driver's hand.

"Put Jelly up front," Jones said.

The young agent placed him in the passenger seat. Otto Reed and Joe Lackey piled in the back of the sedan. Jones followed, and the two cops stood smoking and watching the parking lot, listening to instructions on the route to Leavenworth. They were to take a few back roads just in case they were followed.

The young agent pumped the detectives' hands and then crossed back toward the driver's side of the car.

Jones took a breath and hoisted himself in the backseat beside Sheriff Reed and Lackey. Lackey had propped the shotgun up between his legs, and Jones made the remark he looked like he worked for Wells Fargo.

Cars passed. One of the detectives—he'd later know the name was Grooms—finished a cigarette and smashed it underfoot, making his way to the hot car.

"Hands up," a voice yelled.

A black Chevrolet had stopped beside them, and as Jones turned he heard the words, "Let 'em have it." As Jones bent forward, he saw the young agent chopped to his knees and heard Sheriff Reed's shotgun blast by his ear, the top of Frank Nash's head opening up like a red flower as windows shattered and glass rained down on his neck. As Jones reached for the .45, bullets zipped all over the goddamn place, pinging and piercing, and he heard garbling yells and cries and dull bloody thuds that sounded like a mallet hitting steak.

Lackey was down beside him. He was bleeding, too.

The car shuddered and shook for a solid twenty seconds.

"Stay down," Jones whispered.

The silence was electric and dull, and then buzzing filled Jones's ears, and he heard the crunch of shoes upon the broken glass. A man breathed above him, words as close as if a filthy mouth had been placed to his ear, saying: "They're dead. They're all dead. Let's go."

2

Kathryn had met George Kelly in a Fort Worth speak just before he got nabbed selling some moonshine on a Cherokee reservation just outside Tulsa. She'd been with Little Steve Anderson back then, and George had been with the kind of girl that George tended to be with before he traded up. He'd looked at her and lit a cigarette, a fat ruby ring on his finger, and winked, saying, "Where have you been all my life?" And he said it right there, right in front of Little Steve and the woman he was with, and Kathryn felt like she couldn't breathe. He was big and dark and looked rich. Very rich. And that night she'd snuck away from that sad-sack husband of hers and wrapped her long fine legs around big George in the back of his 1928 Buick, him taking it to her so hard that it about wore out the shocks on that poor machine.

As she'd slipped back into her unmentionables and scooted her silk dress past her knees, she lit a smoke. George had smiled at her and she smiled back, saying: "Just what in the world are we going to do about this?"

"That's the most romantic story I've ever heard," said the girl, a friend of Kathryn's who worked the coat check at the Blackstone Hotel. "That's something out of *Daring Confessions*, or *Good Housekeeping* if you kept out the sex part."

The two sat at a corner table at a beer joint in downtown Fort Worth, the old basement of a hardware store that still smelled of fresh-cut wood and penny nails. The bar was mahogany and the floors black-and-white honeycomb tile. The place was class in spades. Waiters wore white, and the band, Cecil Gill and the Yodeling Cowboys, dressed in satin garb with clean ten-gallon hats.

"I loved him more when I saw how he handled himself," she said. "You know, when he worked a job."

Two more women joined them from the bar. A negro in a white jacket brought them all shots of whiskey and frosty Shiner Bocks in thick glass mugs. The booze not as much fun since drinking was getting to be legit.

"And when he got out of the Big House," Kathryn said, "I was right there waiting for him. We drove straight through to Saint Paul and got married on the spot."

"I like your ring," said the girl.

Kathryn looked at her finger as if eyeing a speck of dust. "I'm getting a new one soon."

"Do tell," said the hatcheck girl.

"It's big."

"How big?"

"So big that I'm through with Texas."

"A bank?"

"There's no money in banks anymore," Kathryn said. "This Depression ruined that. You can't find a decent jug these days."

The three girls leaned forward. They were pretty, all of them wearing stylish new hats cocked just so and expensive little silk scarves. Kathryn pulled out a cigarette, always a Lucky, from a silver case, and two of the girls greeted her with a match.

She smiled self-consciously and took the one nearest to her.

"Where's George?" asked one of the girls.

"Working."

"Did you bring 'em?" asked another.

Kathryn smiled and reached into her little purse, pulling out three spent brass bullet casings. She slapped them on the table and said, "You can probably still feel the heat in 'em. He shot up a barn this morning. You know, to practice."

"Is it true he can write his name in bullets?" asked the hatcheck girl, maybe getting a little too breathless about George.

"Sister, '*Machine Gun*' Kelly can write his name in blood."

KATHRYN GOT BACK TO MULKEY STREET A FEW HOURS LATER so plastered with whiskey and gin she nearly took out a fire hydrant turning in to the bungalow's driveway. The bungalow had belonged to her second husband, Charlie Thorne, and she was glad he'd left her something before shooting himself in the head with a .38, leaving a typed sob-sister note blaming his problems on her. *Can't live with her, can't live with out her*, the note read.

The kitchen light was on.

She closed the door behind her and leaned against the window glass to steady her feet.

George R. Kelly, aka George Barnes, aka R. G. Shannon, aka "Machine Gun" Kelly, looked up from an iron frying pan where he was flipping pancakes. He wore nothing but boxer shorts and blue socks. A cigarette hung loose out of his mouth.

"Where the hell you been?"

"Working."

"Working?"

The boxer shorts were white and decorated with red hearts. His blue socks were held up with garters.

"People are talking about you," she said. "How do you think that gets done?"

"You're drunk."

"So are you," she said, eyeing the empty bottle of Old Log Cabin bourbon on the table.

"Aw, hell," George said. "Is that the way it's gonna go?"

"Why are you cooking so much?"

"We got company."

"It's two in the morning."

"I just got a call," George said. "Verne and Harvey are in town. Don't that beat all?"

"What?" Kathryn asked. "Are you screwy?"

"They needed a place to sleep."

"What the hell are they doing in Texas? They hate Texas."

"Hand me some bacon out of the icebox."

Kathryn plopped down at the little kitchen table and massaged her temples. She breathed, just trying to wrap her drunk mind around what George had done.

"Don't get sore," he said. "Make coffee."

"You make coffee, you rotten son of a bitch."

"Hey."

"Don't you know that we got work to do? Have you even read any of those articles I cut out? Do you know how broke we are? GMAC calls every damn day about the Cadillac."

"I got that covered."

"What? You and Albert are going to go knock over a gas station for ten bucks? This is real money."

"I guess."

"You guess?" Kathryn stood, walked up to her large husband, and rapped on his forehead with her knuckles. "This isn't some bank job in Tupelo. This is the score. And just as we're getting ready, you want Harvey Bailey and that sadistic son of a bitch Verne Miller cutting in. You know they'll want in."

"Maybe we should cut 'em in. They're good, Kit. They're real good. I've worked with them, not you. It's my ass."

"And you want to cut the money another two ways?"

"Goddamnit."

"Listen to what I'm saying."

"That's not it. Aw, hell. You made me burn the gosh-dang pancakes." She took a breath, damn glad she was drunk right now. She half walked, half stumbled back to the bedroom, where she pulled her new dress up over her head, down to her pink slip, and looked at herself in the long oval mirror. She was still good-looking at thirty, still had the curves but not too fat, and the dark hair and eyes she got on account of her Cherokee grandmother. Nice cheekbones. Like the makeup ladies told her at Neiman Marcus, good bones accounted for it all.

A black curl dropped over her eye as she studied herself, turning left to right, watching her profile and trying to remember that pout she'd caught from Claudette Colbert.

She wiped the dark red lipstick off her mouth with a rag and had just plopped into an unmade bed when George stuck his head in the room. "Honey, you mind making up the bed and sofa for the boys? They're gonna be real tired."

She didn't answer, pretending she was asleep, but after he closed the door Kathryn turned over and clicked on a bedside lamp. From the middle of a thick family Bible, she pulled out a handful of neatly clipped newspaper articles from the *Daily Oklahoman*. One of them had been read so much it had grown soft and light in her hands, the folds like lines on an old-time treasure map.

The headline read OIL MAN URSCHEL MARRIES SLICK WIDOW.

The union of the two fortunes will make the Urschels the richest household in the state and one of the richest in the nation. Charles Urschel began his career as partner of the noted Tom Slick, King of the Wildcatters, back when Oklahoma . . .

Kathryn read the story four times, each time with a pleasant smile, feeling much, much better about the world, before clicking off the table lamp and falling asleep.

Sometime about dawn she heard heavy feet and laughter and the clank of bottles and glasses and the smell of more burning bacon.

She lay there staring at the cracked ceiling, thinking of ways to send those two rotten bastards on their way.

THE NEWSBOYS CALLED IT THE "UNION STATION MASSACRE." By the time Gus T. Jones was pulled from the shot-up machine, five men were dead. Sheriff Reed, the two Kansas City cops, Frank Nash, and the young agent. The boy's name was Caffrey. Joe Lackey was shot in the arm, and the SAC was shot in the shoulder. Jones was pulled from the car without a scratch, and he walked the breadth of the brick streets, ringed by onlookers and police, and found the whole thing muted and curious, especially the way one of the big cops lay across the other, like twin boys sleeping in a river of blood.

Jones wired Hoover from the station.

Hoover cabled back that he'd send more men.

The afternoon heat was on them, and Jones stayed long after each man was picked up off the uneven streets by a pasty mortician and his wife and driven away on a flatbed truck. Jones had immediately sealed off the station while the cops put out a radio call for the Chevy. He personally interviewed twenty-seven witnesses, most of whom had been eating a morning meal at the Harvey House. A reporter had spoken to the woman at the Travelers Aid Society, and soon the word was that "Pretty Boy" Floyd and his gang were responsible. The hell of it was that Jones didn't know who'd pulled the trigger or driven the car, or if there'd been two or a half dozen of 'em.

Every story varied. The gunman was short. He was tall. He was dark. He was light. He wore a gray suit. He wore a blue suit. He was handsome. The man was ugly.

When bullets fly, the last thing a person does is study faces.

The hatband on Jones's Stetson had grown wet.

He walked back into the relative coolness of the station, the place feeling even more like a cathedral. He sat down on a long, lone wooden bench. A wide swath of light fell from the windows, and he tilted his face into the sun, pulling off his glasses and cleaning them with a handkerchief.

It was then he noticed the blood and gray matter across the lapels of his jacket.

Old Sheriff Reed grabbing for that shotgun between his legs, weathered hands slipping while trying to take aim at the gunmen, instead blowing off half of Jelly Nash's head. Jones knew he'd take that image to the grave and never tell a soul. He figured Lackey would do the same, knowing Reed worked better for the newsboys as a martyr and not an old lawman with shaky hands.

Jones thought back to a box canyon nearly twenty years ago just outside Pilares, where some greenhorn Rangers and a lone Customs agent had followed Mexican bandit Chico Cano as he drove a herd of stolen horses back to Mexico. The canyon had been nothing but a trap, and soon Jones's friend and the young Rangers had been pinned down by at least thirty bandits, two Rangers escaping and making for a nearby ranch where they got word to Jones. By the time he found the men, they were all dead. Shot a hundred times, faces unrecognizable after being smashed with rocks. The bandits had shot their horses, too, and stolen their saddles and guns. Some political types in Austin blamed the men who escaped for not staying in the canyon and fighting to the death.

Jones would never forget loading up those boys on mule back, the heat more than a hundred, the bloated bodies already busted and the smell so awful that it caused one of the animals to vomit.

It took years. But Jones got the saddles and the guns back.

And Chico Cano's head, too. A gift from Pancho Villa.

"Sir?"

Jones slipped the glasses back on his face, bringing Union Station back into focus. Another young agent handed him coffee and told him he'd drive whenever he was ready to head to the office. Jones thanked him and drank the coffee by himself in that long wash of light. He cleaned his glasses again and, when no one was looking, wiped the brains and blood from his jacket, tucked the handkerchief into his pocket, closed his eyes, and said a short prayer.

Then he stood, checked his weapon, and walked back to the Western Union office.

The next cable to Hoover read AGENTS CANNOT WORK ARMED WITH PEASHOOTERS. PLEASE ADVISE.

THE SONSABITCHES HAD LEFT HER CUTE LITTLE KITCHEN a goddamn mess. Kathryn was no nigger maid—Junie came on Wednesday—and she didn't have time to be scraping out skillets and pouring suds into her big sink to clean up the piles of dishes laden with pancake syrup and cigarette ash. Coffee mugs that smelled like piney gin and sweet bourbon, open bottles of beer and busted poker chips. *Son of a bitch.* Kathryn walked over the black-and-white tile maze of the floor in her gingham housecoat, hair pulled into a tight knot behind her head, her arms elbow-deep into the bubbles, a cigarette hanging loose from her mouth.

The radio was tuned to WBAP, Jimmie Rodgers singing "Miss the Mississippi and You." That yodeler was dead but still singing like the world was nothing but heartache and pain.

She poured in more suds and scrubbed another dish with a brush, rinsing with the clean water, drying with a damp towel, and placing it up on the rack. She grabbed a coffee cup that had been part of a set from her mama, Ora, and she gritted her teeth at the sight of a fat cigar ash in the bottom. *George.*

The back door to her little bungalow opened, and she smiled up at the face of old Albert Bates, the only friend of George Kelly's that she could stand. He was nearly as tall as George, soft muscled, with a high forehead and gentle eyes. Bates was a good egg. A professional thief who was as honest as they come.

"Hey, doll," Kathryn said.

"Jesus H.," Albert said, kissing her on the cheek and setting a suit jacket across a chair. "I miss the party?"

He rolled up his sleeves and began to clear more dishes, whistling along with old Jimmie the brakeman's yodels while Kathryn bopped her head in time.

"Harvey Bailey and Verne Miller stopped by last night."

"They're gone?" Albert asked, nudging Kathryn over with his butt and taking a spot in the suds, handing her the clean dish to rinse.

"I told George to get 'em gone."

"Where to?" he asked.

"They showed George a map, easy-pickin' banks."

"No banks are easy pickin' these days. Nothin' to pick."

He handed her a couple of her mother's cups. Chipped china with delicate rose designs.

"I can't stand either one of those bastards," Kathryn said, rinsing and then drying. "Verne Miller gives me the creeps. Those eyes. Jesus."

"Did George . . ."

"He's not that stupid, thank God," Kathryn said. "This is a two-man job."

"And one woman."

"And one woman."

"Doesn't come much better than Charles F. Urschel," Albert Bates said. "Hey, can I have a smoke?"

Kathryn dried her hands and reached for her pack of Luckies, sticking one into Albert's chiseled mug and lighting it with a kitchen match.

"Oil," Bates said. "Those people shit money. How'd you find 'im?"

"Can you believe it was George's idea?" she said. "He's got a finger man in O.K. City who said this fat cat was ripe."

"Just like we like 'em."

"Al?"

"Yeah, sweetie?"

"You ever get a pain in your heart just 'cause you feel so damn regular and dull?"

"No one would ever call you dull, Kit."

Kathryn smiled and pulled out another smoke. "It sure is good to have some sense in the house."

"Me and George will plan this thing so tight, it'll be—"

Kathryn mashed her index finger to Albert Bates's lips and said: "Shush. Don't be a dope and get all cocky."

3

Saturday July 22, 1933

Charles F. Urschel found the cigar a little dry to his liking and squashed it out in an ashtray while Walter Jarrett dealt another rubber of bridge for the couples. Jarrett was just another oilman in Oklahoma City, someone Charlie knew casually from the club, but he'd seen fit to invite himself and his talkative wife over for a long evening. They'd already played too many rubbers, and despite Betty coming home at eleven-thirty as promised and kissing her mama on the cheek, they continued to stay on the sunporch and talk about government price schedules for low-grade gasoline, a shoe sale at Katz Department Store, and the new president's radio address on Monday night. Charlie lit up another cigar, the same brand, but this one kept much better, and he said, "What the hell, one more rubber," and the cards were all spread around and drinks refreshed. Mrs. Jarrett remarked how pretty young Betty looked in her summer dress, and Berenice was the one who said thank you, because, after all, Betty wasn't Charlie's daughter but Tom Slick's, and as long as Charlie lived he damn well knew the differences between him and his old buddy and brother-in-law, who folks still called King of the Wildcatters.

"You must watch boys," Mrs. Jarrett said. "You can't trust boys. They are ruled by their thingamajigs."

Charlie smiled over at Mr. Jarrett because it seemed to be the thing to do at the mention of peckers, and Jarrett grinned back before he leveled his eyes back at the cards. Jarrett was an uneasy card player who needed complete concentration, whereas Charlie could give the hand one glance, lean back, and enjoy his cigar while working out the basic math and guessing who had what and how they'd play 'em. Didn't matter if you were playing with an oil executive or a driller in some rotten boomtown, people had their systems and rarely liked to break tradition.

"More pay for less hours does not make a lick of sense to me," Jarrett said. "But they say we don't have a choice."

"I have warned Betty, but she won't listen to me about boys and their animal ways," Berenice said. "A new one comes calling almost every day, like tomcats."

"Roosevelt means well," Charlie said. "But you won't see me wearing that goddamn NRA eagle on my breast."

"You can be like that dry cleaner I read about in Muskogee," Jarrett said. "He said the eagle was mentioned in Revelations and that he wouldn't sign a damn thing with the mark of the beast."

"I heard from a woman at the club that one young man tried to hide his in a popcorn box during a matinee movie show," Mrs. Jarrett said, eyes on her hand and then cutting them over at Berenice. "It wasn't even a romance picture. It had Tom Mix in it."

"I'm not one for handouts," Charlie said. "They can have their time with all this NRA nonsense until sharper minds prevail. Have you seen that film *Gabriel Over the White House*? I know the idea of a president dissolving Congress is kind of screwy, but I'll be damned if Walter Huston didn't make a fine leader at that."

"You aren't thinking of getting into politics?" Jarrett asked.

"What did that boy want?" Berenice asked, hand light on her breast. "For her to touch it? My Lord."

"Berenice, would you hush and get us all some coffee?" Charlie asked. "I'd like mine with a kick. Anyone else? Hell, no, I don't care one bit for politics or much for government. Why are you two talking about popcorn?"

The porch had been fashioned from the rear of the mansion, screened in, with comfortable rattan chairs and ceiling fans to scatter away the midnight humidity and cigar smoke. The evening was a pleasant one in Oklahoma City, and the women quickly returned with a serving tray, china cups, and saucers. Hot coffee was poured, a little whiskey added, and Charlie began to flick cards around the table.

Berenice sat directly across from him, Mrs. Jarrett flanked him to the right, and Mr. Jarrett to the left.

Berenice declared no trumps, and so the last game of the evening began with not much thought, the smoldering cigar burning down into Charlie's fingers as he studied Mrs. Jarrett until she led with a ten of spades.

The radio played the orchestra from the Skirvin Hotel but soon signed off, and the weather and Ag reports began. Berenice walked to the cabinet and flicked off the RCA, and the couples were left with the soft evening sounds, a passing car or two, and there wasn't a bit of notice when they heard a car pull into the drive by the garage behind their home, doors click closed, and soft, deliberate steps coming from the walk.

Charlie lifted his eyes from his cards to Berenice, and Berenice shifted in her chair as if the cushion had grown hot. Betty Slick hadn't been home a half an hour and already suitors were driving by with a lot of teenage bravado, probably searching out pebbles to pelt her bedroom window.

Mrs. Jarrett played a jack, and her husband threw across a six.

Berenice met Charlie's eyes with a smile, tossing across a king and winning the trick. He gathered the cards and made a notation on a pad beside him, taking a puff of his cigar, the tip glowing red, and smiling just as two shadows appeared before the screen door.

Men in dark suits and hats walked onto the porch. Both held guns.

The couples froze.

"Which one of you is Mr. Urschel?" the larger of the two asked. He had a square jaw and a thick neck, eyes obscured in shadow.

No one said a word.

"I said who's Urschel?" the man said, with a calm force and without a bit of nervousness, casually holding a Thompson machine gun as if it were a Christmas ham. The shorter of the men, who wasn't that much shorter, only slighter and leaner, held a revolver and kept a gun trained on Jarrett.

The last of the cigar smoke floated up from the glass ashtray, scattering into the ceiling fan as the big clock in the main house began to chime. Charlie could feel the blood rushing through his ears, thinking of that sorry bastard of a night watchman he'd fired only last week on account of him sleeping on the job and listening to *Amos 'n' Andy* when he should have been out patrolling.

The chimes stopped.

"Okay," said the large man. "We'll take 'em both."

Urschel stood.

Jarrett did the same.

The large man gripped Charlie's arm with thick, meaty fingers, walking him to the door as if he were a common drunk being tossed from a party. But the man suddenly stopped as if reminded by his manners or by the interruption of a passing thought. He turned back to the women with a grin: "Ladies, don't say a word or make a move toward the telephone, or I'm afraid we'll have to blow your goddamn heads off."

THE RIDE WAS FOREVER OR MAYBE TEN MINUTES, BUT finally the damn car slowed and doors were thrown open. The driver—the large man—told Jarrett, without knowing his name, to get his ass out. The gunman who sat beside Charlie in the backseat nudged him in the ribs with the revolver and told him to be a good boy and stay put and shut the fuck up. The car had stopped at a dirt crossroads, and with the windows down Charlie could hear a baying hound and see flickering lights from a house a half mile from where the gunmen spoke to Jarrett.

The short one pulled a wallet from Jarrett's pocket and thumbed through it. He lifted his head up to the other man and cocked it like a crow. Heavy headlights from the car seeped onto their heavy black shoes, and the big man with the big gun stepped forward.

"It's not him."

The other man picked out a wad of cash and tucked it into his own shirt pocket before handing Jarrett back his wallet.

"Now what?"

Charles F. Urschel counted the silence, feeling the ticking of his watch against his wrist. He could not breathe, not that he was a great friend to Jarrett, but he didn't want to be a spectator to the man's execution either. He reached for the door handle.

One of the men said: "Start walking, brother."

Charlie let out a long breath.

And the gunmen turned and came for Charlie, but he wasn't the least bit afraid, knowing they were going to hold him ransom just like that city manager's son and that brewer from Minnesota and all the rest, so he let them go ahead and place cotton over his eyes and tape across the bridge of his nose and down between his eyebrows in the fashion of a cross.

He was led back to the car, someone pushing him down into the floorboard and telling him to be quiet and not move, and if they were stopped not to make a peep or he'd not only get himself killed but they'd go back for his family.

Charlie hadn't opened his mouth since the sunporch.

The car fired up, and they rolled away, and Charlie bumped and jostled and closed his eyes, since there was no use keeping them open, but his mind racing all the same, the man resting his feet across his back like he was a stool, calling the driver Floyd. Soon he heard the pinging of rain across the hood and felt the car turn, thinking they were headed south but not knowing for sure as the men were silent. The whole thing made Charlie feel like a scolded child kept down and out of sight with close-lipped parents trying to teach him a lesson. The miles rolled and rolled, and he knew they were on a proper highway again.

As soon as the wheels had touched the smooth surface, the men began to laugh and laugh.

An hour later, they ran out of gas.

KATHRYN SAT AT A SMALL KITCHEN TABLE WITH A DETEC-tive from the Fort Worth Police Department named Ed Weatherford. She'd known Ed since she'd been married to Charlie Thorne, and Ed—a lean, rawboned boy with red hair and big teeth—had been such a good egg he'd made sure all of that mess went away real fast. The hell of it was that he'd only screwed her once, and that must have still resonated with him like some kind of tuning fork in his pecker because goddamn old Ed wore a rickety smile from the moment she'd opened her door after midnight and leaned into the frame just like she'd seen Jean Harlow do a thousand times.

The black satin kimono was just loose enough. And she smelled like fresh powder where'd she'd dabbed it under her arms and in the money patch. She poured rye into two coffee cups, and they sat and smiled at each other from across the table covered in red-and-white oilcloth.

"Aren't you the funny one," she said after they'd had a couple drinks. He played with her naked foot with his clumsy old boots.

"Yes, ma'am," he said, still smiling, Kathryn wondering if his lips didn't hurt by now, squeezed tight over that big crooked smile.

"I appreciate you coming over like this."

"Well, you said you were scared."

"I am scared."

"What about, sweet muffin?"

"You know George."

His smiled dropped fast. "I know George."

She dropped her head into her hands and shook her shoulders a bit, trying out what it must feel like to cry. She really tried to work on the breathing part of it like she was steadying herself or trying to hold herself together, but she knew she could never pull off a good cry like a good actress might.

Ed got out of his chair so fast he knocked his hat on the floor and put a lean hand on her shoulder. "Darlin'."

"He's gone and done it."

"What'd he do? He hit you?"

She shook her head and sniveled. Hot damn, the sniveling felt just about perfect. She opened the hands from her face and wrapped them around the coffee mug full of hooch. "I can't say."

"Who says?"

"George says."

"He threaten you?"

She looked up at him, making her black eyes grow big, and not answering at first. "He's gone and done it. He's gonna take me down with him."

"Darlin'."

She took a drink of rye. She'd had to take a drink the last time with Ed, too.

She reached up and held his bony hand and said calmly, "I'm through with him, Ed. I'm really through."

She squeezed his hand.

"Your daughter here?" he asked.

"She's visiting my aunt."

"And George?"

"He's out of town."

"Daddy's here," said Detective Ed Weatherford. He gripped her hand back.

Kathryn stood from the kitchen chair and let Ed work his lean fumbling hands on her sash until the robe dropped to the checkerboard floor.

"GODDAMN," SAID THE BIG, LUMBERING GUNMAN. "GODDAMN."
He'd been cussing over and over, ever since the other man had gone off for some gas. They were parked somewhere on the side of a ditch, and Charlie could hear the cows making confused sounds and smell their fetid shit through the open windows.

"Goddamn. Goddamn."

Charlie wanted to ask the fella which genius was the one who was supposed to fill up the getaway vehicle, but instead kept his mouth shut.

He heard the snick of a lighter and smelled a cigarette.

"Don't think you'll get much," Charlie said, filling the silence.

"Why don't you just shut up."

"The money's all tied up in trusts. Nobody can touch it. Not even me."

The man said nothing and then leaned forward to open the door, and Charlie heard him talking to the other fella and asking him if he had to walk clear back to Bumfuck, Egypt, to get them some gasoline, and the partner told him he'd had to wake up the attendant to take the locks off the pumps.

"He see you?"

"It's dark."

"You were gone for an hour."

"Son of a bitch."

"I'm not complainin'. I just said it took a while."

"Well, goddamnit, you sure are a grateful bastard."

"Fill it up and let's get gone."

"You're wasting your time," Charlie said again, but wasn't sure if anyone was listening.

THEY SMOKED AFTERWARD, JUST LIKE A CUTE COUPLE IN the movies. The sheets covered Kathryn to the stomach, but old Ed

Weatherford lay naked, the flat of his back in the soft indention worn by George Kelly's big ass, without a stitch on except for a pair of hand-tooled cowboy boots. He stared at the ceiling, hands under his head, and held that Lucky in his lips with a cocky, contented smile.

"Do you like to dance?"

"Sure," Kathryn said. "Who doesn't?"

"My ma," Ed said. "She said dancing was evil. Led to fornication."

"Well, we weren't exactly dancing in the kitchen."

"I wish you'd warned me about that fork."

"Maybe we shouldn't have hopped on that table."

"Why'd you call on me, Kathryn?"

She rolled over toward him, propping herself on an elbow, and played with a thin patch of black hair on his chest. She noticed he had a couple white scars across his stomach like he'd been raked by gunfire at some time, and that excited her more than when they were in the kitchen and he had his boots on and britches hitched down to his knees.

"You got shot?"

"Some crazy nigger got me. I kilt him, though."

"You like me? Don't you, Ed?"

"Sure I like you. Didn't I just prove it to you?"

"What if George were to get me in trouble?"

"Like in a family way?"

"No, real trouble. If he got arrested."

"He rob another bank?"

"Let's say he did and then they arrested me, too. Couldn't you have me called back to Fort Worth? Find something to charge me with here?"

"You call it extradite, darlin'."

"Well, can you?"

"I s'pose."

"You s'pose what?"

"Sure, I could get you extradited here. Make sure you get a fair shake with some friendly judge."

"You swear?"

"Depends on my motivation."

She nestled under his long, skinny arm and plucked the Lucky from his lips, taking a drag and staring up at the big, damp spot on the ceiling where the roof had leaked. She took a few puffs and then reached for him.

"Whew, careful there, darlin'. That ain't no gearshifter!"

CHARLIE THOUGHT THEY WERE DEAD FOR SURE WHEN THE car went veering off the road an hour later, scattering and swerving and then sliding deep down into some kind of gulley or ditch. He'd been rolled up and around, and then found himself in the backseat, hanging upside down. The gunmen screamed at each other, each calling the other stupid. The driver tried the engine, and it turned over, and then there was just the spinning of wheels on mud.

With the tape over his eyes, darkness around him, Charlie Urschel smiled.

"Well goddamn, get out and push, Floyd."

"Quit callin' me Floyd."

"Well, that's your name, ain't it?"

"How 'bout you push?"

"Who's got the machine gun, you dumb yegg? Use your head."

Gus T. Jones barely had time to pack his leather grip with some fresh clothes and his thumb buster before he was on a flight Hoover had chartered out of San Antonio straight to Oklahoma City. He and Doc White stepped off the six-seater by themselves just before sundown and were met by a long black Ford, a couple agents, and the Special Agent in Charge, a fella by the name of Colvin. Bruce Colvin. He was a nice enough guy, and he even took Jones's grip, which Jones took to be on account of respect and not 'cause he was an old man. Colvin was one of the new streamlined agents, not even thirty years old, with grease-parted hair and a tailored suit, and he kept on calling Jones "Sir" and saying "This way," and even held the door open for him. Some kind of lawyer or accountant type.

Jones turned back to the Orion aircraft and watched a mechanic slide some wood blocks under the tires and the propeller sputter to a stop. He could hear the boy a little bit better and leaned in for him to repeat that last part as he held on to the doorframe. Old Doc White threw his bag into the trunk and lumbered back around, asking, "Where do we domicile?"

White still talking like he and Jones were both Rangers, riding the river together with rifles and rucksacks, nothing but hard, wide-open land and restless Mexicans trying to smuggle guns over the border. Back then they hadn't even seen a damn airplane.

"We have rooms for you at the Skirvin," Colvin said, still holding Jones's grip. "We can take you there immediately, let you settle in and get something to eat before we meet with the Urschels."

"Not necessary," Jones said. "Doc?"

"Yep."

And they were in the Ford, riding off the tarmac and hitting a state road into town, two agents in the front and Colvin sitting in back with Jones and White. The sun had just started to dip down, and the glare cut hard into Jones's eyes, making him remove his wire glasses and tuck them into his jacket as he kept on talking.

"What do we know?"

"They let Jarrett go outside the city limits."

Doc had taken off his Stetson—regulation, same as Jones—and balanced it across his knee. His suit wasn't federal regulation like Colvin's; Doc had chosen a Western style, with cowboy stitching at the seams, and a silver belt buckle the size of a dinner plate.

"We know where?"

"Eight miles east on Northeast Sixty-third, right at the river. You know Oklahoma City, sir?"

"I'll take a map to it. Go on."

"Sometime after midnight, Mr. Jarrett knocked on the door of a farmer named"—Colvin looked down at his notes, and, in the light, Jones wondered if the boy had started shaving yet—"Fred Wilson, but Wilson wouldn't open the door. He thought Mr. Jarrett might be an escaped convict. A little while later, he—that being Wilson—saw a car start at the crossroads and head toward Luther."

"What's in Luther?"

"Access to U.S. 66," Colvin said. "Straight to Tulsa."

"Jarrett get a good look at our boys?"

"Said they look foreign."

"Hell, that narrows it."

Doc White rolled a cigarette and lit it, watching the hard country roll by and turning his head back to stare at a small shantytown that had been constructed next to a dry ditch. Burlap sacks flew on sticks like flags. A naked child watched the vehicle pass while banging two tin cans together.

"The wife?"

"Berenice Urschel," Colvin said. "She doesn't remember much."

"And Jarrett's wife?"

"Even less."

"This may be an indelicate question, but just how much are these folks worth?"

"The last estimate of the Slick estate is valued at a little more than twenty million."

Jones gave a low whistle. Doc looked up from his smoke.

"That'll keep the lights on," Doc said.

"I knew Tom Slick," Jones said. "Don't know his wife. Or I should say, Urschel's wife now. Also remember a front man who worked for Slick in San Antonio, fella named Kirkpatrick. You heard his name?"

"No, sir," Colvin said. "Urschel's boys were fishing in Mexico and are headed back. Right now, it's just Mrs. Urschel, her teenage daughter, and some neighbors and friends. We're trying to keep the newsboys away."

"Havin' much luck?" Jones asked.

"You ever been to a circus, sir?"

THE GETAWAY CAR FINALLY STOPPED EARLY THAT MORNING, and Charlie thought they'd arrived at wherever they were headed to chain him up or stick him in a cage or whatever these people do to decent taxpayers. He didn't move from the floor of the backseat, the big feet of the man on his back. The driver got out, and Charlie felt some of the weight lifted from the shocks and then heard some outside banter with someone.

"Gettin' much rain out here?" the gunman asked.

"Not a speck," a woman said in a graveled hick voice.

"Corn gettin' high?"

"Burned up."

"All of it?"

"We still got broom corn. Mister, I get thirsty just walkin' outside."

"You sell Coca-Colas?"

"Sure thing. Cost you a nickel, though."

"That's fine. What flavor you got?"

"We got that grape Nehi, some Dr Pepper, and straight Coca-Colas in that cooler over yonder. Fill her up?"

Charlie thought now was the time to yell, and he filled his lungs, but it was as if the man sitting above him could read his thoughts, grinding the heel of his shoe between Charlie's shoulders, the way you'd put out a cigarette butt. The man whispered, "Stay still. My finger gets jumpy."

"Y'all are preachers, ain't you?" asked the attendant. "I figured y'all for the ministry."

"How'd you guess?"

Charlie squirmed, and the heel inched up to his neck.

"FOREIGNERS," BERENICE URSCHEL SAID. "PROFESSIONALS, I'm sure of it."

"What kind of foreigners?" Jones asked.

"People not born in this country."

"Mex. Eye-talian?"

"They were very dark. Very swarthy. One of them had a neck as thick as a bull."

"What were they wearin'?"

"Light shirts. Dress pants. Both of them wore hats."

Jones made a note. They sat across from each other in the family salon among the velvet furniture, gilded mirrors, and large oil paintings of

well-fed people Jones took to be family. A negro woman came in and set
down two glasses and a crystal decanter filled with water.

"We heard a car drive up on the driveway but didn't think anything
about it, because the children use the drive all the time," Mrs. Urschel
said. "Both of them carried machine guns. I didn't know what those
long black things were, but Mr. Jarrett later told me. We just sat there
and didn't say a word while the larger of the two men walked toward
the card table. The slender one stood by the door and covered us with
the gun."

"You get a decent look at the car?"

"We just heard the motor spurt as it drove away," she said, starting to
choke up a bit. "I didn't get a very good look at the car."

"How 'bout your daughter?" Jones asked. "You said she'd gone
upstairs?"

Outside a great bank of windows, through long pressed curtains,
photographic flashes went off over and over in a strobe fashion, bringing back memories of lightning pockets in west Texas. The lawn of the
Urschel home had looked like a state fair when they'd pulled up, and the
driver had had to honk the horn just to cut through the sea of men with
notebooks and cameras.

"Oh, I'm so thankful that it wasn't Betty," she said. "She thinks these
same two men have been following her for several weeks. She saw them
in a blue sedan when she came back from Tulsa Tuesday."

"You mind if we talk to her?"

"I believe the man from the local office is with her in the kitchen now."

Jones nodded. Doc White was at the front door, talking to three city
cops in plain clothes and giving directions on where to stand post. The
door had been opened and closed so many times that the big house filled
with heavy heat, and White was perspiring through the front of his shirt.

"Did you or your husband have threats against your persons?"

"We have had letters and that mess. But that was some time ago, and
they were all cranks."

Mrs. Urschel leaned forward, resting her forehead in her left hand. A big clock on a very big mantel in the very big room read nearly ten.

"I would try and persuade you to get some shut-eye," Jones said. "But don't expect you to."

"What do we do?"

"Give 'em what they ask."

"And then what?"

"Then we go to work."

"Did I do right calling that telephone extension?" she asked. "I think I woke Mr. Hoover."

"I'm sure he didn't mind."

"It was printed right there in *Time* magazine," she said. "I'd recalled the article about the kidnapping epidemic just as soon as I'd run upstairs. I'm so glad I kept that issue. You'll have to excuse me, I'm as nervous as a house cat."

Berenice Urschel was not a beautiful woman, but she had a nice warm smile and nice warm brown eyes that lit up when she smiled back at Gus Jones. She reminded him a bit of his wife, Mary Ann, only with better manners and no propensity for using bad language. Mary Ann was a true master in the art of profanity and could outcuss any shitheel cowboy or redneck twice her size.

Jones stood and grabbed his hat from the sofa. He followed a long hallway lined with paintings of open pastures and rolling green hills, almost like windows looking away from the city or back years ago when all this was Indian territory.

He found Special Agent Bruce Colvin in the kitchen, talking to Betty Slick while the negro woman refilled a big coffeepot. Another negro was sweeping by a back door where agents and police officers came in and out, tramping in dirt. The negro didn't take notice, just sweeping that same dirty spot over and over, refilling the dustpan and emptying it.

The girl sat up on the countertop, rocking her long tan legs against a cabinet.

Colvin nodded to Jones, a notebook in a loose hand. The girl didn't turn around, staring at Colvin. She continued to stroke long brown hair over her right ear.

"You think you could identify the men who followed you?" Colvin asked.

"Maybe."

"If we showed you a photo?"

"Are you married?"

"Ma'am?"

Jones coughed, and the girl turned to him. She wore a pin-striped linen dress and tall-heeled shoes adorned with pink bows. She had sleepy green eyes, and acknowledged Jones with a soft "Hello" while managing to keep her attention full on that bright-eyed college boy.

Jones grinned a bit when he noted the perspiration pop on the young agent's forehead.

"Miss Slick, we'll do everything we can to protect you."

"Do you all carry guns?"

"Do we?" Jones asked.

"I target-shoot out at a pumpkin farm sometime," Colvin said.

"You don't say," Jones said. "Those pumpkins move much?"

Betty Slick shot him a hot look and then turned back to Colvin with a big smile.

"Mother said there was nothing amateurish about these men. She said, 'They knew just what they were doing.'"

IT WAS ABOUT DAYBREAK NOW, URSCHEL KNOWING THIS because the light changed through the gaps in the hospital tape. A gray, dull light, the rumbling and bumping down the road making him nauseated but never sleepy, tucked and rolled in the womb of the floorboard, and for a while feeling like part of the machine, the gears and the brakes, the cluttering, spurting jumble of cranks and belts digesting the black gold that to Charlie Urschel would always remain hot as the core of the earth and always a welcome sight dripping off the hands and faces of riggers and geologists, always with big, wide grins, from tapping that vein.

The steady, graveling swoosh turned to rolling, piano-key clatter of wood that went on for a good bit—up a bridge and over a river—and then the tires found solid ground again, gears shifting to a purr, and, with a slap of foot on pedal, they were headed somewhere damn fast.

Hours later, Charlie heard clanging and a trunk slam. A man and a young-sounding woman talking. The woman promised to meet them at the ranch, and Charlie strained an ear. But then one of the men gripped him by the neck and pulled him from the car, heels dragging on the ground, and another car door opened, and he was pushed inside and onto a large leather backseat.

"Do you love me?" asked the young woman.

"You know it, baby. You just know it."

"Oh, shit," said the young woman. "Here she comes, sick with the religion, too."

"Get them sonsabitches off my land," said an old woman. "A hellfire abomination."

"Just a minute," said the man.

"They're going," said the young woman.

"Don't think that I won't shoot you," the old woman screamed. "Don't you doubt it, boys."

Charlie twisted his head toward the noise.

"I prayed for you," the old woman said. "I prayed for you both, and you bring this evil to my doorstep. Let us all pray."

The old woman began to hum "Amazing Grace."

"Why don't you plug Urschel's goddamn ears," the man said. "This ain't smart, listenin' to this radio show."

"Hush, you filthy evil man."

They drove the new car faster and harder, and Charlie knew it was a bigger, steadier ride, with an engine as powerful as a truck. He was lulled to sleep for a moment and then awoke when he heard the men talking again, and figured the young woman hadn't come along.

"Did that fella know which way?"

"Head back ten miles and then turn east."

"I told you."

"You didn't say anything. You said you knew where you were. We'd still be traveling down that road if I hadn't stopped."

"What if he's wrong?"

"Would you shut up and let me drive?"

"Go back and ask him again."

"Hell I will."

"Just turn around and let me ask him."

"The son of a bitch will hear you."

"Just let me out and I'll ask."

"I know where I'm going."

"You don't even know what state you're in."

"I'd tell you but then he'd hear me say."

"Goddamn."

"Just lean back and enjoy the ride."

"That's what they tell the bastards in the electric chair."

AGENT COLVIN DROVE JONES AND DOC WHITE OUT TO THE crossroads made famous in the afternoon papers, Jarrett riding with them and pointing them to the exact spot where the gunmen had stopped and the two villains pulled out his wallet and took his cash. Jarrett seemed a little theatrical about the whole ordeal, walking off the paces and acting out the parts as if Jones were interested in some kind of Passion play.

"If only I had a gun," said the rich man.

"And then what?" Doc White asked.

Jarrett started to say something but thought better of it.

He was a well-dressed man with the beaten face and accent of a roughneck. Jones figured he'd spent many a day in the heat with oil deep under his fingernails and sun burning his neck before people started calling him sir.

A full silver moon hung overhead. Big and fat, the way a moon can only look in the country, and Jones didn't even need a flashlight as he found the tire tracks with ease and squatted down, studying the pattern. He found matches in his shirt pocket, filled his bowl with tobacco, and lit it.

He looked up at the long endless road when he got the pipe going, Doc studying the tracks over Jones's shoulder.

"Firestone," Doc said.

"New?"

"Last year's make."

"You boys can tell that just from the tracks?" Jarrett asked.

Jones stood and walked along the tracks, taking the exact direction the farmer had noted. He pulled a small leather notebook from his coat pocket and inked in a few passages.

"He's headed south," Jones said, pipe set hard in his teeth.

"But the tracks go to Tulsa," Jarrett said.

"Yes, sir, they do," Jones said.

"Dirty kidnappers," White said. "Remember when we'd catch fellas like this and chain 'em to a mesquite tree like Christmas ornaments?"

"No, I don't, Doc. You must've confused me with someone else."

"Horseshit," White said. "Those Mexes jumped us outside Harlington? Remember? They'd been running whores and cheating cards out of the Domingo Roach, and we got some of 'em and tracked the rest down a trail where'd they'd laid a fire. Those bastards ambushed us right there, and we shot three of 'em dead? That wasn't that long ago."

"Nineteen hundred and thirteen."

"You said you don't recall."

"I just wanted to see if you remembered who shot who."

"You boys were Rangers?" Jarrett asked.

"Did you know Jim Dunaway?"

"Sure," White said. "He lasted two weeks before being mustered out for drunkenness and insubordination."

The silence was broken by the grumble of a low-flying airplane, and the men craned their heads to watch it pass in the night.

They continued on, following the tracks, Colvin driving slow behind them, the engine ticking and their feet crunching on gravel, moonlight leading the way.

About a half mile down from the crossroads, Jarrett about jumped out of his britches at the sight of a coiled rattlesnake raising its head, ready to strike.

"Holy shit!"

Jones shined his light, and the snake slithered off into the ditch.

"Shoot it," Jarrett yelled. "Shoot it!"

"I'm not gonna shoot it," Jones said. "Has the same right bein' out here as us."

"You ever been bit?" Jarrett asked. "Nearly killed me one time."

"They just actin' according to their nature," Jones said. "Can't fault 'em for it."

"Shoot it."

"No, sir."

Jarrett walked off in the moonlight and returned with a fat river stone he had to hold in both hands. He got within six feet of that old rattler, shaking its tail for all it's worth, and launched the stone at the snake, sending it writhing and turning with a broken back. He retrieved the rock and slammed it back down a half dozen times before the snake, bloody and broken, tried to coil and strike a final time, but only twitched on account of the nerves.

In the moonlight they watched Jarrett spit and try to catch his breath.

"Man can't show anger toward nature," Jones said in a whisper to White. "Any fool knows that. That's what separates us."

5

Monday, July 24, 1933

Okay, so the song went like this: Harvey Bailey and Verne Miller had robbed three banks since Kansas City, none of them worth squat, but the little stash growing into something neat and tidy, a figure to work with, something respectable, and a number that would be well worth telling the dealer, "I'm okay with this. I'm out." They slept in cars and ate by cook fires. They turned their heads from friendly folks in restaurants who wanted to chat about the weather; they wore common clothes and drove common cars. Their lives, their futures, were road maps purchased for pennies at Texaco, Sinclair Oil, and Standard Red Crown service stations. They pissed in drainage ditches and fell asleep with whiskey bottles in their hands, often reaching for guns when a deer would scamper across places where they laid their heads. All in all, Harvey had been having a hell of a time since breaking out of jail. Everything was just that much sweeter.

"So if it's good, why do we bring in Underhill and Clark?"

"Because we need more men," Harvey said.

"Those hicks are the types that find a sexual interest in the barnyard."

"Didn't say I wanted to take them to dinner with us."

"If they fuck up, we leave 'em or kill 'em."

"You run a hard code, Verne."

"You got more patience?"

Harvey shrugged. They stood over the hood of his Buick, parked at the edge of a rolling hill at the foot of the Cooksons, and studied the git out from Muskogee, the People's National Bank. "Big beautiful cage on the left wall," Harvey said. "Safe will be open for business behind them."

"How many?"

"Eight and the president."

"When?"

"Right before closing."

"And then what?"

"I head back to my family," Harvey said. "Wisconsin and all that. And you can go back to Vi."

"Vi's in New York."

"Then you go to New York."

"I think she's fooling around on me."

"You'd have to be pretty stupid to step out with Verne Miller's gal."

"We had some trouble before she left."

"What kind of trouble?"

"She complained that I got a temper."

Dust kicked up on the horizon, and a black speck soon took the shape of a sedan not unlike the black Ford they'd stolen in Clinton. "Mad Dog" Underhill and Jim Clark crawled out, and Harvey and Miller spoke to them. Harvey hadn't seen the boys since the Lansing breakout. Underhill was a bony fella with big mean eyes and dirty little hands. Clark had no neck, thinning hair, and dimples. He was a fat man who shifted from side to side when he walked.

Cigarettes were smoked. The git shown to everyone there just in case Harvey was hit and couldn't drive. Underhill laid down a sharp fart as he studied the map and didn't even say he was sorry.

"I got some aigs and a skillet," Underhill said, scratching his crotch.

"Stole some bread at the Piggly Wiggly," Clark said, and spat.

"Fire's over there, boys," Harvey Bailey said, pointing to the little grouping of stones he'd laid out last night. "Help yourself."

Verne Miller had walked off to the edge of a little hill where the earth had been blasted away to make room for train tracks. He carried with him a little bucket of water, a straight razor, and a mirror. Sitting on an old tree stump, he began to shave as the new boys guffawed it up by the fire.

"Don't think about it so much," Harvey said.

"Mad Dog? You got to be pulling my leg."

"Vi."

"You know, I met her at a carnival," Verne said. "She was working in a kissing booth, and some rube tried to reach under her skirt and touch her pussy."

"And you didn't like that."

"I nearly choked the man to death."

Miller had shaven half his face with nothing but muddy water. The mud slid down off his cheek and into the bucket as he turned to stare at Harvey. He shook his head and slid the razor down his other cheek, the blade sounding like the soft ripping of a paper bag.

"Those morons know about Kansas City?" Miller asked.

"Nope."

"The G's gonna hang us for that," Miller said. "You were right. Jelly Nash wasn't worth it."

"We weren't there," Harvey said. "Don't ever tell yourself anything different."

"People blame me for killing Nash."

"Wasn't your fault."

"Underhill said he heard I killed Nash because he looked at me wrong."

"Underhill doesn't have much sense," Harvey said.

"Why do they call him 'Mad Dog'?"

"You really want to know?"

———

"MORE COFFEE?" MRS. URSCHEL ASKED.

"I'd appreciate it, ma'am," Gus Jones said.

She sent a negro boy back to the kitchen to refill the silver pot.

"I want you to go," Mrs. Urschel said. "I want all these lawmen gone."

"May I ask why?"

"No one will call with every policeman in the state in this house."

"I'd like our people to stay."

"From your office."

"Yes, ma'am," Jones said. "We don't want to interfere."

"Is Charlie dead?"

"No, ma'am."

"Will they kill him?"

"I can't rightly say."

"But they might."

"Yes, ma'am."

"Like the Lindbergh child."

"Yes, ma'am."

"Mr. Urschel is a tough, resourceful man. He's cunning and shrewd and quite strong. He can take care of himself."

"I don't doubt it, Mrs. Urschel."

"Do I call you 'Agent Jones'?"

"'Buster' is just fine."

"Why do they call you Buster?"

"Just what I've always been called. My mother called me that."

"Did she approve of your line of work?"

"She understood it," Jones said. "My father was the same."

"Worked for the government."

"He was a lawman."

She nodded. The negro waited until there was a pause in the conversation to pour the coffee into the china cups. The furniture was stiff and hard, the kind you'd seen in a museum but never used. A large portrait of

Charles Urschel hung on a far wall over a small wooden bookshelf filled with leather-bound editions. Jones would be damned if it didn't seem like old Charlie was staring dead at him.

"Agent Colvin said you knew my first husband."

"I helped him out in a small matter sometime back."

"Charles is much more reserved than Mr. Slick."

"I imagine so."

They drank more coffee. The house had an air-conditioning machine that groaned and hummed and let in refrigerated air while the press and police sat outside in a ninety-degree morning. They ran telephone lines to poles and hustled copy straight from desks fashioned from blocks and beams to downtown newsrooms. Earlier that day, Jones had chased off a grifter selling photographs of the Urschel family.

"Mr. Kirkpatrick said I can trust you."

"You can."

"And you are acquainted with him, too."

"Through your first husband," he said. "Kirk is a right fella."

"He's placed a great many calls on the family's behalf. Some top newspaper editors will be withdrawing their people."

"That's good."

"You don't like them either."

"Never cared for parasites of any kind."

Berenice Urschel smiled at him, and the smile dropped as she craned her head to look at the gilded portrait of her kidnapped husband. She took a sip of coffee and shrugged. "He'll be just fine."

"Yes, ma'am."

THE BANK TELLER LAY FLAT ON HER BACK, SUMMER DRESS hiked above the knee, showing a good bit of stocking and garter. She was a looker, too. Lean and lanky, with red lips and marcelled hair, smelling just like sunshine to Harvey Bailey.

"Sweetie?" Harvey asked.

"Yes, sir?"

"Please, turn over," he said.

The woman—whom Harvey had noted yesterday as Miss Georgia Loving—flipped, face reddened, but no less excited about the show.

"This is a robbery," he said. "Not an audition."

Women were often like that during a job. You offered a little politeness, some little gentlemanly presentation, and they'd work with you. It made the whole thing very safe and enjoyable for everyone.

He checked his Bulova. *Four on the nose.*

Harvey moved across the wide marble lobby—polished shoes clicking under him—and looked out the front-door window to see Verne Miller behind the wheel of a stolen flat-black Buick. Miller met his eyes and tipped his hat.

The street was clean. Two minutes to go.

"Done?" Harvey yelled, heading back behind the cages and scooping up great wads of cash and coin, filling a bag.

"Almost," Clark called from inside the vault.

Underhill stood at the vault door, sweeping his 12-gauge across a dozen or so bank employees and anonymous suckers, face to floor with hands on their necks. He wore a great smile on his unshaven mug, a matchstick in the corner of his mouth, and Harvey knew the bastard was just itching to pull the trigger and let the buckshot fly.

"Head down," Underhill said, jabbing the end of his gun into the bank president's fat ass. "Or I blow you a new hole."

"Easy, boy."

"He moves again and I'll kill him."

"I know."

"You don't believe me? I'll do it. I swear to Christ."

"No need to do that."

"Look at his fat apple cheeks. Just like a hog. If I had an apple—"

"Easy."

The bank president hadn't time to slip back into his coat, and his wide, fatty back was soaked in sweat. You could see the rolls rippling under linen, and his thinning hair had grown hot and matted against his head. Harvey could hear him breathing clear across the room.

He studied Underhill, knowing the goddamn buffoon had gone screwy again, just like when they broke out of Lansing and he wanted to slaughter Warden Prather just because authority made him itch. A loud clock ticked off the minutes, big black fans creaking overhead trying to sweep away the hundred-degree heat.

There was silence.

And then there was everything. Car engines and men yelling and boots clattering up the great steps to the bank door, rattling the lock.

"Who hit the alarm?" Underhill asked. "Goddamn you, Fat Man."

Harvey held up a hand to calm him and walked around to the cages, running a hand under the ledge and finding the small switch. He shrugged and took a breath.

"Ladies?"

Miss Loving and the other teller crooked their heads from the floor.

"Lucky girls," he said. "Lucky, lucky little girls."

The woman craned her neck at him. Harvey winked.

"You can be our hostesses."

Harvey tossed the bag of cash at Underhill and offered a hand to each teller, hoisting them to their feet. The other gal's name was Thelma, a blonde with a fine set of cantaloupe bosoms straining the material of her flowered dress. She hadn't stopped smiling at Harvey since he pointed the gun in her face.

He placed the .38 in the waistband of his blue linen suit and put a palm to each of the women's backs, ushering them to the door. Both of 'em took a deep breath, and the expanse and ripple of it felt like an electric current.

Underhill went first.

With a touch of a trigger, the *blam* sent the boys in blue behind their cars. Verne Miller—*God bless that son of a bitch*—held the Thompson over the Buick doorframe and trained it on the three police cars parked haphazardly on the street.

Underhill nodded. Harvey walked down the steps flanked by the two women, just kind of strolling with a Hollywood air.

Clark loaded the cash in the trunk. Underhill covered Miller, who cranked the engine, and Harvey gently escorted the ladies to the running boards, where he told them they better hold on real tight. As he ducked into the car, he heard a gunshot sounding, felt a white-hot stabbing pain in his heel, and he tumbled on inside and told Verne to get going fast.

Underhill squeezed the second trigger, and the women shrieked as the Buick sped away from the downtown. Harvey Bailey, leg hurting so bad it felt damn good, loved it, laughing and turning back only for a moment to see the cops trying to make chase of that big, beautiful Buick growling and downshifting into a comfortable, violent speed.

His heel bled thick and dark into his shoes, and he tied off the wound at the ankle with his necktie.

When they hit the county line, Verne Miller tossed a box of roofing nails from his window and fired up a Lucky, watching the blowouts in his rearview. For just a moment, through all that goddamn smoke, Harvey noted something on Miller's lips that might've been a smile.

Harvey reached out the window with a bloody hand to give Miss Loving's narrow little ass a nice pat. He knew damn well that the world was a fine place.

6

Kathryn didn't see George again until twilight. He woke up from a whiskey slumber, scratching himself and coughing, and found his way out to the front porch of her stepdaddy Boss Shannon's place. After taking a leak, he lit a cigarette and joined her on the stoop, watching that fire sun slipping down like a nickel into the slotted, flat land. She pulled the cigarette from his lips and offered him some of her gin. He took it because it was alcohol, but she knew he didn't like it. George was the same as every boy she'd known back in Saltillo, Mississippi, who'd been weaned on whiskey.

"You want a quick poke?" he asked.

"Why don't I poke you in the eye," Kathryn said.

"Where's Albert?"

"Boss wanted to show him his mule," Kathryn said. "He claims it can count."

"That mule can't count," George said. "Boss stands over your shoulder and nods his head to make the dang animal tap its hoof. That doesn't take much sense."

"I heard y'all had trouble."

George shrugged.

"Albert said you ran out of gas."

"Albert shoulda brought more gas."

"Weren't you watching the gauge?"

"You see many gas stations on those cat roads?"

"You shoulda thought ahead."

"It worked out."

"Can I see him?"

"No."

She looked away and watched the sun a bit.

"Oh, hell," George said. "Come on. Don't go poutin' on me. I'm too damn tired."

They took the new Cadillac—the same one GMAC threatened to repossess if they didn't make another payment—down a twisting dirt road, scattering up trails of thick Texas dust that coated the midnight blue paint with a fine powder, into the southeast corner of Boss's place, where his son lived with his barefoot and pregnant teen bride. Armon came from the house when he heard the Buick and ran out to meet them, clopping along in unlaced brogans, big overalls covering his naked chest. He wore a big smile on his crooked face and opened the door for her, being more pleasant to her than when they first met, when his hick daddy and her stupid momma decided to make a go of it after meeting in the want ads. Back then, Armon used to try to peep at her through a crack in the bathroom wall. He was that kind of kid.

"Y'all did it," Armon said. "You really pulled it off."

George killed the engine and stood from the car, stretching and groaning, still feeling the long drive from the night before. He lit a cigarette and watched Armon from over the big hood of the Buick.

"What do you say, Potatoes."

"Hey, George," Armon said. "Whew. We got 'im all settled in and even brought him a can of beans. He won't speak or nothin'. I guess he's still kind of upset about y'all taking him. You think he might want a smoke or something? I read in the papers that fellas of his type like cigars. I could go to town and get him some smokes. He might like it. Or you think he'd like some of Boss's 'shine? That might make him feel a little more rested and all."

George looked to Kathryn.

"I think he's fine with the beans," Kathryn said. "Don't make a fool of yourself in town. Just make sure he stays chained up, and you shut your goddamn mouth."

She pushed Armon to the side, walking down the dirt path in her white kid T-straps, the stones making her walk a bit wobbly till she was on the porch and into the hotbox. George was with her—she could feel his breathing on her neck—and she pushed through past a ratty sofa that had been her mother's, a couple broken chairs, and an old organ stuffed in a corner. They didn't have running water or electricity, but Armon had gone ahead and brought an organ home, sheet music and all, so he could buck-dance to hymns or whatever that boy liked.

George cocked his head to a door in the shack and creaked it open, and there he was—bigger than shit—eyes covered in cotton and tape, ears plugged and arms chained through a baby's high chair. Kathryn looked at her big fat baby and smiled, not believing the lug had actually pulled it off. High-dollar oilman Charles Urschel bound and tied like a gift.

George put a finger to his lips and closed the creaky door, walking from the heat of the house and back onto the uneven, slatted porch. He lit a smoke and offered her one from his pack. He clicked open his silver lighter with a little snap of his fingers, and the ruby ring caught the last light of the day. He winked at her, smooth and cool as George R. Kelly could sometimes be.

"How come you're dressed like that?" he asked.

"What do you mean?"

"You look like you came from a party."

"I wasn't at a party," she said. "It's just some frock."

"One of the easiest jobs I ever pulled," George said. "We get four more of these, Kit, and we're on our way to South America."

"Let's get the money first."

"Two hundred grand is nothing to people like this," George said. "They'll pay."

"We'll see."

"They'll pay."

Armon stood by the Cadillac and ran his hands over the silver hood ornament, took out a rag from his overalls' back pocket, and began to shine the winged lady. The wind blew grit into his greasy hair, and he didn't even seem to take notice, just smiling up at the two of them like he sure couldn't have been any prouder.

"Can we trust him?" George asked from the corner of his mouth.

"He'd eat pig shit for you."

"Good to know."

"And your momma?"

"She'd eat pig shit for a nickel."

"We'll have money, Kit. More money than we'll know how to spend."

"I doubt that," she said.

Kathryn turned to George, wrapping her long arms around his neck. She leaned into him, letting herself go in a short fall, and he caught her and planted a big one on her. He reached his big hands around her waist and twirled her around, right there not ten paces from a pigsty and a shack, and kissed her on her ear and cheek and whispered to her that he'd really like to screw her on a big pile of money.

"I can't think of anything I'd like better, doll."

JONES SMOKED HIS PIPE FILLED WITH CHERRY TOBACCO, sitting in the very wicker chair in which Charles Urschel had played bridge just two nights before. He thought it a pleasant summer night, wondering when the real contact would come and how it would come and how reasonable the bastards would be. The toughest thing about a kidnapping was sitting on your ass and waiting. Jones had never exhibited any talent for doing nothing.

"How will we know?" Mr. E. E. Kirkpatrick asked.

"It'll be clear," Jones said. "We'll know."

"Will it be a phone call?"

"Could be."

"A telegram."

"Could be written in tea leaves," Jones said. "But you'll know."

Kirkpatrick was a thin man with a gaunt face and honest brown eyes; Jones thought he recalled something of the man being a newspaperman before joining up as a front man for Tom Slick. His seersucker suit rumpled, tie loosely knotted at the throat from travel, he had that rawboned look of a drinker, although Jones had never personally seen the man drunk. A straightforward fella, although a bit too much of a talker to Jones's liking.

"This would've never happened in Europe," Kirkpatrick said. "They are too civilized. Did you know that in England it's a crime for a family to pay a ransom?"

"Is that what you think Mrs. Urschel should do? Not pay?"

Jones laid his Stetson crown down onto the table. He rolled his sleeves to the elbow and leaned in.

"We can't let people like Charlie just be ripe for the picking. How's an honest man supposed to live his life? Is a rich, successful man fair game for the masses? Does a man have to be surrounded by guards to take a nighttime stroll or go on an impromptu fishing trip?"

"I can't tell the family what to do," Jones said.

"But what would you do?"

"You mean if Mr. Urschel was my family?"

"Or if it were you?"

"If it were me, my wife wouldn't give these people a plug nickel," Jones said, smiling. "But that's based on personal appraisal."

"What if Charlie was your brother?"

"You think Mr. Urschel would pay?"

"I don't think money is of concern to Mr. Urschel," Kirkpatrick said. "Only the principle."

"I believe a grown man being kidnapped is different than a child."

"How do you figure?"

"The person who kidnapped Lindbergh's child is a weakling suffering from some kind of illness. I've always believed that. That whole caper was sloppy. But the ones at work here are different animals; to them this is just a business transaction. Mr. Urschel is nothing more than a flesh-and-blood investment."

"Like a prize steer?"

"Yep."

"You helped out plenty when Mr. Slick had some trouble."

"A man's business should be a man's business. Not ammunition."

"Mr. Slick was much obliged."

"How 'bout we read that letter again?"

The house was as still and quiet as Jones had known it since his arrival, a vacuum devoid of sound that he couldn't quite place. There were police on the premises and agents in the kitchen and stationed in the salon. But the work had subsided, many of the men just drinking coffee and smoking cigarettes and keeping watch on the Urschel family while they all waited for some kind of legitimate contact from the kidnappers. Kirkpatrick coughed and picked up the typed sheets that had been telegrammed to the mansion.

" *'Mr. F. Urschel is fairing well but don't sleep, a trifel nervose.'* Whoever this is could use a remedial course in spelling and grammar. They spelled 'trifle' wrong, and 'nervous,' too, and 'location' in the next sentence. Are all criminals this stupid?"

"Keep going," Jones said, drawing on his pipe. Somehow sitting in Urschel's seat gave him some kind of perspective and feel for how it would unfold, or at least some kind of feel for the man. He wanted to know if Charles F. Urschel was the kind of man to take it or fight it. Or somewhere in between.

" *'Locashun of myself will be revealed in the next notice after I see your dec-i-shun in the newspaper.'* 'Decision' spelled the same way," Kirkpatrick said. " *'Mr. Urschel's release can be secured at small cost and without BLOODSHED.'* They typed 'bloodshed' in capital letters. *'If you follow my instructions, map I will enclose to you at once after I see your ad.'* "

"Read the part about the ad again," Jones said, taking another puff. "From the beginning."

" *'Note you are the go between for the family of Chas. F. Urschel. If so, I can tell you where they are holding him. I will reveal the facts to you if you wish or either reveal them to the detective department.'* Good Lord, nobody can be this stupid on purpose."

Jones listened and smoked some more, watching the smoke kind of hang there in the dull night heat. It had been more than a hundred that afternoon, and the heat didn't seem to want to leave. This was the fourth letter they'd received that day. All of 'em just as phony, but you didn't dismiss a single one. You take one ransom lightly and chances are that would be your number.

" *'But I would suggest you in as much as I thank you'*—I believe they meant 'think'—*'should know and then you could tell whom you wished. If you want this information, signify the same by run add in* Dallas Times Herald *and* Fort Worth Star-Teligram.' *'Telegram'* spelled, of course, as 'I-G-R-A-M.' "

"Chislers," Jones said. "Fakes."

"Surely not scholars."

"That doesn't matter a lick," Jones said. "The writer there hadn't thought through any plan at all. The boys we're dealing with here are pretty shrewd, businesswise, and will have a plan in place. Did you meet that four-flusher today? The one who called himself a 'medium of the psychic arts'? He said he'd try and get in touch with Mr. Urschel's spirit, and Mrs. Urschel asked what if he wasn't dead, and the fella just kind of looked at her, holding his hand out for some kind of payment, not really having an idea what to do next."

"Does it always work like this?"

"They come out of the woodwork, Kirk," Jones said. "This world has no shortage of shitbrains."

"You want another nip in your coffee?"

"Better be getting back to the Skirvin," Jones said, tapping the burnt tobacco from his pipe and reaching for his Stetson. "It's nearly midnight."

He pulled his father's gold watch from his vest and looked back into the mansion's long hallway, studying the open space.

"The clocks have stopped," Kirkpatrick said. "Is that what you were listening for? Charlie wound them every Sunday."

"This house is quieter than a tomb."

"Sometimes you miss the tick," he said.

They were quiet for a moment in the silence, and Jones tapped some ash that had fallen onto his hat brim.

"I think the doctor finally got Berenice to take a shot," Kirkpatrick said. "She hadn't slept since they took him. I believe she loves that man in a way that she never felt for Mr. Slick."

"Maybe I'll take that nip."

"I'm sure glad they sent for you, Buster," Kirkpatrick said.

"Glad to help."

"Even with fakes and chislers?"

"'Specially with them."

THEY DIVIDED THE LOOT BY THE CAMPFIRE. UNDERHILL, with that bony face and big eyes, watching Verne Miller peeling off every bill, stacking every coin on a rock, till they'd come to a shy more than eight grand. Not exactly the Denver Mint job, but not a bad haul, and Harvey was fine with the whole deal, itching to get into a nice hotel, slip that shot-up leg into a bath, and have people bring him things with the jingle of the phone.

"Count it again," Underhill said.

"It's there," Miller said.

Oh, shit.

"We're missing a bag."

"What went into that trunk came out of the trunk, and it's all right there," Harvey said. "Get what you got and let's all get gone."

"We're missing a bag."

Miller stood from the pile of money and placed his hands on his hips, standing tall and looking a bit like that old war hero. He just stared down at the grease-parted hair of Underhill and the pudgy face of Jim Clark, chawing away on a wad of tobacco, the way a man studies an animal in a zoo, with kind of a detached curiosity, waiting to see what they'll do next.

"Two per man," Miller said. "Plus some change."

Miller screwed a cigarette into the center of his mouth and set fire to it. He wore his pants very high and had tucked the cuffs into knee-high boots.

"Why'd you bring him in, Harvey?" Underhill asked. "You gone soft? Everybody knows this fella ain't got no morals. He kills people for dough."

Verne Miller smiled at that and rubbed his movie-star jaw. He glanced over at Harvey, and Harvey had to stifle a grin.

"When would we have stashed the money?" Harvey asked.

"I'm not calling you out, Harv," Underhill said. "Me and Jim was the one did the heavy lifting while you was supervisin'. Your man didn't lift a dang finger. And now we come up a few grand short, this just ain't on the level."

Jim Clark brought his eyes up to Miller and then over at Underhill. He had a stick he'd taken from the edge of the fire and was drawing patterns in the rough earth.

"Why don't you apologize, you damn moron," Harvey said. "You want to break up a gang before it starts?"

"We was a gang in Lansing," Clark said, more of a mumble than words. And Harvey watched him go over and over that dirt line like he had to convince himself that it was there.

"I need a bath," Harvey said. "I need a cigar, a fresh change of clothes, and to get this bullet out of me. I need a woman. But what I don't need is a bunch of monkey business and horseshit."

Verne Miller drew a gun.

"Go ahead, you sideshow freak," Underhill said.

"Come on," Harvey said.

Miller kicked the cash and coin into the fire, and the money started to smolder and burn. He clenched his jaw and slid the gun back into his belt. Sparks flew up from the little campfire, and Clark and Underhill didn't move, mouths open, until it all registered into their small brains, and Underhill reached his hand into the smoldering money and pulled out charred bills, yipping and blowing on his fingers, until he thought he'd felt the weight of four grand and backed away from the sparks and heat.

He clutched the money to his chest and called Verne Miller a crazy son of a bitch, and Miller just kind of smiled at him and shrugged. Clark and Underhill counted off the money and gathered their things.

"No hard feelings," Harvey said.

"I don't take issue with you, Harv," Underhill said. "You broke us out and a man don't forget somethin' like that."

Harvey shook both men's hands, agreeing on a Joplin pool hall to make contact, and Underhill and Clark drove off quick into the darkness and far down the meandering open road.

"Did you have to go and do that?" Harvey asked. "I think you hurt Mad Dog's feelings."

"Yes."

"Because they called you a liar?"

"Yes."

"That's a hard code, Verne." Harvey got down to his knees and counted out the money that hadn't been burned up.

"How's that heel?"

"Bleeding like a bastard. I'm cashing out of this shit. I'm done."

"How much you got squirreled away?"

Harvey didn't answer, as he turned his back to Miller and kicked dirt over the fire until it was just smoke off the ashes.

"I'll drive," Verne Miller said, already headed to the Buick. "Where's that farm you told me about? Kit Kelly's folks' place?"

"Town called Paradise."

7

Berenice Urschel was gone. According to the maid, she'd been seen climbing out a second-story window and shimmying down a rose trellis before making a break for the garage. A couple newspapermen saw her get in a Hudson touring car that sure looked a hell of a lot like E. E. Kirkpatrick's machine, although no one seemed to note the man behind the wheel. And so Jones stayed up waiting till damn-near eleven o'clock, like an old father worried that his daughter might lose her virginity in the heat of a summer evening. He was standing in the drive by the garage when they finally rolled back to the mansion, dimming their lights and crawling from the Hudson with long faces.

"Good evening," Jones said.

"We couldn't take the chance and tell you," Kirkpatrick said.

"Tell me what?" Jones asked, Berenice Urschel not yet looking him in the eye.

"They asked for five thousand dollars and not to tell a soul," she said, soft-like. "They said they'd bring his watch to prove it."

"You get the watch?" Jones asked.

Kirkpatrick plucked his hands into his trousers and pulled out a wristwatch, handing it to Jones.

"Ain't even a watch," Jones said. "The damn hands have been painted on."

"We couldn't take a chance," Berenice said. "You'd have stopped us."

"I wouldn't have stopped you," Jones said. The evening was alive with a radio's music coming from a neighbor's window, and crickets, and the continuous clicking from newspapermen on the dewy lawn, hammering out editorials on the kidnapping and updates on how Charles F. Urschel, Oklahoma City oilman, was still in the hands of the kidnappers, federal agents baffled.

"Makes you angry, don't it?" Jones said.

Berenice walked past Jones and onto the worn path the kidnappers had taken and through the screen door of the back porch. The door slammed, and she sat in a chair with the lights off and just stared out into the empty darkness.

"The less said—" Kirkpatrick said.

"I don't intend to punish the woman," Jones said. "But five thousand is a lot of money."

"They only got a thousand."

"What did these chislers look like?"

"I don't know," Kirkpatrick said. "I drove her out to the corner of Broadway and Main. They told her to come alone, and so I let her out. She went into a chop suey joint called the New Bamboo right next to Branson's cigar shop."

"You see anyone leave the place?"

"They must've taken a back door," he said. "When Berenice came out, she was crying. They'd taken her pocketbook and handed her that fake watch."

"They rough her up?"

"Just scared her to death."

The men heard the telephone ring from inside the Urschels' house. A servant appeared on the back porch and called to Mrs. Urschel in the darkness. After a while she emerged through the porch doorway and walked to the men, the sadness replaced with the woman gritting her teeth. "The language. I can't even repeat what I was just called."

"Who?" Kirkpatrick asked.

"That filthy bastard who took my money," she said. "He had the nerve to call here and complain that I shortchanged him after he didn't produce Charles's watch. I am just a fool. An absolute fool."

"No, ma'am," Jones said. "I'd say that filthy bastard's the fool. We can find out right quick where he made that call and get your money back."

"Vultures," Kirkpatrick said. "Parasites."

"Opportunists," Jones said. "You mind if I take that watch, ma'am?"

THE PAIN HAD BECOME FAMILIAR AND AT LEAST BEARABLE. Charlie would sit in the same position for hours, back to the wall, left arm stretched up in chains to the high chair, listening to the sounds of the farm, for most surely it was a farm, with the rooster and goats, a pig or two, the squeak of an old well, and an old tin cup presented to him with water that tasted of minerals and rust. They did not talk to him, although he tried. He'd comment on the day and the time and how things were awful hot, but there was only the unlocking of the chain and movement to another section of the house, away from the sun, away from the west, and to another part of the old shack, with the creaky floorboards and the smell of dirty clothes and dirty dishes and pig shit.

That morning he'd been given a breakfast of canned tomatoes and canned beans with a tin of cold campfire coffee. "You wouldn't happen to have a cigar, would you?"

No reply.

"You get dust storms?" he asked.

"That's down south," said an old man. "Oklahoma and Texas."

"You got the time?"

"Yes, sir," said a young man.

"Don't see any harm in you tellin' me."

"Better check."

"You got to check with someone to tell a fella the time?"

"I don't have to check with nobody."

"Hush up," said the old man.

The boy returned to the room alone, hours after sundown, Charlie hearing his feet on the slats, and told him it was close to midnight. The hours went like that, although Charlie rarely dozed. "Why don't you get some sleep, Mr. Urschel."

"I can't."

"You want a spot of 'shine?"

"I'd like to use the facilities before I sleep. Is that okay? Or should you ask?"

The young man unlocked him from the high chair and bound the chains tighter at the wrist, checking the manacles on his legs. The boy prodded Charlie on with what he took for the butt of a shotgun, and would tell him to turn here and there, and then grabbed his elbow as they came to the porch and some rickety steps, Charlie nearly tripping over a baying hound awoken from sleep.

The outhouse smelled like a thousand outhouses he'd known, hastily slapped together in the oil fields, but he never had grown used to the stench. He was able to unlatch his pants and sit, and, with his hands loose, play a bit with the tape over his eyes, loosening the cotton a bit and readjusting, moonlight flooding through the cutout in the door. Tattered catalog images of women in their brassieres and slips had been tacked to the leaning walls, and old corncobs were placed in a box at his feet. Flies buzzed from the carved wooden seat and echoed deep within the hole and in the stench of it all, and Charlie Urschel began to plan his escape.

When he finished, with the cotton loose from his eyes, he unlatched the outhouse door and stumbled before the boy. He could see him now through the slits. A short, squatty fella with grease-parted hair and wearing a pair of Union overalls. The 12-gauge looked to have rusted shut long ago.

The boy reached in the overalls' flap and pulled out a cigar. He placed it into Charlie's hands and asked if he'd like him to light her up. Charlie said, "Sure, why not?" and so the boy struck a couple matches and waited until the cigar got going.

Charlie stretched his legs and took in the layout of the little shack, the small hogpen and chicken coop. He saw the old well with a bucket, and in the far distance, perhaps a mile, he saw the lights of another house.

"How does she smoke, Mr. Urschel?"

"Thank you just the same," Charlie said. "But not my brand."

The boy remained sullen all the way back into the shack, where he told Charlie to change into a pair of pajamas. Charlie got settled back against the wall where he could get chained up for the night.

"Just how much of a cut are you gettin', son?"

THE TELEPHONE CALL WAS PLACED FROM A SINCLAIR OIL filling station just across the Canadian River bridge west of the city. Jones interviewed the proprietor of the station near midnight, and the man told him right quick that it had been a couple beggars from down in Hooverville who'd made the call, even bumming the nickel from a customer. The man gave him a fair description of the two, and Jones told Berenice Urschel to wait at the station or he could call an agent to pick her up.

"I want to go with you."

"No, you don't."

"You bet I do," she said. "I can pick him out."

Jones looked away from the gas pumps toward the oil-drum fires burning among the lean-tos and clapboard shelters. You could smell the stink and shit and cook fires even through the cut of gasoline.

"I won't have it."

"Then I'll go myself."

Berenice Urschel was already halfway across the highway following a rutted road into the camp when Jones caught up with her. He didn't say a word as they were swallowed into the wall-to-wall dwellings, women washing laundry in galvanized tubs, nursing babies, and cooking bottom-feeding fish across small fires. A latrine had been dug along the roadway that wound its way to the river where the chamber pots and rotten food had been dumped. The smell was something to behold, and Jones covered his face several times with a handkerchief he pulled from his shirt pocket.

Standing high on the hill, you could see the tin roofs—hundreds of them—gleaming silver in the full moon. The Canadian River moved slow and sluggish in the crook of the bend.

"They live like animals," Berenice Urschel said.

"Yes, ma'am," Jones said. "Every city's got one."

"I never read of this place."

"Ain't a good postcard for the Chamber."

"Where do they come from?"

"The country," he said. "Nowhere else to go, you head to the city, looking for work."

"But women and children," she said. "This just isn't decent."

"These days, it's what we got."

Jones followed Mrs. Urschel, who stumbled for a moment, holding on to some rusted sheet metal and making a big, clanging racket. A tall, skeletal figure appeared from the lean-to and thrust a sharpened stick at Jones. "Who is it?"

The boy's eyes were the color of spoiled milk. Peach fuzz covered his upper lip.

"Looking for someone."

"Who are you?"

"Just looking," Jones said again.

The boy reached out and touched the soft cotton of Jones's suit jacket and moved his fingers across the side where he kept the thumb buster. He stepped back. "You the law?"

"I'm the law."

"You gonna burn us out again?"

"Just looking for a couple hustlers that took this woman's money."

"Wasn't me."

"Didn't say it was."

Berenice hadn't said a word, fascinated by the young boy with the milky eyes. Almost in a trance, she glanced down to see her hand had been cut on the sheet metal, and she stared at it with awe as the drops ran down the length of her arm and twisted back to her elbow. Jones thrust the white handkerchief into her hand and clenched her fingers inward to make a fist.

"What happened?" she asked. "Where are your eyes?"

"These is my eyes," the boy said. "Got caught in a duster. I seen it from forever. You just noticed a line of it, just a line of ink on paper, and then it got thicker and grew till you saw it as a flood. Daylight all 'round you. Birds started to get nervous, animals turning in circles."

"You with your people?" Jones asked.

"Daddy's gone to find work," he said. "Mama's dead."

Jones nodded. "C'mon," he said, Berenice standing still.

"I tried to make it back," the boy said. "I thought we was in End-Times. I covered up my mouth with a rag, but my ears were plugged, and no matter how tight I shut my eyes that dang grit worked in there. Couldn't hear nothin'. Couldn't feel nothin'. I thought I was dead, laying there tasting the dirt, already buried and gone, and I wondered if this wadn't what God had planned for us, that heaven wadn't no reward but the taste of dirt and knowing it."

"You're fortunate to be alive," Berenice Urschel said. "God's will."

"That storm wadn't made by no God of mine."

Jones knew these people, how they lived and scavenged. Only most of them he'd known were down in Juarez or Nuevo Laredo, people burned off their land and out of work, fighting over a pot of beans or milk from a goat. He'd seen human beings turned to pack animals during the Revolution, and this country was being torn apart in the same way, suffering plagues he'd only heard about in a sermon, wandering in the desert and searching for something solid to believe.

Berenice staggered for a moment, re-dressing her wound. And she focused on the boy, her expression righting on her face, determined, and saying, "Well, I don't have any money."

"I don't need no money," he said. "We got everything a man could need right here. Fish and loaves to feed us all."

She touched his face, holding it within her hands adorned with jeweled rings and shiny bracelets. The jewels winked in the firelight, and Jones thought they'd be lucky if they got out of this shithole without a fight. But they walked on, down the sliding hill and toward the banks of the Canadian River, where a group of men stood around an oil-drum fire and sang old hobo songs and buck-danced. One man played a guitar, another a harmonica, the rest singing about the "Big Rock Candy Mountain" and having a hell of a time.

The men in tattered clothes had fashioned a grill from an oil drum and cooked fat T-bones above the flames while passing bottles of bonded whiskey back and forth between verses about your birthday coming around once a week and it being Christmas every day. The men, six of them, were so caught up in the drunkenness that they didn't even see the lady and old man in a cowboy hat walk close to the firelight.

Berenice Urschel just stared at one, the one tipping back the bottle and high-stepping it, and nodded in recognition.

Jones nodded back and stepped close enough to the fire to feel the warmth on his face and to hear the hissing of fat dripping from the grill. The guitar stopped on a dime and the harmonica softly petered out. The men shuffled a bit and then circled around Jones. The man with the whiskey bottle ambled up to him and gritted what few teeth he had in his rotten hole of a mouth.

"Y'all living high on the hog," Jones said. "T-bones and bourbon. Fine ole night in the Hooverville, ain't it?"

"Who the hell are you?" the man asked, tipping back the whiskey bottle. He was unshaven, dressed in rags, with the breath of the dead. He polished off the bourbon, Adam's apple sweaty and stubbled, bobbing up and down as he took the last swallow.

When he saw Mrs. Urschel, he broke the bottle on the grill, sparks scattering, and pointed the bottom directly at Jones's chest. "You shore are a fat little fella. Like a little hog."

Another bum snatched Berenice Urschel's arm and twisted it up behind her back. "Take them rings off," he said, nuzzling his mouth into her ear. "Them things are bigger 'an a cat's-eye. You shoulda never come lookin'."

The broken bottle refracted hard and silver in the fire glow as the hobo lunged for Jones's belly. He sidestepped it easy, and the two men circled each other, the old hobo licking his dry lips. Jones reached for the .45 and aimed dead center at the man's forehead.

"Y'all got ten seconds to hand over this woman's money."

"We ain't got it."

"Decent people live here," Jones said. "And the shit runs downhill."

Jones took a breath and walked forward, gun loose by his side, and went straight up to the man gripping Berenice Urschel's arm. He simply coldcocked the bastard across the temple.

The bum fell to his ass, clutching his face and moaning.

Jones pointed the gun at the hobo with the busted bottle and eyed down the barrel, squeezing the trigger just slightly, the cylinder buckling and flexing.

The man spit in Jones's face, and Jones wiped it from his cheek with the back of his hand. He stepped forward and placed the revolver's tip flat into the man's nose.

The bum waited a minute, breathing hard and sullen, before reaching down and plucking a fat wad of bills from inside a busted boot. He nearly lost his balance, trying to stand tall before Jones but uneasy on drunk feet. "You can't grudge a man for trying to go on the tit."

"Open your mouth," Jones said.

He opened his ragged hole, and Jones smelled a latrine of dead shrimp and whiskey and garbage. Jones pulled the broken watch from his breast pocket and set it on the man's fat tongue. He sucker punched him in the gut, dropping the bastard to his ass, hitting him again in the mouth, breaking the timepiece into shards of glass and busted gears.

"All is forgiven," Jones said.

8

Kathryn didn't get up till almost eleven, worn out from the drive back and forth to Coleman and Paradise. She made a pot of coffee, grabbed her cigarette case, and took old Ching-A-Wee out for a doo-doo on her front lawn. How Kathryn loved that little dog. Lots of folks—including George—didn't realize Ching-A-Wee was royalty. That's God's truth. When she and George had just gotten hitched in Saint Paul and lived in that awful apartment building with Verne Miller and Vi, there'd been an old maid who'd sold Pekingese on the second floor. Kathryn loved Chingy from the start. You could tell he was royal from the way he stood, begged for food, and, hell, even took a dump, legs sprawled and looking you dead in the eye, daring you to tell him it don't smell sweet.

He skittered up the porch steps and, as she settled into a chair, onto her lap, nearly spilling coffee on the robe's monkey-fur trim. She smoked for a while, stood, and checked the mail slot—loaded down with nothing but bills and more bills. The department stores were the worst, always addressing you like this was something personal and not a business transaction, calling her "Mrs. Kelly" and telling her how "unfortunate" it was they hadn't received a payment. The hell of it was, there was nothing unfortunate about it. She and George had blown through that Tupelo money damn-near Christmas, and if Mr. Urschel's family didn't come through she'd be back to making fifty cents an hour cutting men's nails, complimenting fat old duddys on their style just to make a dollar tip or get an invite back to their hotels to make twenty bucks a throw.

"Hey, watch it," she told Chingy. "Settle down. Settle down, little man."

She raked her nails over the nape of his neck and felt for the diamond collar, wondering how much she could pawn it for if things got really rough. Her bags were packed and plans made. She knew every step by heart. She would meet George in Oklahoma City, bring the new Cadillac, telegram to Saint Paul . . . *Hot damn, he'd done it. She didn't think he could, but George Kelly had done it.*

She'd nearly counted off the list for the second time when the gray Chevrolet rolled into her drive and killed the motor, Ed Weatherford stepping from the cab and taking off his hat. "Mornin'."

"What do you want?"

"That ain't no way to greet a gentleman caller."

"What if George was here?"

"I'd sit down and chaw the fat with him," he said. "George knows we're buddies."

"Some buddy."

"What are you sore at, darlin'?" He gave that crooked, two-dollar grin. "Did you want moonlight and roses? I can look in my pocket."

"I know what's in your pocket."

She stood and opened the screen door to let Chingy in. Ed followed the walkway, and Kathryn turned, pulling arms across her chest, the cigarette still burning in her fingers. "If you came here for a throw, I ain't in the mood."

"You are mighty mistrustful this morning."

"Well, did you or didn't you?"

"Aw, well."

"Nerts."

"Listen, doll," Ed said, standing at the foot of the steps and mawing at his hat.

Kathryn stayed flat-footed on the porch and let him stammer.

"There's been some rumors and questions, and I thought I'd be coming out here personal-like and see if there was any truth to them."

"Please."

"Darlin', just listen to me. Isn't that what you wanted from me the other night? Keep an ear open? Well, here I am. So don't throw water in my face. I just wanted to know if George was involved with that oilman business."

"What oilman business?"

"Shoot," Ed said. He looked down at his pointed boots and let out a deep breath. "Hadn't we all had a good time? Me, you, and George— hadn't we shared some laughs? And now you won't even be straight with me for me to help you."

"I've been to visit my mother, Mrs. Ora Shannon."

"I didn't ask where you been, baby. I asked what about George."

"George had business."

"Selling Bibles?"

"Good-bye."

Kathryn picked up her stack of bills, leaving her coffee, cigarette, and morning paper on the porch, and turned to the house. The screen door almost thwacked shut before Ed stuck his big fat foot in the threshold and grinned at her through the screen.

She waited.

He reached down and picked up the *Daily Oklahoman* from the porch floor by her coffee that continued to steam, red-lipped cigarette on the saucer.

"Good likeness of him," Ed said. "I seen him speak one time at the Texas Oilmen's Association. Seems like somebody would've seen them two fellas with machine guns. Say, does George still got—"

"Take it up with him."

Ed made a real jackass show of folding up the newspaper all nice and neat and tucking it back near the coffee cup, saucer, and cigarette. "I can tell your nerves are a bit jangled this morning, and I can see you don't have any sugar to give. I understand. But what you got to know, Mrs. Kelly, is that I knowed this is George's work and I knowed why you were asking me about back doors and legal questions the other night. I didn't figure it was for my good looks."

Kathryn poked out her hip and placed a hand to it, thinking Mae West in *She Done Him Wrong*. "Are we finished?"

"Don't think you need me now the deal is done," he said. "The world can go sour on you anytime. You remember that, baby."

She just looked through the screen at Ed Weatherford and waited for the goddamn, unfunny punch line coming from that goddamn, crooked mouth.

"I want a cut, Mrs. Kelly," Ed said. "And this ain't a request."

"'*A-TRACTIONS OF THE ASTOUNDING NATURE, THE BI-ZARRE, the start-ling and new in entertainment have been gathered from all parts of the universe to make* The Midway—City of a Million Lights *the z-z-zenith of amusement for all thrill seekers,*'" the boy said. "Mr. Urschel, what does that word mean? 'Zenith'?"

"Means 'the highest point,' son."

"Holy smokes," the boy said. "This must be somethin' else. You want me to keep goin'?"

"You have plans to make the Fair?"

"Do I?" he asked. "Hold on a sec, and I'll keep on readin'. '*Located centrally on the World's Fair grounds in Chicago, just south of Twenty-third Street, the many features of this outlay will satisfy even the oldest youngster that visits the Exposition.*' You know, they're calling this thing 'Century of Progress.' That's a heck of a thing, ain't it? A whole dang century in one place? I got to see this. You want me to keep going or you want me to read them *Ladies' Home Journals* to you? They got a story in there about Will Rogers that tickled me plenty. He sure is a pistol."

"I'm so glad."

"Mr. Urschel," the boy said. "You know I don't mean nothin' by chainin' you up and makin' you eat beans out of a can. I don't get no pleasure out of it."

"You could let me go."

The boy laughed.

"What's so funny?"

"They'd kill me."

"Who would?"

"You just messin' with my mind now," he said. "I was told I can read to you but better not talk. So let me go on . . . *'Among the mul-multitudinous features are the many breathtaking rides, an Oriental village with exotic and colorful presentations of the life, rites, and customs of the Far East, a reproduction of African jungles and deserts, its queer villages, its ancient art and weird ceremonies, and "Bozo."'* I think Bozo is some kind of monkey. A relation of mine just got back from Chicago and said they got some foreign dancers who don't wear a stitch of clothes. The women's titties jumpin' up and down got to be worth the price of a ticket."

"You wouldn't happen to have another cigar on you?"

"I can git one," he said. "Hit wouldn't be trouble atall. Thought you said it wadn't your brand."

"It's not. But I can enjoy it just the same."

"Yes, sir. Hold on, Mr. Urschel. Hold on."

"I don't think I have a choice."

Charlie was handcuffed to the bed frame in stiff pajamas he'd worn for days, and, considering it was midday, he felt downright ridiculous. His arm had fallen asleep shortly after he'd been chained and would take nearly an hour to come alive when they'd move him room to room away from the sun's heat. He heard the front screen door thwack close and heavy feet in the main room and coming closer.

The door flew open and two men stepped inside.

"Keys."

A jangle, and heavy shoes moved toward him. A snick, and his dead arm dropped to his side.

"Up, Urschel," said the big gunman who'd brought him to this wretched hole. Charlie was pushed into the next room, and a heavy hand sat him down hard in a chair. "We're gonna take off the tape, but don't turn around and look at us. I really don't feel like killing you today."

They ripped the tape from his eyes, and the brightness of the room blinded him in a white glow. He closed his eyes and rubbed them, the skin feeling wet and soft and raw around the edges.

The big gunman plunked down a cheap paper tablet and a pen on the desk. "Write," the other gunman said. "You can choose who gets the letter. But you tell them we mean business and we want two hundred grand."

Charlie Urschel didn't feel like it, but he laughed like a hiccup escaping his belly. He didn't mean it, but the whole idea was just kind of funny to him, the number so absurd that he wondered how they came up with it. "I don't have—"

"Shut up and write, Charlie," said the big gunman, Charlie recalling his fat, bullish neck.

A thick hand shoved the pen into his fingers, and he caught a glance of a ruby pinky ring on a hairy finger.

Concentrating on the paper and into the glare, Charlie worked about ten minutes constructing the letter to his business associate, E. E. Kirkpatrick. Kirk had handled his affairs for some time and would understand his tone and message beyond these men's obvious mental limits.

A man over his shoulder with hot breath read it and then ripped it up.

"Let's try again," the big man said. "I don't give a tinker's damn about the condition of the Slick Company or what assets you got tied up in stocks and bonds and whatnot. Just say you want the money paid, and we'll handle the rest. Don't think, Charlie. Just write, and smilin' days are ahead."

"The estate's money is in a trust. You just can't cash a check. There are lawyers and procedures—"

"Fuck 'em," the other man said. "Write. Don't think. Thinkin' is our job."

Charlie wrote what the man said, word for word. He heard the man's heavy breathing and even the wet snap of a smile behind him when Charlie signed his name to all this nonsense. No words were said; the gunmen simply left the shack, screen door banging behind them, and a big motor started outside, automobile scratching off in the dust.

"Mr. Urschel, we sure are sorry," said the old man. "Potatoes, get dinner started."

"Sorry, Mr. Urschel," the boy, Potatoes, said. "I got another cigar for you, a gen-u-ine Tampa Nugget. And we got somethin' special for dinner tonight, too."

"That's right, Mr. Urschel. A real home-cooked meal. Don't mind those men none. We just want you real comfortable. Remember, we's the ones who treat you nice."

"Then why don't you let me go?" Charlie asked. "I'll pay you both ten thousand dollars apiece."

Potatoes and the old man didn't say a thing for a long while. The hound trotted over and licked Charlie's hands while the cotton and tape was laid back over his eyes from behind. The dog slopped on his fingers, and Charlie could feel the long, drooping ears.

"That ole boy sure does like you," the old man said. "He don't come 'round to people so quick. He senses you're a gentleman. A just man."

"You should see him take after a coon," Potatoes said. "You want to hear more about the Fair?"

"No, thank you, if you please."

"Yes, sir," Potatoes said.

"Mr. Urschel," the old man said. "If them boys don't make it through what they're plannin' on, you have my word I'll let you loose. I know you don't know me. But my word is fourteen carat."

"I bet," Charlie said. "I could tell you're a pair of real gentlemen."

"I'll go fetch your dinner," Potatoes said. "I think I seen a *Photoplay*, too. Jean Harlow's on the cover and gives an interview, real personal, saying things she ain't said to nobody else before. I get the goose pimples just thinkin' on it."

"DID YOU HAVE TO MAKE HIM SWALLOW THE DAMN WATCH?" Doc White asked.

"They put that woman through hell," Jones said. "Then he tried to slice me with a busted bottle."

"Why didn't you have them arrested?"

"They learned their lesson," Jones said. "I hope they choked on their steak."

"Pretty stupid calling Mrs. Urschel to complain."

"Greedy as hell," Jones said. "Those men were bums before the Depression. It just makes 'em easier to hide."

"No shame atall these days."

"Why don't you tell that to Mr. Colvin?"

"Come again?"

"That little girl is twistin' him in knots," Jones said.

On a stone patio behind the mansion, Betty Slick wore a satin number, something worth a month's pay to Jones, low-cut and tied at the shoulders. Jones had seen such numbers in magazines but never on Mary Ann. Mary Ann was no prude but would've thought paying that kind of money for a dress was a sin on the order of buying a bonnet you only wear on Easter Sunday. Bruce Colvin sat on the ledge of a marble fountain, felt hat in hand, conversing with the girl, who'd hop up onto the ledge in her bare feet and then hop back down. The whole dance of it was making Jones dizzy, and he wished the girl had somewhere to go to keep Colvin's mind on the matter at hand.

Jones took the pipe from the corner of his mouth and knocked the tobacco out with the heel of his boot. "He don't stand a chance."

"What's his story?"

"Worked as a prosecutor in some small town in Mississippi," Jones said. "Joined up a couple years ago. Can't shoot. Can't track worth a durn."

"Dresses regulation."

"Our days are numbered."

"They still need us."

"If you say," Jones said.

Betty Slick laughed and twirled her dark hair and laughed some more, and brought her show closer to Special Agent in Charge Bruce Colvin. Jones noted she was a pretty girl, with a woman's figure and pleasant face. She was the kind of girl that still had the dew on her, and Colvin might as well have had a ring in his nose.

"I think I'm gettin' the piles," Doc said. "Let's take a walk."

"Where to?"

"Out of this mausoleum."

The Urschel place had been cleared of most newspapermen, who had only the day before been working from tents and makeshift offices on the front lawn, on account of not scaring off the kidnappers. They were cleared from the house but not from the story; those bloodsuckers still called every other minute. Four extra phone lines had been added to the house, with agents and police listening to every call, analyzing every telegram, and studying every letter delivered. Simple messages were broken down and straight-ahead words were decoded.

"You go to Sheriff Reed's funeral?"

"No, sir," Jones said. "Couldn't make it."

"He was an all right fella."

"Reminded me of ole Rome Shields."

"From San Angelo?"

"Yep," Jones said. "Rome Shields taught me everything I know."

"Hell, Buster. Just what do you know?"

"The older I get, the more it escapes me."

The trees made a good bit of shade as they walked down Eighteenth along the skinny sidewalk past many smaller homes—bungalows and such—all of them with brand-new cars and children playing on fresh-cut lawns with manicured bushes and trimmed roses. Jones removed his jacket and tucked it in the crook of his arm and over the .45 on his hip. The whole place felt like a hothouse, and he mopped his face a bit. A young agent from the local office slowed his vehicle beside them and asked if they needed a ride somewhere. The older men shook their heads and kept moving.

"This country's going to hell."

"Don't be gettin' soft and senile on me," Jones said. "People have always been evil. Didn't you read the Bible? There weren't too many picnics between wars. Or you want to sing me a song about those gay ole days?"

"I don't recall times ever bein' this bad."

"Don't take as much to be an outlaw, if that's what you're gettin' at."

"How you figure?"

"Remember when we ran the Hole-in-the-Wall Gang?"

"I remember running that posse on Black Jack."

"Well, when they pulled a job it took some effort," Jones said. "You had to blast your way out of the bank and hope your horse kept on till the posse gave up. That's a test of wills and endurance. You planned ahead and saw it through. What you got these days depends on the machine, not the man."

"The best car."

"These hoods are driving vehicles with fourteen and sixteen cylinders. What kind of country sheriff keeps that kind of machine in his garage? They get out of the bank and they're as good as gone. Who's gonna catch 'em?"

"What would Black Jack have done with a Buick and a Thompson?"

"Raise a lot more hell than these folks."

"You know what ole Black Jack said before they hung 'im?"

"Tell it again."

" 'I'll be in hell before y'all eat breakfast, boys,' " White said, stopping for a moment to light a cigarette. " 'Let her rip.' "

"Took his head clean off, I heard," Jones said. "Doc, you ever think you'd see a weapon that could fire thirty rounds in the blink of an eye?"

"That was made for the military, not for gangsters."

"How you gonna keep it out of their hands?"

"Don't take much skill with a full drum," White said. "Sure can chew apart the scenery."

"One man becomes an army."

"It's cowardice," White said. "Not progress."

When they returned, Kirkpatrick met them on the sunporch and opened the door. Maps and telegrams had been laid on the card table along with books and books of mug shots and prison records.

"Anything?" Jones asked.

"Cranks," Kirkpatrick said. "Can you believe that woman had the nerve—"

"Yes."

Jones and White removed their hats, laid them crown down, and took a seat at the card table. A negro woman offered some coffee, and they took it, White discussing running back to the hotel for sandwiches to keep the billing easy for expenses. Jones said that sounded fine, and he filled his pipe again and leaned back into the chair. He could hear the birds in the trees and the cicadas buzzing in the heat. The view was obscured and fuzzy on account of the metal screen.

"This is the screwiest one," Kirkpatrick said. "Received it this morning while I was shaving."

He slid the letter across to Jones. Jones glanced down and read it, getting the fire going in the bowl, and looked up at Kirkpatrick.

"What?" Kirkpatrick asked. "Surely you don't think there is anything to something so outrageous?"

A letter from Charles F. Urschel to you and the enclosed identification cards will convince you that you are dealing with the Abductors. Immediately upon receipt of this letter you will proceed to obtain the sum of TWO HUNDRED THOUSAND DOLLARS (**$200,000.00**) in GENUINE USED FEDERAL RESERVE CURRENCY in the denomination of TWENTY DOLLAR (**$20.00**) Bills. It will be use-less for you to attempt taking notes of SERIAL NUMBERS, MAKING UP DUMMY PACKAGE, OR ANYTHING ELSE IN THE LINE OF ATTEMPTED DOUBLE CROSS. BEAR THIS IN MIND, CHARLES E URSCHEL WILL REMAIN IN OUR CUSTODY UNTIL MONEY HAS BEEN INSPECTED AND EX CHANGED AND FURTHER-MORE WILL BE AT THE SCENE OF, CONTACT FOR PAY-OFF AND IF THERE SHOULD BE ANY ATTEMPT AT ANY DOUBLE XX IT WILL BE HE THAT SUFFER THE CONSEQUENCE. As soon as you have read and RE-READ this carefully and wish to commence negotiations you will proceed to the *DAILY OKLAHOMAN* and insert the following BLIND AD under the REAL ESTATE, FARMS FOR SALE, and we will know that you are ready, for BUSINESS, and you will receive further instructions AT THE BOX ASSIGNED TO YOU BY THE NEWSPAPER, AND NO WHERE ELSE. We have nei-ther time or patience to carry on any further lengthy correspondence. RUN THIS AD FOR ONE WEEK IN *DAILY OKLAHOMAN*. FOR SALE—160 Acres Land, good five room house, deep well. Also Cows, Tools, Tractor, Corn and Hay. **$3750.00** for quick sale. TERMS. Box #—hear from us as soon as convenient after insertion of AD.

An hour later, the postman delivered a letter with Urschel's identifi-cation and personal signature. From across the table, Doc White asked, "Our boys?"

"Yep," Jones said. "See if Agent Colvin might have the time and incli-nation to join us. That is, if his dance card ain't punched."

ORA HAD FIXED A BIG SOUTHERN MEAL JUST THE WAY GEORGE liked it, and they all sat together like a proper family at Boss's place, a mile down the road from where they kept Mr. Urschel. Kathryn let Boss say grace, and George answered it with a big, corny "Amen" and reached for the fried chicken, that long, hairy arm coming clean across the table for a drumstick. Albert Bates complimented her mother on the meal and poured himself a glass of iced tea.

"You send over a plate, darlin'?" George asked.

"Taters brung it," Ora said, her voice grating, filled with a lot of North Mississippi; Saltillo to her bones. "Gave him some sliced tomatoes and field peas, too. Reckon he'll like that?"

"Mr. Urschel should be grateful," Bates said. "A big oilman lives on nothing but sirloin steak and bourbon. Craps out silver dollars like a one-armed bandit."

"He's due for some slop," George said.

"George," Ora said.

"Oh, no, ma'am, I don't mean your cookin' is slop, I'm talking the beans."

"I don't think he's cut out for ranch living," Bates said. "He tried to fight signing that letter, but not real hard. He wants this mess gone."

"And what will you do then, Mr. Bates?" Boss asked. The old man sat at the head of the table in a boiled white shirt buttoned to the throat. He chewed his chicken as he spoke, with a lot of strength in those jaws, looking like a little bulldog gnawing on a bone, thin white hair combed back from his forehead and sticking up like a grizzled rooster's.

"Get back to my sweetie and have some fun," Bates said. "This is it for me."

"What's the next step for you, young man?" Boss asked.

"If I knew, this wouldn't be an ounce of fun," George said with a wink. "You go where you find the action. But I'm figuring they'll answer that ad and play it smart. We'll all be out of your hair by Sunday, and me and Kit will be on the road and Albert will be back with his sweetie."

He smiled over at Kathryn, stopping her from laughing about Boss's hair, and grabbed her knee with his free hand. She looked down at the red-and-white tablecloth and studied the uniform pattern. She hadn't gotten any food, her stomach twisted up in knots. But George didn't have a care in the world, reaching back across the table and grabbing a thigh this time and asking her mother for another helping of field peas. Old Ora lit up with smiles like that big mug had hung the goddamn moon.

"George, when you finish stuffing your gullet, how 'bout you and me go check out the machine?" Kathryn asked.

"Already checked on her," George said. "Fueled up and ready to go. Got a tin of gas and cans of oil. Don't you worry about nothin'."

"I'd like to see her anyway," Kathryn said, moving his hand off her knee, pushing the skirt back down. She reached for the iced tea and poured a glass, wishing these Baptists would wake up to the world and keep some gin in the house.

"Sheriff Faith come by today," Boss said, just as plain as talking about crops and weather.

George stopped chewing. He and Albert exchanged glances.

"Oh, you boys don't get nervous," he said. "I been stashing folks here for years. The sheriff would tell me if the law was onto us."

"May I have some more biscuits?" George asked.

"Haven't you had enough?" Kathryn said.

"Why don't you mind your own business."

Ora hopped up like there was a fire poker in her ass and landed two buttermilk biscuits on his plate. Kathryn just shook her head and walked out the screen door and onto the porch, resting an arm on the column and looking across the pasture at all those goddamn cows mooing at one another, blind and directionless until someone cracked the whip. Suckers.

George sure took his time to join her, door clattering shut. He lit a cigarette and patted his stomach, following her down a path and to the garage he'd constructed with Potatoes and Boss that spring. He found the key in his pocket and loosened the lock and chain, opening up the big, wide barn doors to show off that gorgeous midnight blue Cadillac.

A full sixteen cylinders, with big, fat pontoon fenders, torpedo headlights, and a slant-back grille topped with that gorgeous silver woman with wings. The places she'd see.

Kathryn ran her hand over the paint, which always felt liquid and alive to her, shining wet. She turned and leaned back against the door, crooking her finger at George. He didn't need to be asked twice, but first shut the garage door and lit up a kerosene lantern.

He wrapped his big arms around her and kissed her square on the mouth, not like the men in the movies but like he was kissing somebody to test his brute strength. The way a knucklehead slams his mallet in a carnival game. "Careful," she said. "Don't mess up my hair. I just had it done."

"I love you, Kit."

"Don't I know it."

"That's a big backseat back there, how 'bout we break her in."

She ran a finger down the loose part of his silk shirt and tipped the brow of his fedora back from those murky green eyes, the color of swamp water. "I thought we'd wait. You know. Just like people do before a wedding."

"Wait till what?"

"When you get the money and we're on the road."

"Come on, Kit. I'm hurtin' here. And we're married already, or had you forgot?"

"No, I hadn't forgot."

He wrapped a meaty arm tighter and pulled her in. He reached up under her skirt and was feeling her between the legs and over the panties, and she wasn't feeling in that kind of mood, but it took her, and she had to tilt her head back to catch her breath. "George?"

"You are a peach."

"George."

"I love you, sweet baby."

The garage smelled of polished wood and kerosene and new oil just

waiting to get burned up from here to Mexico. "George, I need you to
do something."

"What's that?"

He pawed at her dress and pulled down a bra strap, pushing her up on
the hood and getting himself good and settled between her legs. With a
real gentleness that she could never believe a big man could achieve, he
laid her flat on her back and put his mouth to her nipple.

"I want you to murder that son of a bitch Ed Weatherford for me," she
said, looking at the tin roof. "He's onto us, baby."

George stopped and stepped back a few paces, shaking his head. "I
don't want to kill anyone."

"George, be a gangster. Really."

He shook his head.

Kathryn righted herself up onto her elbows and pushed herself off
the Cadillac, fingering up her top and smoothing down the dress over
her long legs. She reached into George's shirt pocket and grabbed some
Luckies, lighting the match off the mug's chin.

She blew some smoke and shook her head.

His mouth hung open.

"You'd rather I do it?"

"I didn't say that," George said. "But that's not in the plan."

"Plan's changed."

"Just ignore him."

"Then he'll really be gunnin' for us."

They heard a car's motor from down the road and then all of Boss's
guineas out there, raising hell and making that high, dumb guinea call.
George cracked the barn door and told Kathryn to stay put. He peered
out as she smoked and thought about different ways to kill that bastard
Weatherford.

"Whew," George said, closing the garage. "Thought it might be the
law."

"Who is it?"

"Harvey and Verne," he said. "Ain't that somethin'? Hope they brought something to drink."

Kathryn shook her head and put out the cigarette with the toe of her high heel made of soft white leather. She made a fist with her right hand and rapped on George's forehead as if it were a front door to an empty house.

9

Harvey Bailey eyed the golf ball, lined up the drive from the hogpen, and aimed for Boss Shannon's old barn to the north. He still had a bad limp, the bullet out of him and wound stitched up crooked, but they'd lugged the set of clubs all the way from Kansas City and it would've been a shame not to play. This being the first time he'd a chance to use them, with all the shooting and bank robbing getting in the way of some solid sport. He took a breath and loosened his shoulders and smacked the ball right in the sweet spot, feeling it down to his toes as the ball went skyward and dropped damn near the mouth of the barn, sending some worried guineas up in a flurry of feathers. "Beat that, chump."

Miller plopped down a ball. He was shirtless, wearing the tailored pants he'd had on for days and the handmade wingtips. His upper body was corded with muscle like a fighter's, with skin as white as blanched paper, turning pink in the morning sunshine. He took a few practice swings and sent the ball up and away, and it disappeared somewhere over the weathered barn.

"I say the barn door is the hole," Harvey said.

"Fine by me."

"You want to get a posthole digger?" he said. "I could get a stick and a rag."

"Sure."

"The Shannons seem a bit jumpy, don't they?" Harvey said, hoisting the bag up onto his shoulder and limping toward the barn. A bony coonhound loped after them like a spectator to the sport.

"Boss especially."

"You think he wants us to leave?"

"Could be," Verne said. "How's the leg?"

"Walking helps," Harvey said. "Wound's healing clean, no thanks to that damn butcher who sewed it."

He dropped the bag and chose a number two iron, spying a cat sitting atop a mule plow. The big tom paid the men no mind as it hiked its leg skyward and started to lick its balls.

"I knew a man in Lansing who could do that," Harvey said. "Or claimed he could."

"A man can learn lots of things in prison," Miller said. "I'd rather hang than go back."

"How's Vi?"

"Scared."

"She want you to come up there?"

"Sure," he said. "Brooklyn isn't her kind of place."

"You trust those people?"

"I did a job for them and, oh, well, they owe me."

"And she understands?"

"Vi understands. Always has."

"You love that woman, don't you?"

"Sure."

"You gonna marry her?"

"When all this ends," he said. "Get ahead a little."

"When does this stuff ever end?" Harvey asked. "I got out before this country went in the toilet. That's what happens. You try and go legit, get into some corny business like filling stations, and then the world shits on you. Take what you can get when you can get it."

"One more score," Verne said. "Something big for us both."

"Verne?" Harvey said, setting the ball right for the big tom. "I don't know how many different ways to say it. Next time I walk into a bank, it'll be with a checkbook, not a gun."

Verne met his gaze with those cold blue eyes and smiled.

Harvey tapped the ball with a flick and it sailed within a hair of the big cat, the animal toppling over on his back and scampering away.

"Don't look back," Harvey said. "Don't get greedy. Know your price. When it's met, walk away."

Verne walked around the back of the barn, searching for his ball in some high grass and swatting away some goats set loose to clear it. He switched at the grass with his iron and looked for a good ten minutes before Harvey called time on the hunt.

Behind him, maybe a half mile away, Harvey's eye caught old man Shannon's Model T kicking up dust, heading out to the house where his boy lived. This was the fourth trip he'd made that morning. Twice with George and now twice alone.

"What's going on at Armon's place?"

"That kid needs a swift kick in the ass," Miller said. "Son of a bitch. You saw that ball land here, didn't you?"

"Did you see George's face when we asked if he'd like to take on some work last week?"

"What of it?"

"When's the last time ole George Kelly didn't want to pick up some bucks behind the wheel? He wet himself coming around the Green Lantern, wanting to work a job, and far as I could tell he and Kit aren't rolling in it. You think he got something else going?"

"Maybe."

"With who?"

"Kit's got into something."

"You trust that rancid bitch?"

Miller glanced at him and smiled. He stared out at the farm road and the Model T, growing close and then passing the men in a big old cloud of dust. He reached down and found the ball, tossing it out on some clear land, just a stroke away from a pile of goat shit.

"How 'bout we play up the road a bit?" Miller said. "Might find something that interests us."

ALL THAT MONEY MADE THE BANKER NERVOUS, BUT MRS. Urschel had signed the forms, and there was nothing that the little bald fella could do about it. He watched at the far end of the Slick Company boardroom, leaning into the desk with white knuckles that made Gus Jones smile, while his comptroller and staff worked overtime to log every serial number onto individual pieces of paper. The money was circulated—as requested in the letter that came to box number 807 that morning—all from the Federal Reserve in Kansas City. If Mr. Urschel came back safe, they'd pass these numbers to every lawman, post office, and bank in the country. The gang left little to chance with a letter that spelled out every dance step.

In view of the fact that you have the Ad inserted as per our instructions, we gather that you are prepared to meet our ultimatum.

You will pack TWO HUNDRED THOUSAND DOLLARS ($200,000) in USED GENUINE FEDERAL RESERVE NOTES OF TWENTY DOLLAR DENOMINATION in a suitable LIGHT COLORED LEATHER BAG and have someone purchase transportation for you, including berth, aboard train #28 (The Sooner) which departs at 10:10 p.m. via the M.K.&T. Lines for Kansas City, Mo.

You will ride on the OBSERVATION PLATFORM where you may be observed by someone at some Station along the Line between Okla. City and K.C., Mo. If indications are alright, somewhere along the Right-of-Way you will observe a Fire on the Right Side of Track (Facing direction train is bound). That first Fire will be your Cue to be

prepared to throw BAG to Track immediately after passing SECOND
FIRE.

Mr. Urschel will, upon instructions, attend to the fires and secure
the bag when you throw it off, he will open it and transfer the contents
to a sack that he will be provided with, so, if you comply with our
demand and do not attempt any subterfuge, as according to the News
reports you have pledged, Mr. Urschel should be home in a very short
while.

REMEMBER THIS—IF ANY TRICKERY IS ATTEMPTED
YOU WILL FIND THE REMAINS OF URSCHEL AND INSTEAD
OF JOY THERE WILL BE DOUBLE GRIEF—FOR SOME-ONE
VERY NEAR AND DEAR TO THE URSCHEL FAMILY IS UNDER
CONSTANT SURVEILLANCE AND WILL LIKE-WISE SUFFER
FOR YOUR ERROR.

If there is the slightest HITCH in these PLANS for any reason
what-so-ever, not your fault, you will proceed on into Kansas City, Mo.
And register at the Muehlebach Hotel under the name of E. E. Kincaid
of Little Rock, Arkansas, and await further instructions there, how-
ever, there should not be, IF YOU COMPLY WITH THESE SIMPLE
INSTRUCTIONS.

THE MAIN THING IS DO NOT DIVULGE THE CONTENTS OF
THIS LETTER TO ANY LAW AUTHORITIES FOR WE HAVE NO
INTENTION OF FUTHER COMMUNICATION.

YOU ARE TO MAKE THIS TRIP SATURDAY, JULY 29th 1933.
BE SURE YOU RIDE THE PLATFORM OF THE REAR CAR AND
HAVE THE BAG WITH MONEY IN IT FROM THE TIME YOU
LEAVE OKLAHOMA CITY.

Jones watched as bundles of counted money were loaded in a light-
colored Gladstone bag. The kidnappers being so goddamn specific about
the type, everyone worried that the slightest error might lead poor old
Charlie into the grave.

"Little dramatic," Doc White said, reading over Jones's shoulder. "All that talk about 'double grief.'"

"Well, it ain't a love letter."

"You think Kirkpatrick is up to it?"

"I think he's not only up to it," Jones said, finding the gold watch at his vest. "He's damn well excited about it."

"Give him a gun?"

"You think that's a good idea? I'll be on that train, too."

"But the letter said—"

"Nuts to those bandits," Jones said. "They don't know me. I'll carry the ransom, and Kirkpatrick a dummy bag, in case there's trouble . . ."

"That banker sure is sweating."

"You keep an eye on Mrs. Urschel and the family," Jones said. "I'll call when we reach Kansas City."

"Union Station."

"That's where the tracks lead."

"Why don't you let me take the lead, Buster?" White asked. "Wait it out here. We can't do a thing till Urschel comes back."

"Since when did you become my wife?"

"Since when did you become a touchy old bastard?"

"Hell with you."

"I see."

"Watch the family."

"Watch your ass, Buster," White said. "That station ain't held the best luck. And I ain't calling on Mary Ann for you stepping in a shit pile twice."

"THEY DON'T MEAN NOTHIN' BY IT, KIT," ALBERT BATES SAID. "They're just catching up on old times. George likes to reminisce."

"Well, I hate it."

"I know."

"I was so damn glad when he got out from under those mugs and we got the hell out of Saint Paul," Kathryn said. "I didn't see the sun for four months up there. The ground was nothing but black slush and not a spot of green. All they did was sit around the Green Lantern and drink themselves stupid. George would lie around in pajamas, listening to *Buck Rogers*, for months, and then he'd be wheel on a job and come back with a cheap handout. Harv and Verne throwing him the dog scraps, and George never asking for anything better."

"But you liked Tacoma?"

"I liked George in Tacoma," she said. "He doesn't act like this in front of you or Eddie. He acted normal. He's always putting on for Verne and that bastard Harvey Bailey. I can't stand that big-nosed son of a bitch. Everyone says he's such a gentleman, the 'Gentleman Bandit,' the class yeggman, but he's nothing but a two-bit Mis-sou-ra hick in a hundred-dollar suit with whitewall hair."

"Slow down, Kit," Bates said. "They can hear you."

"Do I look like I care?"

She turned back to the farmhouse window and saw the men inside, the kitchen all bright with a yellow glow, the dumb yeggs laughing and knee-slapping around the makeshift table and plunking down cards, cigars screwed down in their teeth. Old Boss Shannon took up the fourth seat like he was just one of the boys and not some old farmer who ran a rooming house for criminals. Boss had been taking their dirty money since he and Ora met, yeggs from all over the damn country coming to Paradise. All shot up and bloody, suitcases full of cash and with itchy fingers, and offering a teenage girl a few bits for a quick throw, saying it might be their last . . .

"It's okay," Albert Bates said, his hawk-nosed profile crossed in the kerosene light. He fumbled for a fresh cigarette and smiled over at her. "George won't mention it."

"He better not," she said. "He lets these boys in on Urschel and I'll cut his nuts off."

"They're not wise to us," Bates said, cupping a hand and flicking the lighter's flint. "We'll all be gone tomorrow. Your stepdaddy will watch Urschel till we come back and turn him loose."

"That's another screw I worry about."

"Mr. Urschel?"

"Boss."

"He's gettin' a cut," Bates said. "No one wants to whittle this thing down any more."

"You really gonna quit?"

"You bet," he said. "A fella can get set up with this kind of dough."

"Denver, huh?"

"Yep."

"Albert?"

He turned to her, burning down the cigarette and fishing for a new one in his pocket. She pulled a cigarette from her purse, lit it, and passed it on to him. She found a place on the edge of the farmhouse porch to let her legs hang off free and loose, and Bates joined her after a while. The laughter and loud talk had become too much.

"How will I know if there's trouble?" she asked.

"You studied the picture of Kirkpatrick?"

She nodded.

"You see anyone with him, anyone too friendly, you step off the train at any station and call us," he said. "He's supposed to come alone, and that's the only way we'll go ahead with the drop. You unnerstand?"

"You just look out for George."

"Your man will come back in one piece," Bates said, cigarette hanging loose. "I promise."

"It's not him I'm worried about."

"You sure are hard-boiled sometimes, Kit," Bates said. "We're on Easy Street now."

"That's the kind of talk that will get us all killed. Or worse."

"You love him, though?"

"Who?"

"George."

"I married the dumb bastard, didn't I?"

"But do you love him?" Bates asked. "When I think about seeing my sweetie, it makes me feel all funny in the gut."

"Yep," she said. "George makes me feel all funny."

Bates laughed and smoked some more, watching the same herd of cows, following down a line of crooked posts connected with miles of barbed wire.

"The funny thing about you and George is that sometimes he's talking but I hear you coming out of his mouth."

"That doesn't make any sense."

"I don't mean nothing by it," Bates said. "Just something I've noticed for some time. I've known George Barnes since he was running moonshine out of Memphis. And now I see this fella who folks 'round here call 'Machine Gun' Kelly, with his slick hair and two-tone shoes. But I'm not really sure if that's you or George . . . It's all screwy."

"You're the screwy one, Albert," she said. She smiled and kissed him on the cheek in a sisterly way. "You look out for both of you. And don't worry, I'm pretty good at spotting a cop."

"I know, sister."

"No more hard times."

"Welcome to Easy Street."

"Keep the light on . . ."

10

Saturday, July 29, 1933

The men gathered in the shadow of the Urschel house with pistols and sawed-off shotguns and waited for the bank president to arrive with the cash. An Oldsmobile rolled into the drive and flashed its lights twice. Berenice Urschel answered back from the second floor with a flickering flashlight, and they were moving. Jones followed Kirkpatrick, and Kirkpatrick took the grip and got into the car with Jones driving. They headed to the train station, both men holding grips now—Kirkpatrick holding a leather bag filled with old newspapers and magazines and Jones carrying a lighter-colored bag filled with twenty pounds' worth of ransom money. If they were jumped at the station or on the train, Kirk would give up his bag.

They proceeded up into the observation car as instructed, and the strain of it reflected on Kirkpatrick, who let out a long breath, his face covered in sweat, hand reaching into his suit pocket for a silver flask. He took a healthy drink and nodded to Jones, who sat opposite him on a long communal bench and shook his head. So far, the men were alone. Just a negro porter, who asked them for their tickets and if they'd care for anything at all, and Jones had simply asked if they were running on schedule.

Jones checked his timepiece. He lit his pipe.

A half hour left till they were on their way.

The platform filled with dozens of men in straw hats and ladies in summer dresses. Little kids toting little bags and porters carrying steamer trunks on the strength of their backs. Jones looked to the rear of the train, where the glass formed a wide-sweeping window, and saw another Pullman heading toward them, pushed along slow and easy, until it joined to the observation car with a click. The coupling jarred the men, and then there was another hard click, and the porter noted the men's confusion.

"Got to add two more," he said. "Taking on extra passengers in Kansas City to go to the World's Fair."

Kirkpatrick was on his feet, telling the man they had to change cars, they must change cars, this was not acceptable at all. They had been promised an observation view, had paid for the view, and he damn well wanted a view.

They got seats on the last Pullman, Jones and Kirkpatrick taking a seat on two old camp stools pulled out into the vestibule. The air was hot, and it wasn't until the train got going that a good crossbreeze collected over the railing and pushed across their faces, Jones and Kirkpatrick sitting in that last car, watching the brick warehouses and ramshackle houses fading from view until there were only wide rolling fields of dry grass and dead cornstalks.

"Right side," Jones said. "I'll watch the left just to make sure."

They made it all the way to Tyson when the car door slid open and an attractive woman dressed in black with dark lipstick asked if she could join them.

Jones stood and said: "Please."

She smelled just like the flowers Mary Ann cut fresh and kept in the house till they dried and turned. The turning seemed to make 'em even more sweet.

HARVEY AND VERNE WATCHED GEORGE, KATHRYN, AND Albert Bates pile into that big blue Cadillac and disappear down the country road. George said they were going to visit some old speaks, Kathryn wanted to see *Gold Diggers of 1933*, and Albert Bates said in a mutter he had some business needed tending. And Harvey didn't ask any questions, just wished them well as they took off into the night, and he settled onto the porch with Verne and old Boss Shannon, who'd been plied with enough corn liquor to kill a goat. Old Boss talking about how two hundred thousand people had crammed into downtown Saint Louis to march on behalf of the NRA and celebrate all that Blue Eagle nonsense, and he recommended that they all get a solid gun and a piece of land because this country was about to become one filthy fascist nation with Roosevelt no better than Adolf Hitler himself. "You know Hitler treats his own people like animals. If he got one that don't suit 'im, they'll sterilize 'im. God's own truth, I read it in the paper. I wonder what they'd do with an old man like me?"

"How's the farm, Boss?"

"Fair to middlin'," he said. "Don't have enough water. Got me a hog that's turned on me. He's supposed to be ruttin' but the other day damn near tried to kill me. I can't figure it out."

Miller looked to Harvey. Harvey flicked the long ash from his cigar and shrugged.

"Can we go take a look at that hog?" Miller asked.

"Sure thing, boys," Boss Shannon said. "Let me get a lantern."

"Say, Boss," Harvey said, "where's ole Potatoes these days?"

"You know he got that girl from down the road with child? Well, he married her, and now she's knocked up again. I 'spec you could say he's taken on responsibility. He don't like it when I call him Potatoes no more. But I can't seem to wrap my mind 'round it. That kid will always be Potatoes to me. Hold on there, fellas."

Harvey worked on the cigar. The late-night light, not dark but almost purple, still burning deep to the west, almost making him feel like he could see clear over to California and the Pacific Ocean, all wide and endless like a filthy dream.

"Why don't you just ask him, Verne?"

"Where's the fun?" Miller said. "Besides, you think he would talk that easily?"

"He's going to scream."

"Let him scream."

"What if he gets killed?"

"He won't get killed," Miller said. "Whoever heard of a hog killing a man?"

"I have," Harvey said. "You know, I grew up on a farm."

"You don't say."

"I still have a farm," Harvey said. "Just what do you know about me, Verne?"

"I know enough."

Boss Shannon was wearing his finest pair of Union overalls with high-laced boots and an almost clean undershirt. He'd taken a plug of tobacco from a tin in the kitchen and was sucking and spitting as they followed a hog path down along the barbed-wire fence. Pigs wallowed and grunted in a mud enclosure, and nearby the men found a rambling cage of wire and barn wood where a huge hog looked into the lantern light with tiny red eyes.

"What do you call him?"

"Hoover," Boss Shannon said, spitting. "Armon named him. Ain't that a hoot? Hoover. Don't he look just like him?"

"You called him Armon there."

"See?" Boss said. "I'm trying."

"I wish he'd come down and see us," Miller said. "We could have a drink. He might like some whiskey we brought from Kansas City. He could play organ for us. I wonder if he knows 'We're in the Money'?"

"I'll tell him, but he can't leave the house much on account of his wife's condition. 'Sides, he only plays church music."

"They have some company?"

"No, sir," Boss said. "Alone, besides that ole hound. Yep, just Armon and his bride. And like I said, that dog."

Miller drew a .45 automatic from his belt and said, "Take your clothes off, Boss."

"You boys always joking," the old man said with a smile.

"He ain't joking," Harvey said.

"Come on, now. Y'all lost your senses. I don't have no money."

"We don't want money," Miller said.

"What do you want?"

"For you to drop your drawers and crawl in the slop with ole Hoover there," Miller said. "Come on. Let's go."

"You boys lost your mind. I just finished telling you that hog has something wrong with its faculties. He could right kill me."

Miller squeezed off a round at Boss's feet, and the man jumped like an impromptu reel had started up. Harvey laughed and turned his head so Boss couldn't see the smile and think they didn't mean serious business.

"Socks and underwear, too."

"I ain't goin' in the cage with a hungry hog with my pecker freed."

Miller fired off another round. And Boss danced a jig till he wore nothing but his T-shirt, like it was a long flour-sack dress. Harvey slid back the lock on the cage and waved his hand, a doorman at the finest speak in the city. "Your party awaits."

"You two crooked sonsabitches. Want to see me cornholed by a filthy swine. That's a sickness. The plagues will come on you tenfold. You know it."

Harvey slid back the bolt. He got the cigar going again to a glowing red tip. He checked the time.

"How long?" Miller asked.

"I'll say ten minutes."

"I'll say five or less."

"How much?"

"Hundred dollars."

"This some kind of sport!" Boss said. "Goddamn you both to hell in your underbritches."

There was a guttural snort, red eyes in the passing beam of the kerosene lantern. Light scattered from Boss Shannon's hand down into the mud and muck and pig shit before a high squeal sounded that the men took for the animal but would later figure out was only Boss.

Miller only had to ask once, "Just what have George and Kit gotten themselves into, and how can we get a slice?"

KATHRYN BOARDED THE TRAIN IN MUSKOGEE AFTER TAKING another line from Denison, Texas, and waiting it out for the *Sooner Limited*. The observation car had filled with a half dozen drunk businessmen with loose neckties and five o'clock shadows and two sour-faced old women who shook their heads at each other as the men told one another off-color jokes and freely exchanged bottles wrapped in brown paper bags. *"This fella has a trained dog he gives twenty cents that will go to the corner for a newspaper and a bucket of beer. Well, one day he doesn't have change and sends the dog away with five whole dollars. Some time passes, and the dog doesn't come back, so he goes lookin'. He finds the rascal in a back alley really sticking his business to a mongrel bitch. 'I'm surprised at you,' the man says. 'You've never acted like this before.' And the dog says, 'I never had the money before.'"* She stayed there through two stops, not spotting Kirkpatrick and thinking maybe he'd begged off on the plan, but then she decided to walk through the passenger cars trailing behind them, crowded with church and civic groups from Houston, Waco, and Dallas, headed to the big city of Chicago and the big Fair. One group had a little ragtag band with them, and for some reason they launched into "You've

Got to Be a Football Hero," and they thought their antics hilarious as a
few of the boys tossed a ball in the center aisle, nearly sending Kathryn
off her feet. But she recovered and scowled, readjusting her little black
hat and veil, and finding the final vestibule where, through the glass, she
could make out two figures sitting on stools and watching the night pass.

She opened the sliding door, and the older of the men stood, offering
her a seat.

She said thank you, but she wanted to stretch her legs.

Kathryn reached into her purse, grabbed her little cigarette case and
lighter, and had a bit of difficulty in the wind. The men didn't talk, just
watched the snaking tracks, wheels groaning and scraping under them
until the path righted again and they headed due north, the hard earth
and parched farms flickering past. The night was as clear as could be,
and the stars looked like a million winking diamonds.

"Where you men headed?" she asked.

"Kansas City," said the younger man, who hadn't offered his seat.

The older man wore a cowboy hat and smoked a pipe. He got off his
seat again and removed his hat. "Chicago," he said.

"Not traveling together?"

"No, ma'am," he said. "Just passing the time with a friendly drink."

"Would you like some?" asked the other man, and he got to his feet,
using the rail for support. He seemed a bit nervous and a little drunk.
But she as hell recognized him as Mr. E. E. Kirkpatrick of Tom Slick
Enterprises. Two Gladstone bags lay side by side.

She turned her head and said no thank you, stepping back from the
platform into shadow. The sound and vibration of the train coming up
into her feet made her knees a bit weak. There was something about
the old man that she didn't trust or like, and, when the train stopped in
Arcadia, he got up to stretch, looking across to Kirkpatrick, who shook
his head. The old man wore wire-framed cheaters and a gun on his hip.
He was old but had the look of the law written across his wide face.

She told the men good night and crawled off onto the platform, looking for the number George had scrawled on a matchbook from the Blackstone Hotel . . . *If there was any cause, any cause at all, call them at this telephone number.* She checked her watch and prayed there was time for a meet in Tulsa.

"THIS IS WHERE MR. SLICK DRILLED HIS FIRST WELL," E. E. Kirkpatrick said as the *Sooner* pulled into the town of Tryon. The big locomotive hissed and shuttered in rest while folks got on and off in the early morning. The porter brought Jones a cup of coffee as Kirkpatrick drained the rest of the little flask and then reached into his hip pocket for a spare. "Yes, sir. That was back in '05."

"You don't say."

"I wasn't with him then," Kirkpatrick said, taking a sizable swallow, still trying to calm his nerves. "But I know Mr. Slick had some trouble getting leases. Bought space up in the local paper and even joined the Masonic lodge. But he said Tryon people were the most stubborn folks he'd ever met, and he'd had to pull up stakes before they knew he meant business."

"You might want to slow down with the liquor, partner," Jones said.

"My hand is steady," Kirkpatrick said. "My reflexes agile. The drink just keeps the perception a bit more keen."

Jones nodded and drank some coffee. The dawn focused to the east in a dull, gray light, and the old man stretched his legs and studied the porters hauling suitcases and trunks into the baggage car. The car door rolled to a heavy slam, and the steam engine started up again with the conductor's whistle.

"Mr. Slick always got what he wanted," Kirkpatrick said. "He did. Yes, sir. He said he wanted to be a millionaire and didn't rest till he was the King."

"And so Tryon made him a millionaire?" Jones said.

"They blasted every hole with nitroglycerin to shake her loose but ended up with nothing but dusters."

Kirkpatrick grinned a bit to himself and chuckled and took another nip of whiskey, staring straight down the line of tracks from where they'd come, his mind settling on a place that was solid and familiar. He patted the Gladstone bag as he stood. But when he reached for the flask again, Jones pulled it from his hand and tucked it into his coat pocket.

"After the deal, Kirk," Jones said. "C'mon, let's get you some coffee."

The black locomotive steamed and chugged on through Tulsa and over the Cimarron River, taking a hard, clanging turn north. Tulsa's factories bellowing with smoke and the refineries spewing fire soon faded into the lonely glow of old farmhouses and quiet little towns—Bartlesville, Dewey, Coffeyville, and Parsons. Storefronts all shut up with planks over windows and doors. FOR SALE signs across vacant lots and farms. But nothing of the signal. Not even the smell of a fire on the horizon. The old negro porter found the men drinking coffee and smoking in silence as the train jarred to its final stop—the fifty-first from Oklahoma City—and he stood next to them nodding as the Katy's tracks converged with dozens in a wide, sprawling maze of steel and crushed granite. When Jones peered around toward the engine, he could just make out the big cathedral shape of Union Station coming into view.

"They said for me to come alone," Kirkpatrick said.

"And we'll comply."

"I can handle this."

"Don't feel like taking chances on a Sunday."

"You didn't have to take away my liquor," Kirkpatrick said. "Got cold back here."

"Least eighty degrees."

"Perhaps we should take two cabs to the Muehlebach?"

"I'll stay close," Jones said, holding on to the rail and looking east to a bright sunrise. "These folks are having some fun making us jump through hoops."

Jones followed Kirkpatrick through the long beams of lights across the marble floors, train schedules being read over the public address, and right through the front doors he'd taken with Joe Lackey what seemed like years ago. In his mind, he still kept the picture of old Sheriff Reed and that young agent chewed up and bleeding to death on the street.

He arrived at the Muehlebach Hotel minutes later and found the house phone so he could be connected to "Mr. Kincaid." There were potted palms and brass spittoons, sofas as large as beds. Gentlemen and ladies all spoke to one another like they were in a library, and near the registration desk a fella with greased hair played a grand piano. Kirkpatrick finally answered and gave Jones his room number. "Make sure no one sees you."

"I didn't figure on being announced."

Two hours later, the men got a knock on the door. A postal telegram read UNAVOIDABLE INCIDENT KEPT ME FROM SEEING YOU LAST NIGHT. WILL COMMUNICATE ABOUT 6 O'CLOCK.—E. E. MOORE.

11

A hand shook Charlie Urschel awake sometime in the middle of the night, him knowing it was night because he'd heard the second plane pass overhead and on account of asking the boy the time every time he'd heard it. He couldn't see or feel his arm but heard the distinctive click of the chains and felt his dead arm coming to rest in his lap. Then there were hands upon him, rubbing him, giving him the *Mr. Urschel, Mr. Urschel, wake up*, and it was all so rushed and furious that he was pretty well convinced this was it, they'd messed up the deal and now were going to finish him off. But Charles F. Urschel would not give the bastards the pleasure of seeing one jigger of emotion, and he struggled to find his feet using only the good arm. He felt the rip of tape from his eyes, and the whole damn blackness was filled with a harsh morning light coming from the east windows. *Mr. Urschel, here's ten dollars. It's all we got, now run. Jes' remember me in your kindness and prayers 'cause these bastards don't trifle none.* Charlie knew the words were coming from the old man but still couldn't see him, being as blind as a man in a snowstorm, as he allowed himself to be led out into the morning heat and told to *Jes' keep goin', don't look back, don't look back for nothin'*, till he hit the main highway. And Charlie didn't ask questions but loped forward, sightless and fumbling and holding on to his left arm, massaging it with his fingers because it was about the only thing that kept him vigilant and sharp and knowing he was alive. Soon he was able to feel the rocks and stones on his bare feet, the hot wind blowing his pajamas like a loose tent.

He rubbed his raw eyes with his fists until he saw spots, and he tried to move forward, the sun being the first thing that actually had a shape to it, white-hot and burning. He looked down to the ground, the flatness of the hard earth, the thorny weeds and scrub brush cutting and ripping, and Urschel lost his shirt and tore at the cloth, binding the strips to cover his feet. And the shapes were hollow and glowing, and he didn't know if he was headed toward the road the old man spoke of or was wandering aimlessly in whatever godforsaken land they'd taken him to. He was sweating now, and he figured the morning had crept on, maybe two hours since he'd been cut loose. On the horizon, all he saw were gassy mirages and more flat land, in some kind of dusty limbo where he'd walk and lope, growing so thirsty that he didn't know a mirage from a water hole but kept moving ahead until he finally became entangled in a row of barbed wire. Hung in his own personal Calvary.

He took a breath, his legs quivering with the exertion. He unpricked the line from his skin and then touched the wire with his fingertips. The strips of it pierced his hands, but, goddamn, he knew this was a road, and if he could just keep moving ahead it would lead somewhere. The sun was high, and he could see almost regular now, watching a big-eared jackrabbit loping across the dusty plain.

The goddamn jackrabbit didn't need water.

He could go on forever in the morning dew.

The cloth strips had fallen away from his feet, the earth so hot he couldn't sense the gravity anymore. The fence line led to an empty pool of water and then another pool of nothing, and if he could just keeping going there was a road leading back to Oklahoma City and pitchers of iced tea with bridge games and light, leisurely walks for gentlemen after their evening meal, where they patted their stomachs and cleaned their teeth with pocketknives.

He smiled at the thought, bringing his shoulders back, shoeless and wearing only the pajama bottoms, trying to walk like Charles Urschel would. He walked as if people could see him and would know him and could recognize he was a man of great importance in the community.

He figured it to be early afternoon when he about gave up.

But there was a figure in the distance. And he called to it.

The figure called back and waved his hat.

It was Tom Slick himself, covered in top-grade oil up to his knees and elbows, with that rascal grin on his lips.

Charlie, you look like shit warmed over.

"Well, hello, Tom. I sure am in a pickle."

A FEW HOURS FROM THE DROP AND KATHRYN DECIDED THE gang should take in a movie. Not just any movie but *Gold Diggers of 1933*, with Joan Blondell, a picture that *Photoplay* and *Shadoplay* had called a hot-shit masterpiece. There was even a full-page advertisement in the *Kansas City Star* she'd bought at the Tulsa station for a special showing at the Newman Theater that promised some cool, refrigerated air. She wasn't sure if she was more excited about seeing Blondell's gowns or getting out of the damn heat. But after some nonsense from Popeye and Mickey Mouse—George laughing so hard he snorted—the movie finally started up, and there she was with a big mug on either side of her, George dozing off not even five minutes after the lights dimmed, and Albert, who'd kicked his two-tone lace-ups up on the empty seats in front of him, munching a bag of popcorn.

Kathryn couldn't contain it. She saw the whole dream of her life coming together as those chippies danced and twirled on-screen with big silver dollars on their hands and stuck between their legs over their snatches. Hands waving. Feet skipping. Twirling, dancing, and jumping. *We're in the money, the skies are sunny* . . . She wanted to jump up into the screen and join right in.

Here she was. Cleo Brooks. Born in Saltillo, Mississippi. Born on nothing. Born to nothing. She'd been stupid, getting knocked up at fifteen because some boy told her he just wanted to feel it for a second, and then getting involved with that moody bastard Charlie Thorne, who said he'd die for her—and did—and then Little Steve Anderson, who damn near killed her. She remembered being black-and-blue, mouth cut and bloody, his slim, bony hands knocking the stuffing from her every night he got loaded on bathtub gin, and then nearly being sent to prison for pinching a bottle of perfume and a velvet beret. It was George who bailed her out of the can, him being nothing more than a childish scrawl on a cocktail napkin, and the one who told Anderson—that big-dick bootlegger in Fort Worth—that if he so much as looked at her again, he'd rip his goddamn head off and shit down his neck. But somehow every step—from Mississippi to Tulsa and to Fort Worth—had brought her here to Kansas City, where she was finally going to be the woman that she'd imagined. All they needed was that fat Gladstone grip.

We're in the money, we're in the money.

She wanted to dance on the seat but instead squeezed Albert Bates's meaty arm. He ate some more popcorn and gave her a solid ole wink like only a good mug could handle.

George started to snore, fedora over his eyes, and Kathryn glanced behind her in the big space of the movie theater, finding that there were only six people at the matinee. She moved her shoulder, and his head lolled to the side, splurting awake, then finding her shoulder and snoring again.

Albert finished the popcorn and wadded up the bag.

He checked his watch.

It had been a long night, and during a sappy love scene she found herself in the bathroom and washed her face and hands, reapplied her makeup, and ran a comb through her black hair and used some dark wine tint on her lips.

She'd been on a train and in a car so long that her ass hurt. And she hung back from the boys for a bit, leaning into the wall of the darkened theater. She pulled some loose hair from her face and tucked a knuckle under her chin. She'd always felt rich in a movie house. She liked the way this place had long red drapes sashed open, red lamps, glowing like a Chinaman's tearoom, running down the aisles. Lots of brass railings and comfortable velvet seats. You could be anyone in a movie house and dream as big as you wanted without feeling like a sap. She'd worn her best gown and some comfortable T-strap slippers. They'd go out tonight. They had to go out. She didn't care a bit about George wanting them to lay low. What's the use of being rich if no one saw you flaunt it?

She checked her watch. This drop was as slow as Christmas.

Blondell was on the street now in a fine French number, scarf knitted gaily at her throat, watching some poor bastard stoop to his knees to pick up a discarded cigarette. She grabbed the man's shoulder as if in some ballet and lit her own fresh cigarette with his and gave the poor bastard the new one. *I don't know if he deserves a bit of sympathy, / Forget your sympathy.* Now, that was class. That's the kind of rich gal that Kathryn Kelly would be. She'd never forget hard times. *Remember my forgotten man,* she sang. *You had him cultivate the land; / He walked behind a plow, / The sweat fell from his brow, / But look at him right now! . . .* Blondell caressed the lamppost, holding on like the earth was unstable, and moved through the whole moody dream, thinking about those forgotten men, bastards who'd fought and bled in the war and now marched through soup kitchens and breadlines, as she let go of the post. She placed both hands on her left hip, that slight cock of the hip getting Kathryn thinking. She could do that, she could hold that power without the post. *And once, he used to love me, / I was happy then; / He used to take care of me, / Won't you bring him back again? / 'Cause ever since the world began, / A woman's got to have a man; / Forgetting him, you see, / Means you're forgetting me . . .*

Nuts to that.

She checked her watch.

It was time.

WHEN THE TELEPHONE RANG AT A QUARTER TILL SIX, GUS
Jones picked up the receiver while Kirkpatrick paced the hotel room.

"Who's talking?" asked a man with a raspy voice.

"Kincaid," Jones said.

"This is Moore," the man said. "You get my wire?"

"I did."

"Well," the man said, pausing, "are you ready to close the deal?"

"Should be, if I knew that I were dealin' with the right parties."

"You ought to know by now," the man said. "Listen now and follow
these instructions. Take a Yellow Cab, drive to the Hotel La Salle, get
out, take the suitcase in your right hand, and start walking west."

"I figured on taking the suitcase."

"Who is this?"

"I'll be there at six-twenty," Jones said. "I have a friend who came up
here with me—I figured on bringing him along."

"Hell, no," the man said. "We know all about your friend, we saw that
fat old man on the train last night. You come alone and unarmed. You
got me? We get wind otherwise and Urschel's dead."

The phone rang off and the operator came on the line. Jones hung up.

"What did they say?" Kirkpatrick asked.

"They spotted me on the train."

"Hot coffee," Kirkpatrick said. "I knew it. I just knew it."

"Cool your britches," Jones said, reaching for his suit jacket and slipping
into it. He placed some .45 bullets in his pants pocket and checked the load
in the cylinder. "I'll be right behind you. Grab the bag and take a Yellow
Cab to the Hotel La Salle. That's south from here. Once you get there, start
walking west."

"Which way is west?"

"Ask the doorman."

Kirkpatrick nodded and felt for the .38 he'd tucked into his trousers.

Jones looked at him and reached out for the gun with his right hand. Kirkpatrick took a breath and then passed it over.

"Just walk," Jones said. "And don't look back. Just keep walking till they make contact. I'll be behind you. Give 'em what they want. Don't negotiate and don't try to be a hero. Just hand over the money."

"And then what?"

"We pray these moneygrubbing bastards are honest men."

YOU COULDN'T MISS THE SON OF A BITCH. IT WAS THE SAME as watching a drunk man trying to walk straight; they do everything cockamamy. And here was Mr. E. E. Kirkpatrick, executive of Tom Slick Enterprises, trying to act normal. He strolled along the boulevard on a hot Sunday evening with that goddamn beautiful Gladstone grip. Kathryn even loved the color, a light butternut brown. She thought she could even smell the leather from the open window in the big Cadillac, scrunched down in the backseat that would fit four fat men, the Thompson she hocked her life to buy clutched in her arms in case there was trouble. Across the street, in a stolen Chevrolet, Albert Bates had a rifle poked out a side window. And George was in an alley, waiting for Albert to bump the lights, and then he'd move down Linwood Street, down that tony row of dress designers and shoe shops and hatmakers and a dozen places Kathryn wanted to visit, to make contact with the sucker.

She knew this would work out from the first time she'd read the Urschels' wedding announcement. They went to Saint Louis or somewhere for their honeymoon and they both shared some children and all that tra-la-la. But what she read was "Come and get me." Kirkpatrick wasn't twenty paces from the hotel when he set down the suitcase and reached into his pocket for a cigarette. Head skyward and cigarette upturned, he struck a match and glanced around him, lighting it, inhaling and taking in the scene.

Kathryn took a breath, waiting for fat-faced detectives with bad shoes and G-men with bullhorns and billy clubs to come out from the sewers.

But nothing happened as she watched the big, broad back of George, in a two-tone summer shirt and tie, wearing two-tone shoes and a fashionable Panama tilted into his eyes, strolling along in the opposite direction, growing closer to Kirkpatrick, who was trying to remain cool and low-key. She could almost see the bastard shaking.

George passed by the Cadillac, and, with nothing to it, gave her a wink.

Five feet from Kirkpatrick, George R. Kelly said: "I'll take that grip."

Goddamn, she loved him. She loved that smooth, honeyed way he gave directions. *I'll take that grip* . . . She'd remember that forever.

Kirkpatrick was frozen, staring at him. Kathryn leaned into the window and poked the barrel of the gun out of the car, finger on the trigger, teetering over the edge so that nobody could see it even if they were walking close.

"Hurry up," her husband said.

"How do I know you're the right party?"

"Hell, you know damn well I am."

"Two hundred grand is a lot of money," Kirkpatrick said. She could tell his mouth was dry when his voice cracked a bit. "We are carrying out our part of the agreement to the letter. What assurances have we that you'll do what you promise?"

"Don't argue with me," George said, nodding to a row of cars across the street. "The boys are waiting."

"When can we expect Mr. Urschel home?" he asked. "I'm going back to the hotel to telephone his wife. What shall I tell her?"

"You *shall* tell her that this is money well spent."

Kirkpatrick set the bag at George's two-tone shoes.

George bent down and grabbed the handle, and as he reached for it Kathryn shuddered, tongue moving across her upper lip and tasting her sweat.

"Wait," Kirkpatrick said. "*Wait one moment.* You tell me definitely what I can say to Mrs. Urschel."

"He'll be home within twelve hours," George said, the suitcase in his right hand. "Now, you turn and walk back to the La Salle and don't look back. Whatever you do."

George remained on the sidewalk for a good ten paces and then turned back to the Cadillac, Kathryn crawling over the front seat into the driver's side and cranking the big sixteen cylinders, both of 'em watching Kirkpatrick till he disappeared from view. She pulled out onto Linwood and then down to Harrison Street and kept on going south till they found the highway, and she drove for a good six hours, white-knuckled and laughing, with a big, fat moon—a "lucky moon," is what she'd call it—overhead. They only stopped for gasoline and oil, and a couple of sandwiches and pickles wrapped in paper, ice-cold Coca-Colas in small green bottles.

She never left the money. She kept it on her lap after she and George traded places with the driving. George's Panama slipped back far on his head, big, hairy arm hanging out the window. The brand-new radio picking up some signals and then going out, hearing some news about that one-eyed flier Wiley Post making it around the globe but nothing at all about Charles Urschel. There was no music in this dusty, godforsaken land, only preachers and blithering morons talking about the Bible and healing and the road to happiness.

"We're on that road right now, aren't we, Kit?"

"You're goddamn right."

She smoothed her long fingers over the Gladstone, peeking every once in a while at the stacks and stacks of money, the scent of it making her mouth water. She smoothed it some more and rocked that bag back and forth.

A little past midnight, in some no-name town south of Wichita, George pulled into a motor lodge and rang for the manager. The manager was an old woman with a pinched face who said she sure was glad to get a nice married couple and asked them three times if their children were in the machine. And Kathryn gave her an eye like "Beat it," although the old woman didn't quite get it and kept on puttering around till Kathryn had to slam the door in her face.

They were wrung-out, road-tired, nerve-frazzled, and finally alone. George locked the door behind them. They hadn't brought a change of clothes or even a toothbrush. She carried the grip, and George carried some Log Cabin bourbon.

They drank from some tiny glasses found in the bathroom. And they drank some more. Kathryn took a shower, and when she came out George was next to the bed counting the cash, splayed open from the spread to the sheets. Stacks of twenties had been laid out in row after row, and Kathryn walked to him, feeling lazy-eyed from the booze, and dropped her towel, seeing herself in the long mirror over George. George sat astride a ladder-back chair, shirtsleeves rolled up to the elbow, and his eyes moved up from the money and to his naked wife.

He smiled.

She stretched and fell back into the cash, some of the twenties knocked up into the air with a woosh, and she thought George might've been sore. But she should've known better. He about tripped getting off his seat and wrestling for his belt, not even removing his socks, garters, and shoes as he turned off a lamp and mounted her. In the moonglow from the window, he took her hard from behind, making animal grunts and saying how much he loved her and how beautiful she was, and all that tripe, as she pushed back hard against him and stretched out her arms before her, her finely manicured hands breezing through a stack of bills and making sure not a single one of 'em was marked.

They did it once in the bed, and then she straddled him in the chair. He looked good in the moonlight, like a lantern-jawed hero, and she liked the way the glow made her skin soft and white and young. Her arms and legs reached around George R. Kelly. Her hands clutching stacks of twenties as she rode him.

"I love you, Kit. I sure love you."

"I love you, too," she said, soft and meaning it, "you dumb ape."

12

Harvey watched Boss Shannon toss feed from a metal bucket to his chickens, those pin-eyed creatures scratching and squawking and shitting all around them. Boss moped and looked down at his brogan shoes when the bucket fell empty, standing there, hens pecking at his feet and at the empty ground, when he finally raised his head and asked: "Where'd you find him?"

"He was wandering in the pasture," Harvey said, studying Boss's face and coolly slipping his right hand into his pocket, squinting into the early morning. "His feet were all cut up, and he was talking to himself. I couldn't make out a thing he was saying till we got him back to the car. Urschel thought I was Tom Slick. Imagine that. King of the Wildcatters."

"You kill him?"

Boss thought of himself as a hero, the salt of the earth, a hearty country man bred of solid stock, with years of wisdom behind him. But Harvey Bailey only saw a white-haired old fool who was greedy and reckless and would sell out his own boy for a nickel. Harvey studied the man's beaten face and drooped shoulders until Boss grew restless in the open yard, the empty bucket shaking in his hand.

"You gonna kill me?" Boss asked. "'Cause if you are, I need to talk to

Ora just a moment. There are things that need tending, and I'd prefer if I could write my own eulogy."

"How much are they getting?" Verne Miller asked, hopping down from the front porch of Shannon's house. He wore a big .45 in his waistband and a freshly pressed shirt.

"I don't rightly know."

"What was that hog's name?" Harvey asked.

"I believe it was President Hoover," Miller said. "I never saw a hog cornhole a man before, but I believe it could happen. I think he liked the way you smelled. Imagine that wet snout on the back of your neck, Boss."

"Sweet Jesus."

"How much?" Harvey asked.

"Two hundred."

"What?"

"Two hundred thousand."

"Don't lie to us."

"I swear on it."

"Whew."

"What are they going to do with Urschel?"

"Turn 'im loose," he said. "They don't mean no harm to him."

Harvey looked to Miller. Miller shrugged.

"So they're coming back?" Harvey asked.

"Of course."

"And we'll all have a meet," Harvey said.

"Don't seem right," Boss Shannon said, gaining a sense of himself and splatting some tobacco juice into the dust. "Don't seem fair."

"YOU THINK HE'S DEAD, DON'T YOU?" KIRKPATRICK ASKED.

"If you study on the worst, the worst will happen," Jones said. "They were never gonna release him in Kansas City. These are some pretty cunning men we're dealing with. Real professionals."

"You think they're mad at me? For bringing you along?"

"If they'd been really spooked," Jones said, "they wouldn't have made the drop."

"Tell me again what they said on the telephone."

"He called me a fat old man. How do you like that?"

It was the middle of the night when the *Sooner* cut through south Missouri and over the Oklahoma state line, and not once had Kirkpatrick taken a drink. The whole ordeal seemed to have bled the nervousness from him.

"Maybe he was talking about someone else," Kirkpatrick said.

The all-nighter was empty, and Jones stretched out his boots on the seat in front of him. He had a notebook open on his lap, and in the flickering artificial light he worked on a report to Hoover about the whole caper, from the time the kidnappers made contact through the letter to the drop just a few hours ago. The exchange had happened so quickly after Kirkpatrick had stepped from the Yellow Cab that Jones had lagged behind, and when he'd caught up on the street the Gladstone had already been snatched with Kirkpatrick barely seeing a thing.

Kirkpatrick had described the man. The same one Berenice Urschel had described as the big fella with the machine gun. About six feet. Foreign-looking.

"I should've done something," Kirkpatrick said. "If I'd brought my gun I could've forced them to take me to Charlie. If he's dead, I'll never forgive myself. I let down the family."

"If you'd acted like a fool, then he would be dead."

Kirkpatrick nodded. His eyes looked hollow, the skin on his face stretched to the bone.

"Like I said, these men are professionals. They had a solid plan. They carried it out and got their money. Now they'll just look for a safe place to turn him loose."

"What if he knows too much?"

"Quit studying on the worst and the what could be," Jones said, snapping the notebook closed and placing it back in his satchel. "All we can do is wait it out. Mrs. Urschel will need a strong man with some horse sense."

The train clattered and clicked and jittered down the line. Artificial light shone in ramshackle towns and went dark in vast stretches of country, empty and barren.

"What if he's not back in twelve hours?"

Jones shuffled in his seat, reaching for his father's gold watch. "We won't know for another four hours."

"But if he's not back by morning . . ." Kirkpatrick said, the lights in the train car going out and then coming back on. The horn sounded lonely and bovine along the tracks, making their presence known in all that blackness. The moon disappeared under a thick blanket of clouds from the west.

"Then you can worry."

"What if Charlie can identify them? What if he can lead you back to their hideout?"

Jones leaned back into his hard wooden seat and reached for his Stetson. He laid the hat over his eyes and crossed his arms across his chest. "Soon as he comes home, we get to work. Just think about that, Kirk. Until then, this fat old man needs some shut-eye."

The train sounded again, and Jones drifted off to sleep.

KATHRYN SLAMMED THE CADILLAC DOOR WITH A TRIP AND A laugh, feeling about nineteen with a honeymoon glow, while she followed George—him telling the same joke he'd been repeating for the last two hundred miles—up onto Boss Shannon's crooked porch, not seeing Boss, only Albert Bates. Bates just looked at George and slowly shook his head, and she saw George's face change in an instant, and he grabbed the screen door that slammed behind him. Inside she heard raised voices and arguing.

Bates stepped in front of her and put up a hand. But Kathryn tossed it aside and followed George on in, past all of Ora's knickknacks and collector spoons and glasses she'd gotten for free at movie shows, shelved above their brand-new RCA. Her fists were clenched down below her sides, and she marched right next to George, who was talking to that bastard Harvey Bailey.

Bailey sat at her momma's kitchen table, foot up on a chair and holding a cane. He had a preacher's smile on his face as he was trying to talk in a cool, relaxed voice about George coming to his senses.

"Harvey, why the hell are you still here?" she asked.

"George," Bailey said, motioning with his cane, "get her ass out. This is man talk, and we don't need your wife to discuss business."

"There's no business, you big-nosed moron," she said.

"Mr. Charles F. Urschel is some kind of business."

Kathryn stopped, and she could hear her own breathing. Her fists worked at her sides, and she looked at Bailey with a clenched jaw, but she said sweetly, "Have you gone screwy?"

"Mr. Urschel is ready to get home," Bailey said. "Had a real scare yesterday when he decided to take a little walk. But we got him a drink, and he's gone back to sleep. All ready for a drive."

"Don't you even think about muscling in on this, you goddamn lousy, worthless sack of shit."

"George," Harvey said, using the cane to stand. "Please. I don't discuss business with women. Give the lady a boot."

George reached around her waist, and Kathryn relaxed for a moment, thinking George was going to draw her close and tell Bailey to go fuck himself. But instead he picked her up off her feet and tried to carry her out of the house. She broke free and ran for Bailey, wanting to wring his neck and scratch his eyes out. George caught her and hauled her backward, her heels digging deep into a rug all the way out to the porch, where he tossed her out like an unwanted cat.

She landed on her butt and stared up into Albert Bates's mug.

"If that don't beat all."

"I saw it comin'," Bates said.

"Then why didn't you say something?"

"I thought you saw it coming, too."

"What do they want?"

"A third."

"What's that?"

"Sixty-six thousand."

"They can go fuck themselves."

"I agree," Bates said. "But now they have Mr. Urschel."

"He's not with Potatoes?"

"The boy's got him, but he's scared of Miller." Bates shook his head and tossed a butt onto the porch. He ground it up real good with the heel of his shoe.

"The cut's gonna get a little deeper, too," Bates said. "Bailey wants George to use Kid Cann's outfit in Saint Paul for the wash."

"That lousy Jew? Who in their right mind would trust him?"

"Bailey says he's honest. He's usin' him for his own stash."

"That's a hell of a recommendation."

George busted out of the front door, red-faced and sweating, and not the joking boy from the car ride. He grabbed Kit's hand and walked her way the hell out from Boss's house into the parched land where Boss grew his paltry crops. The dry and cracked ground still held the bent and dry stalks of corn blowing slightly in the hot wind. The old windmill twittered and twirled like the hands of a clock wound too tight.

"Listen to me," George said, pulling her hands together at the wrist. "Listen. I talked him down to ten grand. They drive Urschel back."

Kit shook her head and wiped the tears from her cheeks. She breathed in through her nose and kept on crying, goddamnit. Like some kind of baby.

"Kit."

"You pussy."

"Kit."

"Don't you dare take it in the ass from that son of a bitch," she said.

"It's been decided."

"Among men?"

"Yes."

"I think you and your buddies from the Green Lantern Saloon are about as tough as a sewing circle," she said. She grabbed the back of George's big neck and pulled him in close to where their noses touched. Both of them were breathing hard from all the talk and excitement and the heat. Far off in the trees, some cicadas clicked and whirred. An old hound came loping out from the barn and lay down at George's feet, but Kathryn kept on. "I know. I know."

"What?"

"Kill him."

"I can't kill Harvey."

"Not Harvey," she said. "Urschel. You go with that dumb yegg like you're okay with the deal. And when he takes you to Urschel, I want you to take out that .38 and put a hole right in the center of that rich man's head. I never wanted you to take him back anyway. He can make you and Albert. He's been to my momma's house. He's eaten her chicken, for fuck's sake."

George stood there in the heat with his mouth wide open.

Kathryn leaned in and gave him a big kiss on his stubbled mug. She kissed it again and again until his mouth closed and his eyes focused, seeing the sense in what she'd said.

"Do it," she said. "Go do it now."

13

Monday, July 31, 1933

Charlie had resigned himself to his own death for some time. He'd pretty much made sense and order of the affair after meeting up with Tom Slick in the wilderness and now being chained again in this blind purgatory; he knew these people were going to punch his ticket real soon. But life had been good and exciting. He'd been a successful man, raised a good family, and after becoming a widower did the sensible thing in marrying Berenice and joining their fortunes. He would not be maudlin about the day or try to conjure up a prayer. When that bullet hit his brain, he'd just be closed for business, and he knew damn well that time would continue. He just wished like hell he could remember what Tom Slick had told him out there in the vast stretches of land after he'd touched his staff to that parched earth and a black pool of oil had formed at his feet. He'd wanted Charlie to get off his knees and follow him up and over that hill, but as Charlie'd tottered and stumbled, Tom's staff held high, he'd fainted and fallen and dropped in and out of consciousness, looking right into the face of that prize bull with a white face. That's when Tom Slick changed into the figure of a limping man with silver hair and a bandanna across his face, saying, "Well, hello there, Mr. Urschel. Goin' someplace?"

The old shack's door squeaked open, and he was unchained again.

Here we go.

Charlie found his feet, holding on to the posts of a metal bed. He was told to turn around and take the bandages from his eyes. He complied and was led to a crude wooden bench, where he sat down.

He heard a click, and before his blurry eyes appeared the long, sharp blade of a straight razor. He wanted to think of a prayer but just couldn't think of one that fit the situation.

He took a breath and swallowed, knowing it would be his last.

But instead of feeling the blade across his neck, he saw a mug of hot lather slid onto the table, and he looked up into the mirrored image of a man he didn't recognize. Sure, he knew the features and eyes, they'd been with him since birth. But the gauntness and salt-and-pepper beard were those of a much older man.

"Shave those whiskers," the big man said. "You look like a goddamn tramp. *Whoa.* Don't turn around. Don't you dare turn around. You know how this dance is done. We'll bring you a change of clothes and a hat. It's a new straw hat, and I'm pretty sure I got the size right."

Charlie nodded.

He was free. They were taking him back.

He looked into the rust-flecked image of himself and lathered his face in the hot light coming from the west window. The razor was dull and old, and his whiskers took a good bit of pulling and coaxing till they'd be shaved away. Cuts and all, he felt like a hundred-dollar bill.

There was a knock on the door, and Charlie was told to face the wall.

His eyes were retaped, and he took the procedure like a sick man takes the dressing of his wounds. He heard the weathered voice of the old man now tell him that he had a fresh shirt and pants. He'd brought back the shoes he'd worn here.

Charlie didn't answer. *What was he supposed to do? Thank him?*

He just nodded and stood there, blind and dumb. The most well-read man of women's literature in the country.

And then he felt a pair of bony arms wrap his body and pull him tight, and an onion breath in his face told him, "You be careful, Mr. Urschel. Everything's all right. Yes, sir. God bless you."

The door opened and closed again.

"They's gettin' the automobile ready," said Potatoes. "Mr. Urschel, how 'bout a smoke for ole time's sake? I brung you a real good one. I can fetch you some hot coffee, too. It was fresh this mornin'."

"Son?"

"Yes, Mr. Urschel?"

"You can stick that cigar up your ass," Urschel said. "Tell that son of a bitch I want to be taken back to my home right now."

"I'M NOT KILLING CHARLIE URSCHEL AT YOUR FOLKS' PLACE."

"Can you think of somewhere better?" Kathryn asked.

"For five grand, the boys will take Urschel back to Oklahoma City like we promised," George said. "That's on the level."

"Fuck no."

"Harvey said if we don't agree to the deal, they'll just let Urschel out close by where he can lead the law back to the farm," George said. "They said your dumb stepdaddy lost 'im and they found 'im wandering the road to Damascus nuttier than a squirrel, so they're claiming they're owed something."

"Bullshit."

"I know," George said. "But Miller ain't gonna let him go without a fight. What are you gonna do?"

"You're gonna tell Harvey we'll pay out five grand for a finder's fee. And I'll tell him to go fuck himself."

"Kit."

The boys worked out some kind of screwy handshake deal about meeting up at the Green Lantern, where they'd get their cut and change out the rest. Turns out those damn Jews wanted twenty percent to turn the bills, but Bailey was convinced the ransom money serial numbers had been recorded. And, of course, that was something that never even crossed the minds of George and Albert. George only thought a lot about how to spend the dough, not a thing about marked bills.

"Are we still gonna kill 'im?" she asked.

"*We* meaning *me*."

"Either way."

"Let me think," George said.

"I'll hold my breath."

They left the next afternoon, and sometime past ten o'clock, it seeming like they'd been riding forever since Paradise, George slowed right outside the Norman city limits. He didn't speak, neither of them being dumb enough to make a sound with Charlie Urschel all trussed up on the backseat floorboard.

George had finally gotten up the nerve. He stopped the big car, and they got out to whisper to each other.

"Why here?"

"You want to do it in your own backyard?"

"Over there," she said. "Behind that billboard."

A small light shone on a billboard of a little nigger boy eating a huge slice of watermelon and a white man with big clean choppers telling the boy to BRUSH WITH COLGATE, SAMBO!

George got back behind the wheel, and they followed a narrow, rutted path that jumped up and over some railroad tracks and crossed down into a wide, endless scrap-metal yard. Big, fat stacks of junked cars and oil barrels and wagon wheels sat in useless, rusted heaps. It had just started to rain, a few drops splatting the Cadillac's windshield, but when he stopped the car and killed the engine the heavens sure opened up.

George just sat there like he was trying to figure out how to start necking.

Kathryn crossed her arms over her chest and slid down in her seat. She stared straight ahead and bit into her cheek.

George reached for his hat with a sigh and crawled out of the big car. He opened the rear door and pulled Urschel out by his bound wrists and marched him down a narrow space between the walls of rusted cars, down an endless path, and out of sight of the windows.

Kathryn was damned if she wanted to see it anyway. Because if she was ever called to court about being there when Mr. Charles F. Urschel, president of the Tom Slick Oil Company, was killed, she could look that prosecutor right in the eye and say she didn't see a goddamn thing.

The rain fell harder, the first bit of it she'd seen in months, sounding like impatient fingers drumming on the desk. And there was nothing but all that silver pinging on that big midnight blue hood of the Cadillac, Kathryn looking straight ahead past that old silver Indian and leaning forward, squinting to see just a motion or a bit of something. *Son of a bitch.*

Only rain and deep night. Rusted coils and spindles and gears. Old engines and parts of old machines. Stoves and toasters. Useless stuff from machines no one cared to recall.

What if someone was to come along? What if the owner of this goddamn graveyard was to come out of his hole and want to know who was driving this beautiful piece of machinery into his personal shithole? Goddamn, if it wasn't raining, she'd go out and grab George, and, if he hadn't done the deed, she'd take the damn gun and kill the bastard herself instead of sitting in the car like a dog and being left in Shit City . . . *BLAM.*

BLAM. BLAM.

Three sounds. Three strobe patterns.

The figure and shape of that big mug coming back through the wrecks, fedora down over his eyes, gun hanging loose and dirty by his side, and marching straight for the car and slamming the door hard.

"Did you do it?"

He didn't answer.

"We shoulda buried him in a barrel of lime," she said.

He cranked the sweet Cadillac and leaned forward to see through the whole goddamn mess till he bumped up and over the crest of the old rails and back onto the highway, fishtailing and sliding and heading north again.

"Saint Paul?"

"I gave my word."

"To a thief and a killer."

"Verne Miller is a war hero, Kit."

"How did it feel?"

"Why don't you put a sock in it?"

"He was your first, wasn't he?"

"Well."

"Well, how did it feel?"

"Like something that had to be done."

"Amen."

"Turn on that lamp and read the map," he said. "And why don't you shut up till we get back to Saint Paul."

JONES FINISHED WITH HIS REPORT, PECKING IT OUT ON AN L. C. Smith at the Federal Building and sliding it into the mail pouch to Washington. He grabbed his Stetson and returned to the mansion, only to receive a cable from Hoover chewing him out for not being in direct contact during the entire affair. Jones reread the cable, the words chapping his ass, and tossed it in the garbage, following Doc White to the front stoop under the portico, where the newsmen had turned the front lawn into a small tent city.

The pallor inside the house made it feel like a goddamn wake. Urschel should've been home hours ago.

The papers ran phone lines into a wild switchboard under an Army tent. Some of the newspapermen had now brought their desks and were sitting with their feet propped up and taking calls, all the while sweating through their shirts and ties, living through the long, hot night and all day with nothing to add to the Urschel story.

Tom Slick, Jr., and Charles Urschel, Jr., both about fifteen or sixteen, were back from a fishing trip in Mexico. And Betty Slick had decided to bake a lemon pie for Agent Colvin, seeing to it that he ate at least two slices to make sure it was to his liking.

When there was nothing left to do, the family just sat in the salon and waited in silence. Every ring of the phone was like a jolt of electricity.

At nightfall, the wind blew in from the west and the rains came. The first rains in months, and Jones watched from the stoop as the newsmen scampered away, grabbing for their typewriters and copy, chasing stray notes and fallen hats. Tents tumbled down the road, and reporters and cops scrambled for their automobiles.

Colvin approached the men with a smile, watching the show.

"How was that pie?" Doc White asked.

Colvin's face grew crimson. The rain streamed hard and violent across the road and atop the car hoods.

"She's a fine young lady."

"She sure has a crush," Jones said.

"She's just a girl."

"How old are you?"

"Twenty-seven," Colvin said.

"At twenty-seven?" Jones asked. "I was already married. That was back in aught-seven. I'd left the Rangers and joined up with Customs."

Thunder and lightning, a full-out gully washer. Large tree branches shook and small freshly planted trees bent in the harsh wind. Jones took off his hat in fear of losing it.

"Y'all worked the border?" Colvin asked.

"Rode that river half my life."

"You, too?" he asked White.

Doc White nodded.

"You ever see Pancho Villa?"

White and Jones smiled.

"Yeah, we knew Villa," Jones said.

"You met him?"

"Sure thing," Jones said.

"He was a real cutthroat."

"Pancho?" Jones said. "One of the most pleasant sorts you'd ever meet. Would you say, Doc? He was an honorable man. Maybe what got him killed."

They stood there and watched the rains for a while, Colvin and Doc White smoking cigarettes. It was black now, the sun probably not down but the dark clouds smudging out everything and keeping the neighborhood in a queer purple-black glow that usually preceded a tornado.

"The Kansas City office said the telephone call to the Muehlebach came from a local movie house," Colvin said. "They sent an agent to the Newman Theater but came up with nothing."

Jones rubbed his face with a handkerchief and cleaned thumbprints off his glasses.

"He should have been back hours ago," Colvin said.

Jones nodded. He could see clearer without the smudges, the rain softening a bit, a heavy heat and humidity lifting from the ground.

"If they turn him loose," Jones said, "it won't be close to here. We'll have to wait for Urschel."

"When do we start to look?"

"Let's give it till morning," Jones said. "If he doesn't show, we'll understand the situation."

A pack of newspapermen holding black umbrellas approached the front porch and shouted up a couple questions for the agents. Someone inside had tipped them off about the ransom drop, and, boy, they were angry it had taken them almost twenty-four hours to hear about it.

Was it really a million dollars?

Some people say the kidnappers may have taken the Lindbergh baby.

Agent Jones, they call you an Ace Investigator. Is it true you tracked down the last of the Hole-in-the-Wall Gang and forced Butch Cassidy down to Bolivia?

Jones ignored them, loaded his pipe, and strolled down the steps into the soft rain with Doc and climbed into the car supplied to them. They ate supper at the Skirvin, dropped by the local office for any new communiqués, and then headed back to Eighteenth Street and the now-familiar mansion. As the night wore on, the rains continued, and Mrs. Urschel turned on the radio just in case a report in some other state was to come over the wire. It took a few moments for the unit to heat up, and Jones found a comfortable place on the couch under that life-size portrait of Tom Slick, and smoked his cherry tobacco and listened to the *Pabst Blue Ribbon Show* on the radio, someway feeling odd that the nation was okay with alcohol again after spending so many years going after bootleggers.

The Urschel and Slick boys—dog-tired and sick from grief and worry—turned in some hours later. And in hushed whispers by the radio, Betty Slick told Agent Colvin that cotillion or joy of any type had to be canceled. And they soon left, too, and Jones didn't study on it long. And then it was just Berenice Urschel, and the intimacy of them sitting so close with so few in the salon made Jones stand and walk into the kitchen.

She'd been crying a long time and seemed empty of tears and wasteful talk.

He poured a cup of coffee and noted the hour on a clock, growing close to midnight. He'd check in with the boys on the night guard and leave some orders. And then he'd head back to the Skirvin for a few hours of rest. He'd shave and be back here before sunrise.

That's when he heard the commotion at the back door. One of the local agents was arguing with a man who wanted to come inside.

"Mister," the agent said. "You better turn right back around and get back with the other newspapers."

"But I'm not a reporter," said the man wearing a straw hat and soaked short-sleeved shirt.

"No, he's not," said Jones with a smile, offering his hand. "Mr. Urschel, we've been waiting on you. My name's Jones."

14

"W hat the hell, George?" Kathryn said. "Urschel's alive? You lied. I can't believe you lied to me, you rotten son of a bitch."

George mumbled something, his mouth full of eggs and ham, at a ham-and-eggs, no-name joint in some no-name town. Kathryn wasn't even sure what state they were in. But they sure were hungry and had stopped off on the ride north when they'd seen the hand-painted signs for EATS, RESTROOMS, GAS. When she'd come back from the can, she'd seen the front of a *Kansas City Star* someone left with a nickel tip. URSCHEL FREED.

Son of a bitch.

"What did you say?" she asked.

He finished chewing, and leaned in and said real low, "Excuse a fella for not wanting the Chair. What's the point of stirring the pot? We got what we wanted. Why risk it? 'Sides, he almost shit his drawers running away."

Kathryn read on about Charles F. Urschel, head of the Tom Slick Oil Company, bravely making his way from a scrapyard outside Norman to Classen Barbecue, where he calmly got a cup of coffee and telephoned for a cab. He paid the driver a small tip, the newspaperman drawing out that fact to show he was cheap, and was stopped at the back door of his house by a federal agent who didn't recognize his face.

"Says here the kidnappers gave him ten dollars," she said. "Is that true?"

"Why don't you go ahead and broadcast it after *Little Orphan Annie?*"

"Ten whole dollars. You are a sucker."

"Who's that little chatterbox?" George sang. *"The one with pretty auburn locks?/ Whom do you see? / It's Little Orphan Annie."*

Kathryn frowned and fished a pack of Luckies from her purse, lit one with shaking hands, and used the ruby red tip of her index finger to skip from story to story. Charles Urschel's big, dumb hangdog face took up most of the space above the fold.

She smoked the cigarette down to a nub and squashed it out as the waitress in a little paper hat refilled her coffee. George asked for some more toast.

She lit another Lucky and leaned back into her seat. The diner was empty, far too early in the morning for normal folks, and she leaned into the paper and read on. "Says right here that 'FEDERAL ACE GUS T. JONES LEADS MANHUNT.' You ever heard of him? Says he tracked down the Hole-in-the-Wall Gang and was a personal friend to Pancho Villa. Jesus H. How old is this guy?"

"Too old to catch us," George said with a wink. "I bet he still rides a horse."

"Says here he has a government airplane at his disposal."

She turned the page and above an advertisement for Lux soap—*Is Your B.O. Offending Your Husband?*—was a picture of the Federal Ace. Wire-framed glasses, fat man with thinning hair. "Well, son of a bitch."

"What?"

"It's the bastard from the *Sooner,*" she said, laughing. "I knew he was the law. Damn, I knew it."

"The one with Kirkpatrick?"

"No, George. The nigger porter."

"They just put that stuff in the paper to rile us up," he said. "Eddie Bentz says nervousness will trip you up every time. Keep your mind clear and everything is copacetic."

"You can't even spell copacetic."

"Come on now, Kit."

"I mean it," she said. "Ed Weatherford is still out there, too. You know he's gonna turn rat."

"Ed Weatherford doesn't know diddly-squat," George said, scraping some egg onto his toast. He pointed the loaded toast at her. "You wanted me to drive all the way to Fort Worth just to kill a fella 'cause you don't like his smile."

"He's a snake."

"Oh, Ed's all right," he said, grinning. "I think he's a little sweet on you, too."

"You sure are a bright boy, George."

The waitress walked back from the kitchen with more toast and jam and butter. George smiled and winked at her, and the woman blushed because, hell, she had to be at least forty and hard and weathered. But Kathryn Kelly was smart enough to know that *There but by the grace of God*, because if she didn't have a plan, she damn well could be slinging hash in a few years.

"The beauty with these kidnap deals is that no one has to die," George said, wiping his mug with a napkin. "You take the gravy from some rich mug who's swimming in cash while average hardworking Joes out there can't afford a cup of coffee. It's a solid, respectable line of work."

"Since when are you hardworking?"

"How long has it been since you wanted for anything?"

"You made me leave Chingy."

"We don't need a little yapping dog on this excursion," he said.

"How long is this gonna take?"

"Couple days tops."

"And you trust this Kid Cann?"

"He's a businessman."

"He's a crook."

"Harvey's cashin' in his chips with him, same as us."

George nodded and straightened his short red tie. He looked off in the wide, empty space of the restaurant spreading out in a crazy chessboard of blue-and-white linoleum. The place smelled of cigarettes and frying bacon and coffee left on the burner too long. In the darkness outside the glass window, a long, sweeping arrow made of tiny lightbulbs beckoned in the weary traveler.

"Then what?" she asked. "When do we get the money back?"

George smiled. "We relax. Have some laughs."

"I want to go back to Cleveland."

"What the hell for? I want to take you down to Biloxi and put our feet in the sand. We can drink beer on the beach and go dancing on the boardwalk at night. I wouldn't mind doing a little fishing, too."

"Before we do anything, we have to pay off the Cadillac."

"Are you joking?"

"Do you have any idea of how embarrassing it is to get all those telephone calls and telegrams about falling behind on those payments? When we bought that big baby out there, we said we'd be paying by year's end in cash. And now we have it, I want to march right into that dealership and tell 'em to stick it where the sun don't shine."

"That won't prove a thing, Kit."

"You got that damn loan in the name of Boss and Ora! You said your name was Mr. Robert G. Shannon."

"Would you shut up."

"You shut up."

George let out a long stream of smoke from the side of his mouth. He looked her over like he was appraising just how long she'd keep this gag running, and the decision didn't take long as he rested his meaty fist on the table, cigarette burning down to his hairy knuckles, and nodded. "Okay."

"Okay what?"

"Okay, Saint Paul to trade with the Jews and then down to Cleveland so you can play big-time with that two-bit car salesman. Say, I know why you want to do this. You didn't like the way his wife treated you when we had dinner with them. When you told her about the kind of gowns you liked, and she laughed a little like she didn't believe you."

Kathryn nodded. "She was mean to Chingy."

"That goddamn rat shit on her Oriental rug."

"It was an ugly rug."

A few truck drivers walked in through the glass door, a bell jingling above their heads. More bacon frying. More loose talk. Cigarettes and coffee. Hash and eggs. Kathryn picked up the *Star* again and read back over the front page about the Urschel story.

"Does it bother you that your name isn't here?"

"Are you crazy? That's pretty much the point, sweetheart."

"It bothers me," she said. "I read a story last week about Jean Harlow coming to Kansas City to visit her family. They had her picture on the front of the paper just because she came to town. Now, that's something."

"She's a damn movie star with big tits."

"I'm prettier."

"Maybe," George said. "But she's known."

"And now because of us that fat old man is the Federal Ace."

"So what?"

"So, it must be nice."

"What's that?" George asked, grabbing his hat and tossing down some coin. "To get your picture in the paper?"

"For everyone to know you," she said. "Look at 'Pretty Boy' Floyd. He's like some goddamn Robin Hood."

"To hell with Floyd." George stood, tipping the fedora's brim down over his dark eyes as he frowned at her. "Let's see him ever pull a job like this."

"HOW 'BOUT YOU HANDLE KID CANN," VERNE MILLER SAID. "That little Jew has problems with me."

"About what?" Harvey asked.

"One night at the Cotton Club, we had a little talk."

"A talk?"

Verne Miller shrugged and scratched the back of his neck. They were out of the Buick now—Harvey always preferring to buy or steal big, solid Buicks—and they walked in the falling sunlight of an abandoned farm close to the Iowa line. Harvey's heel felt stiff and sore, and he had some trouble keeping pace with Miller's strong, long-legged gait.

"The Kid made a pass at Vi," Miller said, staring straight ahead. His blue eyes like ice. "He told her he'd like to place his pecker right between her titties and ride her like a mule."

"The Kid said that?" Harvey asked, lighting up a Chesterfield and fanning out the match. "I don't even know what that means. 'Like a mule'?"

"He'd been drinking."

"What'd you say?"

"I don't know," Miller said, shrugging again. "I didn't say much. Just stuck a .45 inside his mouth and asked if he'd like to see how little brains he's got."

"He may hold a grudge."

"You think?"

"I do, Verne," Harvey said. "Things like that can stay with a person."

The hot wind off the barren earth felt good on the men's faces, and you could smell the hard earth and dust and dry land. The farm had a familiar old L-frame and a big red barn with a roof painted with the words MERAMEC CAVERNS U.S. 66 STANTON MISSOURI. The shadows were long and smooth across the rough-hewn boards, and the sunlight painted the side of the barn in a soft yellow glow.

"Vi's got you wrapped tight, Verne," Harvey said. "And don't take no offense in this, but if you don't watch your pecker, she's gonna lead you right into a trap."

"What's a man to do?"

"Love."

"Yeah," Miller said with that cruel, twisted mouth. "It's worse than the Spanish flu."

"Now, take George," Harvey said. "That's another matter. He can't even see the trap he's in."

"The pussy trap."

"Snap."

"You're going to thieve their money, aren't you?" Miller asked.

Harvey smiled and pinched the Chesterfield between his thumb and forefinger. He shrugged a bit and smiled again.

"You're gonna get the Kid to switch out the cash on the bank job with Kelly's dough, and we're going to take it all."

"You got a problem with that?"

"I don't have any love for those people."

The Buick sat in the slanting shadow of two big silos crawling with vines. A couple Ford tractors lay rusted and turned upside down in a gully. As the men stepped on the porch, they found a busted door held upright by an old padlock. A note from the bank ruffled in the wind.

"This country is turning to shit," Harvey said, snatching the notice from the tacks and tossing it on the ground.

"Everything is turning to shit."

"They took my gas stations," he said. "They took goddamn everything."

"Who?"

"Fat men."

"Who?"

"Men who feed at the trough of our goddamn sweat."

"You're talking like a communist," Miller said.

"Maybe I am."

"Communism is for suckers, too."

"What do you believe in, Verne?"

"Myself," he said, his face not changing expression.

Harvey Bailey excused himself and walked along the beaten porch of the house, the wind making rattling noises through the broken windows. A door kept drumming with the shotgun wind, and every one of Harvey's steps through the haunted guts of the home was counted until he reached the back stairs and walked out onto that wide expanse of cleared land, an old familiar path now grown up with weeds and destroyed and hidden. But he could walk that path in his sleep, feeling that draw and pull to a shadowed little grove of walnut trees blooming with nuts wrapped in green.

You wouldn't know it to see it. The headstone simply read J. HARVEY BAILEY / SEPTEMBER, 5 1920–JULY, 12 1923. Bailey felt a shooting pain as he got to his knees and pulled away the weeds and vines and straightened the small stone lamb, storm-beaten, and now resembling more rock than animal. He stayed there, smoothing away the moss with his hand-painted tie, until he heard Miller calling for him, and, using the solid trunk of the tree for balance, he got back on his feet.

"You think Harry Sawyer's back up there?" Verne Miller asked as he walked close, toting a shovel.

"Where else would he go?" Harvey asked, rolling the sleeves of his white shirt to the elbow and lighting another cigarette. "We'll head to the Green Lantern first thing. I sure wouldn't mind one of his pork chop sandwiches."

"And maybe Nina's?"

"How can a man go to Saint Paul and not stop by and say hello to the girls?"

"Right here?"

"Right here," Harvey said. "Hand it to me."

Harvey Bailey felt the hot wind push a cloud over the sun, sliding a cool shadow over his face. He slid the tip of the shovel to the known spot and began to dig.

"How much is buried?" Miller asked.

"Just enough."

JONES THUMBED SOME TOBACCO INTO HIS PIPE AND EYED Mr. Charles Urschel. Urschel's face was gaunt and hollow, the flesh around his eyes reddened and blistered. He had changed into fresh clothes that morning—lightweight navy trousers and a white short-sleeved linen shirt. Jones could tell he'd showered and shaved, had his breakfast and coffee. But despite the morning routine, Urschel hadn't stopped tapping his foot and checking his timepiece since he'd sat down.

Jones struck a match and got the bowl going, the cavernous study empty besides Jones and SAC Colvin. The young boy displaying his talents as notetaker, keeping quiet and letting Jones take the lead, the interview continuing from where they stopped late last night, when Berenice Urschel begged Jones to let her husband get some rest. Jones had complied, but then had shown up at six that morning, and had waited damn-near two hours until Urschel said he was ready.

"I hope this won't take long."

"Could take a while, sir."

"I haven't set foot at my company."

"You'll have some time this afternoon."

"But I didn't see anything," Urschel said. "Everything I could know I told you last night. I even told you about the well and how bad that water tasted. You seemed to take great interest in the mineral quality of it last night. Perhaps that will lead to something."

"Yes, sir," Jones said, walking and smoking and moving about in the room, lined from bottom to top with leather-bound volumes of old stories and old tales of murder and adventure, and very serious men taking things very seriously. "Tell me about the boy."

"He was a boy."

"You said he went by 'Potatoes.'"

"I doubt that was his real name. Probably something those crooks made up."

"You never know," Jones said. "I knew a boy in El Paso that everyone called 'Turd Head.'"

"Well, I doubt the moniker."

"But he watched you most?"

"He did."

"And read to you?"

"He did. Yes."

"What sorts of material?"

"Magazines."

"What sort?"

Urschel was quiet for a moment and then said, "*Ladies' Home Journal. McCall's*. Frivolous things in which I had no interest."

"Wasn't your kind of reading?"

"It passed the time," Urschel said. "The boy also had some kind of brochure on the World's Fair and read from that quite often. In fact, I would say he was obsessed with it. Liked to read a portion about native dancers who dance in the nude."

"Did he offer anything personal from the Fair?"

"Just that he planned on going."

"Isn't everybody?"

The more he smoked, the more Jones paced. A flurry of questions came to mind as he paced, smoke breaking and scattering with his steps.

"What about the old man?" Jones said. "You conversed with him?"

"Yes, sir."

"About?"

"Nothing of consequence. We had some bad weather the night before they released me. There was wind and rain, and I asked them if they had tornadoes."

"What did they say?"

"Said they had a lot more tornadoes down in Oklahoma and Texas."

"That was a plant," Jones said with certainty. He strolled behind Urschel's desk and pulled back a thin layer of drapes, seeing the newsmen gather around E. E. Kirkpatrick, who read a statement from the family that he'd typed out over breakfast. The statement basically read that Mr. Urschel didn't recall a goddamn thing about his kidnappers, which was a view that old Charlie kept on sharing with Jones.

"Could you even sneak a peak? Of something? Anything?"

"A few days after they took me, I got the bandages loose. I was able to peer around a bit. They kept me in a shack, like I said. The outhouse was nearby."

"Hold on," Jones said. He sat at Urschel's desk and pulled a small notebook from his satchel. "How many rooms in this shack?"

"Three?"

"Which way did the boards run in the house?"

"The boards?"

"Floorboards."

"Judging on the heat from the sun," Urschel said. "East and west."

Jones nodded. "What about the outhouse? Which direction?"

"West," Urschel said. "I'm sure of it. But, sir, I really don't see the point in . . ."

Jones kept the pipe in his teeth and held up his left hand as he sketched a bit, adding the three rooms to a modest shack, an outhouse, the road Urschel had mentioned last night. That old well where they drew the mineral water. "Did you see animals?"

"Heard them," Urschel said. "Pigs, chickens. The old man and the boy spoke of a prize white-faced bull, and I saw the animal's face when I ran. It was about all I saw when I was running."

"Sun blind?" Jones asked.

Urschel nodded. "I think I lost control of my mind a bit, too."

"Happens with heat."

"The boy spoke of a woman of loose character who lived nearby," Urschel said. "He joked about it often."

"What did he say?"

"Only that there was a teenage whore in the vicinity. I guess she only charged a quarter for intercourse."

Jones nodded. He sketched some more, adding arrows and asking a bit more about where Urschel had heard the farm animals. The man had forgotten about an old cornfield and something he'd heard about a melon patch with fruit just turning ripe. Jones asked about the direction cars arrived from and how they departed, and then he came all the way back around and asked more about the storm and how long it lasted and what he did during the rains.

"I know the rain started before five-thirty."

"And how's that?"

"Well, at five-thirty is when the airplane would pass."

"The airplane."

"Yes, sir," Urschel said. "I really must be going, Mr. Jones. Might we—"

"Tell me more about the aircraft."

"An airplane would pass every day at nine in the morning and again about five-thirty," he said. "I'd ask the boy for the time several minutes after the plane sounded so he wouldn't get suspicious. But I didn't think much of it. Planes fly all over this nation these days."

"What about the rain?"

Urschel looked at him and crossed his legs. His face looked drawn, his dark eyes hollow and void.

"Did that second plane fly the day of the storms?"

Urschel looked up at the ceiling and rubbed his jaw. He thought for a moment and then shook his head. "No, sir. I didn't hear that plane."

Jones nodded.

"Is that of importance?"

"Oh, yes, sir," Jones said, puffing on the pipe. "It most surely is."

15

They arrived in Saint Paul a little before nightfall. Kathryn knew the town, had lived there for a couple of frigid years in a crummy apartment with George, a real honeymoon special, with a Murphy bed and pullout ironing board, him talking her into that frozen wasteland because of his connection with Harvey Bailey, Verne Miller, and the dear departed Jelly Nash. Said they owed him, and that Saint Paul was a wide-open town, the kind of city where those goddamn yeggs could live without ever having to look over their backs. You paid off the detectives, the chief of police, and you were polished gold. Kathryn had liked Saint Paul okay right when George had first gotten out of Leavenworth, and she'd been dazzled a bit with those first few bank jobs—although now, thinking back, they didn't make them rich—and how the big mug would take her out shopping on Main and to R. H. Bockstruck for some baubles and jewels. There were nights at the Parisian, where they had a dance floor as big as two football gridirons, and summers at Harry Sawyer's place out on the lake, skinny-dipping under the moon. The blind pigs and speakeasies were on every city block and in basements, and when George would go down for a meet at the Green Lantern he'd bring her with him, decked out finer and more beautiful than any of those whores of Bailey's or Nash's. About the only one that could come close in looks was Vi Mathias, but Verne had put her on the run, and she wouldn't be in Saint Paul. And maybe since Prohibition was long, dumb history, the whiskey and gin wouldn't taste so damn good as when you knew you were doing something bad and wrong.

Sometimes those were the only things that felt like doing.

"You think he's even here?" she asked.

"It's his place."

"It was his place," Kathryn said, whispering. "It's been a few years."

"I know what I'm doing."

"Did you ever meet the Kid?"

"Yeah, I met him."

"Does he know you?"

"I said I met him."

"Doesn't mean he knows you," she said. "You weren't that known when we were up here. You were just the driver. I don't think you made the papers once."

George placed his big knuckles on the long glass cigar case and gave a low whistle. He called the tobacco shop steward over for a couple of these and a couple of those, and for that big solid-gold lighter, wondering if he could have it engraved.

"Are you even listening to me?"

The cigar steward grabbed what George pointed out and strolled back to the cash register and out of earshot. Toward the front of the cigar shop was a big, tall wooden Indian, standing dumb and silent and proud.

"You were the one who wanted to cut out the middlemen, so here we are. But now you want to doubt me and the plan, and now I'm thinking maybe this wasn't such a smart idea. Do you have any idea how mad Verne and Harv are going to be when they learn we went to the Kid direct?"

"I just don't see the logic in cutting those two fools in when they didn't lift a finger."

George shrugged and didn't disagree. He walked over to the front counter—long stained wood and wavy glass—filled with hundreds and hundreds of cigars wrapped in rich, aged tobacco. The whole store smelled like the inside of an old cedar chest. Every few moments the bell above the door would jingle and in would walk a couple fellas, or a lone fella, and they'd nod to the steward and head back behind a curtain at the rear of the store. George plugged a cigar into the side of his mouth and thumbed his new lighter, having paid a big wad of cash for it. He smiled as he got the thing going, and told her to find a nice, comfortable chair and read the paper or something, he'd be right back.

And as much as it burned her up, she knew she couldn't go behind the curtain, back to the cigar shop's private club, where only dirty egg-sucking politicians, moneygrubbing bankers, and two-timing yeggs were allowed. All of 'em men, with their eye candy left on the settee to read the Saint Paul *Star* about the latest exploits of the Barker Gang and the Barrow Brothers, thousands of Joes showing up at a new agency for home loans, and about those big stores in Bay City, Michigan, being pummeled with stones for not jibing with the NRA work hours. *Ain't that a hoot.* And there was Charles Urschel again, the sheriff in Oklahoma City criticizing the poor bastard for not running to a telephone when George released him. *If Urschel had called me instead of a taxi when he was turned loose, the kidnappers wouldn't have had a chance in a hundred to get away. It was raining so hard that only two roads away from Norman were passable, and he would've found them in less than ten minutes . . .* She scanned the rest, but then her eyes caught the headline: TWO MILLION FOR CLARK GABLE. She passed on over Urschel and some bullshit about the police finding the shack where they'd hid out.

So the *True Story* of this shy and awkward farmer boy who came up from the low, who dreamed his dreams in a logging camp, who worked as an ad taker on a newspaper and as a clerk in a telephone company, finally to evolve as one of the greatest actors and the world's greatest love on the screen, has knocked all records for "reprints" higher than a kite.

No kiddin'. *True Story* sold over two million issues just so the regular folks can read about Clark Gable. Kit could kind of see it but not see it, too. He had confidence and style, and good posture and height. But it would take some to get over those funny jug ears and the space between his teeth.

To the millions of younger men and women who are still dreaming their dreams while they go about the daily round of their ordinary work, this great *True Story* lends the start of hope without which those dreams cannot go on. And to the many thousands of older men and women who are enjoying their first-time fruits of attainment, it lends courage to character, for in the amazing life of this eager young country boy who found himself suddenly without warning caught in the mesh of all the feminine wiles that Hollywood could produce, there has been the lure of enough temptations to shake the character of a saint.

"Ain't that the truth," Kathryn said, popping and stretching the paper and turning over the fold. She knew Gable was swimming in top-shelf tail, and even with the teeth and ears she'd go to bed with the son of a bitch. Mainly because the son of a bitch was Clark Gable, and every time she saw his picture in some dime-store rag or below the movie marquee she'd know she'd made him shake and quiver.

Kathryn lit a cigarette, crossed her legs, and dangled one leg loosely, rocking it back and forth, reading on and thinking that she could use a new pair of good shoes, until George came out of the back room smelling like a Mississippi smokehouse.

"They want it."

"Want what?" she asked, bored and distracted.

"The money."

"Well, of course the Kid wants the money."

"He said it would be taken care of."

"Is he here?"

"No," he said. "They rang him up for me."

"Then hell, no, no one is getting the money," she said. "Tell those Jews you want to see Kid Cann himself, live and in person, or this deal ain't going to happen."

"But Kit . . ."

"Go on," she said. "George?"

He turned around and looked over his shoulder.

"Trade them out a thousand."

"Right now?"

"Right now," she said, blowing some smoke into the ceiling fans. "I want to go shopping."

AGENT JOE LACKEY ARRIVED ON THE MORNING TRAIN FROM Kansas City, his right arm still in a sling from where he took a spray of machine-gun bullets. But he wore a smile on his big-nosed face and stepped down onto the platform in a sharp gray felt hat and blue serge suit. Jones shook hands with him in an awkward fashion and grabbed his old friend's grip as they headed toward the entrance and bright light.

"You sure you're ready?" Jones said. "When Hoover said you were back on the job—"

"Don't you know I'm left-handed, Buster?"

"That's a lie."

"Well, I'm left-handed now. So what does it matter?"

Doc White waited for the agents by the main entrance to the small station, only a couple miles from the Urschel house, deep in the warehouse district. White stepped up and met Lackey, pumping his hand. "I thought you really got hurt. Hell, they just winged you."

"Good to see you, Doc."

"I better get a beer for those flowers I sent," White said. "I thought you were dying."

Jones dropped Lackey's luggage in the trunk and walked around to the passenger side of a brand-new Plymouth the local office supplied. He reached into the front seat and pulled out a folded map that he neatly pulled apart and spread flat across the wide hood of the car. The two agents joined him, the hood still hot as a skillet, and they all leaned over a big, sprawling view of the United States, with all its rivers and man-made borders, state lines, highways, and cat roads. Jones had drawn a big circle in red ink, and in several cities he'd penciled in phone calls, letters, and tips. Every crank, nut job, and honest tip was flagged.

"What we've got is a radius that stretches about six hundred miles," Jones said. "We take in Saint Louis, Kansas City, extend over to Santa Fe on the west and Nashville to the east. I'd put the far point north being Davenport and down south somewhere around Corpus Christi. It's a needle in a haystack for sure."

"You don't think the shack was far," Lackey said in his funny Yankee accent.

"I think they took Mr. Urschel on a little joyride up and around," Jones said. "Hither and yon. They telegraphed they were far to the north. The two yokels who watched him, not the gunmen, had to mention a half dozen times that Oklahoma and Texas were to the south. They furnished him with clothes with the goddamn labels still stitched in 'em showing Joplin, Missouri. This whole deal is south."

"Down on the border?" Lackey asked.

"I don't think that far."

"Just ask Buster if you want to take a flight somewhere," White said, leaning loose and lean as a stick on the fender. "He's studied every airline's flight schedule there is. 'Bout to make us both cross-eyed."

"Saw the report," Lackey said. "You can narrow down the flights?"

"We can narrow the ones that didn't fly the night of the storm," Jones said. "I have two airlines I like."

They were on the fifth floor of the Federal Building ten minutes later. Colvin had given Jones his office, and he'd tacked schedules on a large board, along with maps of Okalahoma and Texas and Missouri.

Telegrams and letters had been sorted in bins, and mug shots were tucked into a half dozen binders on the desk. Jones worked from a small black typewriter on the desk, and at his elbow there was a cup of cold coffee and his cold pipe.

"You're going stir-crazy," Lackey asked, "aren't you?"

"I'm not much for secretarial work."

Lackey took his hat and jacket off and hung them by the door. He closed the door behind the two of them with a light click, but you could still hear the telephone bells ringing and the hard clack of the typewriters and the chatter of Teletype machines. The air was smoky and stale, and all the action of the days since Urschel returned home made the office air smell sour with nervous sweat.

Jones sat on the edge of his desk and crossed his arms. He was in his shirtsleeves and wore a gun rig over his shoulder.

"I'd open a window, but they're painted shut."

"I'd shoot out the panes," Lackey said. "How do you live like this?"

Jones shrugged.

"Listen," Lackey said. "I haven't put this in a report yet. But after you got reassigned, I picked up where you left off on the Union Station massacre."

"Not much to follow," Jones said.

"You remember requesting the phone records for Dick Galatas in Hot Springs? From the pool hall?" Lackey asked. "Well, the son of a bitch called Joplin twenty times after we picked up Jelly Nash."

Jones nodded. "Let me guess."

"That's right, that old grifter Deafy Farmer. It's taken me some time to run down the calls out of Farmer's place, but the wires were burning up while me and you and Sheriff Reed were on that train. We didn't stand a chance."

"Who'd he call?"

Lackey leaned in and placed his elbows on his knees, his short red tie dipping from his neck. "A rental. False names. When we found the place, it was littered with cigarette butts and rotgut gin. They left plates of spaghetti on the counter half eaten."

"You get a description?"

"Two neighbors saw a man ducking in and out. Never made a fuss. Never too social."

"Floyd?"

Lackey shook his head. "Fella was described as pale-skinned with pale bluish eyes. Muscular and mean-looking. He carried golf sticks with him every night."

"Son of a bitch," Jones said. "Verne Miller."

"The witnesses picked him straight out of a hundred photos. That rotten bastard killed Otto, those two detectives, and one of our own."

"Who else?"

"No one saw him, but I'm hearing Harvey Bailey."

"I figured that from the start."

"Miller won't go quietly," Lackey said, working a cigarette from a pack and then finding a lighter in his sling. "Listen, Hoover's been asking about how Nash was killed."

"What'd you say?"

"I said there was a lot of confusion in that car."

"He'll have the bullet reports by now," Jones said. "Hoover knows."

"You think Sheriff Reed meant to kill him?"

"Gun went off while he was trying to set aim."

Someone rapped on the pebbled-glass door, and a nameless young agent walked in and passed a typed note for Agent Gus T. Jones. "How 'bout we get you something to eat?" Jones said. "You like chop suey?"

"What's that message?"

"This?" Jones said, adding the slip to the growing mound of paper on his desk. "Some detective in Fort Worth named Weatherford. I'll call him when I get around to it."

16

George drove Kathryn past all the old Saint Paul places, the Saint Paul haunts and whatnot, chattering on about *The times they had, the nights they danced*, and how all of it was coming around again, sister. The Boulevards of Paris nightclub. The Hollyhocks. Green Lantern Saloon, Plantation—George smiling like a bastard when they rode past the Plantation because he once screwed her there in a toilet stall—and then on to the big brick Hotel Saint Paul on St. Peter Street, where George said Leo Gleckman ran the show on the whole third floor, pointing out the floor like she couldn't count from the bottom. Gleckman was Saint Paul, and the Kid ran Minneapolis, but sometimes those two Jews did business on each other's turf, and in their ancient traditions this all made sense to them. But Kathryn said she could never understand trust between a couple of hoods. She'd met Gleckman once at the Boulevards of Paris, and about the only thing that struck her about the fella was the beautiful camel hair coat he wore and the ruby stickpin—big as a nut—pinned to his tie.

"Whatta you think?" George asked, pulling into the Hotel Saint Paul portico. "We get a suite?"

"We got enough?"

"Couple hunnard," George said, looking in the rearview, with the back window obscured by pretty packages, hatboxes, and bags. "You sure can drop some coin."

"I wanna go to the Hollyhocks tonight," Kathryn said, slumped in the big Cadillac's passenger seat, arms crossed over her breasts. "I want that Hollyhocks steak, cut an inch thick. Blood rare."

"Fine by me," George said. "Hell, I like steak."

"I wanna wear the new dress."

"It's a hell of a dress."

"I like red."

"Red was made for you, sweetheart."

"And the rings. The necklace I showed you at Cohen and Samolson?"

"We'll get 'em tomorrow."

"George?"

"Yeah?"

"Do you love me?"

"You're the Little Wife, aren't you?"

"I guess."

A nigger in a military-looking suit opened the passenger door and about scared Kathryn to death with his big toothy grin, her thinking about the rings and bracelets that she'd buy and plain forgetting they were parked outside the Hotel Saint Paul. He held the door open and called her ma'am in a voice that sounded just like a white person's.

"Checkin' in," George said, with that movie-star grin he practiced sometimes in the mirror. "Kit, we got it. Why not enjoy it?"

"And tonight?" she asked, one foot out the door.

"It'll all go according to Hoyle. Do I look worried?"

They took a room on the tenth floor—a suite, just like George promised—and when she threw open the drapes and unlatched the window she felt a loosening of the nerves, not unlike the way a good martini can loosen your legs a bit. George fetched his cigarettes while she looked down on Saint Paul, at all the rooftops and all those poor bastards punching the clock for some ungrateful fat man. Secretaries. Housewives. Maids. All of 'em suckers.

George was behind her. She could feel his heavy cigar breath on her neck and smell the cigarette burning in his fingers. The city still seemed foreign as hell, with the summer and all. Whenever she thought about Saint Paul, it froze her to the bone.

"You wanna try on those stockings?"

"Why don't you wait, you goat."

"I was just thinking—"

"Thinking what? That you'd get a poke because it's Saturday? I've got to get my hair done. Put some paint on these nails. What do you say I call up the front desk?"

"That's what you do in a joint like this," George said, wrapping his big hairy arm around her small waist and pulling her into him, smelling her neck like a lion on a lamb. "You pick up the phone at the Hotel Saint Paul and it's like rubbing up a genie. Whatever you want, it'll be here."

"Anything?"

"Go try it out."

"George?"

The curtains ruffled in the hot wind and covered her face and eyes, and then there were rooftops much uglier than you'd think, splattered with tar and sprouting vents and hot steam and smoke. Never looked like this from the street. George kept on smelling her and burying his sharp whiskers into her ears. "Mmm?" he asked.

"Screw the Hollyhocks," she said. "Let's order dinner here. And a bottle of gin."

"The day's a waste without it."

"I do love you," she said, nodding to herself.

"'Course you do. My little honey."

"You call about the meet," she said. "I hope it's somewhere that I can wear that dress."

"I'll make sure of it."

Kathryn moved from the curtains and across the open space of the suite, with the big brass bed all made up with big goose-down pillows and soft, cool silk sheets. She found a dressing mirror near the bath and studied her reflection for a bit. The way the long black dress hugged her hips and tits and made her shoulders seem strong and athletic. She unpinned the beret and shook her hair loose, and then found George's hands on her again, unbuttoning the dress from around her waist. She kept her eyes on herself in the mirror as the dress dropped to a heap on the floor and she stepped from it in nothing but her silks and stockings, the new pair of shoes keeping her tall and high up on her toes. Her eyes met George's in reflection, and her first thought was *Goddamn, that monkey needs a shave*, but she passed over the thought and imagined him as Gable or William Powell and not a Memphis bootlegger. She stretched her arms up over her head and, reaching backward, held him close.

George placed his burning cigarette in her mouth. And it was all like that, slow and steady, with the hot wind and bleeping cars from the open window, until they were sweaty and tired and lazy-boned in the silk sheets.

The phone rang, and George said "Yep" a couple times before hanging up.

"You ever heard of the Mystic Caverns?" George asked.

"What is it?"

"A club."

"In some caves?"

"Cann's place," George said. "You can wear the red dress. He said look for the entrance that's an ape's mouth. Now, does that make a lick of sense?"

Kit flipped over on her stomach, nude as Eve, and rocked her legs up to her butt and down again in thought. George had the ashtray on his hairy chest, and she thieved his cigarette and thought for a long while.

"You think we could do this again?"

"What's that?"

"*What's that?* The kidnapping, you dumb mug."

"I don't see why not."

"You pull five of these, George, and we nab a million . . . You know, the Kellys just might be somebody."

"He wants us to bring the money."

"All of it?"

"Yep."

"What if we're robbed?"

"Whatta you think I am?"

Kathryn flipped over again and stared at the ceiling. "I got an idea."

THEY SHOOK HANDS IN THE MOUTH OF THE APE—FANGS AS high as a picket fence; huge eyes, crazy and wide; with flared nostrils and a red carpet for a tongue. Kid Cann reached for Harvey Bailey's elbow and steered him inside the Mystic, all smiles and pride, the tunnels, he said, having been dug out along the Mississippi River cliffs for their sand, now were the hottest nightspot in town. "It's a cool fifty-eight degrees year-round. How 'bout that?"

"What about the winter?" Harvey asked, following the Kid down a long tunnel and turning into a wide cavern. "You'd freeze your dick off."

"We're a hunnard and fifty feet below ground. It gets cold, we turn up the heat."

A floor show had started at the end of the cavern, more tunnels branching off into bars and bathrooms, and probably some places to gamble and whore. A colored orchestra played Arabian music while a white woman prowled around onstage, not a stitch of clothing on, nothing but a couple huge fans made out of ostrich feathers. Men whistled and clapped. The woman was goddamn gorgeous, with wonderful tits and fat nipples.

"You know who that is?" asked the Kid. His hair looked wet from all the oil, slapped down tight on his skull, with an inch part down the middle. He was wide-eyed and weak-chinned, wearing a tuxedo, smoking a cigar, and backslapping and shaking hands as good as any two-bit politician. "Miss Sally Rand, on loan from her World's Fair performance in Chicago."

"Perfect tits," Harvey said. "Wonderful tits."

The Kid nodded and leaned in a bit toward Bailey. A foot shorter, he looked up, and played a bit with his black bow tie. "How much we talkin'?"

Harvey told him, and the Kid's eyes grew big.

"Where you boys gettin' all this money?"

"You talkin' about Kelly?"

The Kid didn't say anything, only twirled the fat cigar in his big lips, hoping the Arabian music would fill up the silence. He shrugged and puffed and puffed, spilling the smoke from the side of his mouth. Miss Sally Rand flitted around on that big white stage, the darkies not seeming to notice as they boomed their drums and played their horns, the white woman covering up her cooch with one fan of feathers and her ta-tas with the other, then switching the two so goddamn fast you weren't sure if you saw the ta-tas or the cooch or even a little ass, and it stayed with you like a drunken memory.

Harvey smiled. "Kelly's with us."

"He didn't mention it."

"Well, he should have. Is he here?"

"I don't want no trouble," Kid Cann said. "I hear you're with Verne Miller."

"He's not trouble."

"Last time I saw him, he broke my tooth with a .45."

"But he didn't kill you," Harvey said. "That's gotta count for something."

The men stood there facing the first tunnel and watched the crowd. Every con man, jewel thief, hustler, pimp, murderer, high-class whore, and top-shelf yegg in the state was in the gorilla's belly, swilling the legal hooch and tossing away their cash on the wheel or cards.

"What's a fella got to do for a drink?" Bailey asked.

Kid Cann motioned with his head toward another tunnel, a dimly lit little elbow where coffins had been carved into the soft sand walls and men in black bodysuits stitched with skeleton-bone designs would jump out at you or pinch a girl's ass all in fun. And Harvey didn't see it coming when some poor bastard grabbed his elbow to scare him and Harvey turned and punched the skeleton right in the nose, sending him flat against the cave wall and sliding down to his ass.

The Kid laughed and muttered, "Christ," and walked to the bar, snapping his fingers at the barman, and the barman reached under the till for a crystal decanter of what would be the good stuff. He poured out two thick measures in crystal glasses, and Harvey pulled out a cigar from his linen suit that he'd taken from Sawyer at the Green Lantern. There was a big painting above the bar all done up in oils and canvas, and Harvey had to do a double take before realizing that was Nina herself, thinking back on times when he'd poked her.

"Switchin' money ain't a problem," the Kid said, before taking a sip, swishing the glass around in his hand. "But I want to shake hands with you and Kelly on twenty percent."

"You're killing me."

"That's a lot of dough."

"I had ten percent in mind."

"A man has to think about the heat that will come with that kind of cash."

Harvey nodded and glanced away from Kid Cann and down the polished mahogany bar that seemed to go on forever, spotting Dock Barker and that ugly mug Alvin Karpis, who was a dead ringer for Boris Karloff, goddamn Frankenstein and the Mummy all in one. Miller had followed Harvey into the caves and stood like a pale ghost at the end of the bar, talking to some bottle blonde, with her big tits crammed into a sequined gown. The lamps' glow was soft and pleasant, and the caverns had a soft coolness, while the negro music from the bandstand rebounded and echoed throughout the walls.

Harvey offered his hand, but the Kid shook his head.

"Let me know when Kelly gets here," Harvey said, and knocked back the whiskey. "Verne's already left my stash with your boy, Barney what's his name."

"Why you need Kelly's dough?"

"Because we got a deal. You really want me to answer all these questions? That would make you an accessory. Now, how 'bout another drink? I want to get back and watch Sally Rand tickle her cooch with a feather."

Little Kid Cann smiled at him, ashing his cigar on the lip of the bar but never for a second taking his eyes off Harvey Bailey. Mean little bastard.

KATHRYN WORE THE RED DRESS, LOOKING LIKE SHE belonged on the cover of *Photoplay*, the wide, regal collar high on her neck, the padded shoulders, the silk material that hugged her ass and legs and draped down past her knees. Most people didn't even seem to mind the big bump on her belly and even moved out of her way and bent over backward to be polite. And she'd smile and touch her protruding stomach and newly done hair. The hotel had sent up a couple women to wash and style while another gave her a manicure. George sitting by the radio the whole time in a hotel bathrobe, listening to *Buck Rogers* with real interest, occasionally nodding to some twist and turn in the plot. But he'd allowed one of the women to cut and oil his hair proper, even giving him a close shave and slapping him down with some sweet-smelling bay rum. He had a new suit, new dress shirt, and a pair of class A two-tone shoes.

She held on to his strong arm as they moved from the sluggish heat off the river and into the big ape's mouth, Kathryn thinking instantly about that monkey Kong and feeling like she was being swallowed whole in the beast. Fay Wray slapping away those big fat fingers that groped her day and night. But Wray knowing that the big beast was just lovestruck over her and that he'd protect her from those crazy darkies with spears, and damn well even climb up the Empire State Building for her. She patted George's hairy knuckles with her free hand, and they were out of the gorilla's soft throat and into the belly, and the whole joint was hopping. A nigger orchestra had the room on its feet, and women danced on white-linened tables, kicking plates and champagne bottles, and men knocked back whiskey and smoked, while a ball of excitement grew in Kathryn's stomach. You felt that way when you were in the place that you were meant to be. This was the heat, this was the action. The bee's knees in the belly of the beast.

"Oh, George."

"What'd I tell you?"

"You crazy mug."

"Whatta ya' think, a girl or a boy?" he said, pointing to her stomach. *This the tenth time he's told the same joke.*

"It's a monkey, for sure."

George snatched a waiter by the arm and thumbed through a fat wad of cash in a silver clip. He tucked a few bills in the man's open pocket and told him to bring a bottle and a setup. And the waiter was back in two seconds with two more waiters, hauling in a table from the back and a couple chairs because there wasn't a free place to sit. George turned and waved to someone, and then Kathryn noted a little man standing near the tunnel to the bar, a short, little Jewy fella with grease-parted hair, puffing on a big fat cigar. He reminded her of a fighter, short and mean and tough as hell because his height had made him that way.

"Who's the gimp with the donkey dick?"

"That's the Kid," George said.

"No foolin'?"

"No foolin'."

The waiter made a big show about the whiskey being bonded and not like that sorry hair tonic colored with wood chips they used to sell at the Boulevards of Paris. They brought ice in a silver bucket and crystal glasses and bottles of ginger ale, and George passed out more wads of bills, all of that money floating away making Kathryn feel just like who she should be, wanted to be, and was. She felt a little hand on her shoulder and saw Kid Cann, grinning, his other hand on George's shoulder, whispering for a moment in George R. Kelly's ear, and then trailing away, with a firm pat on her back, like she was A-OK.

"What was that?"

"Keep smilin', doll."

"What?"

"Bailey's here. Verne Miller, too."

"Goddamn. Son of a bitch."

"You said it."

"Whatta we do?"

"We can amscray or you can birth that baby. We're in a pinch."

Kathryn felt the fat mound on her belly and readjusted the heft. She took a long sip of the whiskey and ginger ale, and contemplated. "Okay. Okay. Only five g's, and don't you dare ask 'em to join us. Those two bastards are going to stink up this whole town for me, ruin my fun, and I'd just as soon be back in the Cadillac halfway to Cleveland."

"Still stuck on Cleveland."

But Kathryn wasn't listening, only taking a breath, knowing the Kellys were cornered, and it was best to brass the son of a bitch out and wait till the next job. *Goddamn George.* She moved her hand from underneath his, thinking how nice it would be if some airplanes would knock him out of his big tree.

"'Twas beauty," she said.

"What?"

"I want a convertible."

"A what?"

"In Cleveland, I want you to trade out your car for a convertible. Cadillac makes the most darling coupe. I saw the ad in *Redbook*."

George reached for the whiskey, pouring it like it was a glass of milk at the end of a long day. The nigger band stopped and then started again with some booming jungle beats, a naked white woman wandering onto the stage holding only a big fat balloon, her pale ass hanging out for all those musicians to see.

"What's this?" Kathryn asked. "The sacrifice?"

17

They brought 'em into Kid Cann's office, a cavern carved behind the club's stage. The walls were smooth blond wood slapped over the sandstone, the joints expertly sealed so that the orchestra sounded like they were playing a hundred miles away or under the river. Harvey nodded at Kathryn Kelly and George, too, but wanted them to know this was all business. The Kid had a small bar padded in black leather by his desk, and Harv helped himself to a little refresher of bourbon with club soda, a little ice and bitters. He stood near the desk and waited for the Kid and his boy, Barney Bernbaum, to get on with the show, take their money, trade it out, and let the whole deal be settled.

"You unnerstand the twenty percent?" the Kid asked.

"Yeah, yeah," George Kelly said, finding a soft, curved leather chair to park in and cross his legs and smoke, resting his hat over his big foot.

"And I don't want no trouble," the Kid said. "What you got goin' with Harv and Verne don't have a thing to do with me."

"It's decided."

Harvey smiled over at George, letting George know the two of them were settled but that he also knew that George was trying to muscle him out.

"Can I see it?" the Kid asked.

George thought for a moment and ran a hand over his big jaw and nodded. Kathryn stood behind him by the door, and Harvey had to look real good to see if she'd gotten fat or if George hadn't knocked her up.

"Yeah," George said, snapping his fingers. "Give it to 'im, Kit."

Kathryn waddled up to the desk, her long, painted fingers on her swaying stomach, and she dropped her big belly on the desk, turning her back to all the men in the room and hoisting her dress. Harvey thinking *Oh, shit, here we go, what's this broad about to pull*, but then the dress reached high over her legs, showing her ass, and stretched over her stomach, and with a big thud on the desk out flopped the ninety g's.

The door opened and in walked the other Jew, Barney Bernbaum, and he was all smiles, holding the door for Verne Miller, who followed, with a tight, twitchy mouth, and coldly looked to each one of 'em before resting his back against the far wall, scouting, and placing his hat back on his head, slow and delicate. All of 'em knowing Miller packed two Army-boy .45s on each flank and could take each one of 'em out without dropping his cigarette.

Barney joined the Kid at the desk and thumbed through the big stacks of dough. Harvey knocked back the drink, poured some more. George was looking up at the ceiling like he was trying to count the tiles. The orchestra played louder now, and you could hear the muffled notes a bit more, the ceiling shaking, and from the minuscule cracks in it came a fine white powder, looking like dandruff or cocaine, splatting Harvey's drink until he looked up to what George saw and knew it was just that natural sand shaking loose.

Barney nodded to the Kid. The Kid's wide-set snake eyes took in the room, and he screwed up his Jew mouth, nodding back. The Kid picked up a big, ornate phone and spoke a handful of words into the receiver before hanging up. "Drink up. Money'll be here in a jiff. Go play the wheel."

"You think we're soft?" George asked. "I prefer to leave this joint with all my money."

The Kid shrugged. "Suit yourself, Georgie." Miller uncrossed his arms, and left his lookout by the door. He joined Harvey at the bar, and Harvey filled a glass with ice and some tonic. Miller lit a cigarette to go with his ice water.

"So you boys gonna tell me the score?" the Kid asked. "You know I'm dying to know."

"You don't know?" Harvey Bailey asked, kind of laughing to himself and taking a last puff from a cigarette and squashing it in a glass ashtray. "You got the most wanted man in America right here in your establishment. Our little boy Georgie has grown up. Look at him—*the master-mind, the criminal genius, the man with nerves of steel . . .*"

"You don't mean . . . ?" the Kid asked. "Come on."

"You betcha," Harvey said. "Can you believe it? Remember how this mug used to stutter, 'S-s-sir, c-c-can I tag along on a j-j-job?' You know he puked in his hat before we robbed that bank in Sherman?"

George played with his hat and would not look at him.

Verne Miller laughed.

George played with his hat and wiped some imaginary dust from his shoe.

"Remember that one job where he double-parked that ole Packard and attracted every traffic cop in that podunk town?" Harvey asked.

Miller nodded and gave a sliver of a smile, knowing what Harv was doing, and took a sip of ice water, rattling the glass. You take a man like George, play with his head a bit, get him off his game, and he'll start thinking sloppy and not worrying about things like counting or watching where fat satchels of cash were laid.

A cloudy head just plain neutered a fella.

HARVEY BAILEY WAS A TWO-BIT ASSHOLE. KATHRYN COULD run down her boy on occasion, but George R. Kelly was still her man, and this was school-yard bullshit that she didn't care for a bit. She prayed to the Lord in heaven that George would just reach into that beautiful tailored jacket, pull out that .38, and plug that big-nosed bastard in the forehead.

"Whatta they call you now, George?" Verne Miller asked, his jaw muscle flexing like walnuts.

George wouldn't look at them. *Look at them, George, meet their gaze, and don't back down an inch.* George wouldn't look at 'em.

Harvey smoked, all delicate and womanlike, and said, "'Machine Gun' Kelly. Rat-a-tat-tat."

"You even know how to fire a chopper, George?" Miller asked. "I can teach you sometime."

George would not look at them.

The big guy just picked a space on the wall behind those two hoodlums and watched it like a cultured man might sit in a museum, or some such fancy place, and contemplate the lines and dots in a painting and make some kind of gibberish remark about the lines and dots forming a whole image. Kathryn had read of such four-flushers in *Collier's*.

"Most wanted man in America," Harvey said. "Got to take off my hat. We didn't think you had the nuts."

"Why don't you shut up, old man," Kathryn said, walking the room and standing behind George and placing her long fingers on the back of his chair and then touching his shoulder. "You think 'cause you stole a bunch of loot in your day? Let me tell you something. Back in the old days, my granny could've busted a jug wide open. Look at you. You can't even walk without a cane. Like an old woman."

Bailey raised his eyebrows and straightened his tie, running the silk through his fingers and sliding the silver clip tight. That nut job Miller just stood beside Bailey, staring at Kathryn, like the staring was gonna do one bit of good and like she hadn't seen that intimidation show a thousand Saturday nights with him and Vi when he'd slap her silly and send her to the powder room with paint running off her eyes.

"Whatta you lookin' at?" she said. "You crazy hophead."

George wouldn't look at 'em.

Not one damn bit.

Wouldn't meet the men's eyes. He reminded her of a schoolkid taken to task.

"Miller, you wanna know why you can't find Vi?" Kathryn asked, the veins running hot and feeling her heart beating double time. "It's 'cause she don't wanna be found. She's prowling New York with some Hollywood producer with a fat wallet while you and Harvey play grab ass for the dregs of what we earned. You know what? She told me you never could please her. Said holding your prick in her mouth was like playing with a kid's pencil."

Miller lurched forward. Harvey Bailey caught his right arm.

Harvey laughed and checked his watch.

"C'mon, George," said the Kid. "Harvey's just having some fun. Drinks on me."

George took a big breath, and put his hands to his knees and stood tall, holding his hat.

"We'll wait outside," George said, mumbling.

He followed her from Kid Cann's fancy-ass office and down a long, long sandstone hall and back into the smoky air and nigger music and ladies who didn't give a shit that midnight was long since over.

"Look at all them knucklehead Cinderellas."

"You got a strange way of talkin', Kit."

She grabbed his arm, feeling his labored breathing against her ribs, as they headed back toward the big ape's mouth, seeing the big ape teeth, and Kid Cann's goons making a show of parting as they came on through, and stepped out of the cool and into the heat. Over the Mississippi, you could see Saint Paul and a couple of rusted-out drawbridges real clear, one of 'em holding a passing freight, with a lot of racket and strain, red lights flashing and flashing.

George sat on the hood of his midnight blue sixteen-cylinder and started a Camel. He motioned to her, seeing if she wanted one. She shook her head and walked near him, kicking away the river gravel with her fine slippers and holding the hem of her dress, catching in the summer wind. The action still playing out the ape's mouth, and if you looked over at the Mystic Caverns you'd think the beast was alive, with those glowing eyes, and the heat and smoke coming from between those picket teeth.

"George honey?"

"Yeah?"

"I'm sorry."

"What're you sorry for?"

"They're just some rotten crooks. You don't have to look up to 'em no more. You outclass 'em all."

George sat on the hood of the car, in the shadow and darkness, and smoked for a few minutes, looking a bit drunk, watching those flashing red lights with all his attention.

"But George? Meet their eyes next time. Let 'em know you're the heavy in this picture."

"I was looking for something."

Kathryn saddled up and skedaddled up onto the hood, pinching his smoke, and watching the gears and whirlycues of the drawbridge lay it all flat and even. Her stomach felt oddly flat and empty.

"The Kid's got a secret door," he said. "Right behind the desk. Looks real good and hid in that fancy woodwork, but it sure as shit is there."

"How do you know it's not a secret safe or some nonsense?"

"'Cause it ain't."

"George?"

They noticed two black Cadillacs, new ones but only eight-cylinder, pull in front of the Mystic Caverns. Some tough Jew boys holding fat grips in their hands crawled out, and the doormen moved the hell out of their way. The business had begun.

"Here we go."

"George?"

"Open the trunk, sweetheart," George said. "And give me your coat."

"What for?"

"To hide the big gun."

"Oh, God," she said, smiling. Knees weak and face flushed. "Oh, George."

"Keep the motor running, and don't turn into a woman if I come out blazing."

18

Thursday, August 10, 1933

Y ou remember ole Pedro Posado?" Doc White asked. He and Jones
were about a thousand feet above North Texas, heading back to
Oklahoma City, in a brand-new aircraft belonging to a buddy of
Urschel's, an executive with Sinclair Oil. White had to yell out the ques-
tion on account of the single engine humming and shuddering the cabin.
But, thank the Lord, it was blue skies today, making it easy work for
Jones to check the rough terrain through a pair of binoculars.

"How could a man forget Pedro Posado?" Jones asked.

"What do you think drove him?"

"Meanness."

"I don't think so," White said. "He was restless. All those Mexicans
were restless back then, the government in collapse, everyone wantin' a
piece, thinking about putting beans on the table."

"Nothing killed that woman but plain-out meanness," Jones said,
studying his hand-inked map and looking back out the oval window,
following the natural borders—rivers and roads and fence lines—across
the flat, dusty earth below them. It was a cloudless day, and everything
from this altitude looked in good order.

"What was her name?" White asked.

"Conchita Ramirez."

"That's right. Conchita Ramirez. Sometimes when I close my eyes, I can still hear the screams."

"I try and not study on the past."

"Pedro ran into that drugstore when he saw us. Where was that?"

"Shafter."

"He pulled a gun on you and—"

"Doc, can we pay attention to the matter at hand?"

"You recall the newspapers?"

"Called us 'killers,'" Jones said.

"Hell, ole Pedro is the one who'd blowed her legs and hands off."

"I was there. You don't need to color a story when a person knows how it goes."

"We find the boys who nabbed Mr. Urschel and we won't have time to blink."

"You don't think I know that, Doc? What am I gonna do, offer 'em flowers first?"

"Verne Miller ain't no Pedro Posado."

"How do you know? Maybe Verne Miller is Pedro Posado's long-lost cousin."

"You see anything?"

"Nope."

"How are you supposed to tell one shack from another?" White asked. "You know how many shacks with pigs and goats there are in Texas?"

"I know the layout."

"And you know absolute this is the route of that airline? The one that didn't fly in that storm?"

"It's down there somewhere. The science'll prove it."

"Science? They'll be long gone."

"Leaving a trail. Like they always do. How's this any different?"

They landed back in Oklahoma City three hours later, ears ringing as they shook hands with the pilot and trudged back to the borrowed car. Jones noted a man at the edge of the tarmac talking with Colvin. The man was youngish but didn't dress like an agent. He had more the look of a local cop, with a dandy's boots and a dime-store suit. Jones greeted them both, and Colvin introduced the fella as a detective from Fort Worth.

"You fly over Wise County?" the detective asked. The man was tall and bony, with giant slabs of teeth and the smile of a tent-show preacher or a roadside huckster selling snake oil.

"We did."

"You find what you're looking for?"

Jones shook his head. "Was getting dark. More to see tomorrow."

"I sent you some messages."

"Give that name again?"

"Weatherford."

"I've been busy, Mr. Weatherford."

"You'll find what you're looking for in Paradise," he said.

"You sound like a preacher."

"Just outside the town is a known hole-up for some Fort Worth gangsters."

"You think they took Urschel? Because from what we know so far, this is too big of a job for some local boys."

"They ain't 'Pretty Boy' Floyd, like the papers say."

"I never believe what I read in the papers," Jones said, opening the door and placing his satchel in the rear of the car.

"Can I buy you ole boys a cup of coffee?" Weatherford asked. "It'll be worth your time."

Doc White joined the men at the car, but no introductions were made. Doc just stood there and hitched up his pants while Jones adjusted his hat brim, the setting sun in his eyes, Weatherford an inky cutout before him. "Doc, this fella's from Fort Worth and says he's done cracked the case."

Weatherford crawled in back of the Plymouth and smiled. Jones didn't like the way the bastard smiled, him watching Jones's eyes in the rearview until they found a small diner just off Eighteenth Street.

On the table between them, Weatherford threw down a mug shot of a fella named George Barnes from Memphis, Tennessee. A bootlegger sent to Leavenworth in '28 for running hooch to some Indians.

"You got to be pulling my leg," Jones said.

THE FAMILY GATHERING TURNED INTO A DINNER PARTY, AND the dinner party to chaos. Charles F. Urschel's nerves were on edge even after taking two strong drinks, before brushing his teeth and returning back downstairs. The staff had cooked up a wonderful meal of roasted quail with red potatoes and summer corn. Big Louise made a particular show of bringing out the platters and talking about how careful you had to be with those little birds' wings or they'd just dry right on up. Water was refilled. Tea and coffee were poured. Kirkpatrick said grace at the end of the table and then raised his glass to Charlie, thanking those present for a job well done. And those present included the nervous young man on his immediate right, taking a seat by his stepdaughter, Betty, Charlie just hearing moments ago that she planned to take the federal agent to cotillion with her that very weekend.

"Thank you, Kirk," Urschel said. "Miss Louise can outcook a gangster anytime."

"What on earth did they feed you?" some society woman Charlie didn't know asked from down the table.

"Humble pie," Charlie said.

And there was laughter and toasts and the clinking of glasses. Miss Louise patted Charlie's back with her fat hand and returned to the kitchen until called again, the door swinging to and fro behind her. But just as Charlie smiled over at Berenice and cut into his quail, the lights faltered and sputtered out. The air-cooling machine went silent, replaced by the sound of nervous laughter and talk. Miss Louise and some of the servant boys brought in candlesticks under their black faces and set them down the long, long table that Tom Slick had purchased on one of his trips to Europe.

"Here's to Oklahoma Gas and Electric," Urschel said.

More nervous laughter, and someone said, "It's just a fuse. Don't worry."

The conversation soon steadied, and Urschel's eyes adjusted in the dark, but his breathing had become a bit squirrelly, and he didn't feel like touching any of the food. "Are you okay, Charles?" Berenice asked from his left.

And he nodded.

"I'll be right back," he said, excusing himself and taking a candle from the kitchen. He mounted the great staircase in bounds of two and three steps, cupping the flame in his hand, until he found his bedroom door and then the walk-in closet, seeking out his shotgun from under some old hats and winter scarves. The shells were found in his hunting coat, and he loaded the barrels and crept to the window, finding the entire street had gone dark. The houses down Eighteenth were blackened in both directions, the streetlights extinguished.

He breathed, and moved over the soft carpet, slipping the weapon behind some tall, thick drapery. The room smelled of Berenice's Parisian perfume and his old cigars, and he had to wipe the oil from his fingers, not knowing if it was from the gun or the quail.

Charlie walked down the steps, the candle's flame sputtering out, as he heard the laughter and dinner chatter, the glow of the dining room giving him light enough to see. When he reached the landing, he found he was nearly out of breath and a bit dizzy, and he held on to a post fashioned in the shape of a pineapple. Tom Slick had said pineapples brought wealth or meant wealth.

Charlie Urschel was quite dizzy.

He breathed, and righted himself, just before the young federal agent walked onto the landing with his annoying clacking shoes. "Sir?"

Charlie looked up at him and studied a face filled with concern.

"They treated me like a dog," Charles Urschel said, mouth completely parched. "Kept me on a three-foot lead."

"Yes, sir," the young man said. His name escaped Charlie. "I know."

"You must find them," Charlie said. "A man can't live like this."

"Yes, sir."

"And when you do, I want to be notified immediately," Charles Urschel said. "I want a chance to speak with them privately."

The young man just studied him, and Urschel turned back toward the kitchen, all of a sudden wanting all these people out of his home, most of them he didn't even know. Society women, garden club members, and members of the club who thought they'd earned a ticket to see the show. He was tired of all the concern and well-wishes and Berenice's pity as she lay next to him in the one o'clock hour, Charlie hearing the chimes but unable to move from the sweaty sheets, arms in spasm, as he lay on his back in complete failure.

Five policemen turned to him in wonder when he walked onto his own sunporch.

Two men guarded the walkway from his house, holding guns and asking if they might walk with him.

Three more policemen sat in the kitchen, listening to the radio with the colored help, the power back on, all of 'em laughing at *Amos 'n' Andy*, while Big Louise finished up setting the ambrosia on a silver platter.

"Mr. Charlie?" she asked with a smile that dropped when she saw his face.

He could only compose himself in the guest bath, and, even after a few minutes, there was knocking to see if it was occupied. He set the lock, turned on the faucet, and ran cool water in the darkness, splashing it on his face. When the lights flashed on, he was still sitting on a closed toilet, gripping a brass handrail, his feet pressing against the wall before him.

With the illumination, his legs dropped, one and two, to the tile. He splashed more water on his eyes and returned to the head of the table, saying he'd been a bit ill but please continue with dessert. Berenice wore a curious expression, and he reassured her with a smile, his shaky hand dropping his linen napkin to the floor.

When he reached under the table, he noted Miss Betty Slick's hand groping that young federal agent right between his legs as if she were kneading bread. Charlie righted himself in his large chair, and added some sugar to his coffee, slowly stirring. "Well now, son. Tell us, how did you come into the employ of Mr. Hoover?"

THEY WERE FINE, FAT, ROSY-CHEEKED PEOPLE FILLED WITH pep and life. The wife was the kind of woman who kept the Lane Bryant catalog by her freshly scrubbed toilet, checking out the latest fashions for portly women, while her old man read Abercrombie & Fitch over a morning bowl of Shredded Wheat, fancying himself the outdoors type, priding himself on crapping regular. They lived in a contented newish bungalow, not far off the streetcar line in Cleveland Heights. And the old man, Mr. K. R. Quigley, probably gave Mrs. Quigley and their precocious—if not annoying—daughter a peck on the cheek before doffing the old hat and rambling down to the automobile dealership, where he'd now sold Mr. R. G. Shannon, prosperous farmer out of Paradise, Texas, two brand-new Cadillacs.

"I have to say I was a bit surprised to see you two, again," Mr. Quigley said. "I figured that custom sixteen-cylinder job would last you some time."

Mrs. R. G. Shannon—*Ora, if you please*—knew why the son of a bitch was really surprised to see the Shannons again and it had nothing to do with the performance of the machine. Mrs. Quigley had called them out at a sit-down restaurant in June as a couple of four-flushers, raising her eyebrows at a couple hicks financing the top-of-the-line Cadillac and doubting that a nice farmer's wife from Texas could even recognize a Hattie Carnegie gown—bought in New York City—black and long, with silver buttons from the top center down to the bottom of the skirt, and done in a very fine wool crepe.

But, my God, what was Mrs. Shannon wearing tonight, along with some quite attractive new baubles? What is that, you fatty old bag? Oh, yes, that's nothing, just a little trinket made of fifty-five diamonds and a square-cut emerald solitaire ring. Nothing, really. Had you not noticed them before, you wretched housewife with mannish hands and bad posture? I don't care if your closets are filled with husky-catalog fashions and your kitchen shelves with Bisquick, Swans Down Cake Flour, and rows and rows of Campbell's soup.

"May I get you more coconut cake?" Mrs. Quigley asked. "The secret really is Baker's. The triple-sealed package keeps it tender and nut sweet. Not to mention sanitary."

"I am quite all right." Kathryn dabbed the corners of her mouth. "A bit rich for me."

"But I followed the recipe," she said. "I'm so very sorry."

"It was quite tasty," Kathryn said. "Quite sweet. But a woman must watch her figure."

The couples sat in a family room with a large window facing a perfect lawn shadowed in maple and elm. The radio had warmed up and broadcast the national news out of New York, and although Kathryn wasn't paying much mind she heard damn well nothing of Charlie Urschel. Apparently there was some trouble with those banana eaters down in Cuba, and they'd gone and overthrown their dictator or some type of mess. There were more NRA parades and Blue Eagle mumbo jumbo, news from the World's Fair, where the station would be live tomorrow, broadcasting Buddy Barnes, from the Pabst Blue Ribbon Casino.

"Was the engine too much, Mr. Shannon?" Mr. Quigley asked, setting down the plate scraped clean of icing. "She can devour some oil."

"Call me Boss," George said, getting all corny and full of himself.

He wore a new navy suit and new oxblood shoes, a new pair of rimless glasses fashioned in an octagonal shape. He'd been told they'd give the angles of his face a new dimension. "No. It wasn't the engine. The little wife here just had her heart set on that sweet little number when she saw it in *McCall's*."

"*Redbook,*" Kathryn said, giving the old stink eye to Mrs. Quigley's fat ass, waddling under the apron's bow, as she picked up their plates and headed into her kitchen domain.

"*Redbook,*" George said, working on his third piece of coconut cake, a cigarette burning on the edge of the plate. "When she saw that little coupe, she said, 'Hot damn. Now, *that's* a peach.'"

"Didn't expect you to pay the entire balance in cash," Mr. Quigley said. "I don't think I ever had that happen."

"If George doesn't drop his pin money somewhere, he'll burn a hole in his pants," Kathryn said, crossing her legs and taking up a smoke, finding great delight when fat little Mrs. Quigley rushed back into the room to flick open a lighter. Must've been some commission.

"'Pin money'?" she asked.

"Of course," Kathryn said. "The other night I sent ole Boss out with eighteen hundred dollars, and the little man here lost the whole thing. Isn't that right?"

George shrugged and pulled out a money clip bulging with cash. "You two ever seen a thousand-dollar bill?"

Mrs. Quigley's eyes went askew and then refocused on Kathryn's face, to see if the couple was pulling her leg. She opened her mouth, but before she uttered a word in skipped the little daughter, stopping the conversation cold, the precocious little moron who had already regaled them with five songs at dinner and two tap-dancing recitals with about as much delicacy as a bloated hippo.

"Well, well, well," Mrs. Quigley said, "Janey wanted to say good night and show you her certificate. Did I tell you she has won an art contest for Rinso soap? She is so very talented. Her little cartoon will be in a national magazine this fall. Can you believe it? It's called *It's Wonderful!* and features the most delightful little story about a woman who just can't get her laundry to smell or look right. You know, Mrs. Shannon, it really is a fine product. If you soak your clothes in it, it'll save you from scrubbing."

"I don't scrub nothing," Kathryn said, blowing smoke from the corner of her red mouth. "I got a nigger woman who does all that."

Little Janey, with her pinned bobbed hair and little sailor suit, looked at her mom and her mom at her. Her mother patted her little butt and scooted her off to bed, the little girl dishing out groans and protests that would've brought a belt from the real Ora Shannon, with her alcoholic breath and ten-cent perfume shining around her like a stained-glass halo.

"Where are the two of you headed next?" Mr. Quigley asked.

George looked to Kathryn and winked. "Chicago."

"The Fair?"

"Figured we got to go," George said. "Everybody in the whole gosh-dang world will be there."

"We were there last month," Mrs. Quigley said, all-knowing and smug. "I felt as if I'd entered another country, different worlds, all in Chicago. They even have an exhibit from Sinclair Oil with dinosaurs that look as real as you and me. They eat and putter about, make noises that scared little Janey a bit. She thought they were real beasts."

"Ain't that quick, huh?" Kathryn asked.

"Excuse me?"

"The kid. A little slow on the uptake."

"We must be gettin' along," George said, hand on Kathryn's back, Kathryn grinning at the woman. "We sure do appreciate the meal. That was a mighty fine pot roast. I hadn't had a meal like that since my youth. Hats off. And those biscuits? Just as fine as my mother's."

"If you change your mind on that coupe," Mr. Quigley said with a wink, "you let me know. Number's on the card."

"I think that little baby out there is just the ticket," George said.

"I think we're gonna drive her flat out tonight and not stop till we hit Chicago."

"An exciting life for a farmer," Mrs. Quigley said, raising her eyebrows.

"You can bet on it, sister," Kathryn said, turning for the door. "See you in the funny papers."

19

D on't feel bad about it, Harv," said Kreepy Karpis, the yegg with the face of Frankenstein. "I mean, Jesus H. Coulda happened to anyone. The son of a bitch ambushed you. That ain't fair."

Alvin Karpis. Alvin *Fucking Kreepy* Karpis sat beside Harvey in an identical leather chair, smoking an identical two-dollar cigar, at Nina's cathouse at one in the morning, trying to give Harvey Bailey advice on how to handle his business. The much younger yegg and that goddamn moron, Dock Barker, had pulled some pretty impressive jobs, but Harvey Bailey had been knocking over banks since Karpis was swiping gum-drops at the five-and-dime and tugging at his pecker in the school yard.

Both men wore Japanese robes provided to them by the management, a steady punch of Kid Cann's who took over when Nina died. The place was class all the way—red velvet furniture, polished wood, brass fix-tures, and burning gas lamps just like in the old days. Jesus, he hoped they laundered the robes.

"So George Kelly kicks in Kid Cann's door," Harvey said, pointing out the action with the cigar tip, "holding that Thompson, and tells the Kid to toss him the coin or he'd spray the whole place, colored orchestra and all. Verne had gone back into the joint to talk up that fan-dancin' snatch, or things mighta been different. But it's just me and the Kid sharing some fine whiskey and talking about the G coming down hard on all the rackets. I'm tellin' you, there was a time when I woulda seen Kelly coming like the light on a fucking freight train."

"What'd the Kid do?" Karpis asked, his hangdog face showing disappointment even when curious. You could stick a knife in the guy's hand and he'd look the same. No pulse, no emotion. "George must have a big set of 'em to bust in like that."

"Or he's fucking stupid," Harvey said. "The Kid tossed over the two grips. Hell, what'd he have to lose? He'd already made the cut and left one bag for me and one for George. I think the little Jew found some amusement in it."

Harvey blew out some smoke, pondering the situation, watching it float up to the second-floor railing that looked down upon the salon and waiting customers, hungry and jazzed for it.

"And he walked out with the two bags?"

"You know the hell of it, Kreeps? You don't mind if I call you that?"

"Not you, Harv. Always looked up to you. I know my face ain't pleasing to some."

"Well, the hell of it is, I don't think George wanted the money," Harvey said, ashing the cigar into a jade tray in the shape of a woman with spread legs. "He wanted to give me the big fuck-you because I laid his ears back in front of his woman. That's just plain pussy-crazy."

"What'd you say to him?"

"I told him he'd about pissed his pants before a job—and that's God's own, I'm telling you. I didn't think he'd pull his shit together. I'll be damned if it wasn't the same nervousness each and every time. I don't know how he pulled this one off. This thing in Oklahoma blows the fucking mind."

"The Urschel job?"

"Can you believe it?" Harvey asked. "I read in *Time* magazine that it was the biggest ransom ever paid. Since we broke out, I been running my tail off around three states on nickel-and-dime bullshit, and here goes big, dumb George Kelly, knocking on the door of the top oilman in the Midwest—*Step this way, please*—goddamnit."

"How much?"

"Two hunnard grand."

"I wish someone would've fingered him to me," Karpis said, crossing his bare feet at the ankle, taking a sip of booze, a hit of the cigar. "Must've been cake."

"You better believe it," Harvey said. "But kidnapping? C'mon. That's not an honest man's work."

"Really," Karpis said, smiling big while biting down on the cigar. "Ain't money respectable?"

"You know the G likes the goddamn Touhy brothers for kidnapping that brewer—what's his name? They might get the goddamn chair for that mess."

"Let me borrow a hankie. I might cry."

"Are you drunk?"

"I'm just plain happy, Harvey. High on life."

"Who's your whore?"

Karpis readjusted in the big, fat chair and pointed up to the railing cut into the ceiling. A redheaded girl, with pink lips and wearing a pink slip, waved down to the men. The girl Harvey had been with joined her, and she stared down, wrung-out, at Harvey, smoking a cigarette and motioning him back up with the crook of her finger.

"I got her all night," Harvey said. "I swear to you, Kreeps, that little girl's pussy is electrified. Does an old man good to get some fresh young tail. Gives me some real pep."

"You goin' after George?"

"He's got my dough."

"There's more banks," Karpis said. "More jobs. I could cut you in on a li'l somethin' we're workin'."

"That's mighty white of you, Kreeps, but Miller kinda got his heart set on acing George Kelly off the board."

"Suit yourself."

"He's right, you know," Harvey said, his cigar failing him, and he reached out to a whore that strolled by and told her to bring him more matches. He swatted her large, meaty ass and sent her on. "You don't steal from another yegg. You cross that line and you're like every egg-sucking bean counter. We lose that and we ain't nothing. Not a goddamn thing."

The whore tossed Harvey some kitchen matches, and he got the cigar going again and leaned his head back, his mouth breaking into a grin, seeing that young whore up there smiling back, a blond angel in the ceiling. If he wasn't so goddamn wise, he'd think the punch loved him. That's why you go to Nina's: whores who could sell it all night long.

"The G won't let him keep it," Harvey said, wresting his hand loose off the chair, cigar burning warm in his fingers. "They'll hunt that poor son of a bitch for the rest of his days."

Over a cold brick fireplace hung an oval portrait of Miss Nina herself, a black-eyed beauty who smelled like sunshine and sweets and could do things to a man that he'd never forget. Harvey recalled her well. What was that, fifteen years ago? There were boundaries then, and rules, and the law knew 'em and the crooks knew 'em, and there wasn't this jack-rabbitin' that was going on today. Today, a criminal was treated like some kind of social outcast. A bum with a tainted mind. A greedy leper.

"I'm done," Harvey said, swilling the drink. "I want my coin, and I'm throwing in the towel."

"There's a guy who can cut your face to look like anyone you please. He can burn your fingerprints off, too. How's the G going to find a man then? You'd be someone else, and no file will say you ain't."

"A man keeps his word," Harvey said. "I just want what's mine. What I earned. What's wrong with that?"

"I don't like to do a whore more 'an once," Karpis said. "You do them more 'an once and they start thinking that you like 'em and they'll want some kind of tip."

"You walk into the bank, put down the cash, and get your farm back," Harvey said. "You take that foreclosure notice and tell them to stick it far and high up their ass."

"Ain't a girl a fine thing?" Karpis said, stumbling up onto his feet, drink sloshing in his hand. "I think I'll have a second helping."

"People today. Greed. Pussy-mad."

THE NARROW, RUTTED ROAD SWOOPED SOUTH SIXTEEN miles from Decatur, the seat of Wise County, Texas, where Jones and Detective Ed Weatherford had just met with the vice president of the First National Bank. The men's badges had opened up the file of Mr. Boss Shannon, a respected cotton farmer who always kept about five hundred dollars in his savings account and was known to pay his mortgage on time. But Jones had also asked where they might find the biggest know-it-all in Wise County, and the vice president laughed and gave the name of their former examiner. And that examiner was called, and, after some telephone back and forth, the vice president raised eyes over half-glasses and told the men the examiner never saw how Boss ever made a living on the few acres of cotton he raised.

Handshakes were made, and they were off in the Plymouth with official papers of the bank, Jones working for First National and Weatherford the new examiner. They'd tell Boss he needed to sign a new note, since that fella in Arkansas had barely paid off the interest.

"How's them charts and graphs and such working out, Mr. Jones?"

"They're coming."

"But they all point to where we headed."

"United Airlines has a twin-engine come out of Fort Worth that flies that route regular."

"But didn't fly during the storm."

"No, sir."

"You brung that map?"

"I brung it."

"If we get into a nest of desperadoes," Weatherford said. "Just want you to know, I'm a fair shot."

Jones replied with a grunt, hot afternoon wind passing through the open car window, as a telephone pole painted white appeared just as the bank examiner said it would. Jones slowed and turned onto an even more rutted, narrow path, the kind built for horse and carriage but not a Plymouth. A dwelling came into view—a slatted-together, tin-roofed shotgun job. No paint, and a stone fireplace barely finding purchase on a back kitchen. As he braked the automobile, scattering a mess of guineas up onto the roof and into a dead mesquite, a smallish man—more like a boy—walked out onto the uneven porch wearing nothing but a pair of threadbare overalls and smoking a long cigar like Jones had seen in the mouths of city politicians.

A barefoot girl holding a child joined him, and they stared with vacant eyes as Jones got out on the running board and offered them a smile. "You Mr. Shannon?"

"I'm Armon. You lookin' for Boss?"

"We are."

"Back the way you come," he said. "Down another mile. Boss is my daddy."

The baby wore a sagging diaper and groped for the girl's fattened bosom, crying for some tit, till the boy told them both to git on inside, the door slamming with a hard thwack behind them.

"This part of his property?" Jones asked. Weatherford crawled out of the car, grinning with his big teeth and removing his sweaty hat from his head and fanning his face. He recognized the layout of the shack, too.

"Yes, sir."

"We come from First National," Weatherford said. "Need a signature on a note he signed."

The boy looked at the two men—in cowboy hats, suits, and boots—and studied their faces in the high afternoon sun, the cicadas going wild in the distant parched trees. Guineas, growing nervous, in a low cackle. His face was a puzzle of confusion, but he didn't say anything, just dropped his left hand inside his overalls and found his pecker to scratch.

"Don't suppose you could spare some water?" Jones asked.

"Yes, sir," Armon Shannon said. "We gots some water. Out back. Supposin' you need a cup?"

"That'd help," Jones said, watching the boy hop from his perch barefoot, waking an old, sleeping hound—a Walker, with long, flea-bitten ears—that loped up and around and down under the shade of the porch.

"How's the corn?" Weatherford asked, giving Jones a sly grin as they walked side by side. Weatherford's shadow had absorbed into his.

"Shoot," Armon said. "Dying or dead."

"You had much rain?"

"A week back," Armon said. "But 'tweren't good enough. Didn't do nothing but bring on the worms. Them worms are greedy as hell, eat down half an ear in a night. You think they'd leave a few kernels."

The boy stopped suddenly and kicked at the dusty, well-worn ground that scratching chickens had made smooth. He pointed to a boarded well with a pulley and old tin bucket. "You can use that ole dipper there."

"Just you and your wife?" Weatherford asked, stepping up as Jones dropped the bucket down deep into the well, hearing it hit bottom with a solid splash.

"Her people live a mile away. My people, too. When you got the kinfolk so close, a man don't want for nothin'."

"And you got 'nother in the oven?" Weatherford asked.

"Wore a goatskin, but the dang thing musta sprung a leak."

"You know you can get 'em made of rubber these days."

"I know," Armon said. "I seen 'em at the drugstore."

Jones pulled the bucket back to daylight and used that old dipper to find a drink just a mite cooler than the air and tasting so deeply of rust and minerals that it soured his face. The action wasn't lost on Weatherford, who foxed those eyebrows and wandered over to a pen with a couple fat sows and piglets wallowing in caked mud and slop, chickens scrambling and clucking at his feet, waiting for them to drop a crumb. Too dumb to find some shade.

"Radio said it might break a hunnard today."

"That so?" Jones said, placing the dipper back on a twisted nail and wiping the rust onto his pressed pant leg.

"Our water ain't cold branch, but glad we got it," Armon said. "Say, would you boys like to share a watermelon? She's a mite puny but just sure would wet the whistle."

The men sat along the open porch, Armon Shannon cutting into the small, round fruit with a pocketknife and handing over generous slices—for the size—to the two men. Jones pulled a handkerchief out of his coat pocket, careful not to expose the thumb buster, and gripped the rind.

"You got some salt?" Weatherford asked, before sinking his big teeth into a slice, the red juice running down his chin onto his silk tie. He took aim at the old hound, who'd come back out from under the porch, and spat seeds at the dog's head.

Armon skedaddled on in, fetching some salt. Door thwacking closed behind him.

"How's the comparison?" Weatherford asked.

"What do you think?" Jones said, tasting the watermelon, and making out the tin of a barn roof reflecting a mile or so to the southwest, thinking he wanted to meet Boss Shannon before the sun went down.

Armon came back with a saltshaker and passed it to Weatherford.

The baby followed, naked as Eve, stumbling for her daddy's leg and tugging for a slice of watermelon, pointing to her mouth like a jaybird. Shannon shook his head and cut off a miserly slice, placing it into the child's tiny hands, the father opening the screen door for the child to wander back through. He finished off the watermelon and said he was headed 'round back to throw the rind to the hogs. As he turned the corner, Jones followed the child into the shack, hotter than the porch, catalog wallpaper of red flowers coming unglued from the walls. He heard the small feet scatter and then stop, and a rusted, tired squeak.

The two doors toward the front porch were shut, but Jones tried one, lightly letting it swing open with the natural lean of the house to find a baby's high chair and a metal bed. *The dead cornfield became the wavy lines in his drawing, the mineral well a well-defined X, and now the southeast room. The high chair. The shaving mirror on a travel trunk.*

He walked farther into the shack and noted a kitchen to the northwest, and the northeast corner filled with a handmade bench and an old organ with sheet music to an old Fatty Arbuckle picture.

He turned back to the porch, walking soft in his boots, the screen door squaring up a big Texas sky, bright blue with heat, and not a cloud for shade. He saw Weatherford's back and his hatless, balding crown. The detective continued to launch seeds into the dusty ground while Jones tried the other door to his right. As it opened, he found the teenage girl sitting atop a bare mattress, her gingham dress pulled astride of her fat, round bosom. Both mother and child turned to the old man, the child going back to the nourishment, but the mother had the look of a coyote, her eyes not leaving Jones until the old door, fashioned of square-headed nails and boards, closed with a final, hard click.

Jones returned to the porch as Armon rounded the corner, coming from the hogpen.

"Our thanks for the watermelon," Jones said.

"I'll tell Boss you come callin'," Armon said, shaking the men's hands before scratching his pecker and looking up high at the sun, as if either one could tell time, and giving an expression like he wished it would get on and set. "Gosh dang, it's gettin' hotter than nickel pussy."

GEORGE STARTED ACTING STRANGE, STRANGER THAN NOR-mal, the minute they got back to the Hotel Cleveland. He'd read off the front page of the *Plain-Dealer*, folded it crisply in half, and said, "Let's get packin', Kit." Just like that. Didn't explain a thing; just "get packin'" at four a.m., after three nightclubs, two cabarets, and one speakeasy. Both of them half in the bag, stumbling and fumbling, and George telling her to lay off when she pinched his ass in front of that sour-faced doorman as that little tan coupe was wheeled around from the garage. So she finally asked, "What gives?" and George told her about the goddamn wire story about a couple of Kid Cann's Jews getting pinched by the G in Saint Paul.

"Did they say it was Urschel money?"

"What did I say?"

"Why didn't you tell me back at the hotel?"

"Because that woulda started a discussion, and I ain't in no mood for discussin'."

"George, you are whiskey mean. You can drink beer all night, but the minute you touch the liquor—"

"Go suck an egg."

They were on Highway 20, halfway to Toledo, before she spoke again, the bumpy road and headlights shooting into nothing but ribbons of road, making her sleepy.

"I got to use the can."

"Piss in a bottle," he said.

"It doesn't function that way, in case you haven't noticed."

"Ah."

"Why are you sore?"

"Those Jews didn't have the money two days before they got sloppy and started to show off."

"How'd they get pinched?"

"How else? Turned in by some lousy bank manager."

"You said the Kid was smart and that he knew people, and no one would be the wiser. You said—"

"I know what I said, 'cause I'm the one who said it."

Hessville. Woodville. Lemoyne.

The bastard drove straight on into the town of Assumption, this being about the time he needed to take a leak, and wheeled on into a road-side gas station and told the grease monkey to fill her up. The monkey unlatched the hood and flipped her open to check the oil, whispering and whoo-wheeing, until Kit got out and found the can herself.

"She sure is cherry," the monkey said. "Her engine ain't even broke in yet."

"And my husband wants to trade her already."

"Come again?"

"He wants to trade her."

"Whatsthematta with him?"

"You name it, brother."

They were back on Highway 20. *Fayette. Pioneer. Columbia.*

And then it was WELCOME TO INDIANA.

"I'm hungry."

"Well, you should've grabbed a pig's foot at the filling station."

"You should go into radio."

"Come again?"

"You should go into radio."

"How's that?"

"'Cause you're a goddamn comedian."

Toast, eggs, and hash in Angola, staring out at signs south to Waterloo.

"Waterloo?"

"What's so funny?" she asked.

"It's where Napoleon got his ass kicked."

She shrugged, and took some more cream in her coffee.

"You wouldn't know that, 'cause you never went past the eighth grade."

"Are you gonna sing me the Central High fight song?"

"I was big man on campus there."

"Rah-rah."

"What's eating you?"

George had a hard time getting settled into the new, smaller car, and about every other mile or so he'd have to tell her about it. Saying they should've never gotten rid of that big beauty and how they wouldn't be having to go through all this mess in Chicago if she hadn't been the one to go show up some salesman's wife.

She crossed her arms across her chest.

"This is no fun at all."

"I didn't promise a rose-strewn path, sweetheart."

"But if we got the money, you said we'd enjoy it. I ain't had one enjoyable night since we left Saint Paul."

"You were having fun last night."

"Pull over."

"What?"

"Pull over, you mug."

And George slowed somewhere on Highway 20 in old Iowa, where the corn seemed to grow straighter and greener. And Kathryn held on to the Cadillac frame and stepped out on the running board, where she puked her goddamn guts out. George had a good guffaw at that, and she crossed her arms over her chest again and then leaned into the window frame, the sweet morning heat lifting the matted hair off her face, and she looked at all that goddamn corn, all those silos and cows. And, goddamn, she wanted to be back in the city again, at a proper hotel.

"I'm callin' Louise."

"Why don't you just take out an ad? Or call up J. Edgar Hoover himself?"

"I'm callin' Louise and have her meet us in Chicago."

"You won't call no one, not even your damn mother, till I say so."

"Louise is fun. You can stay at the hotel and listen to *Buck Rogers* on the can. Me and Lou. We know how to have fun."

"She's a rotten whore. She's worse than a man."

"No woman is worse than a man."

"Bullshit."

There was that rotten, goddamn silence in the Cadillac till they turned up north and could smell Lake Michigan from the open windows and finally caught a big break of solid, civilized road. George pulled off and let the top down, and they saw they were only fifty miles from the city.

"I'm calling her."

"Do it, and I'll break your hand."

"You wouldn't lay a finger."

George rolled up his sleeves to the elbow and plucked a Camel into his mouth. He fished into the back for his matches, but Kathryn took a long breath and reached into her little jeweled purse for a lighter. "You always lose 'em, George. I don't think, since I've known you, you have ever been able to keep a book of matches."

"How we met."

And there it was, a lousy smile on her face. She leaned back into the big, plush seat and stared at the wide, open blue sky. "Yes, George. How we met."

There were people playing in the sand and sailboats way out in the lake. And she had George stop long before they ever reached the city. She pulled off her thigh-highs and tossed them away, running into the sand and touching her feet to the water. George followed, lace-up two-tone shoes in his right hand, smoking and sullen, and found a spot to park his ass. He watched some kids playing on a rickety boat and tossed the cigarette away.

When she'd had enough, feeling a bit more solid and straight, the car no longer up under her and purring and driving and bumping and jostling, she came back to George and parked her ass on over next to him. She laid her head on his shoulder, always knowing that would get to the bastard.

"Say, George?"

"Yeah."

"You never told me who fingered Urschel."

"You never asked."

"Goddamn. Well, I'm asking now."

"You wouldn't believe me if I told you."

"Well, why don't you try me out?"

"What if I said it was Jarrett?"

"I'd say you're a four-flusher," she said. "Jarrett was Urschel's buddy. If you used Jarrett, then how come you two dumb bastards took both of 'em?"

"Maybe, just maybe, it looked better that way."

"Jarrett. Some laugh. Like I said, they should put you on the radio. If only you could sing."

George picked up a handful of sand and let it drop loose and slow out of his fingers till there was nothing left but to brush his hands together and give the thumbs-up sign. "How do you think we knew when to grab Urschel? How come we knew they'd be on the back porch with the screen unlocked? You ever just figure that I might be pretty damn good?"

"It had crossed my mind."

"You wanna screw?"

"Is that all you want from me?"

"Pretty much."

"Room service?"

"In spades."

20

Charlie Urschel dressed at dawn, ate his breakfast in the house kitchen with a negro driver, with whom he discussed baseball and New Deal jobs, and found himself alone on the sunporch with a cold cup of coffee and a dying cigar. He relit the damn thing three times before he had the plug fired up again, and he sat there and smoked, paralyzed, as the early-morning heat seemed to radiate off Berenice's rose garden, already buzzing with flitting bees. The insects tried to fly through the metal screen, bouncing off several times before understanding the constraints and moving on. Soon Betty joined him, pulling the newspaper from under his elbow and, without a word, thumbing violently through the pages until she found something of interest, and sat like an Indian on the porch floor, laughing to herself, until she turned and said, "You must have had a hell of a time, Uncle Charles."

He turned to her and studied the young girl's face.

"You showed those kidnappers a thing or two."

He opened his mouth but closed it, thinking of nothing.

"Say, Uncle Charles? What happened to Bruce?"

"Special Agent Colvin."

"Nuts. He's Bruce to me. He's just a silly boy in a tie."

"What are you reading? The funny pages?"

"Society."

"What's so funny about society?"

"Hey, did you see this? Carole Lombard is getting a divorce from William Powell. Says right here 'They just decided all of a sudden they couldn't agree.' Well, isn't that sad?"

"How's that sad, Betty? You don't even know them."

"Are you kidding? I just saw *From Hell to Heaven* four times."

"Nonsense."

"You think you'll be in *True Detective*? I bet they'll have a picture of the house, and a map to where they let out Mr. Jarrett. That would really be something."

"It would be something."

"Holy smokes! Hey, the newspaper says three men were arrested in Minnesota for passing notes from the Urschel kidnapping. They call 'em 'known hoodlums,' with ties to the Saint Paul underworld. Listen. 'Detectives from both Minneapolis and Saint Paul police departments began an intensive search of gang hideouts and resorts in the Twin Cities.' Say, they are going to catch those rat bastards."

"Betty Slick."

"Well, they are, aren't they?"

"I certainly hope so."

"Why do you think gangsters from Saint Paul had to drive all this way to get you? I mean, no offense, but there's plenty of sugar daddies up there, too."

"Is that what I am?"

"Sure."

"Hand me that paper."

Charlie took it and scanned the headlines, reading the first two paragraphs and getting the idea.

"Do you still have plans to take Agent Colvin with you to the lake dance this weekend?"

"He said if I go, then he has to go as protection."

"Ten years is quite an age difference."

"If the situation was reversed. I mean, if I were the older boy, you wouldn't find trouble with it? Besides, I'm not in love. I'm not ready for that."

"I just don't want you to become upset."

"Mother of Mercy!" she said, clutching her chest. "Is this the end of Rico?"

Betty stood up from the comics she was reading and studied the colored newsprint ink that had bled all over her hands. She showed her palms and laughed, wiping them on her robe, and then turned to the table and plucked the cigar from Charlie's fingers and took a couple puffs, pacing the sunporch and blowing the smoke from the corner of her mouth.

She chewed the cigar into her molars, and said in a tough-guy voice: "You can dish it out, but you got so you can't take it no more."

"Excuse me?"

"Edward G. Robinson. The strange-looking fella in *Little Caesar*?"

"I see."

Charlie looked at the girl over the top of the newspaper headline, but the sun's reflection on the doorframe distracted him. He stared at the reflection for a good while, transfixed by that hook latched tight in its eye, holding the door firm like it always held it. A light summer wind rattled the door, but the frame held. Charlie stood and walked to it, unlatching the hook and then hooking it again, counting the paces back to his seat and rubbing his face as he crossed and recrossed his legs with nervousness.

"Uncle Charlie?"

"How did they know?"

"Are you okay?"

"How in the world did they know we were playing cards?"

"You always play cards."

"Not always."

"They saw the light."

"They knew where to find us. The door was unlocked. They didn't hesitate."

"Calm down. You want me to get Mother?"

"Call your Agent Colvin back here. Right now."

"BOSS, YOU GOT TO COME OUT OF THERE SOMETIME," HARVEY Bailey said, tapping the end of his .38 through the moon cut in the outhouse door.

"Go away. Go away, both you sonsabitches."

"I think he wants us to go away," Verne Miller said.

"I done tole the sheriff. Sheriff Faith knowed you's coming back."

"Sheriff," Harvey said. "Faith."

"You gonna strip me nekkid and put me in with ole Hoover."

"Open up," Miller said, holding the stock on the machine gun, "or I'll spray the shitter with this Thompson."

"Boss, where are George and Kathryn?" Harvey asked.

"Gone. Long gone, and they ain't comin' back."

"They called you."

"I ain't answerin' no more questions. If you boys want to unload your clip on the shitter, then I guess I'll die with my britches on my knees."

"Good Lord," Harvey said.

He walked through the dust and gravel and sat on the hood of the Buick. The heat had to be hitting damn near ninety, and what he wouldn't give to be back in the cool green of a Minnesota lake or down in that fifty-degree cavern where nude women danced with feathers barely covering their snatches. He lit a cigarette and inhaled, thinking, goddamn, he'd already sweated through two shirts that very day.

The old woman came out of the farmhouse just about that time, the screen door slamming hard behind her, and she walked to the men, yelling for them to leave Boss alone, didn't they knowed he'd been having the constipation now for a third day and if they didn't give him some peace they might just bring on the hemorrhoids.

Miller tucked the machine gun up onto his shoulder and shrugged. He walked around the shitter twice and then paused to look at the old woman, who had the same strong jaw and mean black eyes as her daughter.

"All we want to know is where they went," Harvey said. "I know they rang you up or sent a Western Union."

"They said you was coming," Ora Shannon said, dressed in a fifty-cent housecoat and curlers. "They said you'd tried to rob 'em and would come and threaten us, and, by God, I'll call Sheriff Faith."

"Then go ahead and call 'im, woman," Miller said, sneering. "What are you gonna tell him? That we're the only two looking for the most-wanted gangsters in America?"

"Lord God in heaven."

"What?" Miller asked. "You think your hands are clean?"

"You filthy hoodlums. Filthy, shit-ass men."

"I been called many things in my time," Harvey said, adjusting the brim of his hat over his eyes and checking the Bulova on his wrist. "But never 'filthy, shit-ass.' Has a nice ring."

"Go make us some chicken," Verne Miller said. "And slice up some tomatoes from your garden."

"I wouldn't open a can of dog food."

"A cool pie for dessert," Miller said.

"Don't do it, Ora," Boss said from inside the outhouse. "Don't you do it."

Verne Miller squeezed a short burst of bullets into the outhouse door. The old woman screamed. She shrieked so hard that she emptied the air from her lungs and dropped to the earth, pulling out the curlers from her hair. "God . . . God."

"God don't live in the shitter, old woman," Miller said. He rapped on the outhouse door with his knuckles and said, "You still with us, Boss?"

"You sonsabitches."

"Still with us," Harvey said, flicking the cigarette nub end over end into the dust. "Praise the Lord."

They all heard the motor before they saw the dust and were silent, studying the automobile making its way down the long, winding country road. The shithouse door squeaked open, and Boss Shannon peeked his balding white head out, sniffing the air like a scared animal, checking to see what all the calm was about.

Harvey tossed him a pack of cigarettes and then his lighter.

"Go make some chicken."

"Is that the sheriff?" Boss Shannon asked.

"No," Harvey said. "That's 'Mad Dog' Underhill and Jim Clark. And those two crazy bastards are gonna watch you, just like you and Potatoes watched Mr. Urschel. Now, let's talk about George and Kathryn again."

"She left her furs," Boss said.

"Boss!" the old woman said.

"And her jewelry," Boss said.

"Boss!"

"Well, it's true. I know she's your kinfolk, but I ain't dangling out my bits and pieces for the likes of them."

The car, a big green Lincoln, rolled to a stop, and Wilbur Underhill stepped from the driver's seat and onto the running board. The white suit and straw boater looked cartoonish on the skeletal man with the big eyes and farmer's features.

"What'd they say?" Underhill asked. Jim Clark pulled himself from the passenger door and didn't take two paces before he whipped it on out and started to relieve himself on some skittering chickens.

"Miss Ora is gonna make us a big fried-chicken dinner and then—" Harvey said.

"And then what?" Underhill said, squinting into the sun.

"Then we gonna have a little come-to-Jesus meeting."

"Did he just come out the shitter?" Underhill asked.

"That he did," Harvey Bailey said.

"Well, hell. Open the door and let it air out. I needed a commode since the state line."

THE THREE-CAR CARAVAN MADE ITS WAY NORTH WITH detectives from Dallas and Fort Worth, three government agents besides Doc White, Joe Lackey, Colvin, and Jones. One of the boys—a kid named Bryce—was promised to be a real Oklahoma sharpshooter, and, when Jones had doubted him, he'd tossed a poker chip into the air and blasted the center from it. Jones had nodded, said he'll do just fine, and they'd loaded up a little later—three hours later than Jones would've liked—and now, with the sun falling across the hills, he thought about the layout of the Shannon place and having to make their way through the gate and around the house without causing some news-papermen sympathy.

"You know they have dogs," Jones said.

He and Doc White sat in the rear of the sedan. Detective Ed Weath-erford drove.

"You told me."

"Bulldogs," Jones said.

"I never in my life saw a trick like that kid pulled today."

"He shouldn't shoot so near the hotel."

"You called 'im out, Buster."

"Yeah. I guess I did. You see the way he pulled out the poker chip? He'd been saving it, just for this type of occasion."

"They all aren't college boys with neatly parted hair," White said.

"You're one to talk about hair."

"Hell with you."

Jones watched the hills smooth down to nubs and the miles pass by so low and flat you could spot a grasshopper at a hundred feet. And he didn't like it a bit. He checked his watch, knowing the sun would be down long before they made Paradise. The sun looked like the end of a fire poker, melting across the plains. The scrub brush and mesquite flew past the window.

"Colvin tell you Urschel was flying down?" White asked.

"No."

"He wants to go with us."

"Hell."

"He said he'd furnish his own weapon. A sixteen-gauge he uses to hunt ducks."

"Why'd Colvin tell him?"

"He thought he'd put his mind at some ease," Doc White said, rolling a cigarette on his trouser leg and sealing it with his mouth. "Said he'd been a mite nervous since he come back."

"He can't go."

"That's what I told him you'd say."

"Last time I checked, Mr. Urschel didn't sign my checks."

"You don't like the timing."

"I don't think we'll fire a shot."

"But if we do?"

Jones didn't answer, just checked his timepiece and reached for the machine gun at his feet. "Let's hope they throw poker chips at us."

"You know how to shoot that thing?"

"I do."

"Just seems you were against using such a device."

"I was thinking on that. Thinking about the Indians who didn't pick up an iron and tried to fight with the bow and arrow."

"A .45 ain't a bow and arrow."

"Might as well be."

Jones pulled the gold watch from his vest again and wound the stem.

"Would you quit checking that thing?" White said.

"Stop the machine," Jones said.

Weatherford slowed the lead automobile, and Jones crawled out, stretching his legs and putting on his hat. He waited for the other men to join him on the long ribbon of highway. He took his time as they gathered, filling his pipe bowl with cherry tobacco and finding a stick along a gully. The sun was half down on the long plain and cast a long, hot wave of shimmering light on the hard-packed earth and through the dead tree branches.

Jones got down on one knee in front of the men and drew a box for the Shannon place, their barn, a pigpen, and a handful of outbuildings. He noted the direction of Armon Shannon's place and where the trouble would come from if there was trouble.

"And they have dogs," he said. "I don't know how many. But if you got to shoot 'em, shoot 'em. But I'd prefer we keep quiet and not tip our hand."

"How far?" Agent Colvin asked.

Jones looked up at the young man and then at the setting sun. He could feel the heat on his face as he smoked and studied their situation a bit, coming back to that long canyon so many years ago. The dead horses, and Rangers exposed, with only a few boulders for cover.

"Boys, we've got about twenty-six miles to go over slow roads," Jones said. "We might reach the place before dark, but even if we did I doubt we'd be able to finish the job before it got black. There's only one road into it, and that's as plain as the devil. We can't creep up on the place because it's so flat you can see an ant a mile off. The only way to get in there is just head straight in, and for that we need daylight. I've done enough shooting in my time not to want to go barging into a strange place where the odds are all on the other side. My judgment is to back off, go down to Fort Worth, and get a little sleep, then hit this place at sunrise."

21

Saturday, August 12, 1933

They waited the next morning nearly ninety minutes for Sheriff Faith and the deputies he'd promised to show. Jones walked from car to car, idling on the lone highway, clicking the timepiece open and closed in a nervous fashion, while the hands crept up to six, the sun well on its way. He didn't hesitate when he said to hell with 'em, and the caravan moved on northwest from Rhome on Texas Highway 114, passing over the railroad tracks at Boyd and motoring on through the pasture and worthless farmland till they neared the county road turnoff to the Shannon place. The morning sun shone sharp and bright into the vehicle's windshield while Jones unhitched the circular clip of the Thompson, checking the rounds of ammunition, as Doc White loaded the two thumb busters he wore from a belt rig, smoking down the last of a hand-rolled cigarette and spying the farmhouse growing in the distance.

Agent Colvin drove the automobile this morning, some kind of Ford, or perhaps a Chevrolet, and beside him in the passenger seat—much to Gus T. Jones's disliking—was Mr. Charles Urschel, holding a handsome duck-hunting shotgun with a French walnut stock, his pockets loaded down with more buckshot. The man had just had a fresh haircut, the back hairline shaved up high and tight above his earlobes, and you could see the white, untanned skin for a good inch on his thick neck, talcum powder on the collar. Jones shook his head. *Hell, what was a man to do?*

He'd been cabled at the Blackstone Hotel, where they domiciled the night before, direct from Hoover himself, that Urschel was to accompany the raiding party. Hoover said to keep him back from the action, if there were action, as a spectator, requested special by the governor of Oklahoma.

"This is gonna be like kicking over a hornet's nest, Mr. Urschel," Jones said. "And there's no telling what kind of desperadoes will be shooting their way out. So I'd ask that you stay back near the vehicles. Behind them, to be more exact."

Urschel said nothing, just watched the windshield like it was a moving picture, while the automobile wheeled past a crooked mailbox tacked to a cedar post, an open cattle gate, and zipped down a potholed road, kicking up big, thick balloons of dust and grit. The back window dulled with a brown haze so thick that Jones couldn't see the men following.

"Get within a quarter mile of that front porch, Mr. Colvin," Jones said. "Don't even draw your weapon unless you hear a shot."

The eastern skyline lit up hard and clear blue, and soft, rounded shadows fell from the columned, one-story house and lay down long across the rows of dead corn and live beans, trailing and crooking up strings tied to a dozen or so poles. Jones felt he'd stepped back a bit, with a cluttered heap of old wagons, a rusted mule plow, scythes and gears, and the spinning windmill, creaking and turning as slow as the second hand of a watch.

Colvin stopped, and killed the engine. Men piled out of cars, careful to close the doors with a light touch. With shotguns, pistols, and three machine guns, the detectives and federal agents started down Boss Shannon's gully-washed drive, shadows retreating at their feet.

That's when they heard the dog's breath and feet, and saw the little brown shape bound—almost in midair—for the men.

HARVEY BAILEY COULDN'T FALL ASLEEP EARLIER THAT night. Ma Shannon had cooked up four whole chickens, along with some mashed potatoes and slices of tomato. She'd even made a lemon icebox pie—although they'd been so famished the pie was still warm to the touch, but nice with a side of coffee and poor cigars on the front porch. Underhill and Clark had decided to sleep at Armon's shack, where he kept a stack of French naturalist magazines, and Miller slept on the Shannons' couch, smoking and listening to an orchestra from a top hotel in Dallas. Harvey found himself on the porch, lying on a cot and staring across the pasture, sweating like a son of a bitch and wishing they'd go ahead and a get some kind of word on George so he could take a decent shower and kick the dust off his shoes and this godforsaken shithole.

But the stars were electric. Being in the city, he'd forgotten just how many there were, and on a hot summer night, not a cloud in the sky, it was just the kind of blackness up there that led a man to contemplate things, where he was headed, with a few rough directions and some half-formed ideas.

And so he took the cot off the porch and made his way behind the Shannon home, far from the artificial light that spilled from a kitchen window, everyone alone and asleep, the din of the radio-signal static— already signed off for the night—sounding like an ocean's surf.

He found a spot of even ground and used both hands to hoist his bad leg up onto the cot. He lay there, staring skyward, in nothing but a pair of BVDs and black socks, and he lifted a cigarette from his pack of Chesterfields, thinking to himself that he'd once believed in the order of man and church and family and now the only order making any sense was chaos. He wondered if he could go back to the farm with his wife and boy and get back behind a mule, hang up the keys to the big cars and put the fancy suits back on the hangers, to collect dust on the shoulders. You just stand there before those teller's cages and feel your heart up in your throat, hand on the pistol, and, by damn, you feel like God.

Could you get that from planting a turnip? Were you any less a man on the other side of a banker's pen?

Harvey smoked two cigarettes. He wished for a drink, but he drifted off for a few hours without it. At first he thought it was the morning light that had woken him, but, as he turned on one elbow, he heard the automobiles from way off, knowing this was a one-way road to the Shannon place. He reached for the .38 under his pillow, hoping to see a sixteen-cylinder midnight blue Cadillac, as he stood and almost sleepwalked in the early sunlight across stones and pebbles, watching three long black cars appear and, far off, men crawling from vehicles, men in cowboy hats with guns. And the sight of them startled him, sent him scrambling back and jumping onto the porch, pain shooting from his heel up through his calf, as he woke Verne Miller, who clutched his Thompson on the old couch like a spent lover, and told him to get his crazy ass up because the G had arrived and was about to come a-calling.

Miller calmly got up and tucked his pant legs into his boots. He sat on the couch, checking the weapon's load, and placed a fresh cigarette in the corner of his mouth. With those cool blue eyes trained on Harvey Bailey, he said: "Wake the old man and woman. Go fetch Wilbur and Jim and Potatoes. And let the dogs out. Give those G-men a nice welcome."

THEY WEREN'T LIKE ANY BULLDOGS JONES HAD EVER SEEN, brown mongrels with jaw muscles as tight as walnuts, bounding—almost flying—in solid muscular leaps across the dusty ground and launching themselves at Bruce Colvin. He turned his back, careful not to fire and wake the house, but the dog caught a solid bit of his arm and chewed and tore, not letting go. Colvin spun wild and tried to knock the hound away.

Doc White leveled a bowie knife into the mongrel's back, and it yipped and fell away, skittering far off, yelping and spinning crooked, as if chasing its tail, away and wide in endless loops into the dead cornfield.

The other dog followed and grabbed hold of Gus Jones's boot, ripping and thrashing. But Jones didn't feel a thing through the thick leather as he kicked the damn beast ten feet, the animal giving a good cry before darting after the other.

Colvin ripped the material of his suit coat and bound the bloody upper arm, pulling a loose tooth from his torn flesh and gritting his own teeth, trying like hell not to flinch in front of the older men.

"Thanks," Colvin said.

White wiped the blade on his pant leg and slid it into the scabbard.

"Right outta hell," Doc said.

CHARLIE FOLLOWED THE MEN, WHO WERE SPREADING OUT from the gravel road with weapons hanging from their hands, up and over a small hill, and approaching the farmhouse from the front. There were fourteen in all, including himself, and six of them took a wide loop around the house to cover the back of the property near the barn. Guineas scattered high up and into an old oak and stared down with their small eyes, calling out in a high yell that sounded like a woman's screams. The old agent, Jones, hadn't said any more to him, even as Charlie'd crawled out of the automobile with a Browning he'd only fired once and tagged along with the agents in the high, dead grass. The old man using hand signals to send men around to side windows as he mounted the steps at first light and knocked on the door with all the confidence of a Fuller Brush salesman.

He pulled back the screen door, Charlie glancing off at a sprinting rooster, before hearing the six rifle shots from a side window, sending the old man diving from the stairs and scrambling into a gully, where five of them had found lousy cover to return fire, until the whole house was pocked with bullet holes.

"I guess they're awake," Jones said. "Kinda hopin' I could wake 'em gentle."

The old man took refuge next to Charlie and aimed his machine gun at the door, sighting for any movement in the windows. Three more rifle reports—*BLAM, BLAM, BLAM*—from a window. The men ducked, and Jones returned with a long rat-a-tat-tat from the Thompson, elegantly raking the house siding. He reached into his coat pocket for another loaded round and snicked it into the frame. The windows had all been busted out, the doorframe hung loose and crooked from a single hinge.

The guineas and chickens grew quiet. That lone black rooster sprinted back and forth across the fine dirt, too foolish to find cover.

And then there was a hard blast from the rifle and half a dozen shots from a cracking pistol. Charlie could just make out the shape of the man from the broken window, as he'd up and disappear, up and disappear, like a metal silhouette from a Midway gallery.

Charlie took careful aim, waiting for the son of a bitch to pop his head up just one more time. But as he sighted down the barrel he felt the weight of a hand pressing the gun down, and he turned to see Gus Jones, hard light refracting off his glasses, making him appear goddamn blind, or egg-eyed like Little Orphan Annie.

"They're coming out," Jones said. "Hold it."

Charlie didn't see a thing. In the silence, a hawk circled the Shannon property, taking in all the foolishness from a great height. For some reason, Charlie wanted to blow that son of a bitch out of the sky, too.

HARVEY KICKED WILBUR UNDERHILL OUT OF BED WITH THE heel of his shoe, tossed him his pants and machine gun, and told him to load up. Jim Clark was already on Armon's porch, grabbing ammunition for two .45 automatics and packing as many bullets as he could hold in his pants, slipping into his felt hat, even though he only sported an

undershirt, grinning for the gift of a morning gunfight. They'd loaded
into Harvey's Buick, Armon providing useless directions down the one-
way road, and nearly made it to old Boss Shannon's barn before the law
opened up on them, three quick bullet holes appearing out of nowhere,
random and thorough, through the windshield, cracking it as cold as ice
and sending Harvey veering, fishtailing the Buick, but then mashing the
goddamn accelerator and heading straight for the mouth of the barn.
Chickens fell under tires, feathers flying up into the air, as he braked near
the old slatted barn, crisscrossed with shafts of fine light, Underhill and
Clark already out of the machine and scampering high up into the hot
hayloft to find a good vantage point to do some shooting.

Harvey made his way into a stall with a half door and saw three men
in cowboy hats, holding rifles, take aim from atop black sedans.

"Can I get some help?" Harvey yelled up to the loft.

Underhill answered with a violent spew from the Thompson that
shook the entire government sedan, flattening tires, busting out windows, and leaving it pockmarked and sagging, the exclamation of a
busted radiator spewing steam. In the silence that followed, government
men sprinted from behind the automobile and headed for the front of
the farmhouse, right before two quick pistol shots from Jim Clark cut
down one of them at the knees, and a stream of hard chatter from "Mad
Dog" Underhill's reloaded drum kicked up the dust and grit in a trailing poof right up to the fine shoes of another federal agent, while yet
another agent took a flying leap right up and over the chest-high fence
of a hogpen.

One of the men looked to be dead.

Another crawled up and under the axles of Boss Shannon's farm
truck.

The shots continued from the front of the old, single-story farmhouse—
rifles, Thompsons, and some pistols, in a small, merry band—Harvey
knowing Miller could use some help, and maybe, just maybe, they could
get off some shots to clear a way out.

Harvey yelled for Underhill to give cover, as he hurried the best he could on that bum leg across the open chicken ground and rapped on the back door, yelling for the Shannons to open the goddamn door. He turned to see goddamn Armon right behind him, calling out for his pa.

Boss opened up, wild-eyed and sweating, crying that Harvey Bailey had brought the law to his homestead, and Harvey told the old man to put a sock in it. It was George and Kathryn that had landed these bastards on his land.

"I ain't goin' down without a fight," Boss said. "You can't just come on a man's property and start a-shootin'."

"Where's Verne?"

"He got hit."

Harvey followed a crooked trail of blood on the slatted wooden floor into a bedroom, where Miller sat with his butt against a metal bed, wrapping his shoulder with his shirt and gritting his teeth as he tied it up tight. He still held on to the machine gun, his naked upper body covered in blood and sweat, and when he moved to a busted-out window for a look-see, it was on his tail, slow and deliberate, getting a good view of the G-men, hiding like cowards behind a row of vehicles they'd moved down from the main road.

"You all right?"

"Peachy," Verne Miller said, a slight tic in his right eye.

"Wilbur cleared out three of them," Harvey said. "How many out front?"

"Eight. Maybe ten."

"Peachy."

"The Buick still out back?" Miller asked.

"Gassed up," he said. "Keys in it."

"We can't make it down the road. It's cut off."

"We can make it," Harvey said.

Miller shook his head. "What about them?"

"Who cares? Long as we get the boys."

"Young girl's pregnant."

"Where is she?"

"Totin' a pistol. She grabbed it out of my hand."

"And Ma?"

"She's shooting, too."

"Hell of a family," Harvey Bailey said. "Always wondered where Kathryn got her set of balls."

22

Nearly an hour passed, and no one had fired a shot. Colvin ran down through the gully and found Jones conferring with Doc White and Joe Lackey about setting fire to the barn, while Charlie Urschel eyed down the twin barrels of his shotgun, just waiting for one of those chickens to stick its head out. Jones gave the order to toss some kerosene lanterns into the hayloft and told Colvin to shoot down every last bastard who came running from that barn. They had one man dead, two men in some rough shape, one in a pig trough and another bleeding under a tractor. Jones studied the agent's face to make sure he understood all this but only saw the neatly parted hair and eager eyes of that young agent from back at Union Station in Kansas City. "Keep your head down. You hear me, son?"

Jones exchanged glances with Lackey.

Colvin nodded, and scurried back down in the gully to the gauntlet of bullet-filled cars blocking the road from around back of the house. Urschel remained, sighting that damn shotgun, arms starting to tremble from fatigue.

There was the sound of glass breaking, and a few minutes later they smelled and saw the smoke drifting, lazy and slow, in the hot, airless day. The gunshots started again, the rat-a-tat-tatting of the Thompson, the rapid fire of automatics. Young men yelled and returned fire. Jones told a couple detectives from Dallas to keep their eyes trained on the front porch and windows, and he ran for the barn with Detective Ed Weatherford in tow.

Bullets zinged past Jones, and he ducked behind the shithouse, the smell something awful, and Weatherford followed, falling down at his boots.

The lanky detective found his feet, brushing off his pants and grinning, having a hell of a time, as he pointed the barrel of his pistol around the old outhouse and squeezed off some shots.

"You see 'em?"

"I hear 'em," Weatherford said. "You think it's Kelly?"

"It ain't Greta Garbo."

"They got a Thompson."

"So do I."

"He ain't no expert," Weatherford said. "That's just a lie."

"You wanna test that theory?"

Weatherford grinned. "You first."

HARVEY FRIED SOME EGGS IN A BLACK SKILLET WHILE VERNE Miller counted out the rest of the ammunition on the kitchen table, divvying it all out in old coffee cans. Ma Shannon trained a shotgun out the salon window, already brought to tears over her shot-up china and brand-new RCA, while Potatoes held a .22 rifle, watching the rear of the house and the rolling black smoke coming from their barn. Boss was off somewhere, trading duties of watching the child and taking up the gun. The baby girl had run wild through the house, screaming and crying, while bullets had zipped past her in what a superstitious man might call a miracle. Somewhere in the house, he heard old Boss singing a lullaby.

"Y'all got any bacon?" Harvey asked.

"In the icebox," Potatoes said.

"I looked in the icebox."

"I guess I was thinkin' of my icebox."

"You think you could run back to the house and fetch me up a pound?"

"No, sir," Potatoes said. "Not right now. I just seen them two bank examiners run behind the shitter. What in the world are they doin' here?"

"Armon, were you dropped on your head as a youngster?" Verne Miller asked, five guns ready to go. He placed a .45 in his belt and carried the Thompson to the window beside the boy.

"Now, that's a hell of a question, Verne," Harvey said, cracking an egg into the hot skillet. He figured since they were going to be in here a while, there was no sense in starving.

"This is the greatest day of my life, fellas," Armon said. "I sure am glad my family's here to see it."

Ma Shannon turned from the busted window and spit some snuff on the floor.

"You need to get them out of here," Miller said.

"How come?"

"How come?" Miller asked, shaking his head.

Old Boss Shannon walked into the kitchen, rocking the baby girl in his arms, while the child's teenage mother thumbed bullets into her rifle and took careful aim on the law outside.

"Can you give us cover?" Harvey asked the boy.

"I'll die tryin'."

"Potatoes?"

"Yes, sir?"

"I wish you'd quit saying things like that."

THE SMOKE WAS SOMETHING TERRIBLE, AND JONES BURIED his face into his forearm as big clouds of it would scatter on past, bringing tears to his eyes, the heat tremendous. He held the Thompson's grip in his right hand and peered out again at the big barn's mouth, the flames licking up high in the loft, tearing at the walls and boiling the paint, black smoke pouring out of stalls as the timber beams started to crack and fall. A milk cow and two swaybacked horses trotted out and off into a field with heavy-hoofing steps while two black shadows appeared in the barn's mouth, loose hay sparking electricity at their feet. The men held hats across their faces and waved their arms to dispel the coils of black smoke coming through every crack in the barn.

A big crash inside the barn and out rushed a pug-nosed thug in an undershirt, firing off .45s in each hand and running for a Buick that'd been parked sideways out behind the Shannon place. His face was soot black like a minstrel-show player, and his eyes were like eggs, wide with meanness and fear.

The son of a bitch didn't get five feet before the boys opened fire on him, giving him a short pause, him spinning in a comical dance and then falling face-first into a pile of cow shit. He tried to rise up, lifting his head, but his face fell right back.

The second man appeared high in the loft, raking his Thompson back over the automobile blockade and trying to grab hold of a rope pulley. He was bone thin and wore a rumpled suit, scurrying down the rope while holding down the trigger, twirling halfway to the ground before Jones had a hell of a clear shot at the bastard, taking quick aim with a short burst of the machine gun. Maybe three bullets wasted before the man fell and rolled, foot caught up in the ropes, dangling upside down like a broken puppet.

He sprayed the Thompson a final time before it gave out and fell to the ground.

From where Jones stood, he could hear the man crying for the Lord Jesus.

"Funny how they always get religion," Ed Weatherford said.

"Come on."

Jones walked from behind the shitter, up far and around the open land between the house and the barn, while three men now covered the rear of the property. He kicked over the portly man in the undershirt. His face was covered in shit, but a quick eye on his mug told Jones they'd just brought down Jim Clark, escapee from Lansing back in May. And if logic followed . . . He turned and walked a few paces to the man hanging by a single leg and swinging back and forth. *Yep, just who he thought.*

"Hey, Mad Dog."

"Go fuck yourself."

Jones reached into his pocket and tore into the rope with a folding knife, dropping the bastard in a fallen heap, where he rolled and moaned, his teeth bright pink and red in a frozen smile at his last breath.

HARVEY HAD NEVER SEEN ANYTHING IN THE WORLD LIKE the way old Ma Shannon handled a Winchester. She'd spit some snuff and take aim. She'd squeeze off a shot and lever out the round, plugging in a fresh bullet and spitting in a steady rhythm. She turned to Harvey, who watched her in amazement, and said, "Don't just stand there. Pick up a weapon, you fool."

"Yes, ma'am."

Harvey grabbed a pistol, an old .38, and stuffed a handful of bullets into his pants pocket. Verne had changed into a fresh shirt he'd taken from Boss, the material stretched tight against his chest, with the sleeves riding halfway up his muscular forearms.

He put down the skillet of eggs and thanked Harvey.

"Don't mention it."

"If the boy covers us, you think that old Buick will ride it out?"

"You'd rather take a tractor or a cow?"

"I don't care for jail, Harv."

"Jail isn't my biggest concern."

"Potatoes, you see those fellas behind the barn?" Harvey asked.

"I want you to keep firing at them till we get the car turned around. Can you do that?"

Potatoes nodded.

"Good boy."

"You ain't gonna leave us, are you?" Boss Shannon said. "You cowards."

"They're goin' for help," Potatoes said.

"My foot," Boss said. "They're hightailin' it out. You boys just try, and them cops will shoot your insides out!"

"I'm not dying in this place," Harvey said.

"That's what a man does."

"Do I look like Davy Crockett?"

Verne Miller clutched the Thompson and held the handle to the back door. He looked to Harvey Bailey and waited a beat before snatching it open and running for the shot-up Buick, the ground under them seeming to disappear.

THE BUICK DIDN'T MAKE IT A HUNDRED FEET BEFORE THAT sharpshooting kid from the Oklahoma field office blew out two tires and the rear windshield. The machine came to a crashing stop into a heap of old wagons and mule plows, and Jones watched as two men climbed out a side door and went running into the rows of dead corn. Jones looked to Doc White and Weatherford, and they followed, Agent Colvin and the rest of the men turning to the house, where an old man with white hair and in overalls emerged from the front door, hollering, "Don't shoot," while carrying a small child. "Don't shoot, we ain't part of them."

Jones was swallowed into the rows of corn, sunlight bleeding through the brown stalks, seeing the shadow of Doc White moving by his side. Without a word, Joe Lackey had taken a couple detectives with him to run the perimeter, where the gangsters would be flushed out. But soon there was another shadow to Jones's left, and the image startled him for a moment before he realized the silent, hulking shape was Mr. Urschel.

The man was talking to himself, in such a low voice that Jones could not hear—or understand—what he was saying. But Jones suddenly became aware that Mr. Urschel had gone crazier than a shithouse rat.

The rows had been irrigated at one time, but now the earth was hard as stone, gullies dug crooked and without care, the parched cornstalks brushing against each other lighter than paper and dwarfing the noise from the farmhouse and burning barn. The air smelled acrid and burnt, more so in the heat of the day, cicadas gone wild in the trees, Jones feeling the sweat soaking his shirt and his hatband. He had to stop to clean his glasses, and, when he would stop, so would Urschel, almost in shadow of the old agent, and then they would move on deeper into the corn.

There was gunfire. Close.

And then more gunfire, men yelling.

Jones ran, trying to find his way out of the corn, but only finding more and more, turning to see he was alone now, Urschel and White gone. And now more gunfire came within the cornfield, and he turned and listened, but the shots hadn't come from one direction but from all around him. He heard feet, the breaking of stalks, and Jones ran in that direction, suddenly finding himself out of the field and running alongside of it, seeing a loose group of men running for the main road, yelling and pointing, and Jones knew that someone had gotten away.

Another shot from the field, and Jones was back inside now, back in the heat and stalks and loose, lazily planted rows, catching his breath and calling for Doc, finding his knees with his hands and mopping his face and glasses again.

He saw a form at his feet.

"Doc?"

When he looked through the lenses, he stared straight into the eyes of Detective Ed Weatherford, who lay on his back, staring crazy-eyed and widemouthed up at the sun, as if paralyzed by its power. In death, Weatherford still looked as if he was waiting for the perfect moment to speak.

Jones held the Thompson and listened. He spotted some broken stalks—broken down fresh, where the insides still showed a bit of green—and he followed the trail, a wild zigzagging, deep into the heart of the planting, to where he saw the broad, sweating back and freshly cut hair of Charles F. Urschel, leveling his 16-gauge on a man who had fallen to the ground but held himself upright on his elbows with a broad smile.

Jones walked up behind him.

"I have him, Mr. Urschel."

The man didn't answer, only breathed hard out his nose, sweat rolling down from his hair and down into his eyes, making him squint with the sting of the salt.

"I have him."

"No. No, it's not."

"Sir?"

Urschel lowered the gun and rubbed out the salt with his fists. "That's not one of 'em. Who are you?"

The man, now flat on his back, lifted his hands in a small truce, laughing a little bit. The nervous laugh of a man trying to get ahold of the situation.

"Why, Mr. Urschel, that there is Harvey Bailey," Jones said. "The gentleman bank robber."

"Jones," Bailey said. "Been a while."

Jones took off his Stetson and fanned his face. He reached down with his right hand and hoisted Harvey Bailey from the hard earth. "Harvey, if a head bobs up anywhere around here, or another shot is fired, I promise I'll cut you in two with this machine gun."

23

Wednesday, August 16, 1933

eorge was no fun at all. Here he was in the stylish Hotel Fort Des Moines—a suite, no less—with a pile of dough, a new Chevrolet with fresh plates, and two of the hottest babes outside a Hollywood lot, and still he complained about being bored outta his skull. Kathryn had picked up her gal pal Louise at the train station that morning, her carrying a hatbox in one arm and Ching-A-Wee in the other, and they'd spent the day shopping and getting their hair and nails done before coming back to see old sad-sack George, lying on the big king-size bed in his boxer shorts, holding an unlit cigar in his teeth and reading the funny papers, probably *Blondie*, because George sure thought Dagwood was a real hoot, making those tall sandwiches and singing in the bathtub. But he'd been reading the damn thing since they came back and not once had he even cracked a smile.

So what did the good wife do? She and Louise put on a little fashion show for him. Kathryn changed into a very stylish red dress with a shoulder cape, gauntlet cuffs, and a straight-as-straight skirt. Ching-A-Wee sat like a prince at George's feet, yapping and barking with approval and all, because that royal dog had class.

George just grumbled and asked how much dough they'd dropped.

Louise picked out this queer green number to model, with wide, puffy sleeves and a big fat bow at the neck. She didn't bother with the hat, only fussed over her shoes—soft, velvety slippers—turning in time to Duke Ellington on the radio.

George turned back to the funnies, cigar loose and wet, and Ching-A-Wee got pushed off the bed for licking his bare toes.

With their red lips and red nails, Kathryn and Louise were quite a matching pair, just like they'd always been in Fort Worth, ready for a night out after working a double shift at the Bon-Ton barbershop, filing nails and telling grizzled oilmen they were handsome.

George didn't bother to look up from the top fold of the paper when prodded for the next outfits, only grunted again, scratching himself and reaching to the nightstand by the big old bed to put down the cigar and take a pull of bourbon straight from the bottle, a loaded .38 nearby.

"You gonna light that thing or just play with it?" Kathryn asked.

"Yeah, Georgie," Louise said. "Don't be such a fuddy-duddy."

George folded the paper and began to fool with that new lighter he'd bought in Saint Paul, flicking it on and off, and watching the flame with the bored interest of a drunk.

"What kinda luck," Louise said. "Your grandmother dying and leaving you all this dough."

"Yeah," George said, staring over her shoulder and out the window. "Lucky me."

"How's the Bon-Ton?" George asked, not because he cared but because he felt like he had to say something.

And that was pretty damn foolish, because Louise was a hell of a looker. Big brown eyes and full lips, long muscular legs like a dancer. Some folks thought she had kind of a square jaw like a man and were taken aback by the way she talked rough and drank heavy. But that's what made Louise Louise. She was a hell of a gal. If you wanted fun, you rang up Louise.

"Tips aren't bad," Louise said. "Meet some nice fellas."

"Since when do you like men?"

"George!" Kathryn yelled from across the suite.

"And now it's a secret?"

Louise caught George's eye and smiled. George grinned at her.

And so it was like that, a little loosening of that tension that always existed between them. Ching-A-Wee wandered over to the piles of clothes and made a little nest in the silk and lace and turned around three times before lying down.

They'd only just checked into the hotel, getting in from Chicago the night before, and already the whole suite was a goddamn mess. Open champagne bottles and empty bottles of gin and bourbon. Two half-eaten plates of T-bones, fat and gristle congealing into purple and gray, making the poor doggie about go nuts, and untouched desserts they'd ordered at four in the morning, mainly just because you could order such a thing at four in the morning at the Hotel Fort Des Moines if you were staying in the presidential suite. There were newspapers from five different cities, movie-star magazines, and horse-racing tip sheets.

George didn't move from the bed. He only belched and exchanged the funnies for a new copy of *True Detective* that Kathryn had picked up for him at the cigarette stand in the lobby. She knew he was hoping to see some pictures of the Urschel job inside, but instead the issue featured "How the Sensational Boettcher Kidnapping Was Solved." She thought George was studying up on how the G nailed the bastards, but, after several minutes of her and Louise sorting through who had bought what, George looked up from the magazine, with its illustration of a startled man on the cover with a gun in his face, and said, "Do you really think you can learn to play the piano in an hour if I order this course?"

"Son of a bitch," Kathryn said, and tossed her new, spiffy hat onto the carpet.

"Says right here it's a money-back guarantee."

"Just like the course you bought on how to hypnotize folks."

"Worked on Potatoes."

"That's a true test."

George started to laugh and thumped the page with his fingers. "This company also sells rings that say 'Kiss Me, I'm Still Conscious.' Maybe I should order a couple for you gals."

"Yeah, George," Kathryn said, studying some new lines across her face in the mirror. "That'd be a hoot."

She saw Louise standing behind her, holding up the pair of black silk robes they'd bought in both fists, the ones they both adored with the white fur trim. Louise had the devil's grin on her big lips, and Kathryn smiled back, knowing just what the girl planned. And they both scurried off like a couple schoolgirls needing a smoke into that huge tiled bathroom, big enough to park a Cadillac, and they kicked off their clothes down to their silk slips, cocking their legs and tugging on thigh-high stockings and high-heeled shoes with cute little bows. Louise was less curvy than Kathryn, with a flat chest and no hips of note, but she had an athletic look, reminding Kathryn a lot of Babe Didrikson only with a much better face.

Kathryn stood shoulder to shoulder with Louise, each of them in a black satin robe, sash untied, showing off their slips—Kathryn's black and Louise's white—and then the long, tight stretch of black stockings. Kathryn jutted out her hip bone and sank a hand right onto that handle.

Louise grinned at her in the reflection.

"What are you two gonna do?" she asked.

Kathryn dabbed on a little more lipstick and then leaned into the mirror and fingered down the makeup across her left eye. "Whatta you mean?"

"Just hop from hotel to hotel?" Louise asked. "Dance till the money runs out?"

"George doesn't dance."

"Come off it, sister."

"I hadn't really thought about it."

"Looks like Georgie boy needs some action."

"Just like a kid," she said. "C'mon, let's get on with it."

Kathryn went into the room first, George still studying *True Detective*—the back pages, mind you—as she whisked shut the long draperies to block out the hard afternoon light and crawled up onto his right flank, grasping the magazine and throwing it with a flutter to the floor. Lousie wasn't far behind, hopping onto the bed with a giggle and crawling up close on George's other side.

George's mouth opened, and the wet cigar fell to his chest. "Dang it."

Louise lay on her back, the robe opening up wide, and crooked her right leg so she could dangle the other off her knee, kicking the high heel back and forth. "Nice digs," she said, looking up at the gilded fixture over the bed. "Real nice."

"Whatta you think?" Kathryn asked, nuzzling close.

"It's a little dark," George said.

"You said you're getting bored."

"I am bored," George said.

Kathryn leaned into him and kissed him full on the mouth. He didn't resist, not like George Kelly *ever* resisted.

"Why don't you tell your gal pal to take a walk?"

Kathryn gripped his throat with her strong, long fingers and pressed him down to his back, straddling his chest. Louise saddled up to her, walking on her knees, and looked down at George, shaking her head with disappointment.

"What are we gonna do with him?" Louise asked.

"Make him talk," Kathryn said. "See if he's a rat."

"You two broads are crazy," George said. "Damn, it's dark."

"Shut up, George," Kathryn said, slapping him across the mug. "Do we need to draw you a diagram?"

FEDERAL AGENTS REPLACED THE WINDOWS AND FILLED the bullet holes in the old Shannon place the best they could. And for three days they sat on the farmhouse, waiting for George and Kathryn Kelly to drive on back to the homestead and greet the old folks with their newfound loot. But going into late afternoon that Wednesday, Jones knew it wasn't going to happen. Kelly was too smart for that—now thinking of him as just Kelly, trying to figure out the man's mind-set and cunning. A sharp criminal who'd worked with Verne Miller and Bailey.

Jones walked back around the house and followed a rutted path to that big garage Kelly had constructed, his own personal rabbit hole. Inside they'd found all manner of weaponry and bullets, car parts, motor oil, and tins of gasoline. Buried deep in back, agents had also found boxes and boxes of Mrs. Kelly's private things. Fox, mink, rabbit, and monkey coats. Perhaps fifty gowns, and an entire box bulging with the lady's unmentionables—garters, slips, brassieres, and the like—smelling of the sweet lavender of the sachet packed within.

Jones knew that it was a solid plan to study on those you were hunting. From the garage constructed earlier that spring—learning details of the construction from old Boss—he knew that Kelly was an organized man, a man of detail and planning. He'd taken special care of this little rabbit hole, a place to patch up and reload if the heat had come down. But now the son of a bitch was out and on the open road to God knows where.

If the Shannons knew, they sure weren't telling. For two days Jones had sat with them in the county jail, asking questions till they'd fall out of their chairs from lack of sleep, praying to the Lord God for a sip of water. He hadn't talked to that kid Armon, aka Potatoes, for five minutes before the kid pissed his overalls.

Doc White walked through the mouth of the old garage, which was growing hot and stale with the heat and buckets of dirty oil.

"I didn't know any woman could own so many pairs of drawers," White said. "She could pick out a fresh pair for the rest of her life without ever taking to scrubbing."

He held in his hands a telegram he passed on to Jones. He read it.

"Hotel Cleveland?"

"They checked in under the name of the Shannons," White said.

"This was five days back."

"Still a trail, Buster."

Jones closed up the box he'd been searching through and walked out into the fading daylight with White. "Let's head back to Dallas. I'd like a little time with Bailey for Hoover's goddamn paperwork, but we won't get a word. Bailey's a hard ole nut."

"That son of a bitch got caught at Kelly's hideout while taking shots at us," White said. "I figure a little cooperation is in order."

"Hell, I know Bailey. I've known the bastard for about as long as I've known you. He'll say he stopped at the farm to buy some ears of corn."

"I say we go to Cleveland."

"They're not in Cleveland," Jones said.

"We can't keep the news of the raid blacked out forever. The story's gonna break."

"Once the Kellys get word, they'll go underground," Jones said. "It could take months to flush 'em."

Doc looked back at the barn and shook his head. "And all we got is a fistful of panties."

"You reckon she'll come back for 'em?"

"The drawers?"

"The Shannons."

"Everybody loves their momma," White said.

Jones mopped his face and eyes in the fading sunlight and nodded. "Keep the boys stationed here, let's see what turns up. C'mon, let's go talk to Harv."

HARVEY BAILEY KNEW FROM THE START THAT HE WAS GONNA get along just fine with the head jailer, Deputy Tom Manion. A tall, gangly sort, with a contented fat belly and a pleasant weathered laugh.

A gentleman, a genuine Spanish War hero, and, the way Harvey saw it, a fella with a price tag hanging from his nose. On Harvey's third night in the Dallas County Jail, Manion had grown comfortable enough with him to share a cup of coffee and a couple of cheap cigars, talking on the rotten state of things in the world, and how Manion figured he could do a lot better than the current sheriff, who didn't know one end of a gun from another, an elected politico with no heart.

Harvey Bailey leaned into the bunk and studied the end of his cigar. "That's the way of the world. The men who do the real work are never in charge."

"You said it, Mr. Bailey."

"Mr. Manion?"

"You can call me Tom."

"Tom, what have you heard about my affairs?"

"Well, I think that federal man from San Antonio is planning on shipping you to Oklahoma City. He said there's gonna be a big trial for you and the Shannons. He sure is an arrogant little cuss."

Harvey nodded, climbing off the bunk and walking to the narrow little barred window that looked out onto a back alley.

"I want you to know I didn't have a thing to do with that kidnapping," Harvey said, still dressed in a suit but without his tie or shoes. "They just made me the goat."

"I believe you, Mr. Bailey," Manion said. "I know of your reputation."

"I make an honest living."

Manion laughed. "Sure thing, Mr. Bailey. What's it like robbing banks?"

Harvey shrugged. "Not much different from any other job, I guess. You put a lot of work into the planning and detail. A good yegg knows the risks and the payoff."

"You get nervous?"

"Never have," Harvey said, walking toward the bunk. "Just don't have it in my nature."

"You married?"

"Yes."

"You want to talk to your wife?"

"I don't bring her into my business."

"She's kinda in it now."

"She'll be fine."

"I bet she's worried sick."

"She knows I'll be home soon."

"Doesn't look that way," Manion said. "Mr. Gus Jones has a solid case."

"I know that," Harvey said. "That's why I intend to escape."

Manion laughed. "You sure are a pistol, Mr. Bailey. I'd get worried if this wasn't the safest jail in the whole state of Texas. In case you forgot, we have you on the sixth floor. You'd have to bust through me, the jailer working the desk, make your way downstairs, and then out the front door past a whole mess of deputies. And still find yourself an escapee in downtown Dallas."

Harvey shrugged. "We'll see."

"A real pistol."

"I'd just stopped off in Paradise to rest my leg. How was I to know I'd stepped into a federal raid? George Kelly and all that mess. It's gotten to the point you don't know who to trust."

"I do appreciate the company," Manion said, leaning into the ladder-back chair and studying the one barred window. "Usually all we get is cutthroats and niggers. Only good thing about them niggers is, they sure can make music. We just got this ole boy in the other day, came into town from Mississippi and got charged for shortchanging a whore. He plays some mighty fine guitar."

"Well, bring 'im in here."

"I don't know."

"Who'll know?"

"I guess you're right," Manion said, a big smile on his face. He swatted his tired old hat against his leg as soon as he'd made up his mind and jangled the keys on his hip. "Maybe round up a nip for us, too?"

"I wouldn't complain."

"Be right back, Mr. Bailey," Manion said. "Don't go nowheres."

Bailey pointed the end of his cigar at Manion and the cell door and winked. "Don't worry. I'm six floors up, remember?"

A few minutes later, Manion returned with a rail-thin negro, wearing a thrift-store suit and carrying a battered guitar. The negro was just a kid, maybe a teenager, down in the mouth, and looked to be just rousted from his sleep.

"Play a song for us, boy," Manion said.

"What do you want to hear?"

"What songs do you know?"

"I know 'em all."

"You know 'The Wreck of Old 97'?"

"Sure, everybody knowed that."

"Play it."

The boy began to pick the guitar and sing about a cloudless morning on a mountaintop, watching the smokestack below on that old Southern railroad, and the way he twanged his voice and made the words sound pretty, Harvey could close his eyes and think he was listening to a white man. *That ole 97, the fastest train / Ever ran the Southern line.*

"What else you know?"

"'Birmingham Jail'?" the boy said.

Manion uncorked the bottle and took a sip of some bonded Tennessee whiskey and passed it on to Harvey. Pretty soon, a trusty pushing a broom was watching the men through the bars, and he smiled a big negro grin before breaking out into a jig and dancing around. Manion cracked open the door and let him in, and, man, that started it, the trusty walloping around on his brogans, slapping his knees and twirling, the negro guitarist wiping his brow and accepting a tin cup of whiskey from Manion, who was real careful not to let a negro drink from the bottle.

"You Mr. Bailey, ain't you?" asked the guitar picker.

"I am."

"I read about you in the paper," he said. "They say you the best bank robber that ever was."

"If I was that good," Harvey said, "I wouldn't be sitting here."

They finished off the bottle, and Manion tossed the trusty keys to his desk and told him to fetch up another bottle, and the boy returned a short time later. The guitar picker, who called himself R.L., launched into "That Silver-Haired Daddy of Mine" with a grin and a wink, singing that if he could only erase the lines from his face and bring back the gold in his hair.

"Goddamn, you make me feel old," Harvey said. "Sing something else."

"Been working on a little tune," R.L. said, tuning his guitar a bit, "About a 'Kind Hearted Woman.'"

"Damn, you can play, boy," Harvey said.

"Didn't come cheap."

"How you figure?"

"I sold my soul to play."

Harvey turned up the bottle and looked to Manion, yapping it up and slapping his knee, resting his hands on his fattened belly with his tin star pinned upside down on his old chest. Harvey nodded, "Every man's got his price."

The negro was halfway into the song, the trusty using his broom as a dancing partner, when Harvey heard the heavy boots on the jail floor moving closer. Manion was up, slapping his thighs and keeping time, the bottle hanging loose in his hands, and didn't turn till he heard the metallic squeak of the cell door flying open.

In the doorframe stood Gus T. Jones and another old man, carrying a six-shooter.

Jones looked at the scene, his mouth downturned like it was the sorriest goddamn thing he'd ever witnessed. He shook his head with pity for all the weakness in the world, removed his hat, and said, "I sure hope we're not interrupting anything."

———

KATHRYN WOKE UP WITH A SPLITTING HEAD AND A DRY
mouth and only vague memories of a county-line roadhouse where she and
Louise had danced on the bar, with George working out a sloppy slugfest
with two country goons. She remembered there had been a lot of laughter
and fun and a queen's share of gin, but after that most of the details were
fuzzy. She thought she recalled losing Ching-A-Wee when taking him out
for a squirt at the hotel, but she felt the dog breathing between her legs and
knew all was well, and she kicked off the covers and stumbled to the bathroom, making a cup of her hand and lifting water to her mouth.

Her skin felt like paper, and then she looked in the mirror and saw
her face was paper.

Sometime in the night she'd pulled on one of those Part-T masks that
came free with one of those Hollywood magazines, and right now she
was staring cold-eyed into the face of Jean Harlow. She peered out the
bathroom, and there sleeping in the big, rough-and-tumble bed were
George Raft and Joan Crawford.

Crawford had a big hairy leg and a bare chest. Raft was wearing a
pink slip.

She drank the water, the slivers of morning piercing her eyes as she
tore the elastic from her head, remembering patches of how it had all
been such a hoot. The three movie stars out in Des Moines, the big
bankroll in Joan Crawford's thick fingers, laughing and drinking and all
being fine till one of the country boys asked Miss Crawford if she'd like
to suck his pecker.

George didn't hesitate with the knuckle sandwich.

Prison makes a man a little edgy, Kathryn guessed.

She scooped up Ching-A-Wee and rustled at Louise's shoulder until the
eyes opened in Raft's mug and she heard, "Hey, what gives?" Louise tearing the mask from part of her face and then flipping over to face the wall.
More gin and champagne bottles, the trays of food on the carpet this time,
steak bones gnawed clean, and little piles of doo-doo by the front door.

George had thrown his dress pants over a lamp, his two-tone shoes kicked off by the bathroom.

Kathryn slinked into her feathered robe and feathered slippers and carried Chingy over to the elevator, where the nicest old man asked her, "What floor?" and she said, "The lobby," and then the old man asked her if she'd like to get dressed first. And Kathryn said she paid enough money to dress any way she pleased, and, if that didn't please the staff, then so be it.

She bummed a smoke from the doorman and let Chingy take a squirt and sniff a bit. The doorman, growing nervous with the wind fluttering up her silk robe and Kathryn not bothering a bit to pull it down, offered to bring the dog back to the suite.

Kathryn shrugged, the morning sun a real son of a bitch, and elevatored up to the top floor. All along the hallway morning papers had been laid out, all clean and neat. Kathryn scooped up the first one she saw, tripping along to the presidential suite and scratching her behind a bit, yawning and stretching, the fat paper hanging loose in the palm of her hand, above the fold declaring U.S. WARSHIPS TO PROTECT CUBANS, and then flipping on over to see KIDNAPPERS' NEST RAIDED.

And there she stopped and stood, mouth open, not even awake yet, to see a picture of her mother with Boss Shannon and dumb old Potatoes, who was fool enough to look right into the lens and smile. A smaller headline read, "Desperado 'Machine Gun' Kelly and Wife Still at Large."

"Goddamn," she said. "Goddamn."

She threw open the door to the suite, flung open the curtains, nobody stirring in the big bed until she swatted George—still looking like a fool as Joan Crawford—who shot off his ass and reached for the gun, aiming at Kathryn's heart.

"Cool it, Joan," Kathryn said, throwing the paper in his lap. "The G's got 'em. They raided the farm four days ago. They're onto us."

Louise stirred in the bed, complaining and tossing in the tangled sheets until she fell with a loud thud to the floor.

"Get dressed," Kathryn said. "Both of you."

"What gives?" Louise asked.

"We're headed back to Texas to rescue my family," Kathryn said, reaching for the pistol in George's loose hand and then prying the mask from his face until the elastic broke from his thick neck.

"What's that gonna do, Kit?" he asked, looking a lot uglier than Joan Crawford. "It's too late."

"The hell it is," she said. "You brought my kin into this and now you're gonna get 'em out."

"Me and what army?"

"I don't care how you do it," she said. "Take your pecker out of your hand and make some calls to all those hoods that you brag about knowing. Call in some favors, make some bribes. I don't give a good goddamn. Just get my momma."

"Quit your crying," George said.

"I'm not crying," Kathryn said, knowing she'd started.

A toilet flushed, and Louise came startled from the bathroom, carrying her hatbox, already dressed with her hat all crooked. "I think I'm gonna be sick," she said.

Kathryn bit into her knuckles, still holding the gun. "Son of a bitch. Son of a bitch. How'd they know?"

George didn't say a word, keeping a fat finger running over the words in the news story and then turning the page.

"I said how'd they know?" she said.

George didn't say anything for a few moments and then closed the newspaper in his lap. He looked up at Kathryn with the most confused of expressions as he asked, "Who in the hell is 'Machine Gun' Kelly?"

24

That was a hell of a thrilling conversation," Doc White said.

"You expected him to sing?" Jones asked.

"Well," White said, turning to Jones on the steps of the Dallas County Jail, "if I were in that predicament, facing that long of a stretch, I'd be open to some straight talk."

"But you're not in that predicament." Gus Jones affixed his Stetson on his head and squinted into the afternoon sun. A long shadow fell from the jail and sliced down the marble steps. "If it were you, you'd react a certain way. J. Harvey Bailey is a different breed."

"Sounds like you admire him."

"I wouldn't call it admiration, Doc. It's *understanding* the animal."

"Shit, Buster. I never knew you were so goddamn wise."

"You sure are funny today, Doc. You could be Will Rogers."

A government sedan rolled up to the curb below. The wind shooting down the long avenues and through the cracks of concrete and the glass buildings was as hot and dry as the desert. He recalled visiting Dallas twenty years back, and there wasn't a building more than a few stories tall. Now the whole center of town reached to the damn clouds, keeping all the familiar hotels and shops in shadow.

"I just think Harv is pulling our leg," White said. "Said he was only at the Shannons' place to grab some shut-eye. Who's gonna believe that?"

"He confessed he'd just robbed two banks. The man was tired. He has a bum leg."

"You believe him?"

"Now, why in the world would a man confess to robbing two banks if he hadn't?"

"To loosen the noose from the Urschel job."

"Maybe."

"When I got up, you ask him about Kansas City?"

"Shit, I forgot."

"Aw, hell, Buster. You're just trying to be contrary. In the old days, we'd just tie Bailey to a mesquite tree and set his feet on fire till he told us what we wanted to know."

"If Bailey was a weak-minded fool, I'd contemplate that. You think I forgot about those that got killed? But he's not gonna give himself up, or Miller. You could toss a rope around his neck and he'd stick to the same story."

The two men crawled into the black sedan and it pulled away, Joe Lackey turning from the front passenger seat and resting his head on his forearm. "Nothing?"

"Nope," White said. "Buster's gone soft on us."

"He confessed to working two jobs with Clark and Underhill."

"He say where in the hell's Verne Miller?" Lackey asked. He wiped a drop of sweat off his big nose with a forefinger, his face swarthy and wet under his gray felt hat.

"Said he hadn't seen Verne since he escaped from Lansing. Said they played a round of golf."

"Bullshit," Lackey said. "Two men saw Miller dart out of that corn-field. You ask him about Union Station?"

"Said he read about it in the papers."

"Bullshit."

"Well, of course it's all bullshit," Jones said. "You know, I'm getting tired of being second-guessed. I get enough of that from Mary Ann. What'd you get from the Shannons?"

"Good ole Ma sez Kathryn Kelly is a fine Christian woman who has a mental deficiency for bad men."

"And Pa?" Jones asked.

"Nothing new," Lackey said. "Same as before. Said Kelly threatened to kill him and his family if they didn't help."

"Kelly wasn't there when he picked up the gun," Jones said.

"Yeah," Lackey said, nodding. "He didn't have much of an answer for that. And says he never saw Verne Miller. Every time I mentioned Miller, I thought the old guy would piss himself."

The drive took them out of the downtown, past an old warehouse reading PERKINS DRY GOODS COMPANY, and onto the highway headed northwest to Love Field, where they'd arranged for an airplane back to Oklahoma City. They passed roadside courts, filling stations, and new Wild West highway attractions, Passion plays, and Alamo reenactments, the whole town of Dallas spilling out onto what used to be a dirt trail and now had been paved, leading to damn-near everywhere. One of the motor courts had been built in the style of an old Spanish mission, complete with tile and stucco, and it advertised authentic rooms for two dollars a night. Down Highway 77, a roadside diner advertised A MEAL LIKE MOM's for only two bits.

"You can find everything you want out here," Jones said. "Everything a man needs."

Western-wear shops. Steak houses. A billboard facing the road into town read JOBLESS MEN KEEP GOING. WE CAN'T TAKE CARE OF OUR OWN. Another billboard promised that tuberculosis was PREVENTABLE AND TREATABLE.

The driver pulled off the main highway and past a gate opening onto the tarmac. They followed a side road to a large, open hangar where a single-engine silver airplane was being fussed over by several mechanics.

Special Agent Bruce Colvin waited inside along with the young sharp-shooter from his office, Bryce. Bryce held two rifles, one in each hand. Colvin's hair was neatly greased, and he held a perfectly steamed hat in his long fingers.

Jones stood from the machine and tipped his hat to Bryce. Bryce nodded back.

"You boys ready to head home?" Jones asked.

Colvin approached and shook his head, and all five agents, including the driver, walked out onto the tarmac as the airplane sputtered to life and moved out onto the runway, the sound of the engine stopping conversation and deafening their ears.

Colvin simply handed him a postcard from the Hotel Fort Des Moines. *Some heat could be headed your way. Much cooler up north. Will wire gas money soon. Love, Sis.*

"Too late now," Jones said.

"They left in a hurry," Colvin said. "Left a bunch of clothes and receipts. And . . . dog turds."

"She brought her damn dog?"

"A Pekingese," Colvin said, and reached into his breast pocket. "According to personal papers found at her home in Fort Worth, the dog's name is Ching-A-Wee."

"Ching-A-What?"

"We got Kelly ID'd. But now he's traveling with two women. One we're pretty sure is the wife, but we're not sure."

"Never been to Des Moines," Jones said, climbing aboard the airplane.

"YOU THINK HE'LL BE SORE?"

"Who?" Kathryn asked, driving white-knuckled down Highway 69 somewhere in Oklahoma way past midnight, running that little Chevrolet—the one they switched out for the Cadillac coupe in Chicago—just as fast as that standard six would go.

"George," Louise said. "Your husband. Remember him?"

"How can I forget George?" Kathryn asked, taking the wheel in one hand and reaching for her silver cigarette case with the other. Louise flicked open the lighter and got her smoking, as she breezed through another dead town, slowing down for two quick moments to pass over some railroad tracks. "George has the loot."

Louise had begged her to stop off in Kansas City and get some sleep, but Kathryn said she wasn't gonna stop till she got to Coleman. She needed to get back to Texas, talk to Grandma, and figure out some kind of plan to spring Ora from jail, maybe Potatoes and Boss, too.

"They're gonna write songs about you two."

"Thanks for being a sister and not telling George you knew about Urschel."

"How could I forget Charles Urschel? You've been talking about the man for months. Called him your 'sugar daddy.'"

"And you'd be best served to wash that from your mind unless you want the G crawling all over your ass, too."

The highway was open and clear at this time of night, only a train heading north, the Chevrolet running side by side in the opposite direction, light from the passenger cars strobing and flicking across the women's faces. Kathryn smoked and held her right hand aloft, shaking her head at the goddamn insult of it all, seeing her mother in the papers, turning her head from the camera and being called a dirty, rotten kidnapper. The damn nerve, them using a photograph of Kathryn from when she'd been pinched on that shoplifting beef in Fort Worth. It was a hell of a bad photo, with her in a frumpy dress and not looking her best. And now the copper who'd gotten her out of that mess was dead. Poor old dearly dead Ed Weatherford. She just might break down and cry at his passing.

"You don't worry George will leave you?"

"He's right behind us."

"What makes you so sure?"

"I'm sure."

"That's some kind of faith, sister."

"It's not faith, Louise." Kathryn glanced into the rearview and saw Chingy sleeping on a feather pillow she'd stolen from the Hotel Fort Des Moines. "You know, you can train a man just like you train a dog. Only instead of biscuits, you use your snatch. It's true."

"I hear marriage neuters 'em."

"It's a reward system. All men are pussy-crazy. You know that. They can't help it. It's in their damn ape brain. Everything a man does—a real man, anyway—he does it for pussy. Think about George. Why does he take so much time dressing, shining those shoes, and fussing over his hair? You know he has his eyebrows thinned to look like Ricardo Cortez? I shit you not."

"I don't think my pussy has ever trained a man. The only thing my pussy does is get me into trouble. Sometimes my pussy just doesn't think. Bad kitty."

"Listen, we go through Dallas, I'm dropping you at the train station. I'll give you some dough to get home, and then I don't want you saying a word about any of this. You hear me? I want you to amscray from all this mess."

"Sure had a good time," Louise said. "I can't believe that hick told George to suck his peter."

"He told Joan Crawford to suck his peter."

"It was still George."

"It's all mixed up."

"You still never told me about your big plan."

"What big plan?" Kathryn asked.

"What you're gonna do with all that dough."

"I'll tell you one thing that I've promised myself for a long time. The first time I saw it mentioned in *Redbook* magazine. I'm going to that goddamn World's Fair. Everyone on God's green earth is going to be there, and I'm not going to be left out. And we're going to stay at the very top hotels, eat at the very best restaurants, and go to every single exhibit there is even if it's all scientific and boring. Did you know they have chariot races like in olden times?"

"That's fine and all, Kit. But what about after? The World's Fair ain't forever."

"Don't get pushy. You sound like George. I'm sick of that worried mind. It'll kill you."

"I'm just saying . . ."

"It's my road, sister," Kathryn said, pressing down the accelerator and passing a truck loaded down, all crooked and crazy, with chicken coops, feathers crossing over the windshield like it was snowing in August. They scattered and blew away in the hot night air.

"Sorry to hear about Albert, too."

"That's his road," Kathryn said. "He got pinched. His own fault."

"He was a swell guy."

"You screw 'im?"

"Sure," Louise said. "Didn't do much for me. But he sure enjoyed it. I felt sorry for the fella. He'd gotten all sloppy and started to cry. Said he missed his wife."

"You're bugs."

"*You're* bugs."

And they laughed. Kathryn flipping her silver cigarette case over to Louise, Louise taking a cigarette and snapping the case shut, and Kathryn telling her she was thick. She said she wanted Louise to have it.

"Come on."

"Come on, nothin'," Kathryn said. "You're my pal. We got to stick together."

"George is A-OK, Kit."

"I suppose."

"If he meets you in Texas, you better know you got yourself a good egg."

"You really think they'll write songs about us?"

"Sure."

Kathryn mashed the accelerator onto the floor.

"What kind?"

"Who knows?" Louise said, smiling. "Say, you hungry?"

"I'd like that nigger Cab Calloway to sing about me. He sounds better than any ole white man I ever heard. You ever listened to that song 'Minnie the Moocher'?"

"Watch out," Louise yelled, pointing at a pair of gleaming eyes coming up fast, and Kathryn swerved, barely missing a mangy dog with sagging old tits. Knocked up and left on the roadside to starve.

"What about magazines?"

"Of course," Louise said. "This is big. Movies, too. What you and George did is better than being famous."

"What's better than being famous?" Kathryn asked, tossing the spent cigarette into the night air, leaving her hand outside to trail and feel the wind between her fingers, nothing but Mr. Moon to keep 'em company while they headed south on 69, some kind of purpose giving her kick.

"Jean Harlow is famous," Louise said, studying the etching on her new silver cigarette case and rubbing her fingers into the initials KK. "Kit Kelly is infamous."

Kathryn didn't stop smiling until dawn broke over the city of Dallas.

HARVEY BAILEY COULD SLEEP ANYWHERE. HE'D TRAINED his mind to let all the worry and strife go, and doze off in a bed, in a car, on the ground—didn't matter much. He could be on the run, maybe an hour from a job, heart racing a bit, and still he could shut his eyes and take in a nap. You never knew when you needed your wits about you, and it was the suckers and fools who kept themselves plied with coffee or cocaine till the paranoia made them screw up, coppers seeing them trip from a mile away. He was dreaming in jail, as often he did, floating somewhere between memory and fantasy, feeling he was back with his wife and two boys, even the one who died before he could crawl. They were in Iowa on the third farm that he'd bought from his fat bootlegger's roll, where the fields were blanketed in yellow wildflowers and spindly wild onions that made the cows' milk sour but tasty. And he sat at the head of the table, covered in red-and-white oilcloth, that stretched on for miles, and he felt a lot of pride in them all being together like that, saying prayers and all, while he mashed some apple pie with the sour milk, chilled from that creek that cut straight across the land like a vein of good health.

The boy—his namesake—was cuddled into his wife's breast, and he could feel himself smile at the child, a warmth spreading into his chest, and the child turned from the wet nipple to his father, his eyes nothing but empty sockets and limitless space. A great shame flooding from his heart to his toes, knowing that he had killed the boy, backing over him in that goddamn Packard. His heart seized in his chest, and he shot up from the bunk, unable to breathe, tangled in wet sheets and holding tight on to the rails.

"Mr. Bailey."

It took a few moments for Harvey to realize he was on the sixth floor of the Dallas County Jail.

He was locked down solid and fucked ten ways to Sunday, and the thought of it gave him so much relief that he caught his breath and found his feet on concrete warmed by yesterday's sun. As he turned, he faced the negro guitar player from Mississippi, R.L., who outstretched his skinny arm with the longest fingers he'd ever seen, handing him a simple metal cup filled with water.

Harvey took it, wondering how the boy knew his mouth was so parched.

"You was dreaming."

He looked at him.

"You was running from something," R.L. said. "Your legs and arms were pumping something fierce."

"What time is it?"

"Four o'clock."

"When?"

"In the morning."

"Why'd you wake me?"

"I didn't wake you, sir," the boy said. "I was mopping the floor and seen you had some troubles."

"I don't have troubles."

"You spoke the way a grown man talks to a baby. Does that make sense?"

Harvey finished off the cold water and handed the cup back to R.L., who held on to a filthy mop matted with dirt and hair. Light spilled from the metal door down the hall, cracked enough for Bailey to see Manion sitting on his fat ass, smoking a cigar, snorting and laughing it up with a trusty.

"More," Harvey said.

R.L. disappeared back through the cracked door to stand before Manion to ask permission to fill the cup. Harvey walked to the narrow, oblong window, scratching his pecker, and held on to the bars, studying the drop and the route the alley took out into the downtown. He felt the thickness of the metal in his fingers and pushed his face through, just to catch a bit of wind but also stealing more comfort, being inside and paying for what he'd done.

"Once you sell it, you can't take it back."

The boy held the metal cup through the bars. Harvey just stared at him. "You spades always talk in riddles?"

"Your soul," R.L. said, whispering. "You sell it and it's gone. Ain't no return policy on that."

"How can you sell something you don't have?" Harvey asked. "It's all applesauce for simple folks."

"I ain't no simpleton," R.L. said. "Take the water."

The whole jail corridor was dark except for the slice cutting through the door, Manion gone from the chair now but a cloud of smoke left in his place. The boy's face bony and skeletal, big-eyed and serious. "I'm givin' you warning. You be careful for Mr. Manion. He'll rip your guts out. He's not your mark."

"What are you talking about?"

"You make a deal with that man and he'll own you."

"Go peddle your goofer dust somewhere else," Harvey said, tossing the empty cup to the floor, the clang sounding like a symphony along the concrete and metal doors. "I write my own goddamn ticket."

"I know'd an old fella once that could talk to dead folks," R.L. said. "You can say it ain't true. But he swears on it. He said they come to you when you's asleep because then you won't doubt them."

"Leave me alone, boy."

"Watch out for Mr. Manion."

"I'm gonna own that fella."

"Don't take this as disrespect," R.L. said, gripping the mop in both hands. "But I think it's in the reverse."

"Is he gonna steal my soul?"

"Seems like you done sold that long ago."

Harvey heard the skinny boy walk down the hall, the door clanging shut and locking with a final snap, reminding him of a tight cord breaking.

25

The manager of the Hotel Fort Des Moines wore one of those pencil-thin mustaches—the thinnest mustache Jones had ever seen—and smelled like he'd dunked his boiled shirt in some sweet-smelling perfume. All these characters were the same, dirt under their nails and grits in their mouth, till they slide into a suit and get a fancy title, and then they're Douglas Fairbanks. The man had protruding buckteeth, and black hair growing from his nostrils.

"We'd like to see the room," Agent Colvin said, leaning into the reception counter, seeming to take some confidence in standing next to Jones even though Colvin was at least a head taller. Colvin folded his hands on the polished wood and waited.

"The guests never checked out," the manager said. "It's still occupied. You don't have the authority—"

"Didn't I show you my tin?" Jones asked.

"I can't give you a key to a private suite," the manager said. "The Colemans are fine people."

"Give me the goddamn key," Jones said.

"Excuse me?"

"Colvin, grab the key," Jones said. "I'm tired of this horseshit."

Jones nodded to Colvin, who turned the corner of the front desk and snatched the key from the hook, the little man trying to block his escape, holding up a single finger. "You try to stop us, and I'll knock that smirk off your face," Jones said.

The agents took the stairs to the room. The hotel manager trailed like a yippy little dog at their boot heels, telling them they better stop or he'd call the police chief himself.

"I want all telephone tolls from this room and from every pay phone in this hotel," Jones said, taking off his hat and holding it at his side. "I want to interview every bellhop, doorman, and maid. Check taxicabs, restaurants, and down at the train station. Do we know what kind of car they were driving?"

"The two women left in a white Chevrolet sedan," Colvin said. "This year's model."

"What about Kelly?"

"No one saw him leave."

"Sure they did."

Colvin tried the lock with the key and pushed open the heavy oak door into the suite. Lots of newish, streamlined furniture, Oriental rugs, and the like. The hotel manager wedged himself into the threshold and stretched his arms from frame to frame, red-faced and sweating, and the sight of his struggle brought a grin to Jones's face.

"Just how much did he tip you?" Jones asked.

"Excuse me, sir?"

"Kelly."

"You mean, Mr. Coleman?"

"No, I mean Mr. Kelly, you dumb sack of nuts."

Colvin stepped over a pile of clothes and wet towels, already pulling out his leather-bound fingerprint kit to pull prints from the telephone, glasses, lamps, and doorknobs, while Jones picked up a stack of reading material on a nightstand. The *Chicago Tribune. True Detective. Spicy Stories.* On the floor, he found yesterday's *Des Moines Register* torn to pieces.

"Trouble will follow," the manager said, mopping his face with a laced handkerchief. "Trouble."

"You can't get much more trouble than having 'Machine Gun' Kelly in your presidential suite," Jones said. "Don't you read the papers?"

"I think you're confused," the man said. "Mr. Coleman wasn't a gangster. He was a gentleman farmer. They were fine people with beautiful clothes . . . Oh, my Lord."

"You sure stepped in it."

The hotel manger looked down at the carpet, all green and plush and dotted with land mines of dog shit. He lifted up a dandy heel and spun around on one leg, confused as to what to do next. He turned and twirled and about fell over, holding on to his ankle, not daring to set down the wingtip.

"Scrape it off," Jones said. "Listen, partner, you know you're lucky to be alive. You just gave domicile to the most cunning, cutthroat, evil son of a bitch in this United States of America. 'Machine Gun' Kelly gets an itchy finger and he just might shoot up your whole damn lobby and take you out in the process. Human life isn't any more to him than a fly on a cow's ass."

"Oh, my Lord."

"Now, get outta here and let us work," Jones said. "Send up those two agents in the lobby."

"Yes, sir."

"And be quick about it."

"Yes, sir."

"And scrape off your damn shoe," Jones said, stopping the man midtrack at the door's threshold. "You're dragging shit all over creation."

Doc White and Lackey came rambling on inside the suite. White said, "The ladies lit out yesterday 'bout five. Kelly right behind, took a cab to the train station."

"You get a taxi number?"

"Working on it," Lackey said, chewing gum and looking around the suite. "Nice digs."

"Those girls say where they were headed?"

"Nope," White said.

"Mrs. Kelly seemed upset, according to the bellhop," Lackey said. "He said she sure was in a hurry."

"And 'Machine Gun'?"

"Not so much," White said. "Had a couple gin cocktails in the bar before calling the taxi. He tipped the doorman twenty bucks from a roll the size of his fist. While he was waiting, he seemed to be studying things, and told the doorman, 'Don't ever get between your wife and her momma.'"

"What's that mean?" Colvin asked.

"Means she's not too keen on having Mrs. Ora Shannon in federal custody," Jones said. "Where are her people from?"

"Mississippi?" Lackey said.

"Can we send a man from the Birmingham office?"

Colvin nodded.

"Who the hell was this woman with her?" Jones asked. "I wonder if she has kin anywhere else? Doc, you take Bryce and go down to the train station. We got 'em flushed, and now—"

"Now what?" Lackey asked.

Jones walked across the suite to a large wooden dresser and stared into a large oval mirror. Across the mirror someone had written the words GO TO HELL G-MAN JONES.

In the reflection, he watched Lackey, Colvin, and White flank him, reading the words scrawled in red lipstick. Lackey popped his gum. "What the hell's a 'G-man'?"

CHARLIE URSCHEL ASKED BETTY TO TAKE THE WHEEL OF the Packard and just drive, him sitting in silence, as she wheeled around the manicured streets and wide avenues of the Heritage Hills neighborhood, until he made up his mind and told her to go ahead and turn onto North Broadway heading south, and then to cut over and down on Robinson toward the downtown and the Colcord Building, where the Slick

Company had their offices. They found an open space not far from the botanical gardens on Sheridan, and from that spot he could see the Colcord entrance and the parking garage across the street, where the son of a bitch would emerge well before five o'clock in that garish Buick sedan, painted canary yellow, with wire-spoked wheels.

"You want me to wait?" Betty asked.

"I'm waiting, too."

"What are we waiting for?"

"Mr. Jarrett."

"Does Mr. Jarrett need a ride?"

"Of sorts."

"Can I have fifty dollars?"

"What are you going to do with fifty dollars?"

"Buy a dress."

"You have two closets full of the best dresses."

"I need a new one. They're having a sale on summer dresses at Katz's. Lord, it's hot. What's for supper?"

"I don't know."

"I hope Louise makes chicken. I love chicken."

"Betty, we need to talk."

"I knew it. I knew it."

"No one else will listen," Charlie said. "Your mother thinks I should see a doctor for my nerves."

"I don't think you're nuts, Uncle Charlie."

"Then you know why you just can't trust a man of little acquaintance."

"Uncle Charlie, I'm sixteen years old. I know about men."

"No, you don't. You can never know what's in a man's heart. He'll deceive you. He'll look right into your eyes and smile while he cuts you. We can't let him win."

"Uncle Charles."

Charlie reached into the pockets of his suit and found them empty. He patted his pants and looked in the glove box. Betty sighed and reached

into her little pocketbook and gave him her matches. He had a dead cigar
in his mouth and got it going. In the side mirror of their machine—a
Packard sedan of this year's make—he stared into his bloodshot eyes and
uncombed hair and then back at the glass doors to the office, knowing
the bastard would be coming out soon, and that's when he'd grab him,
catching him off guard, and walk with him on his evening stroll back to
his home, back to the house he shared with his family, and sit down with
him, look him dead in the eye, and tell him he knew. Charlie looked at the
little mirror and wiped his cheek, as if he'd felt the wetness of a rotten kiss.

"Not all men are bad." Betty fanned herself with a loose hand, wiping
the perspiration from her lip. "You haven't even given him a chance. All
the boys I know are just that: boys. I'm so very sick of boys, Uncle Charlie."

"The nature of man is deceit."

She turned to him, slinking back into the driver's seat and staring at his
face for a long while. She shook her head and told him that his heart had
grown hard and that he had no right to stop her from her private matters.
But he heard only a bit of it, seeing Jarrett appear from a side entrance
and stroll down Robinson, walking across the street. Charlie felt his heart
hammering in his chest, his mouth dry, and felt the slickness of his hand
on the door handle.

But he did not move. His muscles had frozen.

"Deceit," Charlie said, smoking on the cigar, getting the burn to go
real quick, and stopping for a moment to pick tobacco from his tongue.
"You cannot come into a man's house, eat his food, drink his liquor, and
then stab him in the back."

Betty grew quiet and they sat in the Packard for a long while, Charlie watching the streets and spotting men he knew—friends from the
club, salesmen who dropped by his office peddling useless wares, Masons
with their secret handshakes and antique codes—walk along the familiar route. Shadows slanted, long and soft, with a hazy summer weight.

He smoked down the cigar until he felt it burning into his flesh, feeling
the ropes and chains, tasting that goddamn rusted water in his mouth.

"He did no such thing," Betty said. "He was a gentleman. He does not touch liquor."

The garish Buick rolled out of the garage and headed down Sheridan, out of sight for a moment, and Charlie reached over and mashed the starter and told Betty to just drive.

"He is a liar," Charlie said, muttering to himself. "A goddamn thief of my time."

Jarrett turned south on Gaylord, and Charlie motioned for them to follow. Jarrett doubled back on Reno, well out of the way for a man who should be returning to his family north of town, and then drove flat-out fast, heading east for miles.

The Buick dipped south on Pennsylvania into the Stockyards, and with the windows down in the summer heat you could get a good whiff of the stale hay and fetid cow shit, and Charlie figured Jarrett was about to have what they called "a meet" with some square-jawed hoodlum to divvy up money made as cowards with guns. They would play cards and drink homemade liquor and laugh about all the suckers in the world.

They could not win.

The Buick rolled on, and Betty mashed the brakes hard as a long trailer filled with cattle blocked the road, away from the holding pens, where you could hear the confused animals trying to communicate, shuffling and bumping into one another, their dumb heads sticking out of broken slats in the fence.

Charlie hit the dash and cursed, and then noticed Betty staring and apologized for his indecency.

"Drive me home."

The Packard idled.

"Betty?"

He turned to see his niece with her head in her hands, her delicate sunburned shoulders shaking. He put his hand on her small arm.

"What?"

She didn't answer, just tapped her patent leather shoe from the brake and gently touched the accelerator.

"I won't hurt him," Charlie said. "But he must know I'm not a fool. Don't ever let a man treat you as a fool."

"Bruce is a fine man. He's such a fine man."

She drove slowly for several blocks, under the shadow of a train trestle, until Exchange Street ended, and they were surrounded by a loop of railroad tracks, a turnaround for cattle cars. Charlie just stared, facing the dead end, tossing his spent cigar into some high weeds littered with the broken glass and burned oil drums of derelicts and bums, the losers of this world.

"Which one is Bruce?"

"I APPRECIATE YOU TAKING ME OUT OF THE CELL, MR. Manion."

"Figured you'd like a change of view, Mr. Bailey."

"Appreciate the coffee, too."

"I do brew a fine pot," Deputy Manion said. "Helps keep a man regular. Although I like to put away a bowl of cornflakes if I know I'm gonna drain a whole pot."

They sat across from each other on either side of Manion's old, battered wooden desk. Manion leaned back in a creaky old chair, scuffedup old boots crossed at the ankle while he smoked a thin cigarette and slurped his coffee. Behind him, Harvey saw one of those old pendulum wall clocks, swinging back and forth, marking the hour past ten at night. A trusty was mopping down the long hallways and into Harvey's old cell, the sheriff having decided to move Harvey up to the death cell on the tenth floor. The penthouse suite for the worst criminals, awaiting a hangman's noose and trying to evade a lynching.

The death cell hadn't seemed that much different from any other cell he'd ever seen. A bunk, a sink, and a commode. But the papers sure had a field day with the new home of notorious gangster Harvey Bailey, the mastermind behind the Urschel kidnapping and the Kansas City Massacre.

"So how'd you come into robbing banks, Mr. Bailey?"

"Well, Mr. Manion, I'm not going to mention any particular job."

"Of course."

"But I would say that robbing banks sure beats having a boss man."

"You said it," Tom Manion said, thumbing at a nostril and breathing in a big ole cloud of smoke. "If Sheriff Smoot knew you and I was in here chawin' the fat, I'd be the one he'd be stringin' up."

"What kind of man is Sheriff Smoot?"

"He's political. Fat-bellied and cowardly. To speak in a direct manner."

"Is there any other way?" Harvey asked.

Manion put down the coffee cup and rested his arms across his fat stomach. He yelled down the hallway to the trusty to make sure he unplugged the commode that had made such a mess.

"You must've gotten on the man's bad side," Harvey said, taking a sip of coffee, checking out the row of keys over Manion's head, already noticing the door to the stairwell had a thick lock. The only other ways down were by elevator or to jump six stories.

"No man likes to be recognized for what he is," Manion said. "He knows I know, and that's why he put me here on this shit detail."

"You ever think of running against him?"

"For sheriff?" Manion asked, and cracked a smile. "Shoot . . ."

"Why not?" Harvey said. "Seems like a man with your record against the Spanish and all your service to Dallas would be quite an asset."

"Mr. Bailey, please don't take no offense," Manion said, thumbing at his nostril again and flicking away what he'd found. "But you sure don't know how these elections work. A man don't get elected for being the most qualified. And I'll hold you right there 'cause I'm not sayin' I'm the best man for the job either. What separates any elected official is one thing you seem to know real well."

"Money."

"You are damn right, Mr. Bailey," Manion said. "You know that's what greases the ole wheels."

Harvey stubbed out his cigarette. Manion leaned his fat ass forward and tossed him the whole pack. He got out from the chair with a big heave, pulled the coffeepot from the burner, and poured Harvey another cup.

"Want some sugar?"

"No, sir."

"You don't need to be *sir*ing me yet," Manion said. "Wait till you get convicted."

"The papers already said I'm convicted. They say I killed all those men in Kansas City, too."

Manion sat back down in his creaky old chair, flipped his old boots back on the edge of the desk, and found another cigarette. Harvey noted the edge of the desk had become smooth and worn with familiar heel marks. That wall clock's second hand inched forward again in a herky-jerky jump of time.

The negro trusty walked back from the jail cells holding the wet mop, and even over the fresh scent of tobacco and coffee you could smell the toilet all over him and his wet hands and striped jail shirt and trousers. Manion looked at him and finally nodded in a haze of cigarette smoke, and watched as the negro wrung out the mop and pressed the button for the elevator.

Another sheriff's deputy rolled back the cage and let the trusty inside. The cage door snapped shut, and the elevator headed down.

"How much do you figure?" Harvey asked, leaning back into his seat.

"For what?"

"To be sheriff?"

"More 'an I got," Manion said, laughing, his belly shaking his resting hands.

"But let's say a fella wanted to throw his hat in the ring. What would you need to get started?"

"Oh, hell, I don't know."

"Your best guess."

"I don't know."

"Ten grand?"

"Ten thousand dollars?"

"I'm not talking chickens."

"And just how would a fella come into that kind of luck?" Manion asked, his lips curving into a smile. The dumb bastard not even able to fake surprise. Not in the least. He was licking his cracked lips as he spoke.

"But if he did?"

"For ten thousand dollars, I'd 'spec a man could become governor of Texas."

"I might know how to arrange something like that."

"And why would you do that for me, Mr. Bailey?"

"For the good of the community."

"Might I ask how a fella like you'd be privy to those kind of funds?"

"No, sir."

Manion nodded, standing and stretching. He put a fist to his mouth to stifle a yawn. He opened the glass face of the clock, studied the timepiece he took from his pocket, and fingered back things about five minutes. He paced and smoked. He walked down the hall, leaving Harvey for a good five minutes while inspecting the work of the trusty.

"All goddamn niggers are lazy," Manion said. "Still a mess."

He reached for the telephone on the desk and called down to have the trusty sent back up to the sixth floor.

"When's Sheriff Smoot up for reelection?" Harvey asked.

Manion sat at the end of his desk and stared at Harvey's face to the point that Harvey felt the seat had grown hot, and he shuffled a bit. He just watched the man until life and blood and thinking returned, and Manion just nodded with his thick, fat neck.

"A man could run some kind of fine campaign with that," Manion said. "Would do this community a lot of good. A lot of good."

26

Kathryn had been knocked up by a goofy, redheaded son of a preacher the summer she'd turned fourteen. A boy she hadn't given two thoughts about, but she had agreed to go with him to a nearby creek only after he'd asked her about a hundred times following those two-hour sermons. He hadn't been too bad looking 'cept for that goofy old red hair, and in Saltillo he sure had been somebody, already applying to Bible college and wearing mail-order suits on Sunday while he strolled the rows, passing the collection plate. Studying back on it, Kathryn had to admit it was the collection plate that maybe did it. The church had two of them, and they'd been gold-plated, with red velvet bottoms, and when that dumb boy would stand at the row, waiting for the change and crumpled bills—crumpled so no one knew who was being cheap or too boastful, because, if you boasted on it, the preacher told you there wasn't no reward in heaven—the boy would grin at her like her Sunday dress was made of gauze and he could see right down to her cotton panties. So here comes this lazy Sunday, sometime in the heat of the summer, just like it was now. Maybe that's why Kathryn thought of it now, sipping lemonade and smoking a cigarette on her blind grandma Coleman's porch, remembering them sneaking around the corner of the white clapboard church, cotton fields as endless as the ocean 'round them,

him handing her a Fatima cigarette, while his daddy stood on the front
steps and clasped men's hands with two of his and complimented women
on their silly, ridiculous, cheap hats, and would tear up at word of someone coming down with diphtheria or the piles.

The boy, who was only a couple years older, held the match under the
Fatima and mentioned that it was a "fine ole day for a swim" and asked
why didn't she quit being such an old scaredy-cat. *Oh, hell, how that had
done it*. Nothing could get Cleo Brooks—thinking of herself as another
person back then—all steamed up like someone telling her that she was
chicken. And so she'd shrugged, and said she just hoped he didn't drown
because she wasn't gonna take the time to save him.

"I cleared out the snakes yesterday," the boy said, his mouth opening
wide, showing teeth that now in memory seemed a great deal like old Ed
Weatherford's, and maybe that's why the detective had some familiarity
to her.

She'd eaten lunch with her parents after the service, and while they'd
gone to nap in the front bedroom she'd snuck out a back door and down
a long dirt road for a mile or so, following a trail of barbed wire to where
it had been cut to a path leading to a shaded forest filled with ancient
oaks and hickory trees. The creek breaking into a sandy bend in a wide
cut from her neighbor's pasture.

The redheaded boy was there, still dressed in the mail-order suit, tie
in his pocket and shoes knotted and hung on the root of a tree that grew
straight out over the water. He played with a stick in the sand but smiled
when he heard her swat away the limbs, leaves crunching underfoot.

"There better not be no snakes."

"I swear on it."

"And you try any funny business, boy, and I'll scream my head off."

"I swear."

She walked down a smooth path, the trees giving the whole bend a
nice stretch of cover like the top of a green circus tent. And she'd taken
off her shoes and pulled her dress up to her knees, wading into the

coolness of the creek that dipped over a rocky edge, flowing into a wide
swimming hole that she'd been coming to since she could recall. The
coldness of the water choked her breath, as she found the other side and
took a seat beside the boy on a fallen oak.

He offered her another cigarette. And they sat there and smoked until
the cigarettes were done. He just stood and walked down to the creek
edge and began to take off his suit, hanging it beside his shoes just as
natural as if he was in his own bedroom.

She knew her face must've turned red as she quickly turned away,
eyeing his pale white hide from between her laced fingers, watching him
toe at the water with his ole peter pointing up high and crooked as a wild
divining rod searching for a well. He was skinny like a mongrel dog—
she recalled that—and his ribs and stick-figure arms somewhat comical.

He immersed himself, spitting a fountain of water, and splashed and
paddled around a bit, before calling her "a scaredy ole chicken," and she
told him to shut his damn mouth, with a sly little grin.

"You turn around and close your eyes," she said. "And count to ten. I
see you peeking, and I'm going to go straight home."

"I swear on it."

"I wish you'd say something else. The more you say that, the less I
believe you."

He paddled away and started to count to fifty. Dumb ole Cleo Brooks
began to unbutton the front of her dress, getting down to her bloomers,
and pretty soon those were heaped up on a hot rock, and she jumped
on in the swimming hole, feeling that coolness around her, the relaxing
sound of the creek bubbling over that sandy bend.

The boy paddled toward her.

She paddled away.

He got close, and she turned her naked butt to him.

She found herself in a little rocky elbow hidden under a jutting mossy
boulder. The sunlight broke and scattered like ticker tape above her, and
she reached up with her long, skinny arms to hold on to the rock's point,

shaking her head and telling that boy he better find his own real estate, mister.

"Scaredy-cat."

"I ain't scared of you."

"How come you're shaking?"

"I ain't shaking."

"Scaredy-cat."

"I ain't scared."

He paddled to where he could stand and moved close, his long fingers reaching for her boobies like a fella trying to test the ripeness of fruit.

"Hey," she said.

"That's okay, sugarpie."

"That ain't how you touch a woman."

"You ain't no woman," he said. "You're a girl. And my brother tole me that a girl gets real excited when you touch her parts."

"Cut it out."

"Hold on, sugarpie."

"See how you like it," she said, laughing, and reached out and grabbed his pecker like she was trying for first prize in a tug-of-war, and the boy's eyes got real big, and he toppled over into the water, and stupid old Cleo Brooks didn't run but had to be bold and not a scaredy-cat and found herself on top of the boulder without a stitch, sunning herself from where the light broke out and warmed the stone. She rested on her elbows and closed her eyes, and figured that boy would run off with his sore pecker in his hand, but instead when she blinked in the dimming sun—thinking maybe a cloud had passed—she saw him standing over her, dripping and smiling, kneeling down and grabbing for her ankles.

"Close your eyes, sugarpie."

"I ain't your sugarpie," she said, but let him lay flat on top of her and kiss her hard on the mouth, feeling for his crooked ole pecker and mumbling things he'd probably learned in romance stories from his mama's ragged copies of *Cosmopolitan*. When he called her "darling" and "my love," she snickered, and, boy, that's when he took the chance and stuck it on in, and said, "If you don't breathe, you won't have a baby. It's true."

And so Cleo Brooks took a big breath, closed her eyes, and puffed out her cheeks, as the preacher's son rode her like he was high on an old-fashioned bicycle going down a rocky path.

The whole meeting on the rock didn't take ten seconds.

When he finished, her not feeling a thing, he crawled off her and walked over to his clothes and got dressed. Not looking at her till he knotted his tie tight at the throat. He tossed down a crumpled dollar she knew he'd stolen from the collection plate.

He shook his head and sat, saying, "You tricked me. You got the devil in you. Like all women. You tricked me."

And that was the story that all Saltillo and part of Tupelo heard as her little white belly had grown large and she'd stood before his father on the front steps of the church, the preacher not willing to dirty the sanctuary with the likes of a tricky little girl like Cleo Brooks.

She had a daughter. The dumb boy went off to Bible college.

When Ora said let's pack up and leave Mississippi, Kathryn didn't hesitate. They bundled up the baby, packed two suitcases, and got on the train to Memphis and then onto Fort Worth. She took on the name Kathryn after a fancy woman who used to tip big at the Bon-Ton after a manicure.

Kathryn finished the cigarette on blind Ma Coleman's porch, letting the wind take the ash and scatter it everywhere. She thought about how things mighta been different if she could have stayed in Saltillo, but none of the paths seemed that appealing to her.

She spotted the truck from a ways off, coming down the dirt road, kicking up the grit and the dust, and she stood from the wooden steps and walked blind, shielding the sun with her hand over her eyes until the truck stopped down by that beaten mailbox and out walked George R. Kelly, lugging two suitcases, his fine hat crushed and crooked on his head and sweat rings around his neck and dress shirt.

"Son of a bitch," he said, walking. "Son of a bitch."

Kathryn walked to meet him, not caring if her bare feet tore on the gravel, and stepped halfway up the road. "Where you been, you dumb ape?"

"You're sore at me? If that doesn't beat all."

"Yeah, I'm sore. Took you long enough."

"You and Louise took the car and ten thousand dollars."

"I told you I'd be here."

"You're sore."

"I'm sore."

George let out all his breath, slipping his hat down over his eyes. He shook his head like she was the one who'd gone plain nuts.

"We got to bury the loot."

"Grandma won't be too pleased."

"Grandma doesn't have to know," he said. "She's blind."

"She knows everything."

George shook his head, as if contemplating a hell of an arithmetic problem. "Do you at least have a drink for me?"

"YOU KNOW WHY I CALLED," CHARLIE URSCHEL SAID.

"Yes, sir," Bruce Colvin said. "We got within a few hours of catching them in Des Moines. Their coffee wasn't even cold. Their car was spotted in Buffalo. Yes, sir, we're onto them."

Charlie shook his head. "Not that."

"Yes, sir," young Bruce Colvin said. The young boy always looked spit-polished and clean, suit creased to a knife-edge. Hair neatly parted and oiled, a Phi Beta Kappa key hanging loose from a watch chain. "I see."

"Figured you hadn't had time for a proper meal."

"No, sir."

"Is your steak good?"

"Yes, sir."

"So you know what I want to discuss?"

"May I say something first?"

"Of course."

"She's a fine girl."

"Oh," Charlie said.

The young man had met Charlie at the Cattlemen's steak house right in the heart of the warehouse district, the cows so damned close it wasn't but a few minutes between them taking a breath and sizzling on your plate. He cut a fat slab off the porterhouse and pointed the end of the bloody fork at Bruce Colvin.

"You are an impressive young man," Charlie said. "I know you have the best of intentions."

"Yes, sir," Colvin said. The federal agent had yet to touch his steak, a buzzing conversation of cowboys and roughnecks all around them. A waiter stopped by the table and refilled their glasses of sweet tea and then disappeared. Colvin used his napkin to wipe some nervous sweat from his forehead. "I thought you and Mrs. Urschel might not be pleased, and there are some complications you should know about."

"Because of the ongoing legal matters."

"Yes, sir."

"Isn't this a private matter?"

"Yes, sir."

"Does Agent Jones know?"

Colvin nodded, and took a small bite of his steak. Above him loomed the head of a long-horned steer with yellow glass eyes. The eyes were as large as golf balls.

"There's been some trouble with the Shannons," Colvin said. "We might not be able to bring them back to Oklahoma City for trial."

Charlie listened and continued to chew the meat, along with the fat and gristle, remembering coming here with Tom Slick, the restaurant being one of Slick's favorites because he didn't have to rub elbows with the hucksters always trying to pick his pocket. Charlie remembered Slick sitting right here in this very booth, offering some solid advice on women, talking about one argument or another that Charlie had had with his late sister. What was that? Something about the women who gave you the worst trouble were the only ones worth having. Just what did he mean by that?

"There's a hearing tomorrow in Dallas," Colvin said. "We expect the judge to extradite, but their attorney will no doubt fight. He will appeal, and this could drag on."

"What's Agent Jones say?"

"He said he'll take care of it."

"How?" Charlie asked.

"I don't know. Agent Jones is pretty determined to bring them back."

"I don't give a good goddamn about the Shannons," Charlie said. "They treated me decent."

"They were accomplices."

"They're not to blame. They're simple and weak-minded."

"We will find the Kellys," Colvin said. "You have my word."

"They're not to blame either."

"Sir?"

"I want to tell you something, Mr. Colvin, and I want you to listen. I need you to do me a favor, and I understand it may not be easy."

"Anything, sir."

"I want you to realize this favor has nothing to do with your relations with my niece. You understand?"

"Yes, sir."

"Do you know how to tap a man's telephone line? This damn thing doesn't stop or end with the Kellys."

The boy looked as confused and mindless as the steer over his head. His blue eyes widened as he leaned in and whispered, "Who?"

Charlie looked up from his steak for a moment and then began to saw into the meat closest to the bone. "The son of a bitch who just walked through the door."

Colvin craned his head, and said, "That's Mr. Jarrett."

"That's your villain in this picture," Charlie said. He broke off a piece of toast and sopped up the blood and juices. "He lunches here every day."

"Sir?"

JONES HAD ARMON SHANNON BROUGHT TO THE LITTLE windowless room in the basement of the Dallas Courthouse. Nothing but a small table and a couple chairs, an ashtray, and a pitcher of ice water. The pitcher had started to bead up and sweat in the airless heat. Jones removed his jacket and rolled up his sleeves, exposing his hand-tooled rig and .45. He paced the room, studying on what he knew about old Potatoes's situation, until the boy was hustled in, manacled at the wrist and ankle, and seated with a firm hand.

The deputy locked the metal door behind him.

"You and George are good buddies, I suppose."

Armon said nothing.

"Your daddy says you look up to him."

Armon looked at the floor.

"Would you like some ice water?"

Nothing.

Jones poured a couple glasses and pulled up a chair near Armon. The boy just sat and sulked, not lifting his eyes.

"You're in a hell of a pickle, son," Jones said. "I don't think you need a high-dollar lawyer to explain that. You're looking at a lifetime in prison. You need me to tell you a little bit about those animals who live there?"

The boy lifted his eyes.

"'Spec not. I bet your friend Mr. Kelly might've told you a few of the highlights from when he was in Leavenworth."

"Prison can't hold 'Machine Gun' Kelly."

"'Machine Gun' Kelly. Yes, sir. Desperado hero. You think a man's a hero for holding a gun to a fella's spine and keeping him hostage? You need to get into your thick head that's just plain old-fashioned cowardice.

You need to be thinkin' about your own self. Your wife and that little girl of yours. You'll be feeble and gray before you see 'em again. A good chance that baby will be taken by the state on account of her parents being in prison."

"My wife wasn't party to this."

"How are we to know if you're not talking to us? Your daddy is a smart man. He told us a good bit, and I gave him my word that we'd make that known in court."

"I'm not a rat."

"You learn that from a Cagney picture? Hell, son, you're just a farmer. Look at the dirt under your nails."

"I won't rat on 'Machine Gun' Kelly."

"He ain't Billy the Kid."

"You want me to stand up for the bankers and oilmen?"

Jones rubbed his face, took a sip of water, and leaned back in his chair. "I came to you because I told your daddy I'd try. This is a favor, son, and it won't come 'round again. You need some plain talk and understanding of this predicament. You think Kelly and your stepsister would do the same for you?"

"I know they would."

Jones took another sip and grunted. "You want to bet?"

"Kit told me you coppers would try and buddy up. She said y'all can't breathe without telling a lie."

"I'm offering you time. You're young enough that you can still claim some of it. Your story doesn't have to go like this."

"Go to hell."

"Boy," Jones said, sadly, "that just doesn't sound right coming out of your mouth. I knew you'd be like this, and some of the fellas thought they might be able to get you to tell them where to find the Kellys by stomping the ever-living shit out of you. I told them that wasn't necessary. I figured you had a level head."

"You figured wrong."

Jones stood.

"How much they promise you?"

"They ain't paying me."

"I'd at least ask something for my child," Jones said. "Don't be foolish. You know Kathryn spent up toward two thousand dollars just on panties, shoes, and such? They're living it up. Big parties, spending sprees, booze, and high times. I bet they're laughing at the ole Shannon family."

"They'll bust us out."

"You think George is worried about you?" Jones asked, slipping into his suit jacket and reaching for his hat.

Armon looked down at his manacled legs. "Fuck you."

"Boy, those words just don't fit your mouth," Jones said. "High times. While your youngun is about to be sent to the orphanage, they're popping champagne bottles."

"They'll bust us out."

"Sure," Jones said, reaching for the door. "Did you know Kathryn doesn't even speak to her other kin? They've tried to call and write her for years, but she thinks she's too good for 'em. Just like she thinks she's too high-hat for you, Potatoes."

"That's a lie."

"I'm a trained investigator, son."

"She visits her grandma in Coleman ever since I know'd her. She loves that old woman. Stick that in your pipe, copper."

Jones knocked on the door for the deputy. The door cracked open. "You sure are a tough nut, Potatoes. I just plain give up."

27

Wednesday, August 23, 1933

Well, if the devil don't walk among us," Grandma Coleman said, spitting some snuff juice into an empty coffee can. Her hair was dyed the color of copper wire, framing a wrinkled complexion that resembled the skin on boiled milk. Sometimes Kathryn saw a bit of Ora in her grandmother, and sometimes, when the old woman grew cross, she saw a bit of herself. Mainly it was the way her cataracted eyes would gain some clarity—if only for a moment—and fix on something in her mind. Kathryn knew that look, had seen it in the mirror too many times when George would wander into the bathroom and ask her if she'd like to pull his finger or lift his leg to play a flat tuba note.

"Mornin', Ma," George said, leaning down and kissing the woman's old sagging cheek. He'd showered and shaved, put on a fresh pair of gray pants and a short-sleeved white shirt without a tie. Grandma reached up and wiped away the filth of George Kelly, sticking out her old tongue like she had a bad taste, while Kathryn read the *Dallas Morning News*: SHANNON FAMILY FACES FEDERAL JUDGE.

"How 'bout some ham and eggs?" George asked as he poured a cup of coffee.

"Scat," Ma Coleman said.

"Biscuits and gravy?" George asked, taking a sip, winking at Kathryn.

"I said shoo," the old woman said. "I could smell your brand of evil soon as you crossed the threshold. You smell of sulfur."

"Just some bay rum, Ma."

"Git your own breakfast," she said. "Shoo."

George reached on the table for Kit's silver cigarette case and fetched a Lucky, although he was a Camel man, and took a seat at the beaten table. "Can I have the funnies?"

Kathryn kept reading the front page, all about Ora, Boss, and Potatoes being in court later today and how the federal types had made a motion to extradite all three of them back to Oklahoma City, saying the outlaws had too many friends in Texas. "Son of a bitch."

"I'll give 'em back."

"What?" Kathryn said.

"The funnies. Little Orphan Annie just got caught in a scrap with these pirates yesterday, and I wanted to see how the whole mess turned out."

"George?" Kathryn said, snatching away the funnies.

"Come on, now, Kit."

"Satan!" Ma Coleman said.

"Listen, we got to bust them out."

"Annie and Sandy?"

"Quit trying to be funny," she said. "They want to take my mother back to Oklahoma. They'll hang her, George. I read they're going to make us an example for what happened to Lindbergh's baby."

"Charlie Urschel ain't no baby a' mine."

"I rebuke you," Ma Coleman said, her glazed blue, sightless eyes shut. "Protect her, Lord. Seek the Lord's forgiveness and repent."

"Jesus H. Christ," George said. "Would you shut her up?"

"I rebuke you, Satan," the woman said, slapping the rough-hewn boards of the tabletop. "Bless this sister in Jesus' name."

"Ma?" George asked. "You still got those chickens? I'd like some eggs."

"For all have sinned and come short of the glory of God."

"Sure thing, Ma," George said, slurping the hot coffee. "But can I get some eggs first? Bacon, if you got it."

"We got to get to Dallas," Kathryn said, finishing the story, reading over the last line about the kidnappers and their accomplices facing the chair. "If they take Ora out of Texas, they'll kill her."

"You want me to march into the county jail with my pistol and rescue my mother-in-law?"

"George, bring the machine gun."

"I'd be dead long before I make it inside the joint."

"Call some friends."

"Albert won't be much help."

"Call Verne Miller."

"Have you gone loony tunes? His best friend is in the slammer for something we did. Not to mention, we stole their loot. He's got cause to be upset."

"Then give it back."

"Doesn't work that way, Kit," he said. "Hell, I didn't mean to take it. How was I supposed to know Kid Cann packed all the cash together?"

"They're going to kill my mother."

"You want them to kill your husband, too? We set our path a long ways back."

Kathryn didn't speak, flipping her cigarette case from side to side.

"We got to get out of Texas," George said. "Today."

"Satan," Ma said. "The beast roams the earth as a lion, seeking whom he may devour."

"Shut up, old woman," George said. "I gotta think."

Kathryn lay back and slapped George across the mug. "You've got to do something."

"I've got to fetch up some eggs," George said, rubbing the red mark across his unshaven jaw and standing from the table. "I'm going to take a bath, eat breakfast, and then for the rest of the day I'm going to get good and stinking drunk. You can do all the thinking today."

"That's your answer?"

"I'm not going to Dallas."

"I'm going to Dallas," she said. "They need a lawyer."

"Go," George said.

"Satan," Ma Coleman said.

Kathryn tramped out of the room, the screen door swatting behind her. George wasn't but two seconds behind, Kathryn wishing he'd waited a beat so she could muster up some good sniveling tears, but to hell with it.

"We need a new machine," George said, jabbing his finger into her chest. "I'll give you a few hundred, and you go to town and buy something, anything. Nothing flashy, but reliable. We'll leave the Chevrolet here. Going to Dallas is outright lamebrained."

She nodded, pulling long on a Lucky, burning the cigarette down to nothing but ash and flicking it from her fingers.

"And we need to bury the loot."

"Here?"

"Right here," George said. "When it's safe, we can come back for it. If we get caught, it'll always be here. We take only what we'll need for a couple months."

"Ah, jeez, George," Kathryn said. "This is crummy as hell."

"You want to lose it all?"

George was gone for a few minutes and came back from Ma's old barn carrying a shovel under his arm and a fat leather grip in each meaty fist. "Kit? Go get us those thermos jugs we bought. Some big pickle jars, too, if they got the tops."

So this is how it goes, Kathryn thought, life goes back to canning your goddamn crummy crops and waiting for a rainy day. She watched George walk far into a weedy pasture, where a muddy creek was crossed by a lone willow, limbs hanging loose and breezy over the stagnant water. When she turned, Grandma Coleman had felt her way to the screen door and was staring in the direction of that lone tree, her milky blue eyes seeing nothing as she coldly spit into her coffee can.

Kathryn touched her face without thinking, wondering what it must feel like to have a face like a road map.

"WHAT ABOUT COLEMAN?" DOC WHITE ASKED.

"I sent a couple agents," Jones said. "They turn up somethin', and we'll fly back in the evening. Right now, just keep the motor running."

Jones mounted the steps of the courthouse in downtown Dallas. He removed his Stetson at the door and politely asked a bailiff where to find the Shannon hearing, the man pointing down the hall, and Jones finding the courtroom packed with newspapermen. He brushed past all the men standing in the back row and wandered down to the front, where he spotted a clerk he'd known for some time, tapping the fella on the shoulder.

"Mornin', John."

"Buster."

"Full house today."

"Don't you know it."

"What you got ahead of the Shannons?"

"Two more on the docket," the clerk said. "Shouldn't take long."

"They got counsel?"

"Fella named Sayres," he said. "Came over from Fort Worth half hour ago."

"I know him."

Jones spotted the fat-bellied attorney with the bald head huddled up with Ora and Boss, Potatoes sitting off to the side, flipping and twirling the tie on his neck like a dog with a new collar.

"He's gonna fight it, y'all movin' 'em."

"So I heard."

"What's it matter where they's tried?"

"Let's say I got reasons to distrust who's minding the jail."

The clerk nodded.

Jones leaned into the desk over the man's shoulder and whispered, "Don't burn your britches with the paperwork."

The clerk heard him but didn't say a word, and Jones walked away, back along the wooden walls, finely oiled and polished, and stood among the gaggle of newspapermen that nervously checked their watches and glanced down at the empty pages of their notebooks. He saw one of the men wore a watch with that cartoon mouse on it, and he thought these people sure were of a different ilk.

Didn't take but five minutes before the Shannons were called, and the three of them stood with roly-poly Mr. Sam Sayres of Fort Worth. The judge heard the request from the federal prosecutor to have the family extradited from the Dallas district to that of Oklahoma City, where the crime occurred, and the judge looked over his glasses at Sam Sayres, and Sam Sayres argued that the Shannons were charged with crimes that happened in Texas and would be treated fairly only by Texans. He said it was widely known in the press that the Oklahoma authorities were looking for warm bodies to convict, and this decent Texas family needed a fair shake.

The reporter with the Mickey Mouse watch snorted.

The judge looked down at the Shannons, the ragtag lot of them dressed in clothes that looked to be borrowed from an undertaker. Armon and Shannon both wore black suits from another time, with out-of-date ties, and pants that hung down, loosely pinned and sloppy at the boots. Ma Shannon wore an old gingham farm dress and a small hat with feathers and a dead canary in the crown. They all looked as solemn and sorry as sinners at a tent revival.

"Motion granted," the judge said.

Jones parted the newspapermen, walked down the center aisle, and grabbed a bailiff by the elbow, showing him his piece of tin and telling him he'd be taking custody. Another bailiff joined them, and Ma, Boss, and Armon were marched out of the courtroom through a side door and down a long hallway.

Their attorney shouted for an appeal.

The judge told him to take it up with the clerk.

"Your Honor, those agents are rushing my clients out of the court-room."

"They're within their rights," the judge said. "I just ordered their removal. If I were you, I'd hurry up and file that appeal—I can't make an order without it."

Sayres's fat ass ran to the clerk. Jones passed him before the bench.

"Hurry up, goddamnit."

"Can't do nothin' till I read 'em to make sure all's in proper form, Counselor," the clerk said.

Jones slipped on his hat, tipping the brim at the red-faced attorney shouting at the clerk.

Jones followed the armed men pushing the Shannons down court-house hallways and through concrete bowels till the Shannons were out a side door and marching toward Doc White and the idling government sedan. He held the back door to the sedan open, an armed agent sitting with the family in the back. Jones found a spot up front.

"Go," Jones said.

"You rotten son of a bitch," Boss Shannon said.

"Good to see you again, Boss," Doc White said. "Sit back and get comfortable."

"I got to pee-pee," Ora Shannon said. "I can't hold it till Oklahoma."

"Don't worry, darlin'," Jones said. "It's a short flight."

"Good Lord in heaven," Ora said. "I'm not getting on no flying machine."

"Flying machine? Darlin', this here is 1933. We call 'em 'airplanes.'"

"You'll have to shoot me dead first," Ora Shannon said. "It ain't natural."

"Natural as a crow's wings."

"Oh, pshaw."

"What you did was illegal," Boss Shannon said. "Don't think I don't understand my rights."

"Was keeping Mr. Urschel tied up like a goat legal?"

"Don't confuse a matter of the court," Boss Shannon said, crimson-faced, from the backseat.

"Don't confuse legal with what's right."

Doc White wheeled them past the front gate and onto the tarmac to the waiting airplane, a twin-engine DC-2 the director had chartered that morning. Four agents met the car and opened the doors, Jones noting two of the men carried Thompsons and the other two held shotguns.

The men pulled out Potatoes first, and he didn't give them a bit of trouble as he mounted the aircraft steps, his father in tow behind. But old Ora Shannon was the wildcat she promised, shaking her head and saying, "I've never been in one of those things in my life and I'm not goin' now."

"Suit yourself," Jones said.

He motioned for the agents, and they pulled the fighting old woman from the car, her back arching as she tried to claw at the men with man-acled wrists, until she was held under her arms and by her feet, lifted high off the ground, and taken up the ramp. She launched a final fight at the top, right at the airplane's door, thrashing and hollering, her screams drowned out by the approaching siren.

A sheriff's car had followed them from the courthouse. From the top of the stairs, Jones could see Sam Sayres in the front seat.

"Start her up," Jones said, hollering.

An agent told the pilot. Men spun the props.

Sam Sayres waddled from the official car, hollering and cussing, holding a piece of paper aloft. Jones pointed to his ear and shook his head. White walked past him and into the DC-2. Jones smiled down on the tarmac and waved good-bye just as the wind from the props knocked the papers loose from the lawyer's hands and sent them, scattering and tumbling, toward the tower.

Two minutes later they were in the air, headed back to Oklahoma City.

"GIVE ME A SIP," KATHRYN SAID.

George passed the pint of Old Schenley, straight rye whiskey.

"Bottled in bond under U.S. government supervision," Kathryn said, reading the label before uncorking the bottle.

"Makes me sad to see that."

"I know, George," Kathryn said, sliding up next to him on the edge of Ma Coleman's front porch, the old woman finally in bed, door double-locked in case George decided to get frisky. "You were a hell of a bootlegger."

"You mean it, Kit?"

"Sure."

"Better than Little Steve Anderson?"

"George?" Kathryn asked.

He snatched back the bottle of rye and took a healthy swallow.

"Don't fuck up the moment," she said.

"So that's our new chariot?"

"Best I could do."

"I said cheap," George said. "Not broke."

"The man promised she ran good."

"I haven't seen an old truck like that since I was running liquor."

"Man said those Model A's will run forever if you change the oil."

"All she has to do is get us outta Texas, and then we can ditch her."

Kathryn looked up to the beaten porch, flooded with light from a kerosene lamp, bugs swarming at its brightness, at the spades and picks, a folded-up tent, coffeepot, metal cups, and an iron skillet.

"George, I'm sorry," she said. "I can't go to Mexico. They got my mother."

"If we stay," George said, knocking back more rye, "they'll hang us. That doesn't do anyone any good."

"I 'spec not."

"You can bring Chingy," he said. His eyes had grown bloodshot and his face flushed.

"Sam Sayres wants a thousand dollars."

"Don't you dare wire that money," George said. "You think the G isn't watching his office now?"

"We got to get it to him personal," she said. "I called him today from in town. He walked around the corner and caught the telephone at some café. He says he'll meet me *if* I bring the cash. Said they got Boss and Ora real good, and that they have nothing short of a lynch mob waiting for them in O.K. City."

"Anyone you trust to deliver the dough?"

"Louise."

"You call her?"

"Couldn't find her."

"Go figure." George nodded, and passed back the rye. "Say, why does your grandma hate me so much?"

"She thinks you're leading me down the primrose path to hell."

"Ain't it fun?"

"It was." Kathryn took a swallow and made a sour face. "That's some tough stuff, George."

"Fresh out of champagne," he said. "Say, how 'bout you and me and the pooch head back to Chicago? We'll be protected. Safe. I know some joints where no white man will set foot. Only go out at night, lay low, till somethin' knocks us off the front page and we go back to being Joes."

"You don't get it? Our pictures are in every paper in the country."

"Oh, hell. Haven't you ever been to a party and thought you'd seen some bastard who's famous, but then you start thinking that you're a little loony 'cause the fella is shorter or has different-colored hair or something. That's all we need—a little change in style."

"What can you do to your hair?"

"Go blond."

"That mug doesn't go blond."

"Come on," George said. "You want to go to the Fair. We'll take enough of the loot to have some good times and lay low. Get drunk, lie around in our underwear, and read the funnies for a few months. I know this ole bootlegger up there who's on the square. He owes me from Memphis. They call him 'Silk Hat' Harry."

"Only if we get the dough to Sayres," she said. "He'll drop their case if he doesn't get paid."

"Shit, just give him that new Chevrolet," he said. "That'll keep 'im happy for a while."

George finished off the rye and tossed the bottle far out in the weeds, before leaning back on the porch planks and staring up at the bugs gathering around the lantern. He reached out, pawing at them, trying to touch the light that was too far away. "You're gonna get us killed with that ole hard head."

She didn't speak. She could think of nothing to say.

"Did I ever tell you what Jarrett wanted for fingering Urschel?" he asked.

"Figured the couple grand you took off the top from Albert."

"That was for two cars we ditched," George said. "And gas and the Coca-Cola we bought Urschel."

"So what'd you pay 'im?"

"Not a cent."

"You're off your nut."

"You don't unnerstand, Kit. He said the pleasure was all his, to finger a rotten bastard like Mr. Charles F. Urschel."

"How come?"

"I didn't ask and I don't want to know."

CHARLIE HADN'T SLEPT MUCH IN THE THREE WEEKS SINCE he'd been turned loose. Each night he found himself returning to his sunporch, taking in a cold drink or a hot cup of coffee, always a cigar, and replaying every hand of that bridge game. He'd study on it until the sun would come up, and then he'd return to the kitchen, where he'd greet the federal agents, who sat in cars and walked the perimeter to babysit the Urschel house. But Charlie didn't think much about those sonsabitches coming back. They got what they needed and were long gone by now. They were just a set of rusted parts: knobs and pins, gears and springs. He only wanted to know who wound them.

Agent Colvin walked into the dark porch. No moon tonight. You could hear the crickets and mosquitoes hitting the screens.

Charlie sat alone in a far chair, far enough that even if there had been moonlight he couldn't be seen. He drew on the cigar and didn't say anything, dressed in a bathrobe he'd worn all day, refusing to eat or bathe for the last week.

"We got the Shannons locked up tight."

Colvin stood a fair distance away from Charlie's dark corner, as if he'd catch some dreaded flu.

Charlie smoked and nodded. The boy wore a nice double-breasted blue suit, hat in hand, and, strangely enough, looked to be carrying a gun. Charlie'd never noticed a gun.

"Agent Jones figured they'd be safer in the city. There was some concern of an escape in Dallas."

"Did I show you the latch?" Charlie asked.

"Yes, sir."

"And you thought no more of it?"

"We've made inquiries into Mr. Jarrett's business dealings."

"Any horse's ass can get the key to the city."

"We're still checking, sir."

"I want him arrested," Charlie said, the idea sounding ridiculous and hollow coming from his own mouth. "Or questioned, or whatever the federal police do."

"We don't have anything."

"How did those men know to find me on the back porch?"

"Perhaps the light was on."

"They had no hesitation," he said. "Jarrett unlocked the screen during our game. They had arrived from the front. I never leave the back door unlatched."

"Yes, sir."

"You think I've gone off my rocker?"

"No, sir."

"Timing."

The men didn't speak for a while. Colvin found a chair close to Charlie and asked if it was all right to take a seat.

"Sir, I'd like to take Miss Betty for a soda tomorrow evening after supper," he said, face half shadowed, swatting away a bug that had flown through a crack. "But only if you and Miss Berenice approve."

"Of course," Charlie said, smashing his cigar in an empty coffee cup.

"Agent Jones is very good," Colvin said. "He thinks the Kellys may have returned to Texas."

"That would be foolish."

"Kelly's wife has people there."

"I bet they're halfway to South America, laughing at us all."

"I don't think they're laughing."

"You play cards, Agent Colvin?"

"I do."

"Bridge?"

"No, sir."

"Jarrett cheats."

Colvin nodded.

"He hesitates before pulling a card."

"I don't follow."

"Let's say the player on your right leads with a queen of hearts. And then when it comes to your turn, you have a king, and you're pretty damn sure your partner has the ace. You might hesitate, and toss out a three instead of a king. That way, your partner knows he can take the trick with the ace and lead a low heart back to your king. Does that make sense?"

"Yes, sir."

"Jarrett hesitates like a son of a bitch," he said. "He knew I'd spotted him, yet he continued."

"He didn't change his game?"

"No."

"So what do you do?"

"Confront him."

"So he won't cheat again?"

"Exactly," Charlie said. "A liar must be confronted or he'll continue to rub your nose in his stink."

"Sir?"

"I've invited the Jarretts over Saturday night to play a few rubbers," Charlie said. "I'd like you to be my partner."

28

Shackled at the hands and feet, Harvey wasn't too pleased when Deputy Tom Manion punched the STOP button on the elevator somewhere between the third and fourth floors. He'd grown used to being left alone on the tenth floor, learning he'd been moved to the death cell on account of Special Agent Gus Jones witnessing that little buck-dancing party and complaining to Sheriff Smoot. Stopping partway up on the ride wasn't a good sign. The manacles kept Harvey from even being able to adjust his balls, let alone defend himself. He looked over at Manion and asked, "You forget your blackjack?"

"If you're lying to me, I won't need no rubber hose, fella," Manion said in that countrified, hoarse voice. "What you said the other night, about the money, is it true?"

"Sure, it's true."

"Ten thousand."

"That's what I said."

"How can you get it to me?"

"I can get two grand to you by tomorrow," Harvey said. "The rest will come once I'm freed."

Manion licked his lips and hitched up his pants, using his fancy silver belt buckle.

"This ain't gonna be no cakewalk."

"Didn't expect it to be."

"And if you don't pay up what you owe, so help me Jesus, I'll track you to the corners of this here earth."

"Wouldn't expect anything less, Tom."

"You're gonna be in the death cell," Manion said, biting a cheek, shaking his head. "That's the durned part of all of it."

"Can you move me back downstairs?"

"I'm the one who suggested it."

"It's like a tiger's cage," Bailey said. "Houdini couldn't break out."

"There's a ledge."

"With a barred window."

"And if you get out of that there window, you can shimmy out to the ledge and get to the stairs on the roof."

"You got a blowtorch?"

"I'll get you a file," Manion said, not looking at Harvey, keeping his eyes on the numbers, the stagnant dial marking the floors. "You worry about that money."

"I'll have to make some calls."

Manion nodded. "Figured you wouldn't pull it out your ass."

"The rest of it when I'm free of this shithole."

"This is a brand-new jail."

"And soon it will be your kingdom."

"You really think I could be sheriff?"

"Sheriff?" Harvey said, catching Manion's eye and winking. "Thought you had your sights on the governor's mansion."

"I always ride just one horse at a time."

"May take a couple days."

"Them federal men want you up in Oklahoma City something fierce, already moved the Shannons. The sonsabitches complained about our ability to keep you locked up."

"The nerve."

"Couple days, huh?"

"Yep."

"If I were you, I'd set my mind on Monday."

"Why Monday?"

"It's Labor Day, hadn't you heard? Every deputy in the department asked for time off."

"I'll need a gun, too."

Manion reached over and hit the on button, the elevator jerking hard up out of the still space, knocking Harvey off balance, and heading up to the tenth floor and the death cell. Manion didn't say anything till they stopped and the door slid open to a hollow and silent floor, wind whistling around the building. "I like a man who knows what he wants."

"We got a deal?" Harvey asked.

"Long's as you understand the terms."

KATHRYN BANGED THE EARPIECE AGAINST THE PAY TELE-phone a half dozen times before hanging up, snatching up some loose dimes into a fist, and walking back to the drugstore counter. She saddled up on a revolving stool and ordered a Dr Pepper float, raking dimes back into her purse, and looked at herself in the old-fashioned mirror, deciding the red wig didn't look half bad, even if the frock was something she bought off the rack at the five-and-dime.

Coleman. She hadn't been in this town for years and didn't expect anyone to remember the gangly little teenager who moved there with Ora, the one with the baby on the tit at those church suppers and revival picnics. Ora's little girl. Ma Coleman's granddaughter, who'd gotten in so much trouble in Mississippi she had to move to Texas for a little reformation. If she recalled, which she didn't care to do, there had been an old hotel not two blocks right from where she sat, where she'd first caught the eye of traveling salesmen, who would open up their wallets and buy her flowers, Kathryn having to explain to them that roses smelled real nice but only jewelry got the drawers on the lampshade.

But even her sweet voice hadn't moved old Sam Sayres, attorney at law, on the telephone. She'd used her breathless voice, trying to play sexy with him a bit, the bastard acting coy, like he didn't know who she was when she called herself "his best girlfriend." "And which one is that?" Sam Sayres asked. "The one with the Pekingese dog," she'd said.

He'd asked for her number and said he'd call her back.

A half hour later the pay phone in the drugstore had rung, and there was Sam chewing her ass out for being so almighty stupid as to call him at his practice, and Kathryn saying, "Where am I supposed to call, your barber?" And then regretting it because besides being a fat tub of shit, Sam Sayres was as bald as a cue ball.

"You got to get up to O.K. City, Sam," she'd said. "Today."

"A trial like this costs money, darling," he said, not flirting but talking down to her like she was still that teenager combing the hotels for sugar daddies.

"I don't care about Boss or Potatoes," she said. "They can get corn-holed in the showers, for all I care. But you said you'd take care of my momma."

"You haven't delivered what you promised," Sam had said, finishing it off with "darling." His voice scratchy and strained over the wire all the way from Fort Worth.

"I said you'll get it."

"I don't travel without a full tank of gas."

"I said you got it," Kathryn said, trying not to scream over the phone, knowing the way she felt she could probably make him hear her without the benefit of Ma Bell.

"Sweet cakes, you're as hot as a two-dollar pistol."

"And you're as stand-up as a nickel whore."

"There's plenty of lawyers in this state. I don't know why you always got to call on me."

"Sam? Sam? Don't hang up."

"Don't call my office again."

"How about a brand-new Chevrolet?"

"I won't hold my breath," he'd said, and there was a click, and the operator came on again and asked if she'd like to make another call. And that's when she had started hammering the earpiece on the phone. *Shit, shit, shit.*

She turned around on the stool and drank her float.

When Kathryn looked back at the mirror, she noticed the red wig had gone a little crazy and cocked on her head. She dipped her head down to the straw, eyeing around the counter at the soda jerk refilling the bins of candy and bubble gum, and twisted it a little more to the left.

On the counter, she saw a single dime she'd dropped and decided to call her uncle in town, Uncle Cass, who was a decent old guy and could be trusted to take some of the loot to Fort Worth. He picked up right quick, but before she could get into the pitch of what she needed old Cass whispered into the phone, "I can't talk right now, Preacher. I got some government man over here asking me some questions."

She hung up and raced outside, the bell jingling behind her, out to the old Model A truck, cranking and cranking till it sputtered to a start, winding through downtown Coleman to the dirt highway that would take her back to her grandmamma and George, thinking that maybe she should head the opposite way, out of Texas and away from George, and then remembering those pickle jars and thermoses under the willow and thinking, *Goddamn, this is what you call an ethical dilemma.*

"Where's George?" she yelled to the old woman rocking on the front porch. "Where is he?"

"Sister, let's pray."

"Keep your prayers. Where is he?"

"He has befouled you, my love. Let me touch your face."

Kathryn ran up the steps, looking behind her at the twisting road leading back to the empty highway and then over to that lonely willow by the muddy creek, waiting for a flock of cars to come speeding on down the road any minute, the G-men filing out with their guns at the ready. Son of a bitch. The goddamn G was making her bugs.

"Where did he go?"

All across the old porch were empty bottles of rye and bourbon and gin. The old woman completely unaware of the sin at her feet.

"There is a revival at the river on Sunday," she said. "I want you to go. There is a boy, not even six, who has been blessed with the healing touch."

"Goddamn you and your empty foolishness," Kathryn screamed at the sightless, cataracted blue eyes. "Where is my husband?"

Ma Coleman stopped rocking. The wind crossed her porch and made whistling sounds in the empty bottles.

She spoke light and low, reaching into her cheap, nasty, moth-eaten housecoat—silly sunflowers across her sagging tits and rump—and pulled out a crumpled piece of paper. "This," she said, her lip quivering. "This."

George had written, in that stupid, childish scrawl, a single word: MIS-SISSIPPI.

"Damn fool," Kathryn said.

She was packed within five minutes, George being smart enough to leave the new Chevrolet to pay off Sayres, instead borrowing some old car, maybe even worse than the Model A she'd have to drive. She kissed the old woman on the cheek and bounded down the crooked old stairs, yelling back, "Don't take any plug nickels, Granny."

THEY PLAYED POKER, FIGURING IT WAS MUCH BETTER suited to four men sitting around on a Saturday night, knowing that bridge was a couples' sport. Charlie had invited Bruce Colvin, E. E. Kirkpatrick, and Walter Jarrett to the table. The servants had been given the night off, Betty making sure the men had ice in their whiskey and kitchen matches nearby for their cigars. Jarrett asked if they might sit inside because of the heat, but Charlie insisted on the sunporch, the sunporch being the place where he'd played out the game in his head a thousand times.

And yet Jarrett hadn't cheated on a single hand. The gold teeth in the back of his mouth fascinated Charlie every time Jarrett smiled with his winnings, raking in the chips and laughing it up with that hick accent. Colvin not a damn bit of help, frequently excusing himself to go to the bathroom or fetch more ice or any damn thing to speak to Betty some more.

Only Kirk, who sat to his right, seemed to take a serious interest in Jarrett. And now that Jarrett was knee-walking drunk, they didn't have to be so damn furtive about it. Kirkpatrick excused himself from the table as had been arranged, only the two men left in the haze of squashed cigars, eyes glazed with bourbon.

"I wish that SOB Kelly would try to come back on this porch now," Charlie said, reaching behind him and placing a revolver on the table.

"Nice-looking gun."

"I'd shoot him right between the eyes."

Jarrett just sat there, short-sleeved white shirt all wrinkled on his shapeless form. He played with the cards, running them through his hands, laughing at tricks he'd seen cardsharps work but was unable to perform himself. He cut the deck of cards and tried a fancy shuffle that broke and scattered across his lap and onto the floor.

"You're putting me on," Charlie said. "All that time in the fields, and you can't shuffle better than that?"

"I can't help my winnings, Charlie. Don't be a sore loser."

Charlie smiled, just a little. He reached for his cigar that had burned down a three-inch ash. He tipped off the ash and smoked for a few moments while he watched Jarrett pour a fat helping of liquor and settle into the chair, watching bugs that had collected in a ceiling light.

"You think much about it?"

"'Bout what?"

"Mickey Mouse," Charlie said. "Hell, Kelly. What do you think? What else is there to think about?"

Jarrett turned away from the ceiling and tried to focus on Charlie's face. He lost interest, and leaned into the table to count his money into a sloppy little pile. "I guess I better be goin'."

"Funny how Kelly knew we were here," Charlie said, feeling control for the first time since those bastards had stepped across his threshold. "Funny how they didn't try to snatch me anywhere else."

"I wouldn't call it funny," Jarrett said, pushing back his chair and standing.

"Sit back down."

"Excuse me?"

"Finish your drink."

Charlie reached over and poured out two fingers into his own crystal glass and topped off Jarrett's. "You didn't think it was strange that the back door was unlocked?"

"I never gave it any thought, Charlie," Jarrett said. "Say, what are you gettin' at?"

"If you needed money so bad, why didn't you come to me for a loan?"

"Good night, Charlie."

"You set the game," Charlie said. "You made sure Berenice and I sat here like ducks for that gangster."

"You're drunk."

"You unlatched the back door when my back was turned."

Jarrett reached for the deck of cards, shuffled them out smoothly, reaching for them and sifting through with expert, practiced fingers. He looked up only with his eyes and gave a drunken smile. "Prove it."

Charlie opened his mouth but couldn't find the words.

"You think I sold you out to a couple gangsters?" Jarrett asked. "Then go call Mr. Colvin away from sweet-talking Betty. Go on and lay out what you know—*A back door unlocked? That we invited ourselves over?* You and your fancy wife may find that bad etiquette, but that isn't a criminal case."

"I know it was you."

"I bet."

"I just can't figure out why."

"You got a lot of windows in this house," Jarrett said. "Lots of glass."

"Are you passing out a morality lesson?"

Jarrett reached for the loose bills and silver dollars. The table still littered with sandwich plates and ashtrays, empty beer bottles and fine whiskey glasses.

"How long have you known me?" Jarrett asked.

"You don't recall?" Charlie asked, rubbing his temples with his hands.

"When?"

"Back to Seminole."

"Biggest oil field ever discovered," Jarrett said. "Made Tom Slick one of the richest men in this country."

Charlie nodded, holding the plug of the cigar and waiting, knowing where this was headed, feeling the heat swell in his face.

"You tried to buy my land."

"I made you a fair offer," Charlie said. "Don't turn this back on me."

"I made a fair counter," Jarrett said. "You remember."

Charlie didn't say anything.

"I can't recollect, but I seem to remember I wanted two hundred thousand, an honest price for property that'd later produce nine hundred barrels a day."

Charlie pulled on the cigar. He reached for the edge of the table.

"Thought you wanted me to stay awhile."

"Good night, Walter."

"But you didn't pay me," Jarrett said, getting to his feet. He walked to a sideboard, where his hat had become wet from melting ice. "You just bought up the property next to mine."

"Perfectly legal."

"And you siphoned every drop while I was hustling to buy equipment."

"Do you know how many leases Tom Slick and I worked? How can I recall one deal?"

Jarrett headed for the back door of the sunporch and grinned, stopping to savor the moment, as he fingered the lock open. "Yep, I guess that would be awfully hard to prove in court. I guess that's what you learned men would call 'a conundrum.'"

Charlie Urschel sat back down and listened for Jarrett's car pulling away on the same route Kelly took, sitting there in the midnight silence until the cigar started to singe his fingers.

29

Sunday, September 3, 1933

Kathryn drove straight to Biloxi and then right back around to Texas in that old Model A truck, her ass flying up and off the seat, shifting those crazy, rusted gears all the way across on Highway 80, west through New Orleans and Lafayette, Lake Charles, and over the state line into Beaumont, before cutting up Highway 6 to Navasota, College Station, and Marlin, where she nearly dozed off at the wheel, hitting the clutch, sputtering, and killing the engine, and then starting off again, limping that hunk of junk up to Waco, way past midnight, with a leaking radiator and a shot of gas. She had to drive a mile and then cool down, drive and cool down, that hose spitting and spewing, before finding the Waco Hilton, an oasis in the Texas night. She parked that flatbed truck, shuddering and creaking and steaming, at the front door, and snatched her leather grip, knowing she looked like a damn sight to the bellhop, in her damp red wig and sweat-ringed gingham. The boy stared at her openmouthed as she asked the manager to be right quick in getting her to the finest room they had.

She'd taken a bath and ordered up a steak, baked potato, and Jell-O

salad with a couple bottles of ice-cold Shiner Bock. She didn't wake up
the next day till way past one o'clock, having pulled the shades tight,
and would've slept later if that nigger maid hadn't made all that fuss
about wanting to bring her up some towels and fresh bleached sheets.
Oh, Lawdy, miss. Oh, Lawdy. She paid for the room in cash, got the hose
fixed at a Sinclair Oil station, and headed on up 171 through Hillsboro
to Cleburne, where the goddamn hose—the new one—busted again,
spewing up clouds of steam, the engine running hellfire hot, limping
on—*Another mile to go, another mile to go*—till she saw the billboard for
another filling station, this one a Texaco that promised to sell WESTERN
GIFTS AND NOVELTIES while they checked your engine.

Goddamn George. Goddamn Sam Sayres.

Goddamn all men.

The three miles to that Texaco might've been a million. Kathryn was
more sure than ever that George had found that pretty blond lifeguard—
the one who he'd said resembled a mermaid—and run off to Miami or,
worse yet, headed back to Coleman to harvest their loot and split the country like he always wanted. Either way, brother, she knew she was out of the
picture. Her gingham dress hugged her long body and firm fanny like a
second skin, the slow going of the old truck not giving up a bit of wind, her
mouth parched and dry, aching for a Dr Pepper, the setting sun coming
straight into her eyes. The red wig felt like a winter hat, but Kathryn knew
nobody in Texas figured the infamous Kit Kelly for a daring redhead.

She didn't know who she hated more at that very moment, George R.
Kelly or Samuel Sayres, thinking that old Sam Sayres may have the edge
for making her give up that Chevrolet for this old metal carcass, not having the decency to trust her word that she'd be wiring him the money.
Kathryn kicked in the clutch like she was riding a stubborn mule down
that twisty, two-lane highway, past dead-weed gullies and handmade
signs for the Texaco perched on fence posts. Nothing but cotton around
her forever, making her think that North Texas sure looked a hell of a lot
like North Mississippi, waiting for the next stop to be purgatory.

George R. Kelly sat at a linen-covered table with his tanned whore, a cigar in the side of his mouth, a fist of cash in one hand and the girl's fat Southern ass in the other. Sam Sayres sat at a wooden trough of ice cream, eating and slurping it up like a hog.

The filling station was on the edge of downtown Itasca, population 1,280. The station was a lean, skinny building made out of stone, with two garage doors and twin, globe-topped pumps. Behind the station were stacked junked cars from when they just started making cars, Kathryn wishing she could just add this son of a bitch to the heap because walking to Fort Worth might just be easier.

Two attendants came running out to meet the fuming, jittery truck, as she pulled in and hit the brake and jumped out to kick the tires, just aching to do that for the last forty miles, and then walked to the edge of the highway to light a cigarette. She hadn't said a word to the men, the men being smart enough to figure it the hell out.

She wanted to rip the crazy wig off her head but instead just stared at all those junked cars and the big, endless acres of cotton getting ripe. She thought back about standing at the edge of the Gulf after she found out George was gone and throwing shells out into the water till her arm ached, salt water licking her toes as an insult.

She walked back to the shade of the filling-station roof to where a split log had been laid across some milk jugs. She sat and spread her legs, feeling just the hint of coolness and breeze between them. She leaned back against the stone wall, ran a sweaty forearm across her brow, and looked north at the endless road, crooking up and forgotten, 'round the bend.

She should've known George would've pulled something as boneheaded as this. Maybe Ma Coleman was right. Maybe he was Satan put upon this earth, maybe Kathryn was paying for sins going back to that creek in Saltillo when she let the preacher's son stick his skinny willy in her. Maybe she had lured him there. Maybe she had the same kind of affliction as George and needed to get right in His eyes. Could she change? Could she walk deep into the river—any river—and have her sins and filth and road sweat washed off her and drain on down to Mexico?

Kathryn did something she hadn't even thought about since she'd had a child's mind. Kathryn Kelly, now thinking she could become Cleo Brooks again, began to pray. She started with something simple, about the only thing she could recall, about how great He was, how powerful He was, and how she wasn't nothing but dirt. *O heavenly Father, I'm so damn stupid and trusting . . .*

When she opened her eyes, she saw three figures—shadows, really—in the big blot of the afternoon sun, coming down the road. Two tall and one short. Kathryn was worn-out from the prayer and lit another cigarette, wondering if one of those grease monkeys fussing over her truck might have a spot of liquor on him, knowing she'd give up her last hundred-dollar bill to be good and drunk right about now.

The figures grew closer, coming down the road. She could hear the men knocking around in the garage, but also the cicadas and crows. A nice, new Packard blew past the filling station, scattering up dirt and trash from the roadside. Some of the grit blowing across to her, into her eyes and onto her tongue.

She spat, spread out her legs farther, and used the front pages of the newspaper to fan her undercarriage. JUDGE ORDERS SHANNONS TO OKLA-HOMA.

The shadows became people, and those people became a short man and a taller woman and a little girl in a dress made out of a flour sack. The sack hadn't even been disguised, Kathryn clearly seeing WESTERN STAR MILL written across her middle. The girl trudged along, wearing a pair of oversize men's brogans and kicking a tin can, a sharp stick in her hand. The man behind her looked to be about Kathryn's age but with plenty of wrinkles and scars, wearing overalls and work boots. The woman was slope-shouldered and poor-mouthed, in her tattered flow-ered dress that had been washed threadbare. They stopped a good bit shy of the filling station, and the little girl plopped to her butt, the man rousting through a junk pile to find an old metal bucket where he sat down, not even offering the comfort to the woman or child, and Kathryn nearly laughed at the sight of it.

Another car passed, and the man stepped a long, skinny leg onto the road and put out his thumb.

Those people. They were everywhere.

The mechanic came out after a while and told Kathryn the damage, and it was only going to be twenty dollars, and she reached into her purse and handed him the money without looking at him or making the fuss he clearly expected.

She fanned her face and between her legs again with the newspaper, Boss and Ora's hardscrabble faces staring back.

Advertisements on tin all around her. DRINK COCA-COLA. SMOKE CAMELS. BUY FIRESTONE. She lit her Lucky and waited for another car to pass and kick up a little wind.

"Sure love the smell of a cigarette," a little voice said.

Leaning into the stone wall, legs spread, opening one eye, Kathryn Kelly looked at the little girl in the flour sack standing in front of her. She opened the other eye and muscled her sweaty forearms onto her knees and took in some more of the Lucky, blowing the smoke right into the girl's face and pug, freckled nose.

The little girl winced a little, but then sniffed the air like a rabbit and said, "Yes, ma'am. That's smells right stylish."

"You're an odd little duck."

"Don't take me on account of my clothing," the girl said. "My father lost our suitcase in a card game."

"You don't say . . ."

"He almost won, too."

"Where's your car?"

"We don't have a car," the girl said. "We're just tramping."

"I see."

"You have a car."

"If you can call it that."

"Must be nice."

"What's your angle, kid?" Kathryn asked, crushing the cigarette under the heel of her shoe. The sunset cut across the girl's light eyes and blunt, bowl-cut hair. She wrinkled her nose. "Thought maybe we could hitch a ride, is all. Don't want to be no trouble, ma'am. We just walked a fur piece."

The mechanic pulled the truck around. He had black teeth, and black grease across his red neck, and he winked at Kathryn as he opened the door, at the ready.

"Some town," the little girl said. "Even the people have fleas."

The grease monkey spat.

The little girl turned to walk back to her old bucket daddy, Momma sitting like an Indian beside him. Kathryn wondered where in the hell were those Western gifts the billboards had promised.

She kicked in the clutch and clattered up slow to the girl, having to shout over the coughing motor and through the open passenger window. "What's your name?" she asked.

"Gerry."

"Y'all want a ride, Gerry?"

"Can my folks come?"

"Why not."

A mile down the road, Gerry sitting up on an apple crate beside Kathryn and talking ninety miles an hour, her poor-faced folks in back on the Ford's flatbed, Kathryn started to think about the miracle of prayer and how that family, cresting over the hill with holes in their shoes, just might be some kind of crazy redemption, like they had in the Bible and in the movies.

Cleo Brooks knew she could be good. She just goddamn well knew it.

"YOU SAY SHE'D JUST UP AND LEFT YOU, MA'AM?" JONES asked. "Did your granddaughter say where she was headed?"

"No, sir," Ma Coleman said. "I can still smell him among us."

"How does he smell?"

"Like sulfur and hellfire."

"I think it smells right pleasant, ma'am," Jones said. "Smells like you baked a pie."

"Coconut," she said. "Just starting to cool. Yes, sir, it is."

Jones looked to the ledge, where dozens of flies had gathered over the pie, taking off and landing in a spotted black swarm. He sat across from the old woman, on the other side of a table cobbled together with barn wood, coffee-ringed and beat to hell. Behind her, he had a clear view of the agents walking the land, and he could see young Agent Colvin conversing with that sharpshooter Bryce by a willow growing in the bend of a narrow creek.

A black row of clouds inched toward them, about to blot out the sun.

"It's nice to converse with a fine young man, for a change," Ma Coleman said. "Picks up the spirit. May I offer you some more sweet tea? I brewed it in the sun this morning. My son brought me a block of ice just before you men arrived."

"I don't mind if I do," Jones said, reaching across to grab the sweating pitcher. "I appreciate you inviting us in."

"It's a hot day," she said.

"It's supposed to rain."

"You don't say."

"Yes, ma'am," Jones said, fanning his face with his Stetson. "Sure would cool things down."

"Mmm-hmm," Ma Coleman said, cold and vacant as a broken doll on a ladder-back chair, flies buzzing off from a half-eaten cheese sandwich. "You will find that man she's with?"

"Kathryn's husband?"

"If that's what he claims."

Bruce Colvin walked through the front screen door and was careful not to let it bang closed. He'd sweated through his white dress shirt, perspiration ringing his neck in an effect that looked like a halo. He looked to Jones and shook his head.

There was dirt across the front of his pants.

"She left some things here?" Colvin asked.

"Her furs and trinkets," the old woman said. "Vanity has no shame. He bought them for her. He made her wear them. They feel like dog skins to me."

"I understand," Jones said.

"You are a fine bunch of men," she said, rocking a bit to herself and smiling. "You understand that he's the one to blame?"

"Of course," Jones said, shifting his eyes over to Colvin. Colvin rested a shoulder against the wall, flowered wallpaper peeling from the wood planks, listening. "We only want George Kelly."

Jones reached out his hand and grabbed the frail old woman's arm. "Tell us what you know, ma'am."

Colvin shook his head and looked away from Jones, letting the screen door slam behind him. Jones watched the young man walk away down a rutted path but then turned back to the blind woman, who smiled and rocked. "You do know she has a friend named Louise in Fort Worth? You do realize she's a demon, too?"

KATHRYN RENTED A CABIN IN A LITTLE MOTOR COURT NEAR Cleburne for herself and Gerry and her parents, the Arnolds. Flossie Mae and Luther. She'd left them there to get cleaned up and she'd gone to town to try to phone Sam Sayres again, getting the runaround from his secretary and finally giving up, bringing back some boxed dinners of fried chicken and some fresh clothes for the family. The family sat together on a short bed opposite an identical short bed where Kathryn sat and gnawed on a chicken bone. She was thinking of Sam Sayres being so almighty stupid as to let her momma get sent back to Oklahoma when Luther Arnold coughed in the silence of hungry people eating and said how much they appreciated meeting a real-life angel out on a Texas highway.

"Don't mention it," Kathryn said.

"'Preciate the dress," Flossie Mae said, looking down at the floor-boards and lifting her eyes just for a moment to give Kathryn a ragged smile.

"You gonna eat that?" Gerry asked her father.

"Get your grimy little hands off my chicken," he said.

"You can have mine," Kathryn said. "I'm not that hungry."

She passed over the little greasy box to the girl, who snatched up another drumstick, rocking her feet to and fro on the little bed.

"Where y'all headed?" Kathryn asked.

"Where we can find work."

"Where you been?" she asked.

"We was thrown off our land in April," Luther said, closing his eyes and shaking his head with the memory.

"Where?"

"Ardmore."

"Sorry to hear that."

Flossie Mae shot a surprised look at her husband, and he reached down and tweaked her kneecap.

"Daddy was a good farmer," Gerry said, bright and wide-eyed. "I had me a little goat that would pull me in a wagon. He was a good little goat."

"Hush now, doll," Luther said, cleaning down a breast to the bone. "Quit talkin' 'bout that gosh-dang goat."

"What kind of work can you do?" Kathryn asked, crossing her legs at the knee and lighting a cigarette. She could see her reflection in the mirror over the cheap bureau. A sign read WE HAVE THE RIGHT TO REFUSE LODGING FOR THOSE OF LOOSE MORALS.

"I'll do any work that can feed three hungry people."

"I'm sorry," Kathryn said.

"Don't pity us, ma'am," Luther said, putting a scraggly arm around

Flossie Mae and hugging her close, the woman looking as uneasy as a caught barn cat. "We're together and that's a gift from the Lord Himself."

"Amen," Kathryn said. "Are you all right with God?"

"Gerry was baptized at two."

"I'm glad to hear it."

"Where are you headed, Mrs. Montgomery?" he asked. A long pause. "Mrs. Montgomery?"

Kathryn turned from watching herself in the mirror and said, "I'm meeting my husband, who's on a business trip."

"And what does Mr. Montgomery do?"

"He's in the liquor business."

"You don't say," Luther said, leaning in, rubbing rough old hands together. Flossie Mae stood and asked to be excused, and Kathryn shrugged at her, waving her hand through the smoke. "What kind of liquor?"

Kathryn recrossed her legs, and said: "All kinds."

"I bet you've been to the World's Fair!" Gerry said. "I read Budweiser ran a team of horses with barrels of beer all the way from Saint Louis!"

"Not yet."

"Sure wish we could go to the World's Fair."

"Don't mind the girl, ma'am. Her head is filled with a lot of foolishness. We don't have but three dollars left amongst us."

Kathryn reached for her purse and Luther held up a hand, shaking his head. "We appreciate all you done, ma'am, but the Arnold family don't take no handouts. I work to feed my family."

"I'm sorry."

"Don't think nothin' of it," Luther said, straightening his shoulders and running a hand over his thinning hair, dabbed down with grease. "We do appreciate the hospitality of a fellow Christian."

"I knew you were good country people the moment I set eyes on you," Kathryn said. "Why do such good people always have a road of sorrows?"

"Just the way it is, ma'am."

"I'll take some money," Gerry said brightly, jumping to her feet and twirling before the mirror in her fifty-cent dress and quarter shoes.

"Gerry!" Luther said. "Apologize to Mrs. Montgomery."

She did.

Kathryn winked at her. Over her father's sloped shoulder, Gerry winked back.

The toilet flushed, and Flossie Mae tramped back into the room and sat at her husband's side, head down, waiting for her chance to be asked a question, usually replying in a single word. The room was nothing but a bureau, two iron beds, and a single framed picture that looked to be cut out from a feedstore calendar, a nymph on a rock, looking at the moon, shielding her goodies with an open palm.

"Mrs. Arnold, may I speak to your husband in private for a moment?" Kathryn asked, standing, clicking open her cigarette case, and retrieving a fresh Lucky. "I have a business matter that may hold some interest for him."

Luther hopped to his feet and wiped his nose with the back of his hand. He followed her outside the tourist cabin into the coal-black night, not a sign of the moon; a family two cabins down the line cooked meat on a split oil drum. All the people in the camp had been discussing this big hurricane that had already hit Galveston and was headed their way.

"Yes, ma'am . . ."

"I saw you staring at me, Mr. Arnold."

Luther rubbed his stubbled, weak jaw and nodded. "Sorry, ma'am. I just ain't never seen somethin' so purty."

She nodded. "I don't think that's it."

"Please don't tell Flossie Mae. A man just can't help himself sometimes."

"I know who you are."

"Good Lord in heaven," he said, stepping back to the door.

Kathryn snatched his hand from the handle and leaned in close enough to smell his tired, old onion-and-chicken breath. "You people are good folks, salt of the earth and all that. And you are exactly what I need."

"Ma'am?"

She pointed a long, manicured finger at Luther Arnold's skinny breastbone and said, "You are the answer to my prayers. A gift."

"I don't follow."

"You know who I am?"

"No, ma'am."

"Come on. Don't read the papers?"

"Sure."

"You ever heard of Kathryn Kelly?"

He shook his head. Kathryn stepped in closer and said, "Wife of the desperado and gangster 'Machine Gun' Kelly?"

"You know 'Machine Gun' Kelly? Shoot. If that don't beat all."

"I'm his wife," she said. "Luther, are you a man I can trust?"

"With all my heart."

"I need you to do something for me tomorrow," she said. "I need you to go to Fort Worth and find an attorney named Sam Sayres. Can you do that for me?"

"Yes, ma'am."

"I will pay you fifty dollars in cash for your trouble, and two nights here for your family."

"Sam Sayres," Arnold said, nodding. "Got it. What do I do?"

"I need to find out what's going on with my family's case. You tell him that you are my emissary."

"What's that?"

"You work for me."

"Yes, ma'am."

"I'll give you bus fare that you can take to Cleburne, but you are not to tell a soul."

"Not even Flossie Mae."

"'Specially not Flossie Mae."

"You got my word, ma'am. I swear to it on the Arnold family name."

He put out a small, weathered paw, and Kathryn shook it in the weak light from a single bulb screwed in by the cabin door.

THE FILE DEPUTY MANION HAD PASSED TO HARVEY IN A sloppy handshake only nicked the thick iron bars of the cell wall. It wasn't until he really got his muscles into a solid rhythm, working in the midnight heat, that he made some progress, thinking that goddamn son of a bitch wanted ten g's in exchange for a rusted file and a lousy razor blade.

Harvey tried a downward stroke on the barred wall, the way you might play a fiddle, and he thought of a fiddle and dance music and devil deals with backstabbing bastards, until his mouth went dry again and his hands and arms had about locked in spasms.

He wished he had a watch, knowing he didn't have much time till the trusty would come roaming down the hall to slide his breakfast under the cell door.

The first bar from the wall—Harvey figuring he needed at least three to squeeze through—didn't fall until an hour later, Harvey's arms quivering and undershirt soaked as he reached for the sink, where he scooped out mouthfuls of water. Hard winds shook the building and screamed around corners. That big hurricane blowing off the Gulf had started to tickle Dallas, and Harvey knew if he could time this thing just right the confusion of it just might be a hell of a gift.

Manion promised to meet him at his home out on old Eagle Ford Road, just outside Irving. He said he'd bring another car, a change of clothes, and a rifle, and Harvey would pay him the balance on his freedom, Manion knowing enough about Harvey to value an honest crook. But, goddamn, there was a long way between the cell, ten floors of armed guards, and the road. *A goddamn long way.* And all Manion had seeded him with was rusted junk, refusing to give him a gun but telling him that he'd hid a pistol in the bottom right-hand drawer of his desk.

If he made it down to the sixth floor.

Harvey kept playing that fiddle. The wind pounded the jail, rain pinging the lone window. The light outside was a queer purple, and that made it all the harder to guess the time, as if time itself had stopped, caught in the blurred picture from an old-time camera.

The last bar fell as he heard the gears and pulleys of the elevator going to work, groaning and straining down the shaft. He reached for the razor blade he'd hid under a stained pillow and stuck his head through the gap, facing the open row, and then inched his body through, letting out every drop of air till he could snake out, cutting the hell out of his shoulder before tumbling to the floor and finding his feet.

He hit the ground with such a thud that he wondered if he hadn't been heard ten floors down.

Harvey inched back, watching the barred window of the door. He hoped it would be only one man, like yesterday, unarmed, as was their procedure, and holding cold biscuits, colder coffee, and shithouse gravy.

He found the next cell's door open, and Harvey slipped inside and slid under the bunk. It was very dark, blacker than night, and the storm—it must be a hurricane now—beat the hell out of the tall building, almost feeling like it just might decide to topple all the concrete and steel and make all this effort for naught.

Harvey held on to the rusted blade and just listened to that beautiful storm, the single bulbs hanging from the ceiling flickering off and on, the rain coming down on a parched country like some kind of unnatural act.

He smiled. He hoped that Manion at least had enough sense to pick out a stylish suit and shine his shoes.

30

The guard walked the row, whistling and jangling a set of keys, an old colored trusty at his heels holding a breakfast tray. The whistling stopped when the guard reached the death cell, Harvey inching out from the open cage behind him, the guard stooping to inspect the filed-off bars and yelling at the trusty to put down them eggs and go fetch the sheriff. But Harvey snuck behind them both and held the old razor to the guard's neck, telling them nobody was going to die on Labor Day if they all were slow and steady and did everything he said. "You understand what I'm sayin', boy?" Harvey asked.

The old black man nodded. Harvey snatched up a piece of burnt toast and pushed the two men into the cell, lifting the set of keys from the guard's fingers and locking them inside.

"Sheriff Smoot's gonna tan your hide," the jailer said.

"You tell Sheriff Smoot to kiss my ass," Harvey said, taking a bite of toast and casually walking to the first door and finding the key. Another key unlocked the cage, and he moved past the elevator to the stairwell, the door unlocked, and made his way down to the sixth floor, where he found another cage and a room empty except for Tom Manion's old desk. On the wall hung a calendar that hadn't been changed since Christmas of '29. The Sun-Maid raisin girl held a basket of grapes.

Harvey reached into the bottom right drawer and found a gun, if you could call it a gun. It was a rusted old .44, something Manion had probably carried in the Spanish War. When Harvey spun the cylinder, it fell open into his hand. He noted only three bullets and snapped the cylinder back in place just as he heard steps approaching. Son of a bitch.

Another jailer, just as old and tired as the fella upstairs, walked alongside R.L., the colored guitar player, from a side door.

"Mornin', boys," Harvey said.

"Good Lord in heaven," the deputy said, chaw dripping out of his mouth and onto his chin. He wore a nonregulation Panama hat, slipped far back on his head.

"If y'all would be so kind," Harvey said, nodding back to the row of cells.

R.L. smiled. Harvey winked at him.

"I ain't goin' in there," the deputy said.

Harvey pointed that rusted piece of shit at his chest.

"'Fraid this ain't up for discussion, partner."

"You can't lock me in there," he said.

"Maybe you boys should carry weapons." Harvey reached for the man's Panama and stuck it on his own head.

"That's the row for colored folks, you idgit!"

"Will you be offended if I lock up this fella in the colored wing, R.L.? I don't want to stink up the place."

"No, sir."

"See?" Harvey said. "Now, get your stinking white ass inside."

Harvey locked the deputy in a cell with an enormous black man who sat on his bunk holding a half-eaten bowl of gray mush. The man looked up for a moment and then returned his eyes downward, continuing to work his spoon, not seeing a damn thing.

Harvey flushed the razor blade down the shitter, locked the cell and the outer door, searched for another gun but found nothing but a pair of handcuffs and a worn-out blackjack. R.L. stood over the desk and

watched Harvey, before he turned to the window and the rain hitting
the glass. The young black man seemed deep in thought.

"Fine day," R.L. said.

"Come on," Harvey said.

He grabbed the blackjack, opened the cage, and turned the elevator
key. The elevator clanged to a stop as he held the old revolver in his hand,
aiming into an empty box. Harvey motioned to R.L., dressed in prison
gray, and they both walked inside, knowing the dumb sonsabitches
would never expect Harvey Bailey to skip out the front door with a smile
on his face and a spring in his step. He pulled the Panama down in his
eyes and turned the key. Harvey did all these things without a drop of
sweat or a skip of his heart, something he'd been blessed with from birth.
Nervousness had never been his trouble.

"Guess it's too late to turn back now."

"I do believe."

"You want to come along?"

"Get out Friday."

"So you're stayin'?"

"You know this ain't gonna turn out pretty, sir."

"Who says?" Harvey grinned.

The guard on the first floor couldn't have been more than eighteen,
skinny and slack-jawed, standing at the bars and conversing with a little
fat fella in a suit about getting a right fair deal on T-bone steaks. He had
one hand in his pocket and the other rubbed his jaw, contemplating the
deal.

Harvey pushed R.L. along first and nearly walked past the guard
before the deputy did a double take and asked, "Just where in the hell do
y'all think you're going?"

Harvey turned and said in a calm, quiet voice to keep his mouth shut
and do as he said. The gun hung loose and easy, hidden from the world,
at his right thigh. But the boy sure felt it when it nudged against his ribs.
His eyes grew big, and he nodded his understanding.

Harvey tipped the brim of his straw hat to R.L. The boy looked at

Harvey and gave a loose smile before hitting a button, the elevator disappearing up the shaft.

"How 'bout you escort me out of this shithole?"

The deputy nodded again, hands in the air.

On a far wall, Harvey spotted a gorgeous rack of shotguns and rifles, the old relic feeling like a stage prop in his fingers. As he pushed the boy toward the arsenal, two deputies walked to the front gate, waiting for the deputy to unlock the door, jawing at each other, not even noticing Harvey Bailey, noted bank robber, out for a stroll.

Harvey admired a fine .45 and a 12-gauge with a blue finish from across the room. The deputies called for the boy, and Harvey just nudged him on, turning away from the rack, following the deputy down a short stairwell.

"You got a car?" he asked the boy in a whisper, and followed him to a back door, where the boy unlocked two dead bolts and led Harvey into a back alley, where the rain fell sideways and stung his face. The boy walked across the alley, open and naked, long black electric wires crisscrossing overhead. A river of trash and mud running down concrete gutters and into clogged sewers.

He followed the deputy into an old brick warehouse filled with machines parked in a haphazard fashion, most of them labeled with the official seal of the sheriff. The rain on the roof made it sound like they were inside a huge drum.

The boy pointed out a '29 Chevy. Harvey told the deputy to unlock it and scoot on over.

"Are you gonna shoot me, sir?"

"Kid, I ain't even had breakfast yet."

Harvey placed the .44 under his right leg, started her up with a couple kicks, and then headed north on Houston and then east on Elm. While he drove, he read the handwritten notes pulled from his shoe, the paper wet, ink bleeding on his fingers.

He leaned into the windshield, not seeing shit, and used the flat of his hand to wipe the fogged glass. South on Jefferson. West on Main. Left on Houston again, and then finding Eagle Ford Road out of Dallas.

"You got a dime?"

"Yes, sir," the deputy said, reaching into his hip pocket.

"I don't want your whole gosh-dang wallet. Just a dime."

Harvey made two stops.

One to kick the deputy out of his car.

The second to make a phone call.

Harvey drove down the narrow dirt road, passing slow-moving cars in the opposite direction, spraying up potholes of muddy water, windshield wipers flapping, headlights cutting through the storm. The road had turned to shit, and he just wanted to keep the wheels moving, as he was leaning in, looking for road markers to Irving, that old church where he was to turn off to Manion's house. He overshot it by a mile and had to turn back, the wind almost ripping the top from the vehicle.

The lights were on in a white two-story house with a gabled entrance and crooked black shutters. Harvey killed the motor and sat for a moment in the rain, seeing only a Ford sedan parked outside. The light inside was orange and glowing, coming from kerosene lanterns.

An electric wire had broken free from a pole and skittered up and around, throwing sparks up into the wind.

Harvey lit a cigarette and smoked, the wind rocking the car, until he decided to pull it around back to an old shed and kill the motor. He entered the house by the back entrance to the kitchen.

Tom Manion was eating a piece of buttermilk pie and reading a crisply folded newspaper when Harvey entered, wringing wet and holding the .44 in his waistband.

"Real shit storm, ain't it?" Manion said, training his eyes on the newspaper and reaching for a cup of coffee.

"I could've been killed," Harvey said. "I shoulda been."

"Good day for an escape. You like some coffee?"

"I'd like to get going, if it's all the same."

"Have some coffee," Manion said. "Got your change of clothes right there. Vehicle's gassed up."

Harvey glanced down at a worn-out pair of denims and a blue work shirt. Brogans with broken soles. He took off his Panama hat.

"What about the rifle?"

"What about my money?"

"I'm good for it."

Manion nodded and walked to an old farm sink, pouring out the dregs from his cup. He leaned into the window, seeming to watch the old trees bend and break, limbs littered his yard. When he turned, he held a shiny new .38 in his hands.

Harvey had pulled the old, rusted .44.

"Arms up, Harvey."

"I told you I'd get it."

"I'm bringing you in."

"You got to be pulling my pecker."

"You gonna shoot? Then shoot."

"Naw," Harvey said, letting the cylinder fall from the gun. "Figured I might throw it at you."

"I did me some thinking the other night, and I figured the man who brings in Harvey Bailey could write his own ticket. Don't you agree? When I'm sheriff, I can do as I please. Ten thousand ain't worth that."

Harvey shook his head. The coffee was still over the flame and smelled acrid and burnt. He lifted his hands, Manion marching him to the back door, reaching onto the table for a napkin to wipe the pie crumbs from his mustache.

"You don't think I'll tell 'em about the file and the razor blade?"

"Who's gonna believe you, Bailey? Didn't you flush 'em down the commode like I said? Where's your evidence?"

Lighting cracked close to the house. There was thunder, the rain falling even harder, while Manion pushed open the back door with his pistol. "You first."

The wind shot around the house, blowing a small lace curtain from a door window.

Harvey smiled and picked up his new Panama hat. "If it's all the same, I'd rather square it right here, Tom."

"Whatever you say, Mr. Bailey. I just hate to have to mop my gosh-dang kitchen floor."

Harvey looked down at the linoleum and then up at fat Tom Manion and his shit-eating smile. He almost felt sorry for the sorry bastard as the gun cracked three times, blood spreading on Manion's boiled shirt like spilt gravy, the son of a bitch toppling down to his knees. "You lying cocksucker," Manion said, blood on his chin, flailing a bit before he died.

"How long you been here?" Harvey asked.

A dark figure in a black hat and black rain slicker stepped inside and pocketed the hot .44. His eyes cold and blue, jaw clenching.

"I left the hotel when you called," Verne Miller said. "Let's burn this house down and then go find George Kelly."

"Good to see you, Verne," Harvey said. "You're a swell pal."

KATHRYN DIDN'T GET WORRIED ABOUT LUTHER ARNOLD coming back until about eleven o'clock that night, but a half hour later the grizzled man showed up, wet as a drowned rat, wringing out his hat on the cottage stoop like it was a washrag. Kathryn shooed him on inside, where she handed him a towel, with him saying he sure didn't want to mess her things, as he dried his old head himself, and she told Flossie Mae to fetch up her husband some clean drawers. The rain fell hard and strong, raining all damn day, pinging so hard on the shingled roof that it was hard to talk.

The little girl, Geraline, was asleep, but all the movement and whispering woke her up, and she sat up in her bed and looked over at her father, shaking her head, saying, "Luther, why don't you at least take your shoes off?"

"Hush up, child."

The child reached for a pack of cigarettes, lighting one up and blowing smoke from the corner of her mouth.

"What did he say?" Kathryn asked, reaching for his clean clothes from Flossie Mae. Kathryn wore a black silk robe with gold orchids. Her red wig left to dry on the nightstand.

"Can we speak in private, ma'am?" Luther asked.

"We can't go outside."

They walked into the small bathroom, and Kathryn ran the water, not that it made much difference with the commotion outside. Luther sat down on the commode, with a fist propping up his head. "Well, the counselor said he'd need some more money."

"You ask him about the trade?"

"He said he couldn't put that matter on the table 'less you both come to him in person."

"How are we supposed to both come to him when the whole world is looking for us?"

"You don't look much like your picture," Luther said, taking off his waterlogged shoes and rolling off his socks. "I seen it in the bus station. That woman in the photographs looks like a hardened character. You ain't no hardened character, Miz Kelly."

Kathryn ignored him, listening to the rain against the windows. Luther rolled up his pant legs and leaned forward, with both elbows on his skinny knees. He sniffed a bit and rubbed his nose with a forearm.

"Your husband, Mr. Machine Gun, know about this here deal?"

She kept thinking.

"'Cause that's a mighty white thing for a man to do for his mother-in-law. I know some men wouldn't give a squirt of piss if their mother-in-law's on fire."

Kathryn shot him a look.

"Sorry, ma'am. Didn't mean to curse."

"Just shut up about the deal," Kathryn said. "That's between us and our counsel. What else did Sayres say?"

"Not much," Luther said, rubbing his unshaven jaw. He had the nose of a drinker, bulbous and veined. "Wouldn't let me in his office, though. Told me to go 'round to this alley like I's some kind of beggar, where he didn't come back for a half hour."

"You know any good lawyers?" Kathryn asked. "In Oklahoma? Sam Sayres wouldn't know how to shit outside Texas."

"I know'd a real good counselor over in Enid. You want me to call him up?"

Kathryn reached into her cosmetic kit for a jar of cold cream and began to rub down her face. Luther sat the opposite way, shaking his head and grunting with her complaints. "I don't know where that SOB is, but when I find him he's gonna surrender to the G and get my momma sprung."

"Mighty white."

"So you trust this fella?" she asked, slathering the cream up on her cheeks. "Really trust him?"

"Who?"

"The lawyer in Enid."

"With my own life," Luther said. "He's gotten me out of a scrape or two. Misunderstandings with the law. You understand."

"But of course."

"Mrs. Machine Gun?"

"Call me Kit."

"Kit, you want me to call 'im? I'd appreciate a ride back to town to use the telephone. The weather's mighty nasty to walk the road again. I kept slipping outta my brogans."

Kathryn shook her head and reached for a rag to wipe the cream from her face, staring into her own eyes, thinking about her next move to get out of this goddamn mess. The rain kicked up a little outside, pinging the windows, and Luther turned from the commode and said, "Whoo-whee."

"Scoot over," Kathryn said.

"Ma'am?"

"I need to do some thinking."

He exchanged places with her on the commode and stood, looking awkward and loose, arms folded across his chest and trying to look smart, as she talked out a plan, more to herself than to Luther.

"I want you to take the bus back to Fort Worth tomorrow," she said, holding up a hand, the silk material on her robe draping down her fore-arm like a butterfly wing. "Hold on . . . Hold on . . . I'll pay. But I want you to go back and see that sorry fat bastard Sam Sayres and tell him that he no longer works for the Shannon family. Tell him we're trading up, and that Kit Kelly wants her Chevrolet back."

"He has your machine?"

"Used it as collateral, for him sitting on his ass while my dear ole momma is sent to the gallows."

"You want me to drive the car back here?"

"I want you to go to Enid and hire that lawyer you told me about. I'll take Gerry and Flossie Mae with me."

"Where to?"

"San Antonio," Kathryn said. "You can contact me there care of General Delivery. I'll make sure they're clothed and fed till you get back. Don't you worry about a thing."

Luther nodded.

"He better be good," she said.

"He's the cheese on apple pie."

Kathryn nodded, long legs spread in a solid stance on the commode, listening to herself and making the plan definite in her mind. "Tomorrow morning I'll give you five hundred dollars to advance him."

"Five hunnard," Luther Arnold said, Kathryn noticing the shriveled flesh on his toes and long, curled nails turned yellow. "That'll keep him busy for a while."

"And tell him I want him to put the deal for George on the table," she said. "If the G wants George R. Kelly, they can have 'im. All I want is my momma."

Someone knocked on the door. "Daddy?"

"Yes, muffin."

"I got to pee-pee. What're y'all doin' in there?"

"What if you can't find Mr. Kelly?" Luther asked in a whisper.

"That rotten son of a bitch disappears when you need him most, but he'll show up like a bad penny. I know my George."

31

When Kathryn heard the story, she couldn't tell which parts were true, which parts George invented, and how much of the small stuff he just threw in there to keep it sounding gospel, the details of it coming out of George's mouth like a sinner come to witness about his road of trials. George started with when he'd jumped into a jalopy Chevrolet and headed off Ma Coleman's land, heading right for Biloxi, knowing that Kathryn would understand his note and follow him to his favorite hotel, where they could lay low a bit, put their feet in the sand and drink some cold beer, out of the forsaken state of Texas, down to the Gulf, to vacation from being outlaws for a while. He'd made it as far as New Orleans, George knowing some people in that part of the country from when he'd run booze up to Memphis, and he'd taken a room in the Lafayette Hotel and only left once to get a pint of gin and an Italian sandwich. He said he sat in the room all night, not being able to sleep, reading five different newspapers, all of 'em carrying the same story about her momma's family being taken by airplane to await a fair and speedy trial. And he said it made him so damn sad that he didn't want more company than a bottle of gin, remembering that he'd left the hotel one more time, walking down Canal Street to find a liquor store and a Catholic church, where he wandered in and lit a candle for the Shannon family. That part of the story diverging a bit from the truth of that piney gin, but Kathryn *took the lie as a solid gesture, and let him continue on about driving out of the city the next morning, figuring the one-eyed bellhop sure noticed he could be none other than "Machine Gun" Kelly, and him driving along Highway 90 into Mississippi, following that road through Waveland and into Bay Saint Louis, where he went to the Star movie house and watched a Barbara Stanwyck picture in the colored balcony. Again getting sad, because Barbara sure had a lot of Kit Kelly in her, wandering out of the black night like a crazy dream and staring out at the Bay under oaks older than time, moss in the cool breeze, getting good and buzzed till his heart stopped hurting. He drove on through Gulfport to Biloxi, a town that he knew just as well as he knew Memphis. He headed to the first pharmacy he saw to buy a bottle of peroxide and a shower cap, a toothbrush and some talcum powder, and five* True Detective *magazines, before checking into the Avon, that fine old hotel right off the Gulf.*

For three days, he rubbed his body with baby oil and poured the peroxide into his hair, wearing purple-tinted sunglasses and drinking gin mixed with pitchers of lemonade that the negros sold to the tourists. No one talked to him, and everything seemed fine as moonshine, as he'd sit in a deck chair, dozing to the sound of the surf, letting his cramped car legs unknot, and waking only as the shadows ran long across the combed beach and the sun got ready to disappear to wherever it went at night. In the evenings, he'd order up steaks and hamburgers to his room, some more gin, and would drink all his sorrows away while reading "How the Sensational Boettcher Kidnapping Was Solved, the Baffling Mystery of the Dead Dancer, the Minister—the Love Lyrics—and the Murdered Woman," and then coming across an advertisement in the back pages that promised to help you "Read Law at Home and Earn up to $15,000 Annually," and George said that sure let the snakes loose in his head, thinking, hell, he was earning fifty thousand a year just for knocking over a few banks, and they had to get good and greedy and start in the kidnapping racket, letting the hounds loose on their trail. (This was usually when George would go into that long speech about how he had a different path in Memphis with his first wife—sweet Geneva—and what a good man his father-in-law had *been, much better than his own father, that worthless, mean son of a bitch, and that if Mr. Ramsey hadn't been snuffed out like that, a high beam falling from his own construction site and splitting open his head like a watermelon, old George Barnes—that being George's real name—would be an upstanding member of Memphis society to this day.)*

"And that's how you came to Memphis, George?"

George shook his head, and said, "Gosh dang it. My own fault, we couldn't find each other at the Avon."

He had to pack and move over to the Hotel Avelez, on account of the bellhop studying his profile when he'd stumble down to the front desk to get some fresh towels. He said he'd burned through his Urschel stash in New Orleans and had to dip into those American Express checks he'd boosted in Tupelo.

"You didn't, George."

"Sure did."

"And you didn't think anyone would notice?"

"Didn't have a choice."

"Did you find that woman, that blond lifeguard?"

"Kit, hush up and pay attention to the tale at hand."

"Coppers found you?"

The Hotel Avelez swimming pool shimmered like a glass gridiron the morning he'd decided to eat some breakfast under the oaks and charge it to Mr. J. L. Baker, that being the name he decided sounded best with his tanned skin and yellowing hair. He said he'd grown a little thickheaded, and cocky with his new looks, and decided to drive into the downtown and pick up some shirts and pants he'd left to be laundered. George said he'd also been contemplating wearing a straw boater but sure wished Kit could've been with him because he wasn't sure a dandy little hat like that looked good on a big fella. He said he'd just stepped foot out of his car, looking at some straw hats displayed in a department-store window, when he heard the voice of a corner newsboy yelling with all his might, " 'MACHINE GUN' KELLY IN TOWN!"

George said he nearly shit his drawers.

"What did you do?"

"Left it all."

"Your luggage?"

"Even my .45 and my *True Detective* magazines. Wore the same pair of underwear for three days."

"And that was Memphis?"

"That was Memphis."

George walked to the bus station and bought a ticket. He said his heart didn't stop racing until he crossed the Tennessee state line, and then he worried about coppers waiting for him when he stepped foot off that bus. But he said the sight of the old river sure did his heart some good, as did getting out on Union and walking into the Peabody Hotel, where he used to deliver hip flasks and bottles of bootleg bourbon in a raincoat with a dozen pockets. He felt like no time at all had passed and then realized that it had been nearly ten years since he lighted out for Oklahoma, finding more opportunity in Tulsa, and knowing Geneva and his two sons could get on with their lives without the shame of a daddy who sold whiskey.

"You never told me you had sons, George."

"You never asked for a résumé. Geneva's remarried. They have a new daddy."

George broke his last dollar into dimes and called on the one fella who he knew he could trust in Memphis, ole Lang. His brother-in-law, Langford Ramsey. He hadn't seen Lang since Lang was just a skinny teenager starting out at Central. But George still telephoned him every anniversary of his daddy's death, George usually drunk and telling Lang for the hundredth time how much he respected his father, even taking Ramsey as his middle name out of respect.

"George R. Kelly."

"That's right."

Lang had two listings in the phone book, one his residence on Mignon and the other his law office. George found out that Lang had been the youngest man ever to pass the Tennessee bar, and had just married and had a son, with another child on the way. George had hugged him out of pride at the Memphis train station, and they shook hands over and over, Lang walking with him back over to the Peabody to have a big enough breakfast for an army. George had two plates, since he hadn't eaten since Biloxi, and washed it down with a pot of coffee.

"Did he know?"

"Never even suspected it. I'm just ole George Barnes in Memphis."

"Big man on Central High School campus."

"Why do you always have to say it like that, Kit? You don't know a damn thing about Memphis."

At the end of breakfast, there was an awkward moment where Lang said he had to be getting back to his practice but it sure was great seeing George again. And that's when George had to tell him he was in a spot of trouble and sure could use a loan. Lang said don't mention it, taking care of the check and passing him a twenty-dollar bill. "I'm good for it," George said. "I know," Lang said.

I could use a place to sleep.

I know a fella who owes me a favor.

George slept for ten days on the ragged red velvet couch of a garage attendant Lang had represented in a property dispute over a family goat farm. Tich was a cripple with a clubfoot that dragged behind him when he walked, thudding through the guts of the house, while George would be trying to sleep, as the morning light shone into the house down off Speedway. For some reason, George couldn't close his eyes at night and would just stay up drinking and listening to the radio, Tich having a decent RCA, where he found NBC and the adventures of Buck Rogers in the 25th Century. George said it was all he could do to wait till that broadcast would come on, and he could shut his eyes, maybe a little drunk, and go to far-out lands, planets, and stars, all way away from this crummy earth.

"Did you miss me?"

"Hell, yes. Why do you think I came back?"

"For the money."

"The money, hell. I could've dug up all of it, and your grandmother wouldn't have known."

"She'd woulda known."

"I came back 'cause I love you, baby."

"You're a damn liar."

"You're a double-damn liar."

"You were a fool to run off to Mississippi for some blonde."

"Didn't I just explain it all?"

The horn honked in a Chevrolet sedan, the same one he'd traded out for that little Cadillac coupe in Chicago. The car parked in the dusty driveway of old Ma Coleman's farmhouse.

"Who's that kid?"

"That's a story," Kathryn said. "I'll tell you on the road."

"Where we headed?"

"San Antonio."

"Why San Antonio?"

"'Cause it's a mite better than Dallas or Fort Worth."

The horn honked again.

"The kid's driving?"

"She's a pistol," Kathryn said, not sure what to make of the blond George Kelly with the bloat that came with too much steak and gin. "Her daddy runs errands for me."

"Like what?"

"George, we need to talk."

George stood there in front of Ma Coleman's place, where she knew she'd find him after he'd sent that telegram to the San Antonio General Delivery. It read MA'S BETTER. She knew the G could butt through the cattle gate any minute, but she was out of cash, and, damn, if she didn't ache to see the lousy bastard.

"You want me to turn myself in?" he asked.

"We're talking about my kin, George," Kathryn said, grabbing his big hands and pulling him close. "Something has happened . . . I think God has shown me the light."

———

JONES SPENT THE DAY WITH A GROUP OF YOUNG AGENTS AT
the police department shooting range outside Oklahoma City, a two-acre
parcel of scrub brush, where they'd set up paper targets and kept score. A
head shot was a real winner, but a belly shot earned you enough to stay in the
game. In the end, it wasn't much of a contest, with that kid Bryce edging out
Doc and Jones, scoring a head shot damn-near every time with both his .38
and Jones's Colt .45. They'd practiced a great deal with both the Thompsons
and BARs shipped from Washington, and Jones decided to post the big guns
near the courthouse steps and on the roof of the Federal Building, where he
stood, smoking his pipe in the night and figuring out where and how Kelly
and his gang of desperadoes would be making their attack.

"You think Kathryn's sincere?" Jones asked Joe Lackey.

Lackey placed his hands on the edge of the rooftop and leaned over,
looking down to the squat old houses, churches, and office buildings
around the city. A truck backed up to the building and started to unload
spotlights, as if they expected some kind of Hollywood extravaganza.

"The woman wrote 'the entire Urschel family and friends and all of
you will be exterminated soon by "Machine Gun" Kelly,'" Lackey said.
"That isn't exactly something you put on a Christmas card, Buster. Yeah,
I'd say she's pretty serious. She said she's scared of the son of a bitch, too."

"How many you figure for their gang?"

"You can bet Bailey is back with him," Lackey said, nodding and still
looking out at the city and clear out to the Canadian River. "Probably
Verne Miller, too. Maybe Pretty Boy. Real glad you took out that bastard
Mad Dog."

Jones nodded and puffed on his pipe. "Hated shootin' him down off
that rope and all. But he made the play."

The men watched a couple of agents adding sandbags around a
machine-gun stand by the front steps, and Jones noticed a blind spot
behind the bunker, knowing they'd have to add another gunner. After a

few minutes of running electric cables, the spotlights were lit, the beams crisscrossing the high windows and up into the dark clouds.

"She says she might just turn herself in just so she won't be associated with the coming slaughter," Lackey said.

"She sure likes those words."

"Which ones?"

"Slaughter. *Extermination*."

"Got our attention."

"Nobody's coming in or getting out of this house," Jones said. The wind tipped his hat, but Jones caught the brim, setting it back on his head, before he knocked out his pipe. "We're well entrenched. Ready for those bastards."

"Glad Hoover got us the guns."

"You saw for yourself the kind of animal we're dealing with. Hell, I hope Kelly runs up the steps with guns blazing, that'd save the taxpayers the cost of a trial."

"That's some rough talk."

"You take exception?"

"People don't lynch much anymore."

"Maybe they should."

"You don't mean that," Lackey said. "Rangers keep order."

"Sometimes the Rangers looked the other way."

Lackey reached into his coat pocket for a pack of gum. He chewed, resting his elbows on the ledge, searchlights crossing the sky and the front of the Federal Building. "The Shannons' new counsel says he's never been in touch with Kathryn Kelly," Lackey said. "Said he was hired by a middleman, at his office in Enid."

"Can we track the middleman?"

"Colvin's on it," Lackey said. "We got several men following the counselor."

"Phone lines?"

"Sure. Of course."

"Never ends, does it?"

"What's that?"

"Thievery. Murder. You'd think we'd have advanced past the Old Testament."

"I'm not in the mood to get all philosophical, Buster," Lackey said, chomping on his Doublemint. "Let's go back to the Skirvin and get a whiskey and a porterhouse."

"Now you're talking."

The Venetian Room was on the top floor of the Skirvin Hotel, a swank place that boasted polished, inlaid pecan floors, white linen and silver service, and Bernie Cummins and the New Yorkers on the bandstand. They broadcast a hit parade every night after supper on Oklahoma City's own WKY. But Jones would just as soon hear them on the radio than be interrupted during supper by a man in a tuxedo extolling the qualities of fig syrup to get your pipes running smooth.

Doc White joined Jones and Lackey, and the three men all ordered steaks and bourbon. Doc White rolled a cigarette after getting the T-bone clean and tapped the finger of his free hand in time with the song "Stormy Weather," a big hit earlier that year for some popular colored singer.

They all wore summer-weight coats to hide their holstered pistols.

About halfway into their desserts, peach pie with ice cream, Jones looked up to see a short fella in a big suit really hamming it up on the dance floor with two fat women in evening gowns. He was one of those men who looked as out of place wearing a suit as would a circus monkey. But he'd slicked back his hair and shaved, proving it with bits of toilet paper stuck on the cuts, and the back of his hair was barbered up two inches higher than his sunburned ears and neck. The man couldn't have been much older than thirty but had a large bulbous nose and the reddened cheeks of an experienced drunk.

Doc White ashed his cigarette on a china saucer. "Doesn't that son of a bitch know there's a Depression?"

"Must be family money," Joe Lackey said, a small grin.

There was a split second when the little man couldn't figure out which woman to dance with during the slow part, so he just opened his drunk arms wide and clutched them both close, hands squeezing each of their large rumps. Jones laughed and shook his head, spotting Bruce Colvin walking in from the elevators and flicking his eyes around the Venetian Room. He leaned into Jones's ear and told him that the Shannons' go-between was here.

Jones set down his fork and pushed himself away from the table.

"Right here," Colvin said, pointing to the weathered fella dancing with the two fat girls.

Jones craned his head around to Colvin and would've thought it was a joke had it not been Bruce Colvin. The young man seemed unable to find humor in most situations.

"What do we do?" Colvin whispered.

"Keep an eye out," Jones said. "He resides in this hotel?"

"Yes, sir."

"Follow his every step. Tap his phone."

"Why don't we just pull him in?" Colvin asked.

"So he can clam up like Bailey?" Jones asked. "You got to be patient, son."

Jones finished his dessert. With coffee.

The next morning, hearing nothing from the tapped telephone lines but a slow and dull buzz, Jones rode the elevator to the eighth floor and pounded on the door to have a little talk with the fella. Two minutes later, the hotel manager opened the suite to find a mess of empty booze bottles and a huge pair of pink panties tossed across the headboard. *Des Moines all over again.*

Jones walked to the bed and reached for the big panties, pulling them wide enough to be hung from a flagpole. "Maybe your scientific detection can get us a lead off these?"

Colvin looked down at his neatly shined shoes without a word.

"Do we at least have a name?" Jones asked.

"Registered under Luther Arnold family."

"Be too much to ask where he's headed?" Jones said. "The director might like to be informed."

GEORGE SNATCHED A WIDE SOMBRERO FROM THE STUCCOED wall of the Mexican restaurant and told the waiter to bring him an entire bottle of tequila with cut limes and salt. They'd been in San Antonio now for two days, renting a little apartment, where Kathryn had shared a room with George, Flossie Mae and Geraline in the second bedroom. She'd about had it with Flossie Mae, the woman doing nothing but complaining, complaining more in a "That's fine" or "If you think that's best" kind of way, never really speaking up but never appreciating the hospitality either, somehow thinking she deserved the Kelly family dime on account of what Luther was doing.

Luther'd driven back in her Chevy an hour earlier, and that's when George decided on a big family meal at La Fonda, a short walk from the apartment. And it didn't take but two shots of tequila before he called for that sombrero, throwing back another shot and tipping the mariachi band twenty dollars.

"Why don't you put an ad in the paper?" Kathryn asked.

"Just having some fun, baby face," he said. "Honey pie."

Luther sat across from Kathryn, where he could lean over the table and discuss details of his big trip to Oklahoma City yesterday. Flossie Mae sat across from George, and Geraline was at the head of the table. The table was under a big oak in the center of an old courtyard, with banana plants growing wild under leaking pipes and white Christmas lights crisscrossed overhead like in an old Mexico plaza.

"The hat," George said, touching the sombrero's brim and throwing down another tequila. "Good disguise."

Kathryn noticed Luther had bought a new suit, pin-striped and rumpled and about two sizes too big. He'd also bought a tie and maybe even shaved a couple days back. She guessed for when he'd met with the new attorney.

"Lawyer said the government mulled over your offer," he said.

"Huh?" George asked, turning to Kathryn and winking again. He poured out a shot of tequila for Luther, but Luther shook him off, saying he just didn't have the stomach for no alcohol. Luther looked wrung-out, sick, and exhausted from his journey back to San Antonio. At the head of the table, his daughter, wearing a crisp white dress, her hair in pink ribbons, clutched a huge menu in her tiny fists.

George finished off his drink and lit a cigarette, singing along with the mariachi.

"I hear it's no dice," Luther said.

"Son of a bitch."

"Ole Mr. Mathers—that being the attorney I hired—says he'll try again when they get before the judge."

"But the G won't make the trade?"

"He says they got you cornered."

"Horseshit."

"Huh?" George said, stopping singing for a moment.

"I said *horseshit*," Kathryn said, leaning into George's ear. "The government won't trade you out for Ma."

"Who says the G ain't smart?" George laughed and laughed, slapping his knee. "You know, 'cause your ma isn't worth the trade. Har."

He smiled over at Geraline, and the little girl grinned back, George popping a half-dollar off his thumb into her waiting hand. She passed it on to the guitar player, the band starting into another sappy song about touching a woman's heart with love.

"Did anyone see you?" Kathryn asked.

"Who?"

"The G, Luther. The G!"

"No, ma'am. I traveled with great stealth."

"How much money you got left?"

"Ma'am?"

"The five hundred I staked you."

"Well, there was some traveling expenses, and I paid Mr. Mathers a bit."

"How much?"

"A hunnard."

"You spent four hundred dollars?"

"There was traveling expenses."

"Oh, hell," she said. "How much will you need to go back?"

"Least three hunnard, ma'am."

"Shit," George said, turning the sombrero down across his eyes. He gripped his big gorilla fingers around Kathryn's upper arm so tight her hand started to tingle. "That's him."

"What?"

"The god-dang Federal Ace. Jones."

Kathryn looked over to the opening in the wrought-iron fence and saw a short, squat man in a pearl-colored cowboy hat. She watched the man's face as he spoke to an old woman at the crook of his arm, and Kathryn shook her head. "No, it's not."

"The hell you say."

"That man doesn't look a thing like Jones. He's got a mustache."

"He's got a pearl gray Stetson, too. Boots. He's a tough little fireplug, just like I read in *True Detective.*"

"Goddamn, George," she said. "Did you forget you're in Texas?"

George frowned, removing the big sombrero and tossing it to the center of the table. "I'm hungry."

They ordered pretty much all the menu, the money petering out again, Kathryn knowing they'd have to head back to Coleman this week, not having dug up enough money when she and George were reunited. She also really missed Chingy, and thought maybe George wouldn't get so sore this time if Chingy would be good and not drop any more doodles in his wingtips.

"I sure like being y'all's agent up in Oklahoma City," Luther said, licking his lips, studying the menu, the first time Kathryn noticed *This son of a bitch is faking*, pretty sure he couldn't read a word. "I can report to you any matters of the court."

"The G didn't see you?"

Luther placed the menu on the table and tucked a napkin into his soiled collar. "No, ma'am. I'm positive of it."

"Mr. Mathers think he can free my family?"

"Mr. Mathers has been practicing law a long time."

"How long?"

"Nearly fifty-five years."

"How old is this son of a bitch?"

Luther looked up at the open sky from the courtyard and thought for a moment. "Figure he's got to be close to eighty."

"Could you at least have hired someone who won't die on us?"

"He shore is a tough ole dog," Luther said. "He couldn't believe when he read that your family was flown in a real airplane. He said, 'Hot damn, that's somethin'.' I mean, he was real taken with it an' all."

"Son of a bitch."

"What?" George asked. Three Mexican waiters brought out platters and platters of tacos, enchiladas, refried beans, and guacamole. Cold beer for Kathryn, who ran the iced Shiner Bock across her forehead.

"Luther hired Methuselah to represent Ma."

"Good at cha," George said.

"Can you head back in the morning?" Kathryn asked.

"I 'spec so," Luther said.

They all ate for a while, Flossie Mae for once showing a goddamn smile while she filled her gullet. George picked at his plate of tacos and finished off the entire bottle of tequila, Kathryn having to pin his arm to the chair so he didn't get up and dance with the band. "That's so beautiful," George said, listening to them play under that old oak lit with Christmas lights. "It's breaking my heart."

"It might if you knew Spanish," Kathryn said. "George, we gotta get outta Texas."

"What have I been sayin'?"

"The heat's too much."

"Like I said."

"Where to?" she asked.

"The World's Fair," Geraline said, speaking up loud and strong from the head of the table, a fork pointed right at George and Kathryn. "The G'll never find you."

"Hell of an idea, kid," George said. "Hell of an idea."

Kathryn nodded.

"Goody," Geraline said, going back to eating her enchiladas.

"Oh, no," Kathryn said. "We split ways here."

Geraline shrugged and dug into her beans. The child thought for a moment, as she chewed, and said, "Newspaper says they're looking for a man and a woman traveling together. A 'rough-and-tumble couple,' is what it read. Woman with brown hair and a 'wicked jaw.' Man is an expert machine gunner."

George grinned and nodded. "Damn right."

"What's it to you?" Kathryn asked.

"Nobody said anything about a family," Geraline said, playing with a loose ribbon. "I bet I could pass as your daughter."

Kathryn looked to George, red-eyed and shiftless. George shrugged.

"We could stay a couple nights with your dear grandma and then take 66 over to Chicago," he said.

Luther looked to Flossie Mae and Flossie Mae back to Luther, before staring down at her plate of beans and not saying a word. Luther scraped all the food on his plate into one mess of tortilla, chicken, and beans, and stuffed in a big mouthful, saying, "I shore hate to break up the family."

Kathryn blew cigarette smoke up high into the air. "You'll be paid."

"Well," Luther said, chewing and then taking a tremendous swallow,

"I s'pose if it'll help out you good people, we could part company for a bit."

Geraline winked at George. He smiled and shot her with his thumb and forefinger before asking the waiter for a cold beer. "You sure that wasn't Gus Jones?" George whispered into Kathryn's ear. "I'm seeing that short bastard everywhere. Or have I gone screwy?"

32

Wednesday, September 13, 1933

So we're on?" Harvey said.

"We're on," Alvin Karpis said.

"Been a hell of a trip to Chi with the roadblocks, train stations covered and all," Harvey said. "We've been driving for the last two days without sleep, switching off at the wheel, keeping to the cat roads. I can't stand my own smell."

"How you doin' back there, Verne?" Karpis asked, looking in the rearview mirror of his Chrysler Imperial convertible, spit-shined, with white leather interior. Miller grunted and blew some smoke up toward the front of the car.

"It's worth your time, Harv," Karpis said.

"Sawyer said it's the biggest job he'd ever heard of."

"It's worth your time," Karpis said, driving the streets of downtown Chicago, racing the El train above them, in and out of shadows, looking sharp in a white suit and straw boater, flushed with sun, health, and money. He shifted down onto Wabash and then took a hard turn onto Roosevelt, heading west over a rusted bridge and the river.

"Are we playing a game, Kreeps?" Harvey asked. "We're pretty beat."

"Read about Dallas," Karpis said, smiling over at Harvey in the passenger seat. "Ten floors. How'd you pull that off?"

"I greased the wheels of justice."

"Listen, a couple fellas from the Syndicate came to see me this week," Karpis said. "First thing I thought was, Oh, shit, they know about the job and want a piece."

"Who?"

"'Three-Fingered' Willie and Klondike O'Donnell. Some other fella named Deandre. They wanted to know if we'd thrown in with the Touhy brothers. You ain't in with the Touhys, are you, Verne?"

Miller didn't say anything.

"That's what I told 'em," Karpis said, heading in a straight shot through the West Side, passing the brownstones and corner markets, kids playing under the shade of oaks. "So this guy Deandre says to me to enjoy Chicago, but don't get caught in this personal shit storm between the Touhys and the Syndicate. They're no fans of you, Miller. Said Kansas City was a top-shelf clusterfuck. I hate to say it, but they got it in for you pretty bad, Verne. They'd love to ace you off God's green earth. Killin' those cops in Kansas City was bad business. I'd lay pretty low, if I was you."

"So, what's the job, Kreeps?" Harvey said.

"Federal Reserve," Karpis said.

"Right downtown."

"Right downtown," Karpis said.

"You're nuts," Harvey said. "No offense and all."

"I got an ace up my sleeve," Karpis said. "You know how much money we're talking?"

Karpis told them. Harvey smiled.

Karpis drove them over to this place in Cicero, Joe's Square Deal Garage, where he parked in a side alley, dripping with rainwater, with ferns and weeds growing from the red brick walls. Inside, they found a little fella welding in blue coveralls with the name JOE stitched on the pocket. When he saw the men, he killed the torch and flipped back his shield and smiled. He'd been adding thick steel plates onto a brand-new Hudson. Karpis circled the car, knocked on the glass with a fist, and popped the trunk, studying what looked like a little oil canister connected to an assortment of tubes and wires.

Miller looked over to Harvey. Harvey shrugged.

"Armor-plated. Bulletproof glass. With a flip of a switch, we get a smoke screen that'll cover a city block."

"Trick car," Miller said. "Great, if we make it out alive."

"Why do you think I called you boys?"

Miller looked to Harvey. Harvey looked back and shrugged again.

"You two can stay here," Karpis said. "Joe's got a couple cots for you and a shower to clean up. I'll see what I can do about clothes. Harvey, you look like you belong in a breadline."

Harvey still wore Manion's clothes, and the smell of the dead fat man was still on him. He thanked Karpis and went to the bathroom with a bar of soap and a straight razor, cleaning himself up the best he could and sliding into mechanic's coveralls and some boots without laces.

"You bring 'em?" Karpis asked when he joined the boys back at the trick Hudson.

"Yeah, yeah." Harvey found his golf bag in the trunk of the Plymouth and returned with two Thompsons and extra drums. Harvey admired the cleaning he'd done on the stock and barrel of one of them the other night and passed it over to Karpis.

"Nice," Karpis said.

"Borrowed one of 'em from Kelly."

Joe the mechanic walked over, cleaning grease off his hands with a red rag soaked in gasoline. "George Kelly?" he asked. "'Machine Gun' Kelly?"

Harvey looked at the little guy, not liking that he was an eavesdropper or that he was talking about George Kelly like he was big shit. Karpis smiled, having been with Harvey that night in Minneapolis when George and Kathryn robbed him of ten g's. "What'd he say, Joe?" Karpis asked with a smile.

"He had me put this little Cadillac in storage last month and bought a nice little Chevrolet off me," Joe said. "Now he sez he's gotten himself a Ford and wants to trade out again. Never thought I'd see him so soon—not in Chicago, with the heat all on him. Figured he'd be in South America by now, but he called and sez he'll be here tomorrow. He thrown in with you fellas?"

A CORN FARMER GEORGE HAD KNOWN FROM HIS BOOTLEG-ging days let them sleep a night in his barn not far out of Joplin off 66, the golden road they'd taken since Oklahoma, and would continue to weave off and on till they got to Chicago. Kathryn had run the Ford up into the big barn and killed the headlights, the farmer coming out to hand them some horse blankets and pillows, wandering to a big pile of hay and using his pitchfork to scare off a hog hidden inside. The hog squealed and trotted away, Kathryn saying she'd just as soon sleep in the backseat. The barn smelled of leather tack and pig shit.

"Y'all need some grub?" the farmer asked.

George told the man they'd eaten a hundred miles ago. Geraline still slept in the front seat, snoring, not stirring since the state line.

"Got another couple stayin' the night, too," the farmer said. "Don't let 'em spook you. They's set up in the loft."

Kathryn grabbed the horse blanket, smelled cat urine, and tossed it back to George. George wandered around the big, open barn, holding the lantern and talking to a horse in its stall. "Hello, there."

"Get some sleep," Kathryn said.

"My, my," George said, finding an empty stall, shining his light on a large stack of wooden crates halfway covered with a torn-up quilt.

"Quit talking to that horse and get some sleep."

"God bless 'im."

"What?"

"Likker," George said. "Cases of the stuff."

"That's not yours," Kathryn said, wandering out of the backseat of the car and trying to lead George back to the hay. But George had already opened a wooden crate and unscrewed the top of a jelly jar. He took a big sip. "Smooth as gasoline."

He held the jar under Kathryn's nose, and the fumes about knocked her out.

"That'll make you go blind."

"Mother's milk."

"It's your turn to drive," Kathryn said. "Don't you think you'll sleep it off in the backseat."

"How 'bout a throw, baby?"

"How 'bout you throw yourself."

"Come on, you can be the farmer's daughter."

"You'll wake the kid."

"The kid's asleep," George said. "Let's roll in the hay."

"Good night, George."

Kathryn turned to the Ford but instead faced a thin, worn couple, standing in the door of the barn. The woman held a lantern, and the man shifted in a nervous fashion beside her. George held up the jelly jar and asked if they'd like a drink. Both of them had the hard, bony features of dirt farmers, wearing worn-out clothes and scrapes across their faces. The man had ears as big as Clark Gable's and hair that looked like it had been combed with chicken grease. The woman had mousy brown hair and pale skin, and perhaps would've been pretty if life hadn't been so damn rough. She tramped on through the pig shit and hay in an old-timey black dress and a modern beret. Her shoes were black laced boots like Kathryn had seen on Ora in old photographs.

The man stepped up to George and offered his hand. "You're George Kelly."

George opened his mouth, stumbling for a bit before saying, "Name's Johnson. Travelin' with my family."

The rangy man laughed and took a hit of George's liquor. "I'm Clyde Barrow. But you can call me Smith."

George nodded.

"This is Mrs. Smith."

The woman nodded at George. She had the plug of an old cigar in the side of her mouth and an old revolver hanging from a rope around her waist. She snuggled up into the arm of the lanky man as the man passed the jelly jar back to George. "Where y'all headed?"

George studied the man's face. "You Buck Barrow's brother?"

"I am."

"We're headed north," George said.

"We're headed south."

"Sorry to hear about your brother," George said.

The couple climbed up the barn ladder into the loft, and soon the lantern went out. George finished off half the jar of hooch and made some noise, turning over and over in the hay, until he said, "Gosh dang it," and got in the backseat with her, smelling of barn animals and hay. Kathryn let him get close, figuring they could get clean in the morning, too tired to fight him, and she adjusted, nuzzling up into his chest. From high in the loft, Kathryn heard a rapid knock-knock-knocking, and the sharp, harsh cry of a woman deep in the throes.

George snickered.

"Sure you don't want some moonshine?" he asked.

"Shush," she said. "Who are those people anyway?"

"Just some cheap fillin'-station thieves," George said. "Fella's brother got filled with lead a few weeks back. It made all the papers. Don't know his woman."

Kathryn stayed awake for a long time, the couple up in the loft not waiting but a few minutes before getting back to it, or continuing with it, and then finally they were asleep, too, and she was left with only the sound of the nickering horses and the hot wind through the barn cracks. The little girl sounded soft and light, gently snoring in the front seat.

Kathryn put the flat of her hand to George's chest and felt his heart beat until it lulled her asleep.

LUTHER ARNOLD CRACKED OPEN THE DOOR TO HIS SUITE IN the Skirvin Hotel and peered over the safety chain into the face of Gus T. Jones. "Evenin', Mr. Arnold. You mind if we might have a word?" Jones heard laughter and giggles inside, and figured it to be from the two hefty women spotted with Arnold at the hotel bar. Arnold told Jones he didn't care for whatever it was he was sellin' and tried to close the door, instead finding Jones's boot.

"Won't take long, sir," Jones said, keeping an eye on Arnold from over the chain.

"I said I ain't buyin'."

Jones stepped back beside White and Colvin and then kicked in the door and sent the short, stubby little Luther Arnold down on his ass.

The fat women, one in a silk robe and the other with a towel strained about her girth, both ran for a corner. Empty bottles of Pabst Blue Ribbon fell from a nightstand, a half dozen lying unopened in buckets of ice.

Arnold looked up at Jones and wiped his lip. His skinny, hairy legs splayed, the front of his Skirvin robe halfway open.

"Hell," Jones said. "Cover your peter, son."

Arnold stood, tying the robe with his sash, trying his best to stand tall and take charge of the situation. "I'm a guest of this here ho-tel. And I paid my bill in cash."

The men heard water running, and White pulled his thumb buster from his belt, cracking open the bathroom door. A big bathtub, fashioned of marble and gold, overflowed with bubbles onto the tile floor, some of those suds caught in Arnold's ears and in the big girls' hair. White turned off the faucet and dried his hands on his pants.

"Sir, are you acquainted with George Kelly?" Jones asked. "We're agents with the Department of Justice."

Arnold's mouth hung open, and he slowly shook his head.

Jones slapped the man's face. "Speak up, son."

One of the women screamed, and the other began to scoop up their dresses, shoes, undergarments, and purses, neither of them a stranger to a raid. The women smelled the way whores do, with perfume so sweet and strong that it made your eyes water.

"Agent Colvin, would you escort these ladies downstairs?"

Colvin motioned his chin to Arnold.

"We'll be down," Jones said. "First, me and Doc gonna have a heart-to-heart with Mr. Arnold."

The young man just stood there, looking from Jones to Doc White. Only when Jones shot him a hard look did Colvin grab each woman by the elbow, leading them from the gilded suite.

"High time in O.K. City, ain't it?" Jones asked.

"You slapped me," Luther Arnold said, wiping his pug nose.

"Start talkin'."

"I don't know no George Kelly."

"You know Kathryn Kelly?"

"I don't know no one named Kelly."

"Son, you're tryin' my patience here," Jones said. "Aren't you the go-between with the Kelly gang and that old attorney?"

Arnold ran a hand over his wet hair and rested a hand on the wall. "That's none of your concern."

"Doc, I think Mr. Arnold here might be in need of the cure."

Arnold looked to the older man, and White walked around him and snatched his arms behind his back, forcing him into the bathroom and tossing him back into the claw-footed tub with a hard splash. Jones followed and slowly took off his suit jacket, rolling his shirtsleeves to the elbow, Arnold flouncing and kicking in the bubbles. Doc White snatched his ankles and jerked him backward.

Jones got to his knees and held a washcloth.

"Son, me and you gonna have a come to Jesus," Jones said. "Kelly and his gang killed a friend of mine, and they're threatenin' to murder a fine family. That's somethin' that we won't abide."

Arnold, eyes wide, held his torso upright with elbows perched on the tub lip, while his ankles were still held high by Doc.

"Are you associated with the Kelly gang?" Jones asked again.

"There ain't no Kelly gang."

"Doc."

White yanked Luther Arnold up by his ankles while Jones smothered his mouth with a washcloth and dunked him deep in the tub, holding him to the count of twenty and then snatching him up by the hair on his head. The little man heaved and vomited sudsy water while Jones held him aloft and asked him again about the Kelly gang.

Arnold shook his head.

Jones kept him down in the tub for a count of thirty, the heaving and vomiting even worse when he brought him back up. And Jones let him get it all out before he asked just how did a cockroach like him come into the employ of a professional like George R. Kelly, expert machine gunner.

"All I did was pay the lawyer," he said. "That ain't no crime."

"Where are you meeting with the Kellys?" Jones asked.

"Sweet Jesus. I cain't say."

"Doc, hold 'im straight."

This time, Arnold took himself a big breath of air before Jones smothered his mouth and forced him back into the sudsy water like a traveling preacher. When the thrashing and tossing suddenly came to a stop, White said, "Think he's had enough, Buster. Buster?"

But Jones's mind had drifted from the Skirvin to a train station with long shafts of morning sunlight, to a box canyon ringed by horse thieves and vultures, to the old, weathered hands of Sheriff Rome Shields, passing on his father's old .45.

"Buster?"

Jones turned to White, and White looked downright concerned. Jones pulled up Arnold, but the man had gone limp. They hauled him out of the tub and set him on the cold tile floor. Jones slapped Arnold's back and Arnold came to, heaving water and twisting onto all fours and gagging out a few gallons.

White sat on the lip of the tub and lit a cigarette. He wouldn't look at Jones.

"I met her at a fillin' station in Itasca," Arnold said. "I didn't know who she was till she give me fifty dollar to locate this attorney in Fort Worth named Sayres. My family needed the money. We hadn't et in days."

"When was that?" Jones asked.

"Last week."

"What day?"

"Sunday," Arnold said. "I recall 'cause we was in church."

"Quit your lyin'."

"Yes, sir."

"And you kept the money?"

"No, sir," Arnold said, rolling to his butt, covering himself up with a bath mat, trying to catch his breath. "I give the lawyer his money and gone back to Cleburne to see Mrs. Kelly."

"You said Itasca."

"We met in Itasca, but she rode my family out to this tourist camp in Cleburne."

"How'd you get to Fort Worth?"

"Trailways bus, sir."

"And you came back to the tourist court."

"The lawyer didn't have no good news about her kin, and she got a little hot about that and wanted me to go back and fetch her machine. Next day, Mrs. Kelly drove me and my wife and daughter to Fort Worth on their way to San Antone. She let me out at the bus station and tole me to get her Chevrolet back and then go on and hire this attorney I know'd in Enid."

"But you didn't go to Enid."

"Not right away," Arnold said. "I couldn't find Mr. Sayres, and my resolve had withered," Arnold said, shaking his head with great sadness. "Did I tell you I'd been traveling with my family? We hadn't et in days."

Jones nodded.

"We'd been tossed off our family farm, sir, and didn't have nowheres to go. I hadn't had a square meal in some time, making sure any money we found while trampin' went to my sweet daughter. I guess I'd grown weak in my body and my spirit. Mrs. Kelly give me five hunnard dollar, and when I couldn't find Mr. Sayres that night, well, I found myself goin' to a beer hall. I'm a weak man, sir."

Jones looked up at White. White tried not to grin and just shook his head with the damn shame of it.

"Well, sir," Arnold said, "one beer led to two beers, and three beers led to a dozen. And when I get to drinkin', I get to feelin' lonesome."

"So you got yourself a whore," Jones said.

"Miss Rose ain't no whore," Arnold said. "I made sure when I asked the barkeep for some company he didn't call up some damn ole whore. Just wanted some company, is all. A fine lady. What's the matter with some company in this coldhearted world?"

"Quit your blubberin'," White said. "When'd you see George Kelly last?"

Arnold shook his head and looked down at his pruned toes. "No, sir."

"You ready, Doc?"

Doc turned on the faucet.

"I seen 'im Saturday in San Antone," Arnold said. "First time I'd ever met the feller. He'd been aways, and Mrs. Kelly wasn't too pleased with him, me, being a married man, understandin' the whole situation."

"Why'd you come back?"

"Mrs. Kelly wanted me to pay out her new attorney."

"So you picked up two more whores and rented out the presidential suite?"

"Now, hold on there," Arnold said, gripping the edge of the toilet to stand, bath mat held in his fingers over his genitalia. "I'll have you know these were the same dang whores—I mean, ladies—I picked up last week. They was company, that's all. Who of us don't have sin in our heart?"

"You drove back through Fort Worth to pick 'em up?" White asked. "Must've been worth it."

"Hell, it was on the way," Arnold said. "Sir."

"Your wife and child still with the Kellys?" White asked.

"My wife's still in San Antone," Arnold said. "The Kellys took my baby girl with 'em. Figured it would make 'em look like a family 'case of roadblocks and the like. Promised they'd wire us once they got to where they was goin' and send Gerry back on the train. Lord in heaven, I'm sick with worry."

Jones reached onto the towel rack and dried his hands, rolling his sleeves back down to the wrist and slipping back into his jacket, noticing the wet splatter on his pants that would dry quickly in the summer heat. "Come on."

"Where we goin'?" Arnold asked.

"San Antonio," Jones said. "To wait on that cable from the Kellys."

33

Sunday, September 17, 1933

They drove into Chicago at early evening, finding a furnished apartment in the *Chicago Tribune* classifieds right on State Street down from the Chicago Theatre. They paid the woman a week's rent, and Kathryn lay across a narrow bed while Gerry explored the kitchenette. George just peeked out a window, watching the El train rattle past, glass shaking in the frame, and said, "It ain't the Stevens."

"You said we couldn't stay in a hotel."

"I said we couldn't stay at the Stevens, 'cause we always stay at the Stevens and they know us."

"They know the Shannons. Or were we the Colemans?"

"They know our faces."

Kathryn rolled over on her back and unbuckled her shoes, kicking them onto the floor. "God, I'm hungry."

She looked down at her foot, feeling something strange, and noticed three dime-size holes in her stockings. George stayed at the window, the curtain crooked in his finger, and said, "There's a joint on State that sells waffles."

"I don't want a goddamn waffle," Kathryn said.

"Looks good. Virginia's Golden Brown Waffles. I sure would like a waffle. That'd hit the spot. What'd you say, Gerry? How about a waffle?"

"Can you get a waffle with ice cream?" the kid asked.

"You better believe it," George said. "You can get whatever you want."

"What time does the Fair close?" Gerry asked.

"Too late today, kid," Kathryn said.

"You promised."

"I said we'd go," Kathryn said. "I didn't say when."

Gerry wandered out from the little kitchen, saying the icebox and cupboards were completely empty save for a box of baking soda and two dead roaches. George had bought her a pack of chewing gum back in Missouri, and the girl hadn't stopped chomping and blowing bubbles for the last two hundred miles. Kathryn wished she'd blow a bubble big enough to drown out her talking and then explode it all across her little face and mousy hair in those pink ribbons.

"Waffles," George said, again. "I can almost make out something showing at the picture show. Something about a detective with William Powell."

"Private Detective 62," Kathryn said, more to herself than anyone in the room.

"How'd you know that?"

"Saw it in the paper."

"What's that picture he did with the dogs?" George asked. "Wasn't he a detective in it, too?"

"Kennel Murder Case."

"Doesn't sound like this one has dogs."

"George, I know for a fact it doesn't have dogs. That was another picture."

"Let's go get a waffle," George said. "Kit, where's my bottle?"

"In your luggage, dear."

"Don't need to take that kind of tone," George said. "Just wanted a nip before the picture."

"Are we on vacation?" Gerry asked.

"You bet, kiddo," George said.

"Good Lord in heaven," Kathryn said.

They ate waffles across State Street at Virginia's Golden Brown, and from the booth by the plateglass window, Kathryn watched the traffic light changing colors under the El station, a bolted collection of steel beams and scrolled staircases. Above them, another train clanked and rattled past. The Chicago Theatre marquee lit up the wet brick streets with a cool, even whiteness.

George snuck a bottle of bourbon into his coat and kept refilling his mug under the table. "Who's that?"

"Who?"

"You see him? That man under the El tracks?"

"How the hell should I know?"

Kathryn saw the shadow of a man in a suit and hat, smoking a cigarette. Nothing but shadow, the same as the beams of the El, the streetlamp posts, and the traffic light. George leaned into her and said, "It's the G."

"You need to put down the bottle."

"Ha."

She turned back to the glass, and the man—the shadow—was gone. A tired waitress, with tired marcelled hair, laid down the waffles without a smile, a check to follow. Gerry and George ordered the same—a goddamn waffle with vanilla ice cream, whipped cream, and chocolate syrup. *Who'd ever heard of such a thing?*

"What'd ya think?" George asked the kid.

The girl took a big forkful, making a real corny show of getting an even mixture of all the ingredients, and closed her eyes with the tasting.

"Wow," she said.

"What'd I tell you?" George said.

"Would you two just shut up," Kathryn said. "I'm trying to think here."

She squashed out a cigarette and lit another. She thought for a while and waited for that shadow man to appear. *The G.* George had gone bugs.

The El tracks and girders and beams formed a long, dark, endless tunnel right through the heart of the city. The whole town seeming less like a city but more like a goddamn cage, and the thought of it made Kathryn itch a great deal. The night was slick with a mist that fell over the city, denting puddles and giving halos to streetlamps.

"Gerry?" Kathryn asked.

The girl finished another bit of her forkful, listening, half the goddamn waffle gone.

"What kind of man is your father?"

"He's nice."

"That's not an answer. I mean, can I trust the SOB?"

Gerry finished off another couple bites of the waffle and then looked down at Kathryn's cigarette case. Kathryn rolled her eyes and slid over the case. George worked on his waffle, eyes down, but fished into his jacket pocket for the lighter engraved with her stepfather's initials. He clicked it open and lit the kid's Lucky.

Gerry leaned back into her seat. She shrugged.

"You mean before or after he was in prison?" the kid asked.

Kathryn slammed down the flat of her hand on the table. "A farmer. He said he was a goddamn farmer."

"He was," Gerry said. "But we make most our dough hanging paper."

"How you know words like that?" Kathryn asked. "Paperhanger and the like?"

"Isn't that what you call 'writing phony checks'?"

George mopped up the last bit of waffle, forked it, and stuck it into his mouth. He pushed the plate away and chewed. He gave a lopsided grin to Kathryn, her knowing the son of a bitch was aching to say it. "Salt of the earth? Good country people? Whatsa matter with you, Kit?"

_____

"IT'S A BEAUT," HARVEY SAID. "THAT'S FOR SURE."

He stood next to Karpis across the street from the Federal Reserve
Building on Jackson, fronted by six big Greek columns and two American flags as big as Cadillacs. Two tall iron streetlamps lit up the façade
and an armored truck parked along the sidewalk. It was midnight, and
the two men wore summer-weight suits and straw hats. They watched
and walked, stopping to take it all in as they lit up cigarettes and watched
the streets.

The vault was three floors beneath the street, Karpis said. The trans-
fers from the post office were made at different times on different nights.
Sunday nights were at midnight, same as Thursday night, when they
planned to take the dough.

"Six guards?"

"Sometimes more," Karpis said.

"How many more?"

"No more than two."

They watched as four guards wheeled fat canvas bags on a dolly down
Jackson Street and into the side door of the Reserve.

"How much is the haul?"

"Guess it would be two mil."

"I don't like to guess."

"I like the odds," Karpis said, smoking and continuing to walk down
Jackson before they turned up Franklin to Adam.

"What's the git?"

"We park the Hudson a block over," Karpis said. "When the guards
round the corner at Clark, I'll hit the smoke screen to stop any traffic. You
and the Barkers will take the dough. I'll keep Miller with me to cover
the street. We'll follow the same route we're walking . . . Now, turn here."

They kept walking, turning west on Adam toward the river. Harvey
spent his cigarette and fished into his coat for another, feeling better now
that he was clean and dressed decent.

"We'll have two fresh cars waiting at the garage. New clothes, bandages, morphine."

"You expect trouble?"

"Nothing ventured."

"You trust the Barkers?" Harvey asked. "They ain't the brightest."

"Nobody's better."

"Except me," Harvey said.

The men found the Plymouth parked by the river, and they drove across the bridge, catching Jackson again to the south, down by the train station. Lou Mitchell's diner was half empty at midnight, and they found a small booth where they hung their hats on hooks and ordered coffee and pie.

"You got to lose Miller," Karpis said. "He ain't long for this world."

"He's got a plan."

"How 'bout you?"

Harvey shrugged, stirring his coffee with a thick tablespoon of sugar, shuffling a fresh cigarette out of the pack and clicking open his lighter.

"This thing puts out and I'm headed to Australia," Karpis said.

"No shit?"

"I'm done, Harvey," Karpis said, his sad face drooping and serious. "We got a few more months, tops, before the whole damn government is on us. It ain't like it used to be. And next year will be even worse. How much more time do you think we have hitting banks and making dashes across the state lines? The G's taking over the banks."

"Australia."

"Yep."

"What gave you that idea?"

"I read this story in *Collier's*. Sounded like a nice place. Started by outlaws."

Harvey nodded and then drank some coffee.

"You got to split with Miller," Karpis said. "The Syndicate has money out."

Harvey put down his coffee mug. He ashed his cigarette.

"When?"

"Few weeks now," Karpis said. "He tell you why he killed those cops and Nash?"

A waitress walked over and left the check. The men turned their heads slightly until she had walked away.

Karpis smiled. "You know, I was a kid when I read about that job you pulled in '22."

"That wasn't me."

"Everybody knows."

"I don't know what you're talking about."

"What happened to all that money? You must've gotten half a mil."

"It's never enough, Kreeps. You can lie to yourself all you want. You can sail to the other side of the world, but you'll just find that gun in your hand and an itch in your heart. It's a goddamn disease."

"Come on," Karpis said. "Happy days are here again . . ."

"Why aren't you smiling?"

JONES SAT LUTHER AND FLOSSIE MAE ARNOLD IN THE backseat the next morning with Doc White between them. Jones checked his pocket watch, waiting for the post office in San Antonio to open its doors before following Flossie Mae inside. The first trip was worthless, but after lunch she'd received a telegram. Jones pulled it from her fingers when they climbed back into the stifling car, Luther asking them when they'd be fed.

The telegram was sent from Chicago. Jones sliced it open with a pocketknife and read, "GREETINGS FROM A CENTURY OF PROGRESS. NO TIME TO WRITE. AT FAIR DAY AND NIGHT. SHE'S NEVER OUT OF MY SIGHT, AND BE CAREFUL TO TAKE CARE OF MY CLOTHES FOR THEY ARE ALL I HAVE SO DON'T LOSE THEM. LEAVE FOR SHANGRI-LA APARTMENTS, O.K. CITY. MORE SOON."

"What's it say?" Luther asked from the backseat. "That wasn't meant for you."

"It says you two are going to Oklahoma City."

"That's where you just brung me from," Luther said. "We driving back now?"

"You'll be locked up in the city jail. We'll arrange for you to be shipped back."

"And just where in the hell are y'all goin'?" Luther asked. "And just when are you gonna get us our little girl back? Are you two cowboys listening to me?"

34

Every shadow had become the G to George, and now the bastard had her jumping out of her skin, too. Before they left the waffle joint, a couple joes had walked in and kept on giving sideways glances, and at first Kathryn was sure they were admiring her profile, but then George noticed them, paid the check, and wandered out under the El, Gerry splashing her new patent leather shoes in puddles until Kathryn told her to please act civil. But George just flat-out refused to go back to the apartment and drove them around the city, and for a while it was nice, being in a big, fat town like Chicago and driving past the Marshall Field's windows and across the bridge to the Magnificent Mile, riding past the Tribune Tower and parking by Tiffany's, window-shopping at night, keeping their backs turned to the street and checking out the new fall dresses, shoes, furs, and wraps, letting her mind already drift to the trial—if there was a trial—and how she'd look with that velvet hat cocked just so.

George stood flat-footed at the window of Hart Schaffner Marx, staring at a vacant bust of a dummy. The entire window display bare except for a pair of polished wingtips.

"Hey there," Kathryn said, squeezing his hand. "It's going to be fine. We'll be fine."

"I'm a dead man," he said. "Hope you know that."

"Quit being so dramatic."

"No one gets out of this world alive."

"Dime-novel stuff."

"Another one," he said. "They're across the street. Don't look back. Don't look back."

Kathryn looked over her shoulder and saw a man in a dark suit watching them from over Michigan Avenue. She walked ahead and grabbed Gerry, who was studying what looked to be a small town in a department-store window. Children played on seesaws, chased dogs, and curtsied in their fall prints. Some carried schoolbooks. Her nose was pressed against the glass.

"C'mon, kid."

"Can I drive?"

"You can't drive."

"You bet I can."

"Why didn't you tell us before?"

"On 66, I just wanted to sleep."

Kathryn walked back, told the girl to jump in the backseat, and knocked the starter, driving slow on the Mile for George, who crawled in beside her and took his hat from his head, leaning back into the Ford's seat. "We gotta ditch the car. I tried that rat bastard Joe Bergl ten times."

"Call 'em ten more."

"I don't want to go back there."

"Where?"

"The apartment," he said. "They got us, Kit. They're just making us into fools now. I hadn't even been to the gosh-dang Fair."

"How much of that shine did you drink?"

"Not enough."

Kathryn raced the Ford under the State Street El and turned down toward the apartment, telling Gerry to hop out and get the bags they hadn't unpacked. The kid leaned in and listened, nodding, and scooted on out the door, not needing to be told twice.

"That's a good kid," George said.

"I think you've lost your mind."

"You wanna take a chance?"

"Goddamn you, George."

Kathryn circled around the Loop until she spotted a late showing at the Piccadilly Theatre and let George out with a couple bucks. She said she'd send Gerry in to get him when it was safe. "Aw, hell," he said, stumbling out and craning his neck up to the blinding marquee. "*Gabriel Over the White House?* I've seen this horseshit once and didn't like it the first time."

"Grab some popcorn," Kit said. "Kick your feet up and have a snooze."

She knocked the Ford into first and circled on back down around the street through tall concrete and metal, the guts of the city machine, and headed toward the apartment, the rain starting again, wipers going, leaning into the windshield to see Geraline sitting on their luggage under the El tracks.

Kathryn honked her horn, and the girl threw the bags in and crawled in after them. "Whew."

"Anyone see you?"

"I think the mug is screwy," Geraline said.

Kathryn caught Gerry's eye in the rearview and narrowed her look at the girl.

"I took the service elevator and didn't see a thing."

"Good, kid."

"You gonna let me drive?"

"When we get a new machine."

"What kind are we gonna get?"

"Whatever George can find."

"Hope it's a Cadillac," she said. "I sure like those Cadillacs."

"Me, too, sister."

They drove around the city for a while, Kathryn knowing Chicago better than anyone who ever headed this way from Mississippi and pointing out this and that, the Wrigley Building, City Hall—*blah, blah, blah*—but all of it somehow meaning something to the kid of a dirt farmer. Kathryn checked the time, realizing they'd have to find some new digs, and sent Gerry back into the Piccadilly for George, heading north this time, skirting the lakefront.

"It was worse this time," George said. "Walter Huston as the president gave me the creeps. The whole picture did nothing but blame gangsters for this country's problems. What about the oilmen, the bank presidents, the greedy bastards on Wall Street? It's easy. We're an easy target. Hey, you want some popcorn?"

An hour later they found an apartment far north on Winthrop Street, a place called the Astra, the manager not even minding it being late and showing the good family to the little efficiency with a smile—this place being a hell of a lot cleaner—and talking about all the good folks he'd met from all over the world on account of the Fair.

"We're going tomorrow," Gerry said.

Kathryn ruffled her hair. "Ain't she cute?"

George found the icebox and stared inside until Kathryn came over and let him know it was empty. She gave Geraline a five-spot and told her to fetch up some eggs and beer from a corner grocery she'd spotted.

"Candy?"

"Knock yourself out."

Just as the door closed, she pulled George in close and bit his ear. He just stood there, limp in the shoulder and the arm, and she took a big handful of his sweaty shirt and asked him to do some pretty rough things to her. When he didn't answer, she slapped him across the mug. "What's the matter? We made it."

"I'm going to sleep."

She reached for his thick hand and placed it across her breast. His hand fell away, and he shook his head. "Wake me if I sleep too late," he said, and stumbled off into a bedroom he'd never seen.

Kathryn sat there in the half dark on top of a big suitcase, wondering where the kid had gone, until she spotted something in a far corner, covered in dust and left alone. A fine, solid L. C. Smith & Corona, with working keys and everything, and a fat flat of snow-white paper.

She sat down and played with the keys a bit, the windows cracked open, hearing the night clatter of cars passing and kids up past their bedtime. A dog barking.

She played with the keys. She inserted a piece of paper.

By the time Geraline returned with an apple box of groceries, Kathryn barely heard her come in, Kathryn's temples throbbing and sweat ringing the front of her dress and under her arms. She roused George from his sleep, only a crack of light coming from the bathroom.

"Hold this," she said.

He took it and tried to focus, and then threw it to the ground and turned back over.

She picked it up with her gloves, folded it, and slipped it into an envelope addressed to Charles F. Urschel, Federal Building, Oklahoma City.

CHARLES F. URSCHEL KEPT THE LETTER IN THE RIGHT-hand pocket of the suit Berenice had picked out—a strong navy linen, a crisp white shirt, and red tie clipped with a silver pin. He didn't even think about reading it until he had been seated beside his wife, two sons, and Betty in the federal courthouse, a sweltering hotbox where women waved fans in front of their faces and men used the morning edition of the newspaper to create just a stir of air. Charlie at first thought the letter might not make a bad fan, and only on a whim did he slice it open with his thumb, being used to fan letters, love notes, and crackpots claiming to be Kelly himself. He unfolded it on his knee just as Boss and Ora, along with Potatoes, were led into the courtroom and seated side by side at the defense table. The table was flat and polished neat, a sweating pitcher of water and glasses the only obstruction.

While everyone continued to talk, waiting for the judge, Charles glanced down at the loose sheets of paper from the letter airmailed from Chicago:

Ignorant Charles:

Just a few lines to let you know that I am getting my plans made to destroy your so-called mansion, and you and your family immediately after this trial. And you fellow, I guess you've begun to realize your serious mistake. Are you ignorant enough to think the Government can guard you forever? I gave you credit for more sense than that, and figured you thought too much of your family to jeopardize them as you have, but if you don't look out for them, why should we. I dislike hurting the innocent, but I told you exactly what would happen you can bet $200,000 more everything I said will be true. You are living on borrowed time now. You know that the Shannon family are victims of circumstances the same as you was. You don't seem to mind prosecuting the innocent, neither will I have any conscious qualms over brutally murdering your family. The Shannons have put the heat on, but I don't desire to see them prosecuted as they are innocent and I have a much better method of settling with them. As far as the guilty being punished you would probably have lived the rest of your life in peace had you tried only the guilty, but if the Shannons are convicted, look out, and God help you for he is the only one that will be able to do you any good. In the event of my arrest, I've already formed an outfit to take care of and destroy you and yours the same as if I was there. I am spending your money to have you and your family killed—nice eh? You are bucking people that have cash, planes, bombs, and unlimited connections both here and abroad. I have friends in Oklahoma City that know every move and every plan you make, and you are still too dumb to figure out the finger man there.

If my brain was no larger than yours, the Government would have had me long ago, as it is I am drinking good beer and will yet see you and your family like I should have left you at first—stone dead.

I don't worry about Bates. He will be out for the ceremonies— your slaughter.

Now I say it is up to you; if the Shannons are convicted, you can
get another rich wife in hell, because that will be the only place you
can use one. Adios, smart one.

Your worst enemy,
Geo. R. Kelly

I will put my fingerprints below so you can't say some crank wrote
this.
See you in hell.

Charlie took a breath, neatly folded the letter, and placed it into his pocket, scanning the courtroom for Bruce Colvin. Right as the judge entered and everyone stood, Charlie damn well heard an airplane overhead. He mopped his brow with a bleached handkerchief and excused himself, making his way from the courtroom, feeling like he was going to vomit.

In the public restroom, he steadied himself at a sink, splashing cold water in his eyes. As he dried his face and looked into the mirror, he spotted Bruce Colvin, standing over his shoulder.

"Betty was concerned."

"I'm fine."

"We've tapped two lines," Colvin said. "Jarrett's office and his personal line at home. We can put every conversation on phonographic records. It's very clever stuff."

Charlie steadied himself with hands on the porcelain sink.

"That won't be necessary."

"We have suspicions, too."

"I said that won't be necessary," Charlie said, turning from the mirror and facing Colvin, the boy's face withering in the volume of his voice. "My concerns were unfounded. I haven't been well."

"I don't believe you."

"Do I need to call Mr. Hoover myself or will you please drop this matter? Walter Jarrett is not a crook."

"May I see what's in the letter?"

Charlie snapped it into his hands like a piece of trash on the way out. "Why don't you just find the Kellys, so my family can sleep. Or are you having too much fun playing house?"

35

Kathryn lost George not long after he'd wandered into the Golden Pavilion of Jehol to find a toilet. She'd said to him, "Go ahead, George, take care of yourself just as we were about to see the Dutch dancers after missing them two days in a row." Ever since they'd been at the Fair—their first day being Tuesday—George had been downright crazy for the Dancers of Tunis featuring the Amazing Iris, drinking gin from his hip flask, feeling like he was invisible with his blond hair and white suit, Panama hat, and purple-tinted glasses. All she wanted to see was one lousy traditional Dutch dance and to spend a little time on the Streets of Paris. But keeping track of George was the trick. And God knows where Gerry went—Kathryn wasn't her mother—the girl showing up at the same time both nights on the Avenue of Flags, where they'd all wait in line for the Sky Ride, stretched high across the Fair, dodging spotlights, the pavilions lit up like ancient pyramids in blue, green, and yellow lights, neon wrapping the streamlined buildings. George would be full-on plastered and proclaim himself the real Buck Rogers and make folks in the Sky Ride laugh. He'd grown *that* goddamn cocky.

Not two seconds after stumbling out of the temple, he wandered up to her and asked her again about the Dancers of Tunis. "Don't you know those girls aren't from Africa," she said. "They're from Brooklyn. Two of 'em are nothing but common bubble dancers."

"The hell you say."

"One thing, George. I asked to see one thing."

"So they dance in wooden shoes," he said. "Where's the kid?"

Kathryn shrugged. She lit a cigarette. They walked down the wide avenues hugging the lakefront. Signs pointing to every corner of the earth. LONDON. PEKING. DARKEST AFRICA.

"I bet she's at the Enchanted Isle."

"She doesn't go for that kids' stuff," she said. "Told me she wanted to see where they made the beer."

"Bavaria," George said. *"Heigh-ho, the gang's all here. Let's have pretzels, let's have beer."*

The streets were fat with people, most of the men in crisp white shirts without ties and women in flowered dresses and straw hats, pouring past George and Kathryn, who walked in the opposite way, crowd pushing around them like water around a river stone.

"Did you call?"

"Hell, yes, I called," he said. "What do you think took so long?"

"I figured the temple has a nice toilet."

"Some fella keeps telling me that Joe will call me back. Said they're working on getting us a car. Forged papers, all that stuff."

"And then what, George?"

"I'll figure it out."

"We leave the country?"

"This country doesn't want us anymore," he said. "Maybe Mexico. Maybe Cuba. Maybe Memphis."

"Memphis?" Kathryn asked. "Are you kidding?"

"I'm tired," he said. "Let's get a drink."

"WHAT ARE THE CHANCES?" DOC WHITE ASKED. "I'VE WALKED from one end of this damn Fair to the other twice and my feet done swoled up."

"Let's take a seat."

Jones and White followed a crowd into a bigmouthed amphitheater, where some kind of spectacle was about to begin. This Fair wasn't short on spectacles, Jones and White not being able to walk ten feet without some carny barker trying to lure them into some forbidden land, exotic culture, or a temple built to some damn company. He'd never seen a church as large as the worship halls they'd built to General Motors, Plymouth, and Hudson. Firestone and Goodyear. He took a seat by Doc White and pulled out some money for a boy selling Coca-Colas from a crate hung 'round his neck.

"The cable was sent from the Fair," Jones said.

"That was two days ago, and Kelly ain't that goddamn stupid," White said, taking off his Stetson for a moment and running a forearm across his brow. "There's no tellin', and we're wasting time."

"Did you buy your wife somethin'?"

"Got 'er a souvenir spoon. You?"

"Bracelet," Jones said, reaching into the pocket of his linen suit and finding a sterling silver band stamped with different exhibits from the Fair.

"Kelly ain't here."

"Today I seen things I never even considered," Jones said. "Sixteen midgets emerged from a Chevrolet. A colored boy made a puppet whistle and dance. Belly dancers, sword swallowers. I walked the canals of Holland, the streets of Paris, and journeyed deep into China. A man even asked me if I wanted to meet someone named Freida Fred, an individual he noted was born with equipment of both sexes."

"Did you see it?"

"Hell, no, I didn't see it."

"Well, lookee there," White said, pointing up to the sky, a silver dirigible floating out across Lake Michigan, the city of Chicago spouting from the ground in steel and concrete to the north.

"*Science Finds, Industry Applies, Man Conforms.*"

"What's that?" White asked.

"Words written over the gates of the Fair."

"I just noticed the belly dancers and that fella dressed as Mickey Mouse."

The loudspeakers crackled to life and announced that the show was a journey through the history of transportation, showing some poor man dressed in goatskins walking an oxcart, followed by racing Roman chariots and some conquistadores on horseback. The announcer seemed to get real excited about traveling the West in a stagecoach. An old Wells Fargo wagon rambled on out of the gate, chased by some banditos on horseback, bandannas over their faces, shooting up guns to the sky the way bandits did in movies but never did in real life 'cause they wouldn't waste a bullet. Doc sipped a Coca-Cola and leaned on his bony knees, signaling another boy for a sack of peanuts.

He shelled the peanuts and absently watched. He'd seen that show before.

The stage stopped and the bandits circled, a woman in a frilly dress and ankle boots, pushed out on the dirt, screaming when her pocketbook was snatched. The gates opened again, tinny, silly music came from the loudspeaker, and there was some stupid son of a bitch riding a white horse.

"You come at 'em straight like that, riding high, and you'll be shot clean off your saddle," White said, nodding to himself. "Who doesn't know that?"

TO GET TO THE STREETS OF PARIS, YOU HAD TO ENTER through a phony steamship that adjoined the display of baby incubators featuring REAL LIVE BABIES. Kathryn had a hell of a hard time prying George away, him pressing his drunk self against the glass and waving at the little babies behind their own glass, just trying to get some sleep after being born into this nuts world and now having to deal with crowds of monkeys pointing and staring at them. She finally got George by promising him a cold beer in the steamship's lounge, and soon they sat up on the top deck of this boat built for land, George sipping on his Budweiser, looking out across Lake Michigan with a self-satisfied smile.

"That little girl's gonna be a hellcat when we send her packing."

"She's fine," George said. "A good girl."

"She thinks every day with the Kellys is the goddamn Fair."

"Hasn't it been?"

"She didn't have to drive from Biloxi to Fort Worth in a jalopy truck looking for you."

"I told you I'd be back."

"You told Ma Coleman you'd be in Mississippi."

"I wrote the word *Mississippi*."

"Which meant for me to drive to Mississippi, knowing you'd be in Biloxi hunting up that lifeguard gal."

"If I was trying to scare up some tail, why'd I tell you where I'd be?" George widened his eyes and pointed at Kathryn with his free finger. "We hit the road tomorrow. Lay low in Memphis and then head back to Ma's farm for the dough. Maybe Cuba. Cuba's looking good."

"A real cakewalk. I'm sure the G will open the cattle gate for us."

"You want some more of my beer?"

"I have champagne."

Kathryn lay back in her seat and crossed her legs. She'd bought a new burgundy dress for the fall, with a square neckline and bloused sleeves at her elbows. She tilted a smart ladies' fedora into her eyes.

"Remember that bootlegger in Tulsa who used to cut apple juice with grain alcohol and call it an 'Oklahoma cocktail'?" he asked.

"It hurt to pee."

"Good times."

"Sure."

"You remember stealing Little Stevie Anderson's bulldog after you packed up to leave him?"

"Of course."

"What happened to that bulldog?"

"I think you sold it to that bartender in Muskogee."

"We'll be fine in Memphis," George said. "Don't you worry about a thing. Ole Lang will take care of us. When his sister and I busted up, he couldn't have been more than twelve. I had to be the one to tell him, him looking to me as a father, I think, on account of what happened to Mr. Ramsey and all. He didn't speak to Geneva for a year after that, blaming the bust on her and not the moonshine I was running. He's a good egg, Lang. You'll like him. He doesn't know I'm George Kelly. You'll have to call me Barnes."

"You want to see your boys, don't you?"

"Yes."

"Figured, the way you were looking at those babies."

"I was looking at the babies 'cause I like babies. What kind of fool doesn't like babies? That's like a man who doesn't enjoy a cold beer. Sister, I missed real beer."

"I miss my girl, too," Kathryn said. "I'd like to see her before—"

"Before what?"

"So you're not gonna turn yourself in?"

George finished off his beer and wiped his mouth with a napkin before lighting up and leaning back. He squinted into the smoke, pretending like he was contemplating the question.

"I knew you'd chicken out," she said.

"It's a fool's deal, Kit," George said. "If I got a guarantee in blood, I still wouldn't believe the G would turn your mother loose. I turn myself in, and they'd just lock us up right next to them. All this for nothing. How'd you feel then?"

"But if we were assured?"

"How do you make sure of that?"

A crowd had gathered around a small tub of water, where a skinny, muscular man started to monkey up a high ladder to a diving board. George smiled, watching him make his way higher and higher. Over

the top of George's purple-tinted sunglasses, he raised his eyebrows at
Kathryn.

She finished the glass of champagne and put down two dollars.

George reached his hand under the table to her leg and inched his way
over her stockings. She snatched it away, shaking her head and turning
back to the fella on the high dive, just cresting the top. There must've
been five hundred people below, right outside the entrance to the Streets
of Paris, craning their necks, staring right into the sun like crazies, and
waiting for him to jump. Even the folks over by the incubators had
finally left those poor babies alone, and quiet came over everyone as the
man lifted his hands high, a cool breeze cutting across the lake, stirring
him a bit, before the nutso bastard turned and flipped and crested like a
bird with holes in its wings to a big, goddamn splash.

The crowd just got loony.

"I wish I could live here."

"We do live here, George."

"IT'D BE PRETTY FUNNY IF WE SAW SOME FELLA WALKIN'
around the Fair wearing a sandwich board that read 'MEET "MACHINE
GUN" KELLY, LIVE AND IN PERSON.'"

"They could charge a handsome admission," Jones said.

"Do they really have a feller here with both sets of plumbing?"

"So I was told."

The sun had started to set, and Doc leaned over the railing at the
Sinclair Oil exhibit, the most realistic-looking dinosaurs you'd ever seen
growling and chomping on some grass that hung from their mouths, red
eyes all lit up. One of the beasts was as large as a Greyhound bus, with a
diagram hung on the fence about how their old carcasses had turned to
lubricant.

Doc broke a peanut in half and threw the shell down into the pit.

"How many men we got working on this?" White asked.

"Here in the city?"

White nodded.

"Figured about twenty," Jones said. "The SAC here, Purvis, says he's got men watching brothels, known watering holes for hoodlums."

"Watering hole sounds pretty good right now," White said, flipping more shells down to the dinosaur as if the beast would suddenly change course and start foraging for real food. "What do you think about that Purvis fella?"

"Hell, all those college boys look the same to me, Doc. At twenty feet, I thought he was Colvin."

"When I walked into the building, he asked me for my thumb buster," White said. "Tole me I couldn't walk around a real city armed. What the hell does he mean 'a real city'?"

"He's just jumpy, is all," Jones said. "Following regulations."

"Kelly ain't here."

"You said that already."

"They'll tip us off in a telegram," White said. "Always do."

"I think if George Kelly is in town, he'll announce it bigger than a telegram."

THE FINAL PLANS WERE LAID OUT OVER A FOLDING CARD table set up in the back room of Joe's Square Deal Garage, with maps of the city marked in pen and opened cartons of chop suey. Karpis wouldn't let any of them drink, saying if they wanted a nip to settle their nerves they'd pass a bottle about go time. But he said it was going to be a hell of a long night, for them to lie out on the cots, think about the details of the job, every step, from the Reserve to the git. At half past twelve it was "Go, go, go, that's the rhythm of the day," just like Fred Astaire says. Harvey squashed out his cigarette and stretched his legs, Miller flat on his back on the floor, not using the cot, eyes wide open, a Thompson like he carried in the war by his feet. The Barker boys were giving a final check over the Hudson, the greased hillbillies more excited about the ride out of town than the dough. And Karpis checked over the map once more before folding it up all nice and neat and tucking it into the side pocket of his suit jacket.

Harvey walked to the bathroom to find a fresh suit of clothes resting on a hanger, new shoes and socks. He shaved and dressed, tying his tie just as someone started beating the hell out of the door and telling him to shake it off and come on.

At first, he thought it was the cops. Or, worse, the Syndicate, looking for a cut.

But, goddamn, it was that hillbilly Fred Barker, telling him he was about to shit his drawers. Bailey left the bathroom and walked across the wide concrete floor to Miller, kicking at his shoe. Miller's bright eyes sprung open, not dozing for a second, waking up like some kind of animal.

"We split the dough, and I want you gone," Harvey said. "You hear me? I'll find my way."

Miller nodded. "Vi's in Brooklyn."

"Go to Brooklyn, anywhere but Chicago. Karpis told me Frank Nitti blames you for the world's problems. You *sabe?*"

Miller nodded.

"Verne?"

Miller pulled up his body to his crooked knees, wrapping his arms around them, and lit a cigarette. Karpis walked back into the room, and Harvey turned to watch him, the light from the single bulb cutting a swath up to Karpis's feet.

"Fred's sick," Karpis said. "Real sick. He's got problems coming from both ends. Said it was the chop suey. Did you guys eat the pork?"

"Give 'im a soda," Harvey said.

"We did," Karpis said. "Shits running through him like a freight train."

"We'll make do," Harvey said.

Karpis put his hands in his pockets, trying to rearrange the whole plan in his mind. But he shook his head. "Nope. Won't work."

Harvey looked down to Miller, and Miller cut his eyes up to Harvey, Harvey knowing this was Miller's last chance, the last few hours he could make a score in Chicago. If there had been another way . . . any way.

KATHRYN WAITED FOR GEORGE AND GERALINE AT THE FENCE to the racetrack on the Enchanted Isle, the little girl and the big lug in the same toy car, zipping around turns, Gerry at the wheel while George laughed and held on to his hat with one hand. They came skipping out from around the exit, George having turned the front brim of his fedora up so that he looked like a stooge. Still wearing the sunglasses after the sun had gone down.

The three of them walked side by side down the Avenue of Flags, where a couple women had chained themselves to a pole, one wearing a stitched cloth that read PROTEST FASCIST TERROR. GERMAN CONSUL HERE. Men stood by and watched the broads like they were sideshow freaks, a couple of coppers standing by, waiting for a key or someone to cut the chain. About halfway down the wide avenue, Kathryn spotted two men, elbow to elbow with thousands of sweaty folks with sore feet, walking back into the fairgrounds, the crowd splitting around them, the two fellas talking and walking in a casual, relaxed way. One was a tall and skeletal thing, wearing a Western suit and boots, the other, in a white linen suit, was shorter, and thick around the middle, wearing Western boots and a pair of glasses.

She clutched George's arm and pulled him into her, a loving couple after a fine old day at the Fair, resting her head on the mug's shoulder, reaching down and gripping Geraline's sweaty little hand. The girl looking up at Kathryn and narrowing her eyes with that goddamn "What gives?" that she'd gotten down pat.

One of the men tipped his cowboy hat to the fine family and kept on walking. George started to whistle "Stormy Weather" as they passed.

"George?"

"I sure am hungry."

"Did you—"

"What?"

She pulled him in closer, following the fat, heavy crowd, bustling with souvenir hats and balloons and pinwheels for the kiddies, out onto South Michigan, walking damn-near a goddamn mile south to find the big open lot where they'd parked that road-tired Ford. Geraline crawled in the backseat and lay down without a word, tuckered out from the long day.

"I shoulda got a hot dog," George said, knocking the car into gear and heading west over the river and back over to Cicero to dump the Ford. They'd get some sleep at the Astra, George said, pack and leave for Memphis in the morning. *Goddamn Memphis.* George excited about heading home, talking about places he wanted to show her.

"You really think we can make it to Cuba?" she asked.

"You can practically see the place from Key West," George said. "We have a nice drive down the coast and then hop a boat."

"I remember *Havana Widows*. Lots of nightclubs."

"You bet. And rum."

"Shoulda known you'd care for rum."

"Joan Blondell sure was a knockout in that picture."

"Why don't you ring her up, then?" Kathryn said. "See if she'll iron your shirts."

The traffic thinned out over the river but nearly stopped when they got outside Cicero, streets closed off for this big, crazy NRA parade, with tons of folks carrying banners and American flags, pictures of Roosevelt on sticks. Lots of blue eagles and all that hooey.

"Think about all the people we've put to work," George said, smiling, mashing the clutch, shifting to neutral, the engine chugging behind an endless line of cars. Window down, arm hanging out the window. "You bet ole Uncle Sam is in overdrive, paying those G-men to look for the Kellys."

"Maybe you can get a blue eagle tattoo on your ass."

"Maybe I will."

George pulled into the alley beside Joe's Square Deal Garage and killed the lights. Kathryn reached back and tried to shake Geraline awake, but the girl was exhausted, and they left her in the backseat, taking a side door and walking into the big open space where several boys were giving a big Hudson a once-over.

One of the men leaned back out from under the hood and smiled.

Harvey Bailey wore a big shit-eating grin.

Verne Miller walked in from a back room, holding a Thompson loose in his right hand. Alvin Karpis. One of the Barker boys. *Shit. Shit. Shit.*

"Hey, George," Harvey said. "Think you got something that belongs to us."

George looked to Kathryn, back to Harvey, and squared his shoulders.

"Guess you don't have it on you right now," Harvey said, grinning.

George shook his head. Kathryn was about to tell that bastard to go straight to hell when Harvey asked them if they'd be interested in a little business proposition.

Kathryn stepped in front of George and said, "Start talking, and make it fast."

36

Friday, September 22, 1933

Karpis drove the Hudson, the armored tank with the bulletproof glass, the steel-plated doors, and the revved-up eight-cylinder engine. Harvey and the boys piled into George's dusty Ford since ole George wanted to lose the car anyway, Karpis telling Joe Bergl and some grease monkeys to switch out the smoke machine into its cab. When they snatched the dough, they'd leave the Ford on Jackson Street, pile into the Hudson, and be on their way. But, brother, Kathryn Kelly wasn't having any of it, didn't want her man involved in some two-bit snatch and grab, even after learning Fred Barker had a mean case of the shits. Harvey decided not to lecture her on the nature of the country's fine Federal Reserve system, instead only telling her that there were banks and then there was *The Bank*. She shook her head, came back with some little kid rubbing fists in her eyes, telling Bergl to pull around their new machine or she'd go straight to Frank Nitti himself and tell him his word wasn't worth chickenshit. She got her a Chevrolet sedan, clean papers and all that, but George wouldn't go, telling her he needed to square this thing with Harvey and Verne and that they both could use the extra dough.

"You did the right thing," Harvey had told them at a little past eleven, the lug down in the mouth after Kathryn slapped him across the jaw and told him he was a fool.

"Say, is that my gun?"

Miller looked down at the Thompson and nodded. "Collateral," he said.

"Keep it," Kelly said, following Harvey and Verne and Dock Barker into the Ford. "That gun's nothing but trouble. I don't want to be 'Machine Gun' Kelly anymore."

"Who are you, then?" Harvey asked.

"Just George."

They crossed the river at eleven-thirty and had found their spot on Jackson where it met Clark Street, where the mail carriers and the Reserve guards would be rounding the corner at midnight with those gorgeous fat sacks of money fresh off the train in from the U.S. Mint.

Harvey checked his watch. No one in the Ford spoke. George sat at the wheel, chewing some gum and watching the sidewalk.

All the men carried machine guns except for George. George refused to take anything more than a shotgun, a .38 for his hip pocket, and some extra shells. Beads of sweat had popped out on his forehead while he loaded the pistol and looked over the git with Karpis and made a deal with Harvey that ten grand would be shaved off his take, whatever the take may be.

"Then we're square," Kelly had said.

"And then we're square," Harvey said, offering his hand.

They would all split the city after the job, Harvey getting word to his wife through a friend of Harry Sawyer's that he'd be coming for her and his boy tomorrow and to bring only one suitcase. They'd drive west till he saw a good place to cross the border into Canada, like he'd done a thousand times in the old days. They'd become new people. Start over. Start living, and leave this crummy country on its own. Karpis was right. He'd go fishing. He'd drink some beer. He'd farm a little.

George kept the Ford's engine running with no lights. A few minutes later, he flicked his lights into Karpis's rearview mirror.

Harvey turned to see four men rounding the corner, two pushing the mail cart and the two guards walking along, jawing and loosely holding a couple shotguns. The four men in the Ford fixed bandannas across their faces and waited till the guards reached that halfway spot between Clark and LaSalle. George pulled out on Jackson—a loose, lazy flow of traffic at midnight—and smoothly edged up to the curb, all the gunmen piling out with guns drawn.

From the backseat, Harvey punched the button, and dense black smoke began to pour from the cab of the Ford, inking out Jackson Street. The guards already had their hands up, and shotguns clattered to the sidewalk, scooped up by George and Barker, Miller telling them all something hot and clear, making them turn and face the walls of the Continental Illinois National Bank. The men hoisted fat canvas bags, throwing the loot into the Hudson, slamming the trunk, with Karpis back behind the wheel.

The whole thing not lasting thirty seconds, the doors not even slamming closed before Karpis was driving through the thick smoke, breaking clear on the other side and running west on Jackson, the men laughing and talking, pulling the bandannas off their faces.

Harvey sat up front and lit a cigarette.

"What'd I tellya," Karpis said. "What'd I tellya?"

He drove fast up to Adam and then west across the Chicago River, back toward Cicero, to divide up the loot and find each of their new cars, serviced and fueled up.

"The smoke was a nice touch," Harvey said, relaxing a bit, leaning back into his seat. Karpis drove at a nice clip, not fast, but not so slow as to be noticed. "What kinda bank has two guards for all that dough?"

Karpis hit a little bump in the road, the tail of the Hudson scraping the pavement, just as they were set to cross Halstead, a green light speeding them on to Joe's Square Deal Garage. That's when that damn little Essex coupe came out of damn-near nowhere, honking its horn and T-boning their Hudson right toward a streetlamp. Karpis tried to right the car, but it kept going straight for the light, scattering two beat cops right before the car crashed.

Everything was still for a few seconds. Cracked glass and busted machine parts in the road. Harvey felt like his heart had stopped but now could feel it jackhammering in his chest.

And then Harvey heard the women scream from the Essex, and that was everything.

"I WANT TO SEE MR. NITTI," KATHRYN SAID.

"Mr. Nitti ain't here."

"You tell that wop son of a bitch that I know where he can find Verne Miller and Harvey Bailey."

The fella shrugged his shoulders and walked away.

"Who's that?" Geraline asked.

"Some stooge."

"Thought we're leaving."

"Let me tell you something, sister," Kathryn said. "Don't ever let a man tell you the rules. Set 'em yourself."

Geraline nodded. She was smoking and drinking a Pabst Blue Ribbon beer at the Pabst Blue Ribbon Casino, which stayed open after most of the lights along the Fair Midway had dimmed. Kathryn fished for another cigarette and tapped the end of her silver cigarette case on the edge of the table. Those bastards had no right to force George on a job at midnight, right while the heat was all over them, Gus T. Jones and the G-men crawling all over the city. They shoulda done him a solid and let 'im skate.

"I like your hat," Geraline said.

It was a fine little beret she'd bought along the Streets of Paris, sold to her by some gal who walked those streets with a mirror on her back.

Kathryn reached up on her head and tossed the beret to the little girl. "Take it."

"You're all right, Kit," the girl said, trying on the hat, a Lucky hanging from the corner of her mouth.

"You gotta go back."

"I don't wanna go back."

"Your parents are sick with worry."

The girl shrugged. "They don't care a rat's ass about me. My daddy always said I was nothing but another mouth to feed, and he'd be good and goddamn glad when I could look out for myself. And so here I am."

"You can't go with us."

"I can carry your bags," the girl said, taking a sip of beer. "Your guns. I can run errands. Get your clothes pressed, shine your shoes."

"Don't do that," Kathryn said. "Don't ever play the stooge."

The fella walked back into the casino bar and leaned down to Kathryn and whispered in her ear. She tossed a dollar on the table and followed, walking down the empty streets of the Fair, the neon and bright lights all gone, leaving nothing but the barren, weird shapes of the exhibits.

"What'll they do with all this stuff after the Fair?" Geraline asked.

"Tear it down."

"They built this just to tear it all apart?" she asked, mouth hanging open. "What a waste."

"The American way, sister."

The fella led them up the steps, twenty-seven of them, Kathryn knowing because Geraline was counting under her breath, up to the House of Tomorrow, an octagon-shaped building with a garage occupied by a little airplane, making it seem clear that every family would be zipping around the skies in the future. The house walls were made of plate glass.

He left them on the top of the house, rails wrapping the sides, where she soon saw a big black Cadillac pull down the drive and kill the lights.

"Who's Frank Nitti?"

"The kind of guy that doesn't have any boss."

"George doesn't have a boss."

Kathryn smiled and squashed a cigarette under her toe.

Nitti bounded up the steps, a crisp wind cutting off Lake Michigan, Geraline nearly losing the beret. Nitti was short and swarthy, with a fat mustache, slick hair, and a hundred-dollar pin-striped suit.

One of the two gimps on each side of him asked, "You know how to find Verne Miller?"

She nodded.

"What you want?" the other stooge asked.

"I want you to get Verne Miller outta my hair."

Nitti nodded. Kathryn told them about Joe Bergl's garage.

"There's another fella with him," she said. "My husband. I want him left alone. You *sabe*, Frank?"

Nitti caught her eye and nodded before turning and heading back down the steps.

"That's it?" Geraline asked.

"You better believe it," Kathryn said.

"I heard in the future, we'll only take pills and not eat or drink."

"The future is a bunch of hooey," she said. "Stuff for weak-minded saps. Come on."

THE HUDSON'S RADIATOR BOILED OVER AND STEAMED UP into the flickering lamplight as the men dashed out onto Halstead, carrying their guns and canvas bags, the two coppers running toward them telling them to stop. One held out his hand and reached for his gun while women screamed from inside the Essex, a man slumped at the wheel. A young woman wandered from the car with blood across her face while Miller stood in the middle of the street and mowed down the copper, machine gun chattering, toppling off the cop's hat and sending him to his knees and face, and then he scattered bullets at the other cop, who jumped behind a newspaper stand. Sparks of electricity rained down onto the top of the Hudson from the broken streetlamp, and a fine rain misted the street.

The copper was dead, a new path set, and Harvey grabbed two bags himself, while Karpis stopped a Plymouth and yanked a man from behind the wheel.

The other copper took shots from inside the stand, hitting Barker's fingers. But the pain just made Barker madder, and he squeezed off six rounds from his pistol with his good hand at the fleeing cop.

The men tossed the bags into the Plymouth's trunk, and Karpis yelled for Miller, who kept on spraying the clapboard newsstand to shit, kicking off the magazines hung from clothespins and busting up the lot of white lights hung from the roof. "Come on, goddamn you," Karpis yelled, clutch in, racing the motor and then tearing off down Halstead, taking some wild turns before doubling back and heading back toward Cicero.

"Clockwork," Harvey said, catching his breath.

"I didn't see 'em," Karpis said. "That bastard came outta nowhere."

"You coulda swerved," Verne Miller said.

"You didn't have to kill that cop," Karpis said.

"Fresh out of flowers, Kreeps," Miller said.

"Son of a bitch," Karpis said.

"What?"

"We're outta gas."

They drove for another mile and then bailed out and stole another car, pointing a Thompson between the driver's eyes. Harvey sat beside Karpis with Miller, George Kelly, and that moron Dock Barker in back, Barker whining about a bullet knocking a ruby from his pinkie ring. The men didn't say another word till they pulled through the bay doors of Joe's Square Deal Garage and closed them shut.

Karpis popped the trunk and grabbed a bag, Barker and George Kelly grabbed the others, all of 'em tearing into them with folding knives and emptying out the fat sacks onto the card table.

Harvey said he needed a drink. Joe Bergl passed him a bottle of rye. He took a pull and handed it to George Kelly, who took a longer pull.

The table filled with fat, tightly bundled stacks of envelopes.

Karpis tore into another to find the same.

And another, until letters littered the oil-stained floor.

Harvey sat down in a rickety chair and rested his head in his hands. Miller stood across from him, white-faced and still holding the Thompson. Dock Barker started to open every goddamn letter as if it were a letter from Momma.

"We just stole the goddamn mail," Karpis said, and started to laugh. "What a hoot."

"I don't get it," Dock Barker said, ripping open a couple more envelopes. "What do ya mean?"

"We got the mail, you idiot," Harvey said. He lit a cigarette and leaned back into the hard chair, shaking his head. Karpis started to laugh like a maniac, looking more and more like a fella you called "Kreeps."

George Kelly rubbed his lantern jaw, shrugged, and reached for the rye on the table.

But Miller clenched his teeth, dropped his machine gun on the floor, and kicked it to the wall, sending it spinning across the smooth concrete floor and shooting off a short burst of bullets.

"Take it easy, Verne," Karpis said. "This stuff happens. Have a drink. Get laid every once in a while. I hear Vi's screwing half of New York."

Miller turned and came for him, reaching for Karpis's throat and choking the ever-living shit out of the ugly bastard before Harvey and Dock could pull him off. Harvey had to reach a forearm across his friend's throat and pull him back like a dog.

When Harvey felt Miller relax, he followed him into the back room they'd shared for the past week. He watched him pack his suitcase: a pressed shirt, two pairs of trousers, a regulation .45, and some fresh drawers. A rusty faucet dripped, hanging crazy and crooked from a back wall.

"Where you headed?" Harvey asked.

Miller shrugged.

"You know Karpis was talking out his ass?"

"He was telling the truth."

"You don't know that."

"She can do what she wants," Miller said. "See you 'round, Harv."

He offered his hand, and Harvey shook it.

Harvey, wrung-out, walked back to the card table and sat down. Miller walked out of the back room and reached for the latch on the bay door, rolling it open.

A large car sat idling outside, headlights shining bright into the big garage. Four men crawled out of the car, and they stood in loose shadows with shotguns hanging from their hands. Harvey started to stand, and Karpis put his strong hand on his shoulder. Barker stopped tearing into the envelopes, mouth wide open.

In the bright light—so bright you had to squint—Miller looked back at Harvey. He offered him a weak smile, walking outside and moving to the car's backseat. A shadowed hand went on his arm, but Miller tossed it aside, getting into the car himself. Harvey could now see the car was a Cadillac as it backed into the alley and sped away. Verne Miller's battered suitcase stood alone by the door.

"You goddamn son of a bitch," Harvey said. "You called Nitti."

"You know better," Karpis said.

"You're a goddamn liar."

"If I were a double-crosser, you'd be with 'im," Karpis said.

"I'm going after those bastards."

"You want to be dead?" Karpis said. "Go ahead."

Harvey stood and walked to a brand-new Ford parked sideways near the bay doors. He looked around the big garage and then back to Karpis. "Where the hell's George?"

JONES STOOD AT THE CORNER OF ADAM AND HALSTEAD A few hours later. They'd pulled a white sheet over the dead policeman—a long-faced cop by the name of Cunningham—and before the man was hauled away, Jones saw he'd been mauled up pretty good. He'd figured it for a machine gun even before the women in the Essex had confirmed it, along with the other beat cop who'd been hit in the shoulder. Doc White stood over at the newsstand and spoke to a little runt of a fella who sold newspapers and movie magazines. The man was pointing to the bullet holes and shredded magazines, saying God had protected him with big stacks of the evening editions.

The newspaper boys had taken their pictures, asked their questions, and gone.

A few onlookers stood and watched at first light. But the streets had been cleared, the cars towed and the glass and metal swept up.

An hour earlier, he and Doc had been on Jackson Street, interviewing the bank messengers and the guards. They'd searched that Ford and found the smoke machine. In the Hudson, they'd found a first-aid kit and two boxes of .45 ammo.

The men had worn bandannas at the robbery, and no one at the wreck recalled much. The fella that owned the newsstand said he was pretty sure they weren't colored.

"Kelly?" Doc White asked them as they walked back to their vehicle.

Jones nodded. "Fits. He's here."

"One of the women gave a description sounds a hell of a lot like Verne Miller."

"What about Bailey?"

"Didn't hear of anyone sounded like Bailey."

Jones watched a city worker take a wrench to a fire hydrant and start hosing away the beat cop's blood. "Lot of misery for a few sacks of mail."

"Any other night could've been more 'an a million."

"You want to stay here?"

"Only sure bet is the Arnolds."

"What Colvin do with 'em?"

"Did like Kathryn Kelly asked," Doc White said, striking a match and cupping his hand around a cigarette. The morning wind sure felt like fall. "Holed 'em up in the Shangri-La Apartments in O.K. City till she gets word."

"Could they be tipped off?"

"Colvin was careful."

As they walked to their car, a big truck with slatted wooden sides ambled up to the shredded newsstand, dropping off morning copies of the *Tribune*, local police blaming Kelly for the robbery and the cop killing. 10,000 LAWMEN HUNT "MACHINE GUN" KELLY.

37

Saturday, September 23, 1933

Kathryn took a drink with George's brother-in-law, Langford Ramsey—just calling him "Lang"—on the front porch of his bungalow in a fine Memphis neighborhood, right around the corner from Southwestern College. He had a fine car and a fine little wife and a fine job as a local attorney, George telling her twenty times that Lang was the youngest man in the state in practice. She liked Lang from the start after they'd rolled into Memphis that morning, dog-tired and muscle-cramped, and here this young boy and his wife had set their dining-room table with fried chicken and potato salad, iced tea, and lemonade spiked with gin. The lemonade just hitting the spot after they'd taken to the porch while George washed up and changed, expecting his sons at any minute.

"I'm so glad y'all are here," Lang said.

He was a nice-looking boy, skinny and rich, a doughy face, but with nicely cut hair and beautiful manners. He called her ma'am, which annoyed her a bit. But he'd also blushed when she'd crossed her bare legs and lit a cigarette, and after their third lemonade he'd confided a bit about his wife, who was a restless girl from a good Memphis family who Lang said was under a doctor's care for frigidity.

"Hell, just get her drunk, Lang," Kathryn said. "Always works."

"I like you," he said.

"Back at you."

"Your little girl is beautiful."

"Yeah?"

"She was so helpful in the kitchen."

Kathryn wanted to warn him to watch his valuables. But instead she just smoked and took in the smooth green lawns, blooming crepe myrtles still spotted from a morning shower, and the young oaks that had grown just tall enough to shade the street. Fallen leaves skittered down the streets in bright little whirls. You noticed those type things when you were a bit high.

"You have to realize we were all taken aback to hear from George."

"How long has it been?" Kathryn asked.

"Until he came through Memphis a few weeks ago, I hadn't laid eyes on him for seven years," Lang said. "I didn't know till then that he'd been remarried."

"We'll be married three years tomorrow."

"He did well for himself," Lang said. "Anyone ever tell you that you look like Joan Crawford?"

She smiled at him. "George says nice things about your sister."

Lang nodded. "We miss him. His boys miss him."

"He got so nervous when you said they were visiting."

"I think it's only right," Lang said. "They should know their father. Don't get me wrong, F.X. is a fine man and a good husband."

"What's he do?"

"He's a big-time advertising executive. Have you seen those ads for Rinso soap?"

"That woman with the awful BO? You bet. The way her friends don't want to take her to the movies and her husband stays late at the office. It's a riot."

"He came up with that."

"On the level?"

"On the level," Lang said. "Listen, I wish you all could stay here, but with Geneva and her new husband, I thought it best—"

"It's sweet that you found a place for us."

"George stayed with Tich last time," Lang said. "His wife and kids are in Paducah visiting her mother. He said it's no trouble at all. He's a funny little guy, kinda ornery, but don't let him fool you. He'd give the shirt off his back for my family. Did I tell you he was a cripple?"

"You want me to speak to your wife?" Kathryn asked.

Lang reached for the pitcher of lemonade and gin. "About what?"

"Being frigid," Kathryn said. "A fine catch like you . . ."

Lang's boyish face grew red.

"Buy her something nice," Kathryn said. "Girls like that. A silk nightie. Make it red, with lace trim. Some French perfume. That stuff just sets me off."

Lang smiled. He had the jacket to his wool crepe suit hung over the back of his rocking chair. When he stood to light a cigarette, she could tell he'd grown a little drunk. The afternoon was breezy, a little warmer than up in Chicago, a restless wind with the changing seasons, the dead, skittering leaves and all that.

"Are you a good lawyer?" she asked.

"I try."

"You work with many criminals?"

"Mainly property."

"Oh."

A shiny new blue Buick rolled down Malvern and turned into Lang's driveway. A car door opened, and a short blond woman in a summer dress walked around and opened the back door. Two boys in Eton suits came bounding out; George Jr. was seven and Bruce was six. They were good-looking boys, with their dad's jaw and blue eyes. The woman was a looker, too, fair, but maybe a bit mousy. She smiled up at Lang. Lang waved back at his sister and she got back into the Buick, her husband backing out and pulling away.

"She said they'd go over to Overton Park for an hour and then pick 'em up for dinner."

"That's F.X.?" Kathryn asked.

Lang nodded.

"He wasn't smiling."

George must've been watching from a window, because he opened the front door fast, not looking at Lang or Kathryn but walking slow down the front steps and hanging there in his best suit, charcoal gray, with a tailored shirt and tie. She noticed he wore the sterling silver tie clip she'd bought for him at the Fair.

The boys kept their heads down. But George dropped to a knee and opened his arms wide, and the whole thing made Kathryn seize a bit in her chest, turning her back to them, pouring out some more lemonade for her and Lang and asking if there was more.

The boys chattered up something fierce, there was baseball and trips to the zoo, and George walked back to the Chevrolet and gave them both souvenirs from the World's Fair. Two toy zeppelins, two CENTURY OF PROGRESS coins, and two official World's Fair badges.

They said "Wow!"

"Do you boys listen to *Buck Rogers?*"

They both nodded hard.

"I knew it," George said, snapping his fingers. "I dang well knew we're on the same airwaves."

George told them he was a federal agent on a special mission. He explained that's why he'd been away so long. He told them both he loved them. And Kathryn felt that uncomfortable, goddamn pain in her chest again and drank half the glass.

"Is George's father still living?" she asked.

"You don't know?" Lang asked.

She shook her head.

"George despises his father. I never knew him to say one good word about him. After his mother died, his father remarried. He's still in Memphis."

"But he loved his mother?"

"Very much," Lang said. "She died when he was at Central High."

"And he loved *your* father?" she asked.

"I don't think George ever got over the accident," Lang said. "He was talking about it again this morning. Said he hadn't been in church since, blaming God for what happened."

She felt like an eavesdropper up on the bungalow's porch, but Lang had made no move to go inside the house. She could hear some kind of radio show from the open windows, where she hoped Gerry was listening and not sorting through the Ramseys' jewelry boxes.

She stood and put a hand to a column, watching George sit on the stoop, showing the boys how to wind the zeppelins' propellers, and then stretching his legs to reach into his pocket to peel away two twenty-dollar bills from a fat roll.

He gave one to each and told them to go buy the best bicycles they could find.

"Goddamn him," Kathryn said, and marched into Lang's house to hunt up some more of that Royal Knight gin that sure hit the spot. "Goddamn him to hell."

"YOU HAD NO ACCOUNT TO DO ME LIKE THAT," LUTHER Arnold said. "I ain't no criminal."

"We had an emergency situation," Jones said. "Did you read about what happened in Chicago?"

"I haven't read nothin' but the scrawlings on these jail walls."

Agents had brought Arnold into an empty jury room at the Oklahoma City Federal Building and sat him across from Jones at a long conference table. Arnold, looking forlorn and pissed off, jostled the handcuffs on his wrists. Jones smoked a pipe.

"'Machine Gun' Kelly and his gang robbed the Federal Reserve and started a Wild West shootout in the middle of downtown. Killed an officer, and nearly killed another."

"I didn't cause that."

"Didn't say you did," Jones said. "I'm just explaining why vigorous methods were needed for you to come to Jesus."

"Wadn't fair."

"Life ain't fair, Luther," Jones said. "Only wet brains and half-wits think that's true."

"The Kellys done stole my daughter. You don't think I'm sore about that? That child is probably scared outta her mind. She ain't but eleven."

"From the way your wife tells it, you took two hundred dollars to rent her out for a while."

"Mrs. Kelly said they wadn't goin' but two hundred miles and they'd bring her back in a few days."

"Didn't work out that way? Did it?"

"'Spose not."

"You need anything?"

"Could use some fresh drawers and a toothbrush."

"I'll see to it."

"Maybe a pint, too?"

"Anything else?"

"I'd love to see my sweetie. Where you keepin' Flossie Mae?"

"She's safe," Jones said. "You have my word."

"You shook my dang hand before you tried to kill me in the ho-tel tub."

"I didn't try to kill you," Jones said. "You're my ace in the hole, Luther."

"How you figure?"

"You're the Kellys' only contact back here," Jones said. "Before they make another move, you'll be the first to know."

"But I'm in jail."

"Says who?"

"Flossie Mae's still at the Shangri-La," Luther said, nodding with a slow understanding. "You all is waitin' for the Kellys to knock on the door, bigger than shit, when they bring Gerry back."

Jones sat silent.

Luther started to laugh. "Old man, nobody's that foolish."

Jones nodded, blowing pipe smoke into his face. Luther tried to stand up to it but broke into a coughing fit. "Pardon me."

"You sure take pleasure sticking that boot up my ass."

"Wouldn't say it gives me pleasure."

"Mrs. Kelly told me George was going to bust her family out. She said y'all won't even know what hit you."

Jones shook his head. "A man couldn't fart near the Federal Building without us knowin'."

"What makes you so mean?"

"Just doin' my job, Luther."

"Don't mean I have to like it."

"It's a free country."

"I got interviewed by six different federal agents, all of 'em young enough to be your offspring," Luther said. "Why don't you and that other feller just hang it up and go fishing, or try some porch sitting for a spell. Just what do you have to prove?"

Jones reached for his Stetson that hung from a hook by the door.

"Those boys told me they got a whole school in Washington where they're doin' nothing but educatin' young fellas in all matters of science," Luther said. "You didn't even know electricity when you was their age."

Jones pulled on the hat. He smiled. "I've been to that school. Still learning."

"You just keep on pluggin' away? Is that it, old man?"

"Dinosaurs stood still, and now they're greasin' our cars."

"What in the hell are you talking about?"

KATHRYN AND LANG HAD GOTTEN PROPERLY PLASTERED before Lang led the way to Tich's place south of the city on Speedway, a working-class neighborhood with simple houses and old cars. He parked in the drive and woke up Tich, a small cripple with a bum leg who hobbled down the steps but was strong enough to help Lang carry in George from the backseat. Just as soon as his boys drove off to dinner with their momma, George must've drank three pitchers of the lemonade, talking with Lang about what a good man Mr. Ramsey had been to him and how if he'd lived, things in George's life would've been real different.

Kathryn had had enough of that talk and waited outside with Geraline until he passed out.

She and the little girl followed Lang and Tich, who carried George inside like a fat sultan and plopped him on an old sofa.

"Can't we find a hotel?" Geraline asked.

"No," Kathryn said. "Go get yourself washed up and go to bed."

"I'm not tired."

"It's dark," she said. "When it's dark, children sleep."

"I'm no child."

"You want to go back to trampin'?"

"No, ma'am."

"Good."

Kathryn walked with Lang out to his car. He was glassy-eyed but coming out of the drunk and gave her a big hug before saying, "You two can stay here until it's safe to leave. I'll help George with anything in this world. I love him like a brother."

"What are you talking about?"

"Ten thousand lawmen hunt for 'Machine Gun' Kelly."

"How long have you known?"

"Since he pulled the Urschel job, and I saw his picture in the paper."

"But you didn't tell him."

"I didn't want to hurt his feelings."

Kathryn wobbled and sat down on the curb. She looked up at Lang and shook her head. She felt grimy, sweaty, tired, and parched from all that gin. "You mean it? You want to help George?"

"I don't know much criminal law, but—"

"We have a lawyer," Kathryn said. She turned back to the house on

Rayner Street and saw Gerry's pug nose pressed against the glass in the lighted room. When she spotted Kathryn, the kid let the curtain fall.

"She's gonna kick and scream, but that little girl is going home."

"That's not your daughter?"

"My daughter is with family," Kathryn said. "Do I look like the kind of mother who would let her child be mixed up in something like this?"

Lang smiled.

"Lang?" Kathryn asked. "You think you could run a little errand for us?"

"Anything," Lang said. "Where?"

"Coleman, Texas," Kathryn said, clicking on her lighter and firing up a Lucky.

HARVEY BAILEY ARRIVED IN MEMPHIS AT SIX-TWENTY THE next morning. The light on the train platform was weak and gray, and as he headed down the marble steps and into the terminal he realized he hadn't eaten or bathed in two days. He'd left Joe Bergl's soon after Nitti had snatched Verne, and he'd found a flophouse where he'd dyed his hair black and changed into a sorry suit and raggedy hat, a corn farmer gone to town. Some round, gold-framed glasses gave him a quiet, studied look, the kind of fella who could quote passages from the Bible and the *Farmer's Almanac* equally and had a stout little wife back home elbow-deep in canning. Harvey crossed Main, over to a corner diner called the Arcade, where he found a back booth and studied the menu, snatching up a copy of the *Press-Scimitar* someone had left beside a half-eaten plate of bacon and eggs. He and every lawman in the country looking for George Kelly, George being blamed for just about every crime from snatching the Lindbergh baby to killing Lincoln.

Harvey looked around and ate the toast and bacon.

A Greek in an apron came over and took away the plate. When he returned, Harvey ordered black coffee and counted out the coin from his pocket.

Harvey had known George Kelly since 1930, when they robbed that bank in Ottumwa, Iowa. There had been a lot of others—Nebraska, Texas—and when you spend that kind of time mapping gits, lying around hotels planning a heist, and driving thousands of miles, you get to know a fella pretty good. George loved talking about Memphis. *Memphis, Memphis, Memphis.* He talked about his ex-wife and his boys, and his brother-in-law—Something Ramsey—like the middle initial George had taken for his own. Harvey knew he was studying to be an attorney, and if that's where George had headed, he'd be easy to find.

Harvey finished his coffee and rode the streetcar toward the downtown, past all the warehouses, machine shops, and garages, wishing to God he'd never met the Kellys. The streetcar rambled on into the shopping district, Harvey now knowing he didn't care if he had to kill poor ole George to get his money back. Hell, it would probably put the sorry bastard out of his misery from being married to Kathryn. He stepped off the streetcar right in front of the Orpheum Theatre. GABLE. HARLOW. *HOLD YOUR MAN.*

Hold your man. Harvey wondered how long till those suckers in Hollywood made a picture about those two. He could imagine the movie poster, George in a fine tuxedo with the machine gun, Kathryn dressed in a glittering gown, her husband's nuts squeezed tight in her hand.

Harvey followed Main down to Union and strutted right into the lobby of the Peabody Hotel, past a sign advertising a colored orchestra at the Sky Lounge, and found a bank of phone booths. With his last few nickels, he arranged for a car and a little stake of cash. He snatched out a page in the telephone book for a Langford Ramsey on Mignon Avenue and decided to walk while he waited for the car. He walked up and over the Memphis bluffs and down to the Mississippi River, where he sat on a park bench for a long time and watched the long, sluggish brown water.

38

The trick with dodging a hangover was just to stay drunk for as long as you could, parceling out the sips slow and easy without getting sloppy. Kathryn drank straight gin over cracked ice for most of the night until she heard Lang knock on the back door, rousting Geraline from the couch, the girl none too happy about the plan. "I'm not going," she said.

"The hell you aren't," Kathryn said.

"My parents don't care."

"How's Lang supposed to find my grandmother's place in Coleman?"

"And you swear he'll bring me back?"

"Just as soon as he picks up a few things."

"Your furs and your Pekingese dog."

"That's right."

"I'm not a sap."

"Didn't say you were, sister," Kathryn said. "The boy can't find the farm himself."

Geraline packed her little suitcase, arranging items they'd bought her at the Fair along with three packs of cigarettes, a small cigar box, her new little dresses, frilly socks and panties, and what have you. Kathryn walked outside and saw Lang hand Tich a twenty-dollar bill before Tich

hobbled down the steps to head to work at first light down at the Peabody Hotel garage.

"He won't talk?" Kathryn asked.

"He's loyal," Lang said. "Worked for my family for years."

"Goddamn, my head hurts."

"Where's George?"

"Still passed out in the back bedroom," she said. "Hasn't stirred a bit."

"Tich will get rid of the Chevrolet," he said. "He promises to bring
back something better with Tennessee plates."

"I don't know what to say."

"George is my family, Kathryn."

She leaned in and kissed him on the cheek, whispering into his ear,
"After you get our dough, ditch the little smart-ass at the first train station you see."

Lang nodded.

"You'll need cash to get there."

He shook his head. But she tucked a fat roll of twenties in his hand.

"If something goes screwy, send a telegram to Tich."

He nodded. They heard George stumble from the back bedroom and
pad out into the hallway with bare feet, wearing only an undershirt and
boxer shorts. He rubbed his stubbled jaw, and smiled when he saw Lang.
"You headed to church or somethin'?"

Lang smiled, holding a brand-new straw hat in his hand.

"He's going to be calling on Ma Coleman for us," Kathryn said.

George walked close to Lang and put his hands on his shoulders,
smiling at him, and Lang looking a little uncomfortable, probably from
George's gin breath. But George didn't notice, only wrapped his big arms
around Lang and gave him a big old bear hug. He patted his back.

"Don't get yourself killed," George said, and padded into the bathroom, where they both heard him start to take a leak.

Geraline stood at the door, dressed in her brand-new flowered dress,
new shoes, and that beret Kathryn had bought on the Streets of Paris.
On her collar, she wore a button that read CENTURY OF PROGRESS.

"C'mon, Lang," Geraline said, chewing a big wad of gum. "Quit your yappin'. We got a long day ahead."

HARVEY WATCHED THE YOUNG LAWYER AND THE LITTLE girl he'd seen with Kathryn in Chicago leave the little bungalow on Rayner Street. He'd followed Lang all the way from North Memphis, the man not once making him out in his rearview mirror, not even when Harvey pulled in down the street and killed his lights a little before dawn. On the seat next to him, he had a pack of Camel cigarettes, a .45 automatic, and a copy of the morning newspaper with more trial coverage on the Shannons in Oklahoma City and news that Verne Miller and George had been spotted at a diner in Minnesota. He also had several maps of Iowa he'd bought at a Standard service station—he planned to cut through there on his way up to Wisconsin to pick up his family.

The only sleep he'd gotten was when he'd closed his eyes for maybe two seconds on the river. A short time later, a nervous negro met him at a downtown filling station, handing him the keys to a Plymouth, afraid to look the famous bank robber in the eye.

When the lawyer and the girl pulled away from the house on Rayner, he tossed his cigarette out the window and laid the .45 in his lap. Only a fool would bust into the back door in a fella's hometown, no telling who George had in there or if George was in there at all.

A prowl car passed outside the car's windows, and the way it drove lazy and relaxed was enough for Harv. He started the car, knocked it into first, and drove back toward the downtown.

"HAPPY ANNIVERSARY," KATHRYN SAID, JOINING GEORGE IN Tich's rumpled bed.

He reached to a nightstand and grabbed a pack of cigarettes and his lighter.

"I'm gonna buy you the biggest ring in Havana," he said.

"I don't need it."

"We're going to go to all those fancy clubs and drink rum. I'll smoke cigars and fish."

"What can I do?"

"Any damn thing you want."

"Then what?"

"You want more?" George asked.

"I don't like to be bored, George. I hate being bored."

Kathryn turned her head on his chest to look at him. He ashed the cigarette into his palm and scatted it onto the floor, passing the cigarette to her. "Lang's lemonade sure sneaks up on you," she said.

"The trick is to keep on drinking."

"So I heard."

"Kit, pull the shades."

"You got to be kidding."

"We got the house all to ourselves."

"This place is depressing."

"Bed still works," he said, rocking it back and forth with his butt, making the springs squeak.

"Come on."

"It's our anniversary," he said.

"You read the papers?" she asked.

"Always bad news," he said. "Take off that nightie."

"I'll leave it on," she said. "Just be quiet."

She kicked out of her panties and straddled him, George flat on his back and looking up at her with puppy-dog eyes. She reached for him, and he told her that he loved her.

She reached for him again, knowing this was going to take some work.

Kathryn slapped George across his face and told him to try a little harder. The strap of her slip had fallen off one shoulder by the time they finally got the show started, and she alternated with a firm hand on his chest and dropping them both loose at her sides, feeling him inside her,

George with his eyes closed, Kathryn thinking that, in the weakened light, he really did favor Ricardo Cortez, and for a while there was a pleasant moment when he was Ricardo Cortez and this wasn't a crummy nest of a bed but the biggest, fattest bed in Havana, with silk sheets, and guitar music floating in from the brick streets. And the air smelled like sweet flowers and tobacco, and she arched her back more, her mouth parted, and then reached her nails into George's shoulder and said, "Did you hear that?"

"Damn it, Kit," George said, opening his eyes and crawling out from under her.

She pulled down her silk slip.

George walked to the window and peeked outside. "Nothing. Not a damn thing."

"Come on," she said. "Let's finish."

"I need a drink."

He started slamming cabinets in the kitchen, looking for some more gin but instead finding Tich's stash of Log Cabin bourbon, bottom-shelf kind of stuff, that George poured over ice. He turned on the radio, saying he was listening for any news on them but only finding some kids' show again. He drank and brooded there on the sofa until the shadows fell across the floor. Tich was back sometime later, dragging that old foot and bringing them an angel food cake from his church service and a .45 automatic he sold to George for $17.50.

George grabbed the gun but didn't eat a bit of the cake, and he and Kathryn both went to bed sometime late that night, not really knowing when, all that time kind of getting mixed together. They slept apart, Kathryn not waking until she heard Tich had returned, and the ugly little man handed her a telegram from Gainesville, Texas. HAD SEVERAL TOUGH BREAKS . . . DEAL FELL THROUGH. TRIED TO GET LATER APPOINTMENT. BEST PROSPECT WAS AFRAID. IMPOSSIBLE. CHANGED HER MIND. DON'T WANT TO BRING HOME A SAD TALE. CAN GO ON IF ADVISABLE. WIRE INSTRUCTIONS HERE.

"Where's the bottle?" she asked.

HARVEY WALKED UP THE DRIVEWAY OF THE LITTLE HOUSE
on Rayner early that Tuesday morning after sleeping a night in the car at
a tourist camp over the river in West Memphis, Arkansas. With the .45
loose at his side, he checked the back door and found it unlocked. He
pressed on, not knowing who all was in the house. The kitchen was bare,
a black skillet left cold on the burner, with the grease turning white and
hard. He shifted the gun in his hand and moved into the main room,
where a bunch of pillows and blankets was left on the couch, full ashtrays and half-finished glasses scattered across the room. He looked for
suitcases, satchels, anything where they'd keep his dough if they had it
with them at all. But he'd take whatever they had, fight over it if it came
to that, and then he'd be on the great, beautiful, open road.

He heard sounds coming from a back bedroom.

He crept forward, and through a narrow crack saw the nude back
of Kathryn, who was on top of George and riding him. He only saw
George's hairy legs and big feet and was glad he couldn't see more, finally
spotting a fat leather grip at the edge of the bed.

"Hope I didn't stop you from the morning routine," he said, tipping
his hat at Kit. She crawled off George and covered herself with the entire
sheet, George stumbling to his feet.

He walked up to Harvey as naked as you please and shook his head.
"Take it, Harv."

"How much is left?" Harvey asked. "I only want what's mine."

"Three grand, give or take a few hundred," George said. "Rest is hidden."

"I'll be wanting the rest."

"How were we to know you pooled your goddamn money with ours
at Cann's place?" he said. "Your own fault."

"Good luck, George."

"Where's Miller?"

"Dead," Harvey said. "Nitti snatched him."

"How'd Nitti know?"

"Pussy sure can make a man blind," Harvey said. "You better get your eyes checked, George."

"Skip the commentary, you rotten SOB," Kathryn said. "Get what's yours and get gone."

Harvey tipped his hat, the leather grip feeling heavy and fat in his left hand. He hoisted it onto the table and opened the top, a breeze through a cracked window fluttering the loose bundles of cash. He caught sight of two garbagemen conversing with a fella who'd just parked across the street. The man opened his hood and stood against the fat fender.

The garbagemen had good haircuts. The man with the busted car shifted his weight, placing a hand on his belt, the son of a bitch carrying a rod. All three men glanced up at the bungalow, trying not to stare, first light still an hour away.

Harvey didn't say a word, only snatched up the grip and walked out of the kitchen, hopping a fence to another house and then another, before finding his machine parked out on Speedway, knocking it into first, and thinking what a beautiful day it was going to be.

KATHRYN WOULD LATER HEAR HOW MA COLEMAN HAD rebuked Lang and Geraline three times before shooing them away and telling them federal agents were everywhere. Lang tried his best to get back to that willow tree he'd been told about, Geraline pleading with the blind old woman to let her inside, saying that Kathryn missed her little Pekingese dog and needed her furs for the winter. But the old woman wildly aimed a little .22 and said they wouldn't last a mile if they picked up Kathryn's things. "If they knew what was good for 'em, they'd get back in their car and keep driving till they were out of Texas." The whole thing didn't seem to bother Geraline but rattled poor Lang so bad that the little girl had to hold his cigarette while he lit it. She even told Lang he didn't have the nerves for gangster work.

He ignored the kid.

And then fifty miles down the road, she started in on how much she missed her folks and started to primp up to cry.

"You told Kathryn you wanted to go back to Memphis."

"Please," Geraline said. "I want my momma."

And he'd found a station, walking inside with her and purchasing a one-way ticket to Oklahoma City. He handed her a five-dollar bill and wished her good luck.

He wasn't gone five minutes before she used the money to wire a message to the Shangri-La Apartments, Oklahoma City. MEET ME AT ROCK ISLAND STATION. 10:15 TONIGHT. GERRY.

Gerry had a fine time on the late train, finding the Sunday funnies section on a vacant seat. She probably laughed and giggled the whole way, with no more concern about what she'd done than Chingy showed when he killed a songbird.

The train arrived on time and clattered to a stop at the station. Geraline grabbed her fattened suitcase and politely declined help from a kindly negro porter. She stopped on the platform, the engine still hissing and steaming several cars ahead, and soon spotted old Luther and Flossie Mae, her momma and daddy, waving to her by a large clock atop a metal post.

Geraline lugged her suitcase, not in any particular hurry, and became annoyed when some old man came in step beside her and asked if she was tired.

"What's it to you?" she asked.

"I'm a friend of your parents'."

She noticed he wore a fine pearl gray cowboy hat and polished boots. He was short and sort of fat and wore a pair of gold-rimmed cheaters.

"Must have been some trip."

"Sure thing, pops."

Flossie Mae ran to her and tried to hug her. But Geraline just stood there limp while the woman put on some kind of show, kissing and cooing, for the cowboy. "Can we get something to eat?" Gerry asked.

"Little girl, how'd you like an ice-cream cone?" the cowboy asked. "We have a lot to discuss."

Gerry looked to her parents and back to the man. She saw that her daddy had a hell of a shiner.

"WILL YOU RECONSIDER LETTING ME COME WITH YOU?" *Charles Urschel asked.*

"We appreciate you arranging a plane."

"Kelly won't go easily."

"Don't expect it."

"Will you kill him?"

"If the situation calls for it."

"I'd hate to have another trial," Urschel said, speaking to Jones in the rear of the government vehicle on the way to the airstrip. *"My family has been through enough."*

Jones said nothing. It was past three in the morning.

"How many men?"

"Me and Doc," Jones said. *"We're meeting four men from the Oklahoma City office, including Special Agent Colvin. Six more in Memphis."*

"What do you think of Agent Colvin?"

"You don't need my opinion, sir," Jones said. *"Think you already got that figured out."*

"You know Betty broke that young man's heart when she took up with the club's new tennis pro?" Urschel asked.

THEY LANDED IN MEMPHIS AT HALF PAST FIVE THAT MORN-ing. The police met them at the landing strip, and a briefing was held inside an airplane hangar. The locals had arranged for a garbage truck and some uniforms for Agent Bryce and Joe Lackey. Agent Colvin would drive a car and park across from the house on Rayner, where he'd feign having engine trouble.

A little after five a.m., Jones got word there was no movement in the house, and they figured Kelly—if inside—was still asleep. Jones pulled a machine gun from the back of a Memphis police car they'd parked six houses down on Speedway. Doc White carried a sawed-off Browning 12-gauge. The six detectives brought pistols, knowing this would all be close work inside that little house. Bryce could watch the front door and windows with a scoped rifle he'd stowed in the front seat of the truck.

Jones checked his timepiece and nodded to Doc White.

"IF KELLY IS KILLED," CHARLIE URSCHEL SAID, "YOU'D BE A hero."

"I made my way for twenty years trying to stay out of the papers."

"The country needs something like this," Urschel said. "Strong leaders. People are restless as sheep."

"Folks follow money," Jones said. "Always have. Greed is the root of it all."

Charlie Urschel turned away.

JONES CROSSED THE SMALL, SLOPED LAWN AND MET DOC White, circling the house from around back. He was slow up the walkway and front steps, recalling the Paradise raid, trying the front door and finding it unlocked, a clear view of a big open room through to the glass cabinets of the kitchen. A small fella lay on the sofa, a half-empty bottle of whiskey in hand, and Jones was careful to open the front door slow and easy, while Doc touched the shotgun to the man's nose and the man opened his eyes wide, frozen.

Bottles of bourbon and gin lay all around the house. Ashtrays overflowed. Jones spotted a copy of *Master Detective* wide open to a story called "My Bloodcurdling Ride with Death."

Jones's boots beat heavy steps on the wooden floor, and he waited any minute to hear gunshots. He walked along the hallway to find a bed-room door wide open and a nude woman, who lay tangled in a pile of white sheets. The first light of the day crossed the room and over the back and shoulder of Kathryn Kelly. A piece of her hair had caught in her mouth during sleep, her mouth slightly parted, eyes closed.

When he turned, a shadow crossed the wall, and Jones turned and raised his Thompson.

"THOSE MEN HUMILIATED ME," URSCHEL SAID.

"Yes, sir."

"It hasn't been settled in my mind."

"And won't for some time."

"Did Agent Colvin discuss with you my suspicions?"

"He did."

"I made a mistake."

"As us all."

"Those people took Mr. Jarrett at gunpoint," Urschel said. "I don't want his personal conversations placed on phonographic records."

"Mr. Hoover cabled that Mr. Jarrett should be left alone. Is that to your liking, Mr. Urschel?"

IT WAS KELLY, LOOKING HEAVY AND TIRED, HIS THICK HAIR bleached bright yellow. He stood not five paces away in the bungalow's hallway, aiming a .45 at Jones's chest. He wore only a pair of boxer shorts with red hearts.

"Drop that gun," Jones said.

"I've been waiting for y'all all night," Kelly said with a smile, as if he found the whole situation to be funny.

"Well," Jones said, "here we are."

Kelly stepped forward but did not lower the gun.

_____

"DO YOU HAVE CHILDREN?" URSCHEL ASKED.

"No, sir. We wasn't blessed with them."

"When I received that letter from Kelly, I purchased pistols for all my children. I even gave Betty one to carry in her purse."

"I never found that letter sincere."

"I don't let my children out of my sight."

"I suppose that faith is the toughest part. Being a family man."

"I don't even trust my own safety. A shadow startles me."

JONES INCHED HIS FINGER ON THE TRIGGER; JUST A LITTLE pressure would scatter the entire drum of bullets. He wondered if Kelly thought the gun was his own and that Jones had stolen it from him. He thought back on Paradise and then on Kansas City, Sheriff Otto Reed and those two dead city detectives lying like twin boys in the blood along the brick road.

Kelly just smiled down at Jones. Jones knowing goddamn well that Kelly thought it was kind of humorous being drawn by the much shorter, much older man.

"Are you the Federal Ace?" George Kelly asked.

"I'm Gus T. Jones of the Department of Justice. Now, drop your weapon."

Kelly smiled some more, Jones hearing a stir in the bedroom and Kathryn calling for her husband to come back to bed. George chuckled. He lowered the .45 and placed it with a light touch on a sewing machine that had been pushed against a wall, covered with discarded rags and a fine dust.

It would take fifteen minutes before Kathryn agreed to put on some clothes. She emerged from the bathroom wearing a black dress that hugged her fanny and fanned out at her feet like a mermaid. As she was pushed into the Black Mariah with handcuffs on her wrists, Jones heard her say, "Officer, an agent of mine is returning from Texas shortly with all my furs and jewels and my Pekingese dog. Please make sure these are returned to me."

George was sullen and silent. Jones only saw him grin once more after the arrest. The desk sergeant asked his name, age, and where he lived. "My name is George Kelly. I'm thirty-seven years of age, and I live everywhere."

39

Harvey Bailey cut through Memphis without trouble, the bluffs falling away behind him, and he drove over the Mississippi River at dawn with a wide smile on his face, that gorgeous light hitting the muddy water and shining like gold across the Arkansas Delta like something out of the Old Testament. He had the window down, the air bright and cool, a full tank of gas, and a full satchel of cash beside him.

He nearly missed the roadblock.

Slowing, trying to remain confident. He rolled down the window and smiled.

Four coppers pulled guns on him. Harvey shook his head, held up his hands, and told them they were welcome to help themselves to what's in the bag if they'd just let him pass through.

One of the coppers grabbed the bag and plunked it on top of the Plymouth, tossing out the thick stack of bills, reaching deeper to pull out magazines and a phone book and what looked to be kids' undershorts and socks.

"You trying to bribe us with fifty-two dollars and some dirty drawers?" the copper asked. "You got some set of balls, Mr. Bailey. Now, put your goddamn hands up where I can see 'em."

KATHRYN KNEW THE SCORE FROM THE MOMENT THAT SNOT-
nosed kid pranced into the courtroom in a hundred-dollar dress and
patent leather shoes. She wore a full-grown woman's slouch hat, and told
Flossie Mae—who held her hand down the aisle—to go and sit down
and be quiet. Flossie Mae lowered her head and did what she was told.
Geraline took the stand with a little jeweled pocketbook that Kathryn
knew was just bulging with that money she'd switched. She nudged
George in the ribs at the defense table, but he didn't take any interest,
sitting there in a nice suit with a dull smile.

They tried them together after convicting Bailey and Bates, Ora and Boss.
Potatoes and the hot-money Jews from Saint Paul. Kathryn had tried to
explain that George would've killed her if she'd tried to leave him. But all the
saps were turning a deaf ear, the judge and the prosecutor just over the moon
with the dumb kid who'd taken the stand, a real flavor of the month, with
headlines across the country reading GIRL, 12, NABS "MACHINE GUN" KELLY.

Kathryn didn't see how telling the G that they were in Memphis
amounted to anything. But the Arnolds sure had put in for the ten grand
in reward money, and already there was talk of a Hollywood movie, with
the girl from *Dora's Dunkin' Donuts* in the role of Geraline.

The little girl sure as shit gave Kathryn the high hat when she finished telling her little tale of meeting while her parents were hitching,
all the way through to the Fair and then down to Memphis. It was a real
sob-sister act, and, as much as Kathryn hated it, she grinned to herself a
bit when the rat walked past.

George never seemed to mind Kathryn telling a story of George being
the brains behind it all and how he said he'd kill her and her family if
she didn't go along. He seemed to know this was all part of the game and
even patted her goddamn hand when she returned from breaking down
on the stand, remembering, of all the horror from their time on the road,
what the big gorilla had forced her to do.

But nothing could save them. Even Chingy would've been convicted in that lousy court. She knew it was all a sham when they rode the elevator up for sentencing. She turned to kiss George on the cheek, but that cowboy federal agent Doc White pushed her away. And like he deserved, she slapped that old bastard across his face.

He grabbed her hand and snatched her up at the elbow.

In manacles, George turned to try and break his grip. But all that old man did was pistol-whip George till the elevator doors opened, leaving him with a good-size egg and a handkerchief on his split lip as their verdict was read.

They were sentenced to life.

When Kathryn was released twenty-five years later, she remarked to a reporter, "I guess the thing that impressed me most on my first trip out was the fast traffic. I was honestly afraid to cross the street."

George never did get out.

September 1934

The train was a midnight special, taking the highball route from the federal prison in Atlanta, tracks cleared all the way to Leavenworth, and then steaming right for the California coast, where a hundred and three of the very worst in the system would be locked up tight on Alcatraz. Hoover had put Jones in charge of the move, and he hadn't even been able to tell Mary Ann his assignment, only saying that he'd meet her in San Francisco at the Mark Hopkins Hotel. They'd have cocktails, and she'd try to talk him into retiring like Doc White.

The train's windows had been covered with bars and a metal screen, and the doors could only be unlocked from outside, the openings covered in welded lattice, easy to slip the muzzle of a machine gun through and start shooting if there was trouble. By morning, they all felt the heat wave without even a small crack for a crossbreeze. Some of the men went on a hunger strike, most of them unshaven and stinking. Many he knew on sight—*Bailey, Bates, Kelly*—as he patrolled the aisle with a Thompson in hand. George Kelly nodded to Jones every time he passed, like an old friend, asking him once, when they stopped in a train yard to let the prisoners stretch, smoke, and drink water from tin cups, if it would be okay to write Charles Urschel a letter.

"I don't think it'll change his mind."

"It's not supposed to," George said. "I just want someone to hear me out."

"Maybe try a more cordial tone this time."

"You know I didn't have a thing to do with that mess in Kansas City." Jones nodded. "We got Miller's prints off the gun."

"Guess he won't be facing the chair."

"Facedown and nekkid in a drainage ditch," Jones said. "Why do you figure they had to make him be nekkid before they killed him?"

"Nitti wanted to shame him," Kelly said. "He'd like you G-men to lay off the Syndicate. Never were fond of the freelancer."

"I know Bailey was there, too," Jones said. "Someone knows. We got him. And we got time."

"Hell, he didn't kidnap Charlie Urschel," Kelly said. "He was framed for that."

"Ain't it a shame."

Dear Mr. Urschel—

I hope I am not pulling a prize blunder (or should I say committing a "faux pas"?) in writing to you. Don't think I am merely writing this letter to try to get into your good graces. You can rest assured I will never ask you to do anything towards getting me out.

I feel at times you wonder how I am standing up under my penal servitude, and what is my attitude of mind. Maybe you have asked yourself, "How can a man of even ordinary intelligence put up with this kind of life, day in, day out, week after week, month after month, year after year." To put it more mildly still, what is this life of mind like—and from whence do I draw sufficient courage to endure it.

*To begin with, these five words seem written in fire on the walls
of my cell: "Nothing can be worth this." This—the kind of life I am
leading. That is the final word of wisdom so far as crime is concerned.
Everything else is mere fine writing.*

"What are you going to do when you get us all locked up on that
island?"

"Plenty," Jones said.

"Won't be long till you nab every yeggman in the country."

"Worse headed this way."

"The Depression?"

"Worse than the Depression," Jones said. "The country has worse
problems than a bunch of hoods with guns."

"Like what?"

"The Germans, for one. Filthy Nazis. Did you know that son of a
bitch Hitler won't let churches use 'Amen' because it's a Hebrew word.
That ain't right."

"And you can't wait to fight 'em."

"Won't be long till they'll be coming for us."

"That's screwy."

"Our borders are wide open," he said. "They'll look to Mexico."

"And you'll take up the gun."

"If it comes to that," Jones said. "I can speak Spanish."

*I feel splendid and am in perfect physical trim. My one obsession is the
climate of this island. I am constantly bothered with colds. My cell,
made of steel and concrete, is always a trifle chilly; but I've come to
believe that man is so made that the presence of a small superficial
irritation, provided the sensation is acute without being symptomatic
of any serious trouble, is a definite aid to his mental equilibrium and
serves to keep occupied the restless margin of his consciousness. He
regards it, too, as a sort of ring of Polycrates, for I suspect that there is*

in all of us, always, an obscure sense of fate, inherited from numberless
ancestral misfortunes, which whisper: "We are not sent into this world
to live too happily. Where there's nothing to worry us, it's not natural,
it's a bad sign."

"You know she wrote me in Leavenworth," Kelly said, the morning clear and bright. They ate their eggs with plastic utensils. "The lawyer we hired sued for all the jewels and furs. That big, gorgeous Cadillac, too. She had a sixteen-cylinder engine. You could steer clear across this country like that car was a yacht."

Jones nodded, watching him eat, holding the Thompson over him.

"She told me she still loved me," Kelly said.

"Yeah, I read that letter. You know your mail's censored? I think she was hoping you'd help bust her out."

"That might be a little tough," Kelly said, raising his manacled wrists.

"They put her in prison with her momma," Jones said. "That has to give you some comfort."

"You think she used me?"

"You want to know the truth, son?" Jones asked.

But I must be fair. Being in prison has brought me one possible
advantage. It could hardly do less. Its name is comradeship—a rough
kindness of man to man: unselfishness; an absence, or a diminution,
of the tendency to look ahead, at least very far ahead; a carelessness,
though it is bred of despair; a clinging to life and the possible happiness
it may offer at some future date.

A person in prison can't keep from being haunted by a vision of
life as it used to be when it was real and lovely. At such times I pay,
with a sense of delicious, overwhelming melancholy, my tribute to
life as it once was. I don't believe it can ever be like that again—
but you can bet your last oil-well George won't lose any sleep
over that.

How's your bridge game? Are you still vulnerable? I don't mean
that as a dirty dig, but you must admit you lost your bid on the night
of July 22, 1933.

I hope you will not consider my writing an impertinence, if you
do, just tear this letter up and forget it. With best wishes, I am

Very truly yours,
George R. Kelly
Reg. No. 117

The seats in the train jostled up and down, metal wheels scraping
against rails, anonymous towns of light and smoke flying by the windows, just slightly cracked. Jones sat across from George Kelly on that
final stretch, having so many questions about him and Kathryn but
deciding what went on with his woman was of a personal nature. He got
his pipe going and stretched out his shined boots, the front of his shirt
clinging to him, with sweat drying in the coolness of the night.

Kelly faced the rear of the train, Jones in the seat opposite him, toward
the engine.

The men both took turns staring out the barred windows at the lonely
landscape. One view forward, one behind.

"You want to trade places?" Jones asked, checking his gold timepiece.

"Not on your life."

Acknowledgments

Background information provided by: *Public Enemies: America's Greatest Crime Wave and the Birth of the FBI, 1933–34*, Bryan Burrough; *Machine Gun Kelly's Last Stand*, Stanley Hamilton; *A Man Named Jones*, George Ellis; *Crimes' Paradise*, E. E. Kirkpatrick; *Robbing Banks Was My Business: The Story of J. Harvey Bailey*, J. Evetts Haley; *American Agent*, Melvin Purvis; *Inside the F.B.I.*, John J. Floherty; *The Texas Rangers and the Mexican Revolution: The Bloodiest Decade, 1910–1920*, Charles H. Harris III and Louis R. Sadler; *"King of the Wildcatters": The Life and Times of Tom Slick, 1883–1930*, Ray Miles; *John Dillinger Slept Here: A Crooks' Tour of Crime and Corruption in St. Paul, 1920–1936*, Paul Maccabee; *Cars of the 30s*, Editors of Consumer Guide; and *The 1933 Chicago World's Fair: A Century of Progress*, Cheryl R. Ganz. I'm very grateful to the assistance of the FBI Archives for providing nearly ten thousand pages of files. As always, thanks to the University of Mississippi library for their interlibrary loan program and to the great reporters of 1933 for their top-shelf coverage of the Kansas City Massacre and the Charles Urschel kidnapping in the *Kansas City Star*, the *Daily Oklahoman*, and the Memphis *Commercial Appeal*.

An extra special thanks to Jack Ruleman at the Shelby County Archives in Memphis, who put me onto this story and tracked down invaluable records on the Kellys' arrest. The Texas Ranger Hall of Fame and Museum in Waco provided terrific background on the Ranger days of Jones and White. As always, Esther and Neil make this work possible and give it purpose. My ultimate thanks for our fourth book together.

Also a great deal of appreciation to Sara Minnich at G. P. Putnam's Sons for her consistent and sharp eye. I'd also like to thank the continued support year after year of the following folks: Maggie Griffin at Partners & Crime, Cody Morrison and Slade Lewis at Square Books, David and McKenna Thompson at Murder by the Book, Patrick Milliken and Barbara Peters at the Poisoned Pen, Mary Gay Shipley at That Bookstore in Blytheville, Thomas and Cheryl Upchurch at Capitol Book & News, Jake Reiss at the Alabama Booksmith, and Ted O'Brien at the Garden District Book Shop.

The usual suspects played a huge role of support while I was working on this project: Larry and Dean Wells for their friendship and knowledge of bridge, former political boss Richard Howorth for insightful comments, Tim Green for years of support, and, of course, my entire family.

This book is better thanks to the wife, Angela, who always gives it to me on the level, a woman who might've taught Kathryn Kelly a thing or two. And most of all, to my son, who constantly reminds me that the world is a funny place.

Ace Atkins
Oxford, Mississippi, 2009

Behind the Story

Somehow poor George Kelly gets lost in the shuffle of Depression-era gangsters. Dillinger, Bonnie and Clyde, and "Baby Face" Nelson all get plum roles in movies and books, often with parts that glamorize or exaggerate their real lives. "Machine Gun" Kelly and his wife, Kathryn, seem to be the footnotes in the history books, their one big score—the kidnapping of Oklahoma oilman Charlie Urschel—relegated to faded headlines and one B-movie from more than fifty years ago.

Bryan Burrough, author of the excellent *Public Enemies*, called Kelly the most inept of the era's criminals. Kelly hasn't fared much better in other books on the period.

Hell, he never even killed anyone.

I came across the Kellys' story by a fluke. I was in Memphis at the criminal court clerk's office researching another novel in the summer of '08 when the clerk told me about recently finding their file from 1933. He shared with me details about the G-men raid on the Kellys' hideout in south Memphis, with federal agents and city detectives posing as garbage workers.

I asked for a copy out of curiosity, knowing next to nothing about their story.

Then I read the file.

It didn't take but a moment to set aside my project and start working on the manuscript that would eventually become *Infamous*. George— and most important, Kathryn—were not at all what I expected.

They were better.

This wasn't the same old violent ride to the death, but instead a true comedy where every piece of bad luck and worse choices lead to capture. This was a gangster story as directed by the Coen Brothers. Real life that mirrored scenes from *Fargo*, or better yet, *Miller's Crossing*.

Perhaps I was also drawn to the setting. I'd had no idea that I'd lived in "Machine Gun" Kelly's world for nearly a decade. Kelly, born George Barnes, was a good Catholic boy who was raised in Memphis and attended nearby Mississippi State. Kathryn Kelly was born and raised Cleo Brooks in Saltillo, Mississippi, not far from my home and where my father grew up.

I knew these people. The only gangsters from my Deep South.

I had a great deal of information about the Kellys' capture and made frequent trips to the sites. But I didn't really understand the wild summer of 1933—the Urschel kidnapping and the national manhunt by the Department of Justice—until I turned to the FBI archives.

This story, unlike any other I had written, had been covered from every angle with documents, reports, and photographs, in a file of nearly eight thousand pages.

This didn't even include the separate files of never-released material on bank robber Harvey Bailey and FBI Agent Gus T. Jones. Or the newspapers, whose insatiable coverage of George Kelly, the first Public Enemy, stretched out for months. (You have to keep in mind that John Dillinger didn't become a household name until 1934.)

What emerged was a story of a great American road trip. Fifty-six days on U.S. highways after the kidnapping, nearly twenty thousand miles across Middle America and the South. The Kellys drove Cadillacs, Chevrolets, and Fords, crisscrossing across the United States of the Great Depression as FDR worked to get the country back on its feet. As I wrote the novel, sometimes the headlines of our current financial crisis blended into stories about the National Recovery Act.

You could follow the Kellys' big trip through the luxury hotels where they stayed—places like the Skirvin in Oklahoma City to the LaSalle in Kansas City—almost all of them still open. I worked to re-create hotel lobbies and suites through vintage postcards and photographs I found on eBay. The online auction site also became a great resource on the Worlds Fair of 1933. I found maps and tourist guides, and even home movies of the big fair in Chicago.

But when I started to write, the novel changed course a great deal. George Kelly—as in real life—began to take a supporting role to Kathryn. Kathryn became the central figure in *Infamous*, calling most of the shots, second-guessing George, and eventually leading to their capture. Or, as J. Edgar Hoover said, "If ever there was henpecked husband, it was George Kelly."

I guess in a strange sense, you could also call this book a love story.

Although she grew up not far from Memphis, Kathryn was of a much different class than George. Saltillo, Mississippi, was a farming community on the outskirts of Tupelo, and she grew up poor, had a baby at fifteen, and lived her early years as Cleo Brooks. By the time she met George she'd become Kathryn Thorne, a glamorous party girl in Fort Worth. She liked to drink and smoke, and she loved fast cars and fine clothes. She was a gray-eyed, long-legged brunette with a wicked jaw.

George didn't stand a chance.

He grew up the son of an insurance executive in Memphis, and although he had a strained relationship with his father, he never wanted for anything. George was the only one of the Depression-era criminals not to be raised in poverty, not only graduating from high school but attending college, even if it was only for a semester, his highest grade in personal hygiene.

I don't believe George had any ambition. I think he robbed banks so he wouldn't have to work.

It was Kathryn who had an insatiable desire to be known . . . and that's the core of the novel.

Maybe that's why, when I wrapped up the book earlier this year, I could not stop thinking of her. I had a pretty good feel for Kathryn based on newspaper accounts and endless FBI interviews and reports. More files than anyone I had ever written about.

But I wondered if there was any family left in Saltillo who remembered her.

I enlisted the help of Patsy Brumfield, a good friend who writes a column for the *Northeast Mississippi Daily Journal.* She wrote about George and Kathryn, about how Kathryn had been raised in Saltillo and how George had robbed the Citizens Bank in Tupelo in 1932.

Even though Kathryn Kelly/Cleo Brooks left her hometown in the 1920s, she was not forgotten.

I heard from numerous members of the Brooks family.

The strangest connection was a longtime friend of mine in Oxford who just happened to be Kathryn's cousin. She works at my bank, a fact we later laughed about. Her mother had exchanged letters with Kathryn's mother for years.

Another cousin recalled stories of an aunt visiting Kathryn—her family still calling her Cleo—in Fort Worth in the spring of 1933, and getting rides in her sixteen-cylinder Cadillac and coveting Kathryn's gorgeous clothes. Kathryn would later send a studio portrait to her family in Saltillo signed: *With all my love, Your Girl.*

The photograph is something out of classic Hollywood, Kathryn decked out in furs and jewels, her hair marcelled. Even before the kidnapping, Kathryn was working on her public image.

But the strangest piece to shake out from the column came from the daughter of Homer Edgeworth, the head teller at the Tupelo bank Kelly robbed seventy-seven years ago.

She simply wrote: *Would you like to meet him?*

At 102, Homer Edgeworth still recalls the day "Machine Gun" Kelly came to town and stuck a pistol to his head.

A few weeks ago, I drove down to Clinton, Mississippi, where Homer is now living in a nursing home, spending his days watching *The Price Is Right* from his bed. When his daughter Cecelia introduced us and said I was the man who'd come to talk about Kelly, he asked to be propped up to pay better attention.

"I'll remember it for the rest of my life," he said.

In a cracked voice, Homer recalled Kelly walking up to the teller's window on the morning of November twenty-eighth, 1932. He asked Homer to change out a twenty-dollar bill, and while money was being passed, Kelly coolly asked about how many employees worked there, and then he left.

Homer would see Kelly one more time, just as the bank was closing, when Kelly entered the bank lobby with a machine-gun carrying man, later identified as Albert Bates, and they locked the door behind them.

Kelly walked over to Homer and placed a .45 automatic right behind his ear. The gangster told him to do as he said and he wouldn't be shot.

"Was he rough with you?" I asked.

Homer said: "He was a pretty nice guy. Polite."

So goes George Kelly.

Kelly prodded Homer to the teller windows to fill up his pillowcases while Bates looted the safe. The most tense moment came when the vice president of the bank craned his neck from the floor. Albert Bates threatened to blow his head off.

Within twenty minutes, Homer said, the pair had gathered the money, thirty-eight thousand dollars cash, fifteen thousand dollars in negotiable bonds, and ten thousand dollars in traveler's checks, and exited Citizens Bank.

They left only a two-dollar bill.

Homer called the police and followed the pair out onto Main Street. He noted a third person at the wheel of the getaway car before they sped away from the downtown. He didn't get a good glimpse of the driver.

Of course, I'd like to think it was Kathryn.

"I didn't see Kelly again until the FBI flew me out west to identify him," Homer said. "I pointed right at him. He called me a son of a bitch and said I only knew him from the papers. I said, 'I don't know your name. I just know you're the man who robbed my bank.'"

You can still visit that safe Kelly robbed in Tupelo, the house where the Kellys were captured in Memphis, Charlie Urschel's mansion in Oklahoma City, and even the Shannon farm in Paradise, Texas, where Urschel was kept prisoner. Not to mention all the train stations, hotels, and restaurants from Chicago to San Antonio. You can follow the Kellys' escape route with ease, making for a hell of a road trip.

One of Kathryn's relatives recently asked me why the Kellys weren't more known, remarking: "Kathryn is a lot more interesting than that Bonnie Parker."

After taking this long trip with the Kelly family, I'd have to agree. They were complex and contradictory. Every time you thought you understood the couple, they'd turn on you. In the end, I don't know if they had much of an agenda other than just to have a good time.

And like Homer Edgeworth, it will be some time before I will forget them.

Ace Atkins
Carrefour Farm
Oxford, Mississippi
2009

Turn the page for a preview
of Ace Atkins's new novel...

THE RANGER

Available June 2011 in hardcover
from G. P. Putnam's Sons!

From the acclaimed, award-winning author comes the beginning of an extraordinary new series about a real hero, and the real Deep South.

Northeast Mississippi, hill country, rugged and notorious for outlaws since the Civil War, where killings are as commonplace as in the Old West. To Quinn Colson, it's home—but not the home he left when he went to Afghanistan. Now an army ranger, he returns to a place overrun by corruption, and his uncle, the county sheriff, dead—a suicide, he's told, but others whisper murder. In the days that follow, it will be up to Colson to discover the truth, not only about his uncle, but about his family, his friends, his town, and, not least of all, himself. And once it's discovered, there is no turning back.

This is the series Ace Atkins's fans have been waiting for.

Quinn headed home, south on the Mississippi highway, in a truck he'd bought in Phenix City, Alabama, for fifteen hundred, a U.S. Army rucksack beside him stuffed with enough clothes for the week, and a sweet Colt .44 Anaconda he'd won in a poker game. He carried good rock 'n' roll and classic country, and photos from his last deployment in Afghanistan, pics of him with his ranger platoon, the camp monkey, "Streak," on his shoulder, Black Hawks at sundown over the mountains. Things you bring back home after six years away, from Third Battalion Headquarters at Fort Benning to Iraq to Afghanistan and back again, when you didn't really intend to return home so fast, if at all. He drove south on Highway 7 and then down 9W, and kept heading south into the winding hill country that had been logged down to nothing decades ago, leaving the people scrub pines and junk trees and squashed beer cans and bottles. This part of the state had always seemed used up to him as a kid, and it looked just as used up in the headlight glow of the truck. He was headed back down to Jericho at midnight, not wanting to see a damn soul till the funeral tomorrow.

He figured nobody plans being away for that long, but when you join up at eighteen and earn your tab just before September 11, a soldier can keep pretty damn busy. He tried to recall the last time he'd seen his mother (not caring if he ever saw his father again), and wondered about his sister who hadn't called him in two Christmases. At home there was an ex-girlfriend who'd dumped him not long after basic, and good friends he hadn't spoken to in years.

He turned up the radio, a Johnny Cash version of a classic Western ballad. Quinn knew the song by heart but loved hearing it every time.

The old truck ran at seventy on a steady ribbon of blacktop unfolding from hill to hill, a path cut through endless forest that once had been traveled by horse and wagon, Tibbehah County being one of the most remote counties in north Mississippi.

After years of marching and maneuvers, sitting still seemed odd to him, although at rest he could fall asleep at will and wake up just as fast. The Regiment had whittled him down to a wiry, muscular frame built for speed, surprise, chaos, and violence. His hair was cut in the standard high and tight, not even an inch thick on top and shaved on the sides, making his face seem even more chiseled in the rearview mirror, sharp angles thanks to a Choctaw grandmother about a hundred years back, mixed with the hard Scotch-Irish who settled the South.

The truck's heater was cranked, and Quinn's hand was on the wheel, sitting comfortably in a black T-shirt, blue jeans, and cowboy boots. In the ashtray he kept a half of a dead cigar that he'd smoked about a hundred miles back while drinking some bad coffee. The trip was only five hours, but it was a hell of a long time alone with your thoughts.

Another bend, another curve on the highway, and there was a speck in the light. He touched the brakes—finding them a lot less tight than the salesman had promised—thinking the speck was a spooked deer or a dog but then seeing it was the bare back of a woman, turning on long spindly legs and caught in his high beams.

He shanked the steering wheel to the right, the truck coming within an arm's reach of the hair rushing across her blank face. He was in a ditch, and stuck, back wheels spinning into mud.

Quinn got out and tromped over to the girl, still standing there on the double yellow line, her breath audible against the quiet of the motor and hot ticking of the engine. There were cows calling from someplace across a barbed-wire fence, and a train whistled far off. A lonesome midnight moon glowed, and Quinn called to the girl, just spotting a logging truck cresting the hill. He grabbed her hand and pulled her toward the shoulder, finding her face in his truck's headlight.

"You okay?"

She nodded.

"What the hell you doing in the middle of the road?"

"I didn't see you."

"You didn't hear my truck?"

She didn't say anything.

"Shit, I about killed you."

The girl wore cowboy boots, a miniskirt, and a sequined halter top busting at the stomach. The girl, maybe eighteen or nineteen or sixteen, was blond and light-eyed. She had tight curly hair, a small upturned nose, and was well on her way with child.

"You from here?" he asked.

She shook her head, breath clouding in the cold.

"I'd give you a ride, but—"

She said it didn't matter and turned away, and kept walking south.

Quinn hopped back in the truck and cranked the ignition, the F-150 older than him kicking to life, and he knocked it into four-wheel drive just for the hell of it, thinking he'd never get out of that ravine. But the tires spun, and it lurched forward a foot and then five feet, and he was back on the road, following the girl. He let down his side window, slowly, and told her to get in.

She stopped and didn't say a word. She just stood there, back roads leading nowhere all around, with nothing on her, nothing to her, and then she climbed inside the cab. Quinn accelerated fast in case she decided to change her mind.

"Headed down to Tibbehah County," he said. "Jericho."

He didn't realize he'd left the radio on, catching a staticky local station. A talk-radio-show host offering his views at the decline of American morals and the nearing of the end times.

"How old are you?" he asked.

"How old are you?" she asked.

"Twenty-nine."

"You look a lot older."

Quinn and the girl didn't speak for nearly fifteen miles.

"You can let me out here," she said.

"Nothing here."

"I can walk."

"Where you from?" Quinn asked, keeping the same speed.

"Alabama."

"You walked from Alabama?"

"It's a fur piece," she said, staring straight ahead.

"'Specially in those boots."

"You from Jericho?"

"Grew up there."

"You know a man named Jody?"

"Haven't been home in some time," Quinn said. "What's his last name?"

The girl didn't say anything. She just stared out at the headlights hitting the ten feet of darkness ahead of them, not much to see along the road but trailers perched on some cleared land and homemade signs offering fresh vegetables, although the season had passed months ago. The nights had turned chilly; past cotton harvesttime.

"What you're doin' is dangerous," Quinn said.

"Thanks for your concern."

"Just tryin' to help."

"Why are you going back?"

"It's time."

"How long you been gone?" she asked.

"Six years and a few months."

"You do something bad?"

"Why would you ask that?" Quinn asked, a little edge in his voice.

"Just trying to talk."

"You have money?"

"You can let me off in town."

"You have people?"

"Jody," the girl said, not sounding too excited about the prospect.

"The boy without a last name."

She stayed silent and leaned her head against the window glass, a few stray cars passing, high beams dimming over the crests of hills, all the way till they reached the Tibbehah County line, the road sign spray-painted over with the words AIN'T NO HOPE. Quinn recognized some things, Varner's Quick Mart, the small high school stadium where he'd played football long after they'd been state champs in '78, JT's Garage—but JT's looked like it'd shut down a while back. The downtown movie theater where he'd seen *Fievel Goes West* with his kid sister had been turned into a church. He passed the town cemetery where he'd probably be buried alongside both sets of grandparents and a few kin beyond that, and then they were circling the town square. A small gazebo stood in the center as a monument to all the boys who'd been killed in action since the Civil War.

"Is this all there is?" the girl asked.

"Pretty much," Quinn said. "Can I get you a place to stay?"

"I'll make my own way, thank you."

"Some churches and places might could help. Hey, look, there's a motel right across the railroad tracks over there. I'll pay for your room tonight and then you can make your way fresh in the morning. I have to check in, too."

"I know that song," she said, turning to look at his face.

"I'm not shy," he said. "But I draw the line at pregnant teens."

She didn't say anything. He gunned the motor and crossed over the tracks, circling down into the Traveler's Rest, an old U-shaped motel where the units faced outward to the highway. Quinn remembered it used to be thirty bucks a night back when the couples needed to be alone at prom time. Now they advertised bass fishing in their pond and free Wi-Fi. You used to could drive past this place at midnight and know which girls had finally given in to their boyfriends or who was stepping out.

Quinn grabbed his bag, paid for the rooms, and tossed the girl her key.

"Good luck," he said, heading to his room.

"I'll pay you back in the morning."

"Not necessary," he said. "I got a funeral to be at anyway."

"Who died?" she asked.

THE FUNERAL STARTED AT NINE A.M. SHARP, EVERYONE noting that his uncle sure would have appreciated the punctuality. There were about twenty people there. Quinn expected more, but understood it was a cold, rainy morning, and it being Thanksgiving Day and all. Most were men, old veterans who'd been buddies with his uncle since Korea, long before he'd become sheriff back in '73. They held their baseball hats, decorated for whatever military branch they'd entered, over their tired hearts as the body of Hampton Beckett was lowered into the ground to the sounds of a twenty-one-gun salute, some of the old men looking like they sure enjoyed getting out the rifles and firing off a few rounds. Every damn snap made Quinn recoil a bit, and he hated himself for that, watching the flag being folded and handed to a frizzled waitress from the Fillin' Station diner, a woman that Hamp had been seeing since his wife had died five years ago. There were nice words and handshakes, and then it started to rain harder and everyone ducked under their umbrellas and ran for their cars, snaking out of the county cemetery and starting the real bit of the ceremony at the VFW club.

As Quinn reached for the truck's door, Luke Stevens waded through a ditch to shake his hand. He hadn't spoken to Luke since they graduated from high school, but he looked pretty much the same: shaggy brown hair, with a handsome face and confident grin. His gold glasses were spotted with rain, and his suit drenched. He just gave a brief smile to Quinn, shook his hand, and then wrapped him in an awkward hug. Luke still feeling bad about taking Anna Lee away, even though Quinn was the one who'd left. Luke being the one who'd gone to medical school at Tulane and come back to Jericho to live and die.

Quinn started to speak, but Luke had turned back to his car, where Quinn caught only the back of Anna Lee's black dress as she climbed inside and shut the door. Hell, he didn't know what to say anyway.

THE VFW BUILDING WASN'T MUCH BUT CINDER BLOCK AND tin, murals of Europe, Vietnam, and Iraq painted on the walls. A sign outside advertised BINGO SATURDAYS, and a CATFISH FRY from two Sundays back. Quinn removed his damp dress coat and loosed his wet tie and sat at a table with three old men. One of them looked around the empty room, more for show than from worry, and pulled out a bottle of Wild Turkey; another headed to the kitchen to fetch some coffee mugs.

"You been to see your mother yet?" asked old Mr. Jim, a Third Army man who from his barbershop pulpit told stories of meeting Patton, even keeping the prayer card he'd been issued since before they rolled into Belgium. His nose resembled a rutabaga, his eyes narrow and a washed-out blue.

"No, sir."

"She'll want to see you."

"Yes, sir."

"Don't be angry."

"He was her brother," Quinn said. "Doesn't seem too much to show up at his funeral."

"They hadn't spoken for some time," Mr. Jim said. "Bad words said."

"Those two argued over the color of the sky," Quinn said. "Hamp didn't talk to her for nearly a month after she called John Wayne a pussy."

Old Judge Blanton, small and white-haired in a black suit, cracked open the seal on the bourbon and uncorked the bottle. Luther Varner, a Marine in Vietnam, owner of Varner's Quick Mart, returned with four mismatched cups. Varner lit a long, cheap cigarette. Quinn wished he'd brought in cigars.

He felt odd sitting with them, the men always just a "Sir" and a polite handshake. Quinn was never part of the boys, sitting around drinking coffee in the morning at Varner's. But here he was after doing what was expected of him in the Army, and the old boys seemed to say, "Sit down, and sit a spell. You're one of us now."

"You didn't wear your uniform," Judge Blanton said.

"I've worn it enough."

"You gettin' redeployed?" Mr. Jim asked.

"We just got back," Quinn said. "Third Batt did six months in Afghanistan."

"You see much action?"

"We always do."

"Y'all boys get called in when the shit hits the fan," Varner said. "In case of trouble, break the glass and call in the rangers."

"I just don't know why he did it," Mr. Jim said, making a clicking sound with his cheek. He was staring into a blank spot in the corner of the VFW, not listening much to what was going on around him.

Quinn watched. The other men exchanged glances. All looked down at the table.

There was a good twenty seconds of silence when all Quinn could hear was breathing and rain pinging on the roof. He sat and waited.

"You didn't know," Mr. Jim said.

"Know what?"

Mr. Jim looked to Varner and Varner to old Judge Blanton, Quinn noting Blanton must've been elected their spokesperson.

Judge Blanton took a big swig of whiskey. "Sorry, Quinn. Ole Hamp stuck a .44 in his mouth and pulled the trigger. Go figure."

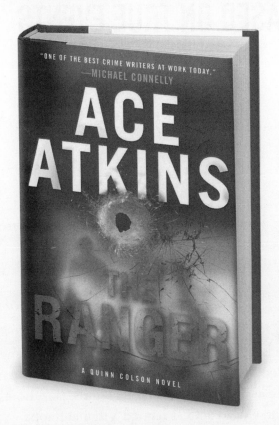

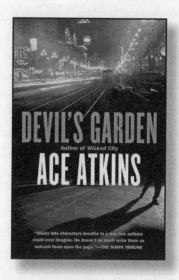

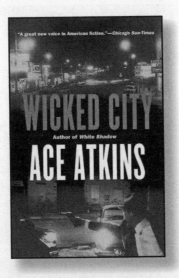

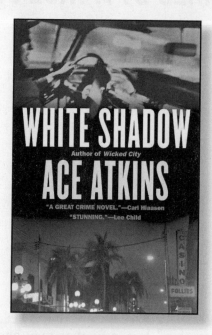